I0762925

BY PRIYA PARMAR

Exit the Actress

Vanessa and Her Sister

The Original

The ORIGINAL

HOLLYWOOD

The ORIGINAL

A NOVEL

PRIYA PARMAR

BALLANTINE BOOKS
NEW YORK

Ballantine Books
An imprint of Random House
A division of Penguin Random House LLC
1745 Broadway, New York, NY 10019
randomhousebooks.com
penguinrandomhouse.com

Hardcover ISBN 978-0-593-98413-0
Ebook ISBN 978-0-593-98414-7

Printed in the United States of America

1st Printing

FIRST EDITION

BOOK TEAM: Production editor: Jennifer Rodriguez • Managing editor: Pam Alders • Production manager: Sarah Feightner • Copy editor: Briony Everroad • Proofreaders: Barbara Greenberg, Andrea Gordon, Amy Harned

Frontispiece: TheMountBirdStudio/iStock

Book design by Ralph Fowler

The authorized representative in the EU for product safety and compliance is Penguin Random House Ireland, Morrison Chambers, 32 Nassau Street, Dublin D02 YH68, Ireland. https://eu-contact.penguin.ie

For Mama
who tells me to scribble, scribble
and
for Anthony

"Sometimes people leave you
halfway through the wood."

—*Stephen Sondheim,*
"No One Is Alone," INTO THE WOODS

"We, none of us, know each other, do we?
Not too well."

—*Katharine Hepburn*
interview with Clive James, 1985

The
ORIGINAL

LOS ANGELES

We don't take cowards here. In the young, we accept vice, avarice, stupidity and vanity, but not cowardice. We will spit you out for that and send you back on the dusty bus to wherever you came from. Not her. She was brave and was always going to end up here.

When she was young, before the suicides, she preferred the sunshine sports: golf, sailing, swimming, croquet, climbing trees. She could ski—all the old money kids in Connecticut can ski—but she didn't like it. She liked hot air on her arms, sweat, and the way her scalp itched after a day in the sun. She wore her brother's clothes and never looked in the mirror.

When she was older, we reached for her. She was on Broadway then. Arguing with directors, getting fired, quitting, getting married. She could have stayed that course; she had already married a Main Line man. Their address was listed in the Philadelphia phone book: Mr. and Mrs. Ludlow Ogden Smith. "Luddy"—prep school boys always have names like that. They ordered letter-pressed writing paper, opened joint bank accounts, the works. Would a child have changed her mind? No? Maybe. Regardless, the scooped-out belly and the thin white scar were inevitable. Anatomy is anatomy. It cannot be persuaded.

Where most people are accepting: *I will not be a professional ball player, I will not sing at Carnegie Hall, I will not live in Paris, no one will write articles about me, there will never be an audience;* Kate said no. She would never be happy with a good, small life.

And we offered her love here. Blazing love. We were not stingy about that.

Suppose it did not happen the way you think it did? Frame by frame, the way you remember—think you remember. Memory is a creative animal. See the washed-out photograph of the fruit bowl and you will remember the ripe juice of the fruit. In the end, all lives are secret.

PART ONE

THE EAST COAST

KATE

HARTFORD, CONNECTICUT

1921

To understand her, you should start with him. She begins with him.

But you don't have to.

The girl also begins with salt and fir and glacial soil. With a family that talks about bodies and disease and reads at the table. The father believes in water, the chemical properties, the health benefits: cold baths, ice shocked skin and nude swimming. The mother believes in Margaret Sanger, Bryn Mawr, votes for women, New England and her husband.

One night in November, in the big yellow house, the girl's parents give a dinner party. The new daily maid has arranged the flowers and laid the second best family china. She drops a knife and wipes it on her skirt. No one sees. She is annoyed and wants to get home. On a junior doctor's salary, the Hepburns cannot afford for her to live in like Fanny. Bus fare is five cents. Nickel there, nickel back. She plans to ask the Hepburns for a raise.

Friends of the Hepburns sit around the couple's oval table. They discuss the country's poor, how to help, what to do. The Hepburns are still young. They look at each other often, soft, blunt gusts of affection. They look for approval, yes, but more for love. The girl will always be proud of the way her parents love each other. But a child can never really know a parents' marriage. Sitting at opposite ends of the dinner table, the Hepburns are enclosed, like a phrase. Kit Hepburn observes the old rules, one never sits next to one's husband.

On this night in November the new daily maid stands by the swinging door, waiting for a gap in the conversation, a moment when the guests chew, or cough. When it comes, she goes in to tell them that a man without a home has come to the kitchen door looking for food. She moves toward Mrs. Hepburn, knowing Mrs. Hepburn would want to feed the man without a home, bends to speak low into her ear but the girl's father does not like anyone to be that close to his wife. The new daily maid straightens and speaks so all at the table can hear. Irritated at the intrusion—they have guests after all—Dr. Hepburn tells her that they cannot receive a visitor at this time of night. He looks at his wife, for approval, for love. And then he swallows his food.

If you are looking for the girl, she is not here yet. She will arrive soon, two years after him. After the boy. They will be called Tom and Kate.

. . .

There are six of them at their peak. After Kate come four more. All flame-headed and freckled but smaller, less articulated. Maybe that happens when there are six? The last ones get a little out of focus? Mrs. Hepburn was always sure she was going to be the kind of mother who checks to make sure her children comb their hair and keep their fingernails clean. She assumed she would want to stand over them while they brush their teeth and to patch their clothes herself. But she has found that raising children is tedious work and she has other things to do. She wants to be a person in the world. By her third child, she has resumed her suffrage work. By her fifth, she is president of the Connecticut Women's Suffrage Association. But Mrs. Hepburn, a natural leader, can delegate. There are so many of them and they have each other. And she does not want to make them soft. At night, she reads to them. They pack the bed like a fish crate, all fresh socks and pajamas, wet hair and clean teeth. Eight pages of George Eliot before lights out.

In the winter they live in Hartford, near Dr. Hepburn's hospital, but in the warm months, they live here, in the shingled summer house sitting on a finger of land, across the narrow causeway from Old Saybrook. Birds fly low over the roof and land on the long stripe of gun blue water. It is called Fenwick, this circle of houses that hug the sandy road, grouped around the small private golf course. The houses tend to be large, baggy, with front porches that need painting. It is not the thing here to be pristine. This is salty New England country and it does not do to be showy. Dr. Hepburn is from Virginia and wants the porch painted. Mrs. Hepburn tells him she will get to it soon but does not call the painters. Better to do it in the winter so that it will look broken in by summer. And, anyway, it will just need it again next year.

The Hepburns believe in vigor, *noise*. The walls here are thin and none of the doors close properly but no matter. "We have nothing to hide," Dr. Hepburn says. He means it. They are a medical family. The body is not mysterious. They are the sort of family who are not fazed by nudity or sex but refuse to discuss fear. Dr. Hepburn teaches his children to rise early, shower in cold water before confronting the day. Kit Hepburn teaches them to blow on hot soup, chew with their mouths closed and to never use contractions. She says shortcuts are a sign of a lazy mind. The Hepburn children like heights and dares and are proud when a bruise turns from blue to green. They can always be found on roofs and up trees. Dr. Hepburn sends them up to clean gutters on autumn afternoons and to push the snow off the gables in the winter. He likes that the neighbors talk about the rowdy Hepburn brood and warn their own children to take care when they go to the Hepburn house. Dr. Hepburn does not speak to the old guard Fenwick neighbors himself; Mrs. Hepburn does that. He is still worried he will sound like backroads Virginia. Mrs. Hepburn knows they are not popular with their neighbors. Kit Hepburn does not care.

. . .

The small Hepburns pile their shoes at the base of the ash tree and climb barefoot to get a better grip. Kate climbs highest, up to where the branches thin. Tom watches from a low, thick limb. Children are tribal, they form their own governments. The Hepburn children have divided into camps: older, younger. The younger Hepburns try to keep up but there is no room for them in Tom and Kate.

. . .

There is a lot of yelling the summer Kate cuts off her hair. Tom sits on the rolled edge of the bathtub that Saturday morning and watches as Kate shoves her skinny fingers through the scissor rings. She slices off a panel of her red waves, leaving a pad of bristle over her right ear. She keeps going, clipping off long rectangles, and does not look in the mirror. The scissors make a fibrous, grassy sound; they are not sharp enough. She finishes, drops the scissors in the sink and looks at Tom, her head terraced with uneven red stumps.

Tom cannot quite look in the sink. The scissors are lying half open on the white enamel. Red hair still tangled in the mouth. He feels it's too private, too female, something personal he should not see. Tom does not join in the kitchen table discussions of bodies and medicine. Instead, he keeps a *Buster Brown* comic book on his lap. He does not open it, his father would not like that, but he feels safer knowing it is there.

He looks at Kate. "You're a mess."

Kate reaches in and pulls the scissors from the sink. "Fix it."

Tom tries to neaten up the sides and the back of her neck, the way the barber always does to him. Kate closes her eyes and drops her head forward, unafraid as the blades slide over her skin.

When he is done, they stand side by side, looking into the bathroom mirror.

"You look like my brother," Tom says.

"I *am* your brother."

They go downstairs. Tom will come back up after breakfast to sweep up the bathroom floor. He is not a boy to leave a mess for someone else to clean up.

The family gapes.

"It was in my way," Kate says, shaking salt onto her eggs.

"Good god," her father shouts, banging his open hand down on the table, clattering the dishes and jumping the spoons. "*What* were you thinking?"

Bob and Dick giggle but one look from their mother and they bite their lips, hard, and sit up straight.

"Kate! Answer me!"

Kate does not answer.

Dr. Hepburn turns to his wife. Quieter, he doesn't want to rattle his son. "*What* has she done? Why? *Why* has she done this?"

"She seems to have cut her hair, dear," Mrs. Hepburn says. "It is summer. It is hot. We let Tom, Bob and Dick keep short hair. Why not Kate?" Kit Hepburn is trying to pry open the tight air in the room.

"Tom did the back," Kate speaks up and then looks at her brother and wishes she hadn't.

"He *what*?" her father said, turning on Tom. "You did this to her?"

Tom swallows, turns. "The line wasn't straight," Tom says, "so I straightened it." His words slip back down his throat and he struggles to project his voice, to calm down, the way he and his mother have been practicing. Fanny puts a plate of eggs down in front of him and quickly cups his cheek. Tom is her favorite.

"I think you've done a very good job," Mrs. Hepburn says. "Especially around her ears. The ears are always the hardest." Mrs. Hepburn hates it when her husband snaps and her eldest son flinches. It has been getting worse this year.

"This is a *ridiculous* conversation," Dr. Hepburn shouts. "No one should *see* her ears. Her ears are supposed to be *under* her hair! She looks like a tufted baboon."

Dick and Bob giggle. "*Baboon*," they repeat.

"It is ugly." Dr. Hepburn rises from the table. He does not like females to be ugly.

Dick and Bob stop giggling.

Kit Hepburn and Fanny are women who understand each other. Fanny steps in.

"*You*, Kate, are getting hair all over this kitchen," she says, brushing the red strands from Kate's stiff shoulders. But the words are empty. Fanny cannot help. They always say she is part of the family but she knows she isn't, nor does she want to be. She has her own family.

Kate is locked to her chair. Her mind colds with silence when her father shouts.

"I think you have great ears," her mother whispers.

And she does; small, curved harps fastened low above the hinge of jawbone. Encouraged, Kate steadies, roots, but now Tom's left shoulder is twitching. Bob flinches but does not look away. He would not do that to his brother. Now, Tom's right shoulder joins in. His body bounces in ragged time. The rhythm spreads to his head, yanking it to the side. Dr. Hepburn looks away. He cannot watch. He has also been practicing with his wife and does his best to rein in his temper. He can see the boy is getting worse. At first, the family joked about it but that lightness wore off quickly and now Bob and Dick no longer tease. Everyone sits in silence and waits for it to pass.

Privately, when they speak of it, Mrs. Hepburn calls it by the medical term, St. Vitus' Dance and Dr. Hepburn calls it his son's "affliction." When Kate talks about it with Tom, she calls it the twitches. Best to call it what it is; it takes the sting away. Now, she reaches for Tom's hand under the table, presses her thumb into the meat of his palm. He squeezes back. Their mother takes his other hand, boldly, on the tabletop. Tom's head slows, balances; his shoulders lower. The table waits. No one looks at Dr. Hepburn. He knows what they are thinking: if he had not shouted about Kate's hair. No. If his son were less sensitive. That is what would solve the problem. Dr. Hepburn abruptly stands and leaves the room. He is late for surgery and does not want to have this fight today. He will speak to his wife later.

They have heard it all before. Seven doctors, seven examination rooms, seven clipboards, seven diagnoses, all the same. Dr. Hepburn says they need another opinion. He will not accept that his son cannot conquer his own body. The first doctor told them that it was psychological, that it stems from the stress; the second doctor told them it grew out of a fear of competition and the third doctor suggested it could be the product of nervous parents. "Nervous in the *clinical* sense," the third doctor emphasized, as if the stamp of medical certainty could improve his implication. "It can run in families," he finally said. Dr. and Mrs. Hepburn did not respond. They do not want to talk about what runs in their families.

"Withdraw him from all athletics at school," the last doctor advised and Mrs. Hepburn nodded her head but already knew she would not do it. Tom never twitches at school; the competition is all at home.

. . .

Mrs. Hepburn sits alone in her husband's study. It is the one door the children will not open. Did her father jerk and spasm? Did her uncle? She cannot remember. She was sixteen when her Uncle Frederick walked to the rail yard with the pistol in his coat pocket, younger still when her father went. They must find another doctor; she opens her address book.

. . .

Kate is already in her bathing suit. No cap, she wants to see what it feels like to swim without the tangle of hair clouding the water. She wants to be unencumbered, sleek and bullet fast.

"The creek?" Tom asks.

"The sound," Kate says. It is deeper.

Barefoot, towels around their necks, Tom and Kate leave the house together. Fanny makes two sandwiches, wraps them in wax paper and leaves them on the kitchen counter. Always two. They put them into their bicycle baskets and ride out over the shell driveway into the wide day.

. . .

The neighbors notice. The postman blinks, and the greengrocer on the corner of Water Street does not recognize her when she puts salt water taffy on her mother's account. Kate's friend Florence tells her mother, her mother telephones Mrs. Hepburn. Kate and Tom crouch on the stairs and listen to their mother's side of the conversation.

"Yes, Mrs. Miele, everything is fine."

"No, Mrs. Miele, Kate is not ill."

"Yes, she did it yesterday and I knew all about it."

"Thank you Mrs. Miele, but I believe Kate just prefers it short."

"Why should she not do it herself? It *is* her head?"

"Goodbye Mrs. Miele."

That is one thing about the Hepburns, they fight as a pack.

. . .

Mrs. Hepburn is going out for the evening. She is meeting Mrs. Sanger. It is not just the politics. Both women grew up in Corning, New York. Although, Kit Hepburn's family owned Corning Glass and Margaret Sanger's brothers worked in the factory. But growing up in the same town binds the two women and Kit Hepburn is one of Margaret Sanger's top lieutenants. She meets Mrs. Sanger on Tuesday evenings. On Tuesdays, Tom has his piano lesson and then stays over at a friend's house. Mrs. Hepburn prefers he not come home when she is out.

. . .

Dr. Hepburn says Tom will follow him into medicine. Kate looks to Tom who looks back at her. She will never be a doctor, nor will he. They have already made a pact. Tom will write and Kate will act. Kate wants to be on the stage where everyone will applaud, right there, in front of you. Tom wants to write for the movies where, if they film a scene and it is not perfect, he can rewrite until it is. Whatever life they choose, they promise, they will always do it together.

. . .

In the private, red brick school in West Hartford, Tom's grades are slipping. His teacher sends a note home. The principal asks for a meeting. To discuss options. Mrs. Hepburn does not show the note to her husband but tucks it into her file on the Connecticut Women's Birth Control League. Her husband will not look there. She telephones her friend Mary Towle in New York. Kate and Tom need to be away. Once they are out of the house, she will talk to her husband about the note, the meeting. She has already made an appointment at Andover. Boarding school will be better for him. He will be happy twenty-four hours a day instead of eight. Kit Hepburn knows Kate will miss him but she will adjust. Children do. She has not told Tom yet but she is sure he will like it. A mother's instinct. Her husband will resist; he will not like the thought of strangers raising his son but Kit Hepburn does not plan to lose this fight.

. . .

The day it happens, Kate wakes up happy. Tom and Kate are in New York, Greenwich Village. They are visiting Aunt Mary Towle who lives in the cobbled, crooked part of the city that looks like a Christmas tin. The raffish heyday of these streets has come and gone. Most of the bohemians have left; moved to cheaper apartments in Paris and London, but the neighborhood is faithful and it cocks its hat low over one eye and remembers them. They will be back. Bankers who aspire to be bankers will never be at home here. Aunt Mary is a solid woman, a squat, paint spattered rectangle built of conviction and sugar cane. When she visits Fenwick in summer, her bathing costume is Victorian black and comes to her knees. This Easter visit, she has shown Tom and Kate her town, taken them to galleries on the West Side, up to the Cloisters to walk in the high garden behind the wall, to Midtown to see a picture, *A Connecticut Yankee in King Arthur's Court* and to Huyler's on Jane Street for molasses candy. Tom, at fifteen, brushes his teeth afterward. Kate goes to bed with a sticky mouth.

Later, Kate will remember that Tom shook her awake, long after she had fallen asleep.

"You're my best girl, right Kath?"

"What?"

"You're my favorite girl in the whole world."

"I'm sleeping?"

When she wakes, she cannot remember if it really happened.

Kate is a morning person. This day, like other days, she is up early and spends her minutes carelessly. The nine minutes when she falls back to heavy sleep. The three minutes she watches the street from her bedroom window. The rubber yawn, the stretch, the swish of water in her cotton mouth. The four minutes to get dressed.

Later, Kate will grind through these minutes again and again, re-birthing the day.

She runs up the narrow steps and knocks on the door. The attic room is low, whitewashed and set under the raw roofed eaves. By June, it will be too hot to sleep up there. Each time they visit New York, Tom chooses this room and gives Kate the large bedroom downstairs with the slab of featherbed and the faded wallpaper. She knocks. The white paint is flecking off the door in places, but it will not be repainted. No one comes up here. She knocks again. Louder. Later, she will remember it differently, recall a stab of premonition, a gut thud of fear, but at the time, she just feels hungry and impatient. She leans hard—the door swells in the heat and will only open if you give it a good shove.

At first, there are only the logistical thoughts. Practicalities. She knows there is no urgency, no reason to run for the doctor. Not really. Medicine will not help but she wants a doctor anyway—the authority and the black bag.

She cannot leave him there. She has to pull him down.

Kate is strong for thirteen—fourteen in May. She can hoist herself up and swing by her knees on the trapeze their father built on the front lawn of the house on Hawthorn Street. Tom worries about the height but not her. Not when their father is watching. She can climb tall trees. She can swim in the March gray Long Island Sound. Her family watch from the beach as she snaps on a rubber bathing cap and dives, sinking through the water's skin. Tom follows, after a finger's width of hesitation, a second beat. Kate never hesitates. What's the point? Later, she will be less sure, but she is not there yet.

The bed sheet is looped around and around the low beam. No knot—but it has held. His knees are folded and his feet touch the floor.

His feet touch the floor.

The heft of this fact, it is a bullet slamming into bone. Her breath shakes in her throat, her ribs tighten around her stone hard lungs.

She will lift him. Could she? Did she? She will remember later that she did; will be able to recreate the feeling of his too long legs and cotton pajamas. She will tell herself she lifted him. Newspapers will say she didn't. The police report will say she didn't. She will remember that she did.

He is light. Too light for a boy of fifteen, their father says. Their father teases him that Kate is the faster runner, the stronger, deeper swimmer. The words shear the pride from the boy. He is left slick, new lamb bare and cold. Movement comes easily to Kate, she does not deny it, but in front of her brother, she does not push herself to do all she can do. If she allows it, her narrow, blade body can carve up air and water until the elements fall into tissue thin strips. She takes it for granted. Air and water are thicker for Tom.

She tugs hard and he lands. The noise. She remembers a noise. Later, she rinses the sound from her mind: unraveling it wave by wave until cotton white silence. This will become her habit. She will sand the raw, jumpy memory down to a smooth grained ball she can fit in her pocket and hold in her hand.

She shunts him onto the bed, straightening his legs in their thin pajamas. His best trousers are folded on the dresser. His overnight case is set on top of them, a weight to keep the crease. Their father believes there is beauty in a sharp crease. He isn't cold yet; she notices that.

Downstairs, the morning is going on as before. Kate will think about this later. When you do not know a thing, it has not happened yet. That unrealized joy. To Aunt Mary, Tom will be down in a few minutes and she is worried that they will miss their train. Aunt Mary is making toast, eggs and bacon for breakfast. The hot, slick smell gums up the air and sticks to the walls.

Kate cannot leave him alone but what comes next? Think. She pulls herself in. Binds herself tight. Practicalities. There is always a before and after. A fracture when the shell of before cracks open, exposing the narrow spine of after. This is where fragility starts.

Her parents. She exhales a soft buckle of relief. Oak strong and fearless, they will leave Connecticut and come. They will catch the first train to New York. Her mother will know what happens next. She has been through this all before.

The doctor's house is four doors down. Kate runs to tell him her brother is dead.

. . .

The police file their report. Afterward, among themselves, the three policemen who stood in that hot attic room discuss the boy: his small weight, his height, the angle, his ruthless lean into the noose, his determination, his toes, his feet. They speak with admiration. Courage demands respect. Two of them leave work early that night. They want to get home to hug their own boys.

Kate's father gives interviews. That is his mistake. *The Times*, the *Hartford Courant*. The versions of the death of his son: it was murder, there was an intruder, it was an accident, it was a trick he had seen in a film, in a play, it was from a story he had heard from a former slave in Virginia, it was insanity, it was not what it seems. The father's son becomes abstract, a story, a reflection, a shame. The most obvious answer is often the right one, people say.

The story runs on page six of *The New York Times*. When the verdict comes, it is suicide. Her father stops giving interviews.

. . .

Kate's mother is busy. The body—she calls her son "the body"—has to be brought back to Connecticut. The funeral home, the plot, the date, the headstone; she has lists for all of this. Mrs. Hepburn is a strategist and a better field commander than her husband. She can distill a thing to its elements and go from there. And Kate's mother knows how to lose. She is practiced and can do it with stony New England grace. First her father, then her mother, on the long white ward with the other ladies dying of cancer, then her uncle with his favorite revolver. And then came the safe run of years when the battles were smaller, less mortal, but still painful to lose. In 1920, the Democrats asked her to run for the Senate seat in Connecticut. Dr. Hepburn preferred she decline. Some limelight on his wife was good, real brilliance was not. Mrs. Hepburn declined.

"Two weeks is a long time to wait?" the funeral director says, standing in the front hall at the house on Hawthorn Street. "Of course, we understand, the family needs time to prepare," he says using all the euphemisms people in his business use, "but perhaps they could be ready sooner?" His sentence wobbles at the end. He is uncomfortable. He does not like to keep children in the basement refrigerator too long. Usually, these things did not need to be spelled out. The daily maid hovers by the swinging door. She tells herself she is listening because it is her job. Should she bring in tea? The funeral director is not sitting down. Is he a guest? She goes to ask Fanny. She wants to repeat the overheard conversation to someone.

"Grief swallowed is grief doubled," Fanny says.

The daily maid is not sure what that means.

Bob and Dick do their homework at the kitchen table now. They do not want to be alone in their bedrooms. They do not look up when the daily maid leaves.

No, Mrs. Hepburn will not invite the funeral director to come in and sit down. She does not want him in her home one moment longer than necessary.

"So, you wish to wait until the thirteenth?"

"We have family coming from Virginia, but we do not want a service," Mrs. Hepburn says, ignoring the funeral director's question that is not really a question.

"And, you wish to *wait*?" The funeral director treads delicately, but Kit Hepburn is not a delicate woman. He can see she is made of fire forged iron. Mrs. Hepburn does not answer.

"At least the April daffodils will have come up by then," the funeral director says and then regrets it. He is filling empty air. Nothing sounds right. He is usually better at this.

Kate has stopped speaking by then. No words make sense so she gives them up. Not much to talk about anyway and if she tries, she is sure her heart will push up her throat, tip over her teeth and fall out her mouth. This will all get away from her if she gives it an inch. Better to close down the whole business of being a person. School is unimportant so she stops that too. A private tutor is engaged but Kate mostly plays golf and climbs trees. Kate keeps forgetting it has happened, that is the worst part. The gut drop of remembering. Lifting her feet off the bike pedals or swinging from a tree branch, she will feel a wild thump of happiness. She will drink up the blue of the day, step on a pad of fresh cut grass and her jaw will loosen. Her teeth will un-grip like puzzle pieces coming apart and her skin will resettle on her bones. But then, she will see that there is only one bicycle, one pair of shoes kicked off at the base of the trunk. Sitting on the high branch, she hears papery tree noises and a silence that will only break if she breaks it. She will remember that she has forgotten and rush hot with shame. So, she works hard at remembering, making it part of every minute. She goes quiet, withdraws. If he can't be here, she shouldn't be here. The voiceless air grows thick, like river ice in winter, and she loses the habit of living.

"You're my best girl, right Kath?"

"What?"

"You're my favorite girl in the whole world."

. . .

At first, she looks for the boy her brother had loved but she never sees him again. Her brother Dick says he has changed schools. She had wanted to give that boy something: a thing ripe with her brother but she could not think of anything real enough. No thing can bottle up a life and keep it alive. By the time Kate is speaking again, everything important she could have given him is gone. All that is left are the empty things, unlived in shells without history: unread books, model ships he hadn't liked, starched sheets smelling of washing powder and new shoes that Bob and Dick will grow into. Tom had never told Kate about the boy, not straight out, but, in their family, such feelings are never called by name, and anyway, Tom did not need to tell her. They were of a kind. She already knew.

When Kate decides to change her birthdate to his birthdate, her parents don't speak of it. What is there to say? They can see she needs to celebrate her brother's day more than her own. Later, in interviews, she will stick by the lie. Now she is an autumn baby.

Kate knows the neighbors are talking about them.

"The eldest son," Mrs. Pruitt says at the South Congregational Church that first Sunday.

"What a tragedy," Reverend Fitch says. He is an unimaginative man.

"Did you read it?" Mrs. Rampling says.

"In the *Courant*? Mrs. Fitch clipped it out." Reverend Fitch says.

"The story keeps changing. Now, they are saying it was 'accidental.'" Mrs. Pruitt lowers her voice.

"Dr. Hepburn must have had a word with the editor," Reverend Fitch says.

. . .

The neighbors bring casseroles and lemon pies. As if you can feed the hole in the Hepburn family and the flesh will grow back. Mrs. Hepburn's suffragette sisters send cards. Mrs. Hepburn reads them standing up and then throws them away.

. . .

Dr. Hepburn's Virginia family will arrive, and then Mrs. Hepburn's New York family. Mrs. Hepburn's rich Uncle Houghton from upstate New York will not stay long. He is uncomfortable, and, as he points out, he has a company to run. *Corning Glass*, the neighbors whisper. They whisper about other things too. They say his two brothers did it; that Tom got it from that side of the blood; that urge to slip free and die young. These things can be passed down. Tom once told Kate that their mother's father used a gun, a pearl handled revolver, but Kate never knew where he had heard that. Later, he said that he should not have told her. Tom also knew that their mother's Uncle Frederick had done it with the same gun, out along the railway line, but he never told Kate. One shot each. The Houghtons are not the sort of people to miss.

But, it could also have come from the Hepburn side. Years ago, Dr. Hepburn's elder brother leapt out of a window and was stabbed through by the wrought iron fence below. His wife was talking to him from the other room when he soundlessly jumped. He was alive when they took him off the fence, it was more painful to pull the metal out and there was no question of saving him, but they could not leave him there.

Six days before Tom's funeral, Dr. Hepburn's younger brother does it. He and his wife are meant to leave Virginia, catch the train from Richmond and travel four states northward to Connecticut for Tom's funeral. They have already bought the tickets and telephoned long distance to book a room at the Hartford Grand. Instead, Dr. Hepburn's younger brother Sewell comes home from work late on Wednesday, puts the car in the garage and leaves it on. He balls up his overcoat under his head and lies down on the cement. His wife finds him the next morning, his handkerchief folded and folded again in his hand. Was he going to cover his mouth and nose? Delay and live a small moment more? His wife will say he looked peaceful but Kate will not believe it when her father tells her why her Aunt and Uncle Hepburn are not coming. She knows better. Dead people are not peaceful; they are just gone. Kate's father decides not to travel down for that funeral. Kate's mother wishes her husband had not told the children.

Now, Kate's father will not speak of his brothers, he will not speak of his son, but after a scotch in the evening, he will talk about his wife. Her monied, aristocratic, intellectual blood. Dr. Hepburn says there is weakness there, and blood will out. Blame is easier to push outward.

. . .

As they drive away from the cemetery, Kate knows they will never come back. Never. They will not be one of those families who know the florist by name and pile into the car on Sundays. Tom's small rectangle will grow knotty and wild; no one will come to weed that patch of earth. Kate understands. Her parents see no point in keeping something alive when it is dead.

Kate is squashed in the back seat with Bob and Dick. Marion and Peg are too small to come and are at home with Fanny. Marion will always believe she can remember how her brother Tom pushed her on a backyard swing once, but she never mentions it to her family. They would say she was too young to remember. She is sure she can feel the moment the swing arced upward and the way her stomach dropped to her knees. Peg will remember nothing except for the pool of quiet around his name and the way her mother stiffens whenever she meets anyone called Thomas. Really, what the younger Hepburn children know is that there is something broken where there was once a sense of triplicate, three daughters, three sons, teams of children paired together like dancing partners, or harnessed oxen. They know they are lopsided.

It is over and the car pulls around in a wide left turn. Kate slides into Bob. She twists around to look back. That's it. They will leave him there, on the damp, spring ground, inside a short, brass handled box.

A List of Missing Things:

A red Schwinn bicycle, the one with the loose handlebar and white seat, a silver snow shovel—someone else will wake up early to clear the front walk, a tennis racquet from the mudroom basket, a set of golf clubs—given away, a jar of white sea pebbles kept by the bed, a school blazer and camel hair topcoat—donated to St. Michael's in

Bridgeport, eight pairs of socks and a pair of blue mittens—also donated, a knitted Christmas stocking, the bedroom at the end of the hall—a guest room now but no guests will be invited to sleep there, a yellowed, soft paged copy of *The Count of Monte Cristo,* a place setting and chair at the kitchen table, a name mentioned at prayers, a name mentioned at all.

. . .

Kate looks like Kate but she is hollowed out, un-twinned. The days keep happening, weeks piling up. She is surprised by this basic fact. Some things should be so big that the days stop, that the mechanics of the planet fail and the sun doesn't come up, out of respect. Kate resents each new month.

In their bedroom, her parents are disagreeing. Her mother wants to let Kate get on with it her own way and says they should just leave her be. Her father wants to push Kate to be *more.* More vivid, more alive. He says she should be sharper, quicker. He wants to shake her out of her dense silence and tell her to fill up the space. She has to pick up slack, be son and daughter. He wants her to study medicine, to take her golf more seriously and get out to the tennis court early to work on her backhand, her ground strokes. The only place he does not push her is in the water. In the water she is beyond all of them.

Her family could get closer. They could pull the planks from her windows or get under her siding if they wanted, but they don't. The Hepburns are loud and known for their bold ideas and knife sharp conversation, but they are not a personal kind of family. No one came to speak to Dr. or Mrs. Hepburn when they lost their favorite people in this world, the ones they could not live without. Now, they do not know how to speak to Kate. In any case, Dr. Hepburn believes speaking of one's personal life is weak and Mrs. Hepburn was raised never to air dirty laundry.

"Other people are other people," Mrs. Hepburn says. "Always remember that."

"Children are resilient," Dr. Hepburn says. "Expect excellence."

So, they leave Kate boarded up. Dr. Hepburn watches his wife, quick to take every chance to lay the blame at her door. Mrs. Hepburn watches her children. Will any of them start to twitch? The younger Hepburns watch their parents. They learn which questions cannot be asked. They learn that a soul is a private beast.

Kate sinks. Kate grapples. Her body regains noise and bounce. At first it is fake, she is pretending, if only so that people will stop watching her. Pretending blurs into being. Her appetite for movement picks up again, slowly—the habit of living is spongy in the greasy muscles and the juice seeps back, not right away, but eventually. Her golf game improves, as does her tennis. Two sports she will play all her life. "See," her father tells her mother, expect more and she will be more. She just needed to be pushed.

. . .

College, graduation, and then New York. Acting and elocution lessons during the week. Her father says it is a silly pursuit and will not pay for the lessons outright but agrees to send her his bridge winnings. Bad money, he calls it, but it is more than enough. And on the weekends? You can find her golfing, swimming and even loving, but she is separate. It is intentional. Why kick for the surface? She knows what is up there. All the prepositions of grief: getting over, moving on, getting past; they are insulting. There is no such place, nor should there be. Some things ought to take more than one lifetime. Recovering will be someone else's problem.

. . .

It is 1932. Kate is living in New York; older now, taller, but still sparrow light and she always wishes on a New Year's Eve. She does it alone. Kate is devoutly private; life is a closed affair now. In her four years at Bryn Mawr, she never once ate in the dining room. But, on New Year's nights like this, her wishes grow thick, feathered wings. At midnight, when she should be singing or drinking or kissing her husband, or lover, she wishes. She slams down her eyelids, squeezes her teeth and blows her wish skyward.

LOS ANGELES
APRIL 1932

Go East. To the Morosco Theatre, West Forty-fifth Street. Broadway. You'll recognize her. The woman never outgrew the girl's countertop flat surfaces and drinking straw hips. She is still rangy, horsey. All bones and freckles and sheets of milk water skin. She wears no makeup and smells of Ivory soap. Sometimes, she scrubs her face with rubbing alcohol so that it shines, clean and tight under the lights. She is playing Antiope, in gold short-skirted armor. She has impressed the critics. In Act I, she leaps down the stairs and hurls a dead stag at the feet of her sister, Hippolyta, the Amazon queen. The audience gasps. It gets applause every night. She's feral, musky and wild. You can imagine her this way, primitive, fast. This is illusion: good lighting, mediocre writing and lots of leg. Out of costume, Kate is citrus clear and afraid of jungle things. Years later, when she is on a steamboat in the Belgian Congo, she will have to pull leeches from Humphrey Bogart. She will bite her cheek to keep from screaming.

But now, she is young. Watch her, this redhead with the long stride. She wants you to watch, throws a look over her hollow boned shoulder to make sure you are there. But she will not stop. Not for you. Not for anyone, really. All that astringent confidence looks like bravado, but it isn't. At her root, she is straightforward, not the enigma she will become. It is simple—she bets on herself, in case no one else will. She is still new to this business and on the stage she is raw and often not much good, but a director in Hollywood has seen her screen test, seen an unlit power and is sure he can make something of her. Something new.

She has twenty-two shows left in the run. After that, she will pack it in and go west. No parts yet but she has done two screen tests in New York, one for Warners, one for RKO. Already, her photo is passed around meetings; the white border is smudged with gray thumbprints and sticky with mustard from a cinematographer's sandwich. The ID numbers for her RKO screen test are written on the back in green ink. Black can bleed through. Men in shirtsleeves sit at folding tables and talk about her height. Five foot seven. Not many men are tall enough for her and they do not want the apple crate problems again. John Barrymore has only an inch on her but if they photograph him from below it will give the impression of size. The big head theory.

See them? There, on the RKO lot, in the upstairs office? The short, rounded director and the taller, beveled producer. They are director George Cukor and producer David Selznick and they are talking about casting a new picture, *A Bill of Divorcement.* They need someone fresh, unseen. John Barrymore is a big name and can carry the billing. George Cukor is the one with the affected enunciation. David Selznick is the one with the loud voice. People say they look alike and when you don't know them, they do. They have lots in common. Both from New York, both wearing glasses, waving imprecise hands, with kind, fleshy, rectangular faces framed by dark curling hair. But the similarities stop at the skin, you'll see.

At first, producer David Selznick does not see it. He has heard about her, this Miss Hepburn. He has seen the screen test. The director, John Ford, over at Fox, wants to test her too. Knowing another studio wants her makes David Selznick want her more but he still feels a resistance. Miss Hepburn chose a good scene but did the whole damned thing with her back to the camera. Irritating. George Cukor doesn't mind. He sees something else. There is a moment when she sweeps forward, puts down a glass and George knows they've found her. It's a certainty. Selznick rewatches the test, looking for that moment. She isn't one of those Oklahoma farm girls who have to relearn how to walk for the camera, he'll say that for her. Cukor thinks the girl has East Coast breeding and class. Normally, the studio has to pay for comportment and elocution, Kate Hepburn has it all built in; Selznick thinks of the money they'll save. Cukor is already trying to imitate her glassy vowels and narrow consonants.

They have it all wrong of course. She is not rooted in ease and privilege. Her family just had a head start in pretending.

Later, in his living room, David Selznick describes Miss Hepburn to his wife, Irene. Irene watches, her legs folded under her on the sofa, as her husband describes George Cukor's belief in this girl. She watches him describe George's perception until he is convinced it's his own. Half listening, Irene is watching to see if his hands shake, if his nose runs.

Someday, David Selznick will say that he spotted Katharine Hepburn's beauty and talent right away but he didn't. It is Irene who sees it first. When she watches the test, she sees what George has seen. Kate Hepburn does not move like other starlets. Her strides are long, her arms swing wide, her voice is metallic, her mouth turns down, her lips are thin and her nostrils flare, but none of that matters. This woman does not apologize. There is no calculation, no hesitation. Here is something *new*, Irene Mayer Selznick says and Irene's opinion matters. She is steeped in the movie business, born to it in a way none of the rest of them can ever be. David worries Irene might tell her father about the screen test and then Louis B. Mayer and MGM will grab this new and magical girl. And so, he bids for Miss Hepburn. Her agents, Leland Hayward and David Selznick's own brother Myron don't tell anyone, but Kate Hepburn has insisted she set her own price, and she has set it high. Leland Hayward tells her it is an outrageous figure, but he is wrong. Kate Hepburn knows that something feels more precious if it is expensive.

Now, her name has been sent to the printing firm on Wilshire, the one upstairs from the greasy blue-tiled café. RKO uses them to print up the names for the chairs: white letters on navy canvas. The designers have spelt her name wrong and it will have to be redone. It is Kath-a-rine with an a not an e. George Cukor and David Selznick want it to be right. They have plans for her. And so, Kate is part of it now; part of the sporty, rich film glamour, that bright bolt of electric youth lighting up the left side of the country.

And watch them. The circus acrobat, the Catholic and the boy who can fly. They have already left and are on their way to meet her. They will intersect on the wide sun-wet avenues of Los Angeles under the coconut palms. White toothed and young, they will push their sunglasses on top of their heads to get a better look at each other.

. . .

Hollywood is a storied place. There are things that happen and things that don't. People talk. Everyone says they were there; they saw it. But people lie. They say they were on the Paramount lot when Clara Bow first saw Gary Cooper. They were at the Chateau Marmont the day Garbo jumped into the pool in gold heels. They were at Mocambo when Tallulah Bankhead left with Billie Holiday. They were playing five card draw, at the Clover Club the night David O. Selznick lost ten thousand on one hand. They were at the counter at Schwab's when Harold Arlen wrote "Get Happy." They were still at the counter when Ava Gardner worked the soda fountain. They were at the Brown Derby when Louella snubbed Hedda. They weren't. People who were really there don't talk about it. They don't need to.

KATE

NEW YORK CITY

MAY 1932

It is nearly eight. The room is rinsed in light. Kate is up and dressed but the woman in the bed has not moved although she is awake. Kate pins up her hair and does the Manhattan arithmetic: a cab at this time of the morning will take fifteen minutes, walking will take twenty. She'll walk to the apartment on Thirty-ninth. She wishes she had her bicycle. Kate sweeps back the sheet and bites her lover's soft hip, where no one will see the mark, pulling the red blue blood to the milky surface. Laura leans into Kate's squared off teeth. An invitation. Kate rests her head on Laura's thigh, sips in the comfort, and then stands, looking around for her shoes. Practicalities.

The alarm. Eight A.M. Damn.

Laura twists back to turn it off, sucking her stomach back to her spine; she still thinks Kate has not seen her doughy belly, but Kate gets up in the night. She sees the soft middle, the red welt where the girdle has cut across flesh, the yeasty thighs. She likes Laura's figure, the scale, the arc, the seagull curves. She likes everything about Laura, more than she admits.

Kate is usually up and out earlier than this but she has left it too long. Will the overnight doorman tell the daytime doorman that Miss Harding's guest has not left?

LAURA
NEW YORK CITY

Eleven stories up, Laura watches her lover leave the building. The top of Kate's head, a reddish smudge as she turns left and passes out of view. Laura feels the air dim when she goes.

Laura Harding's heart will break. You should know this now. Sure as sunrise. Her heart will crack along the bright nerves, unstitching the chewy flesh from the blue valves. That is how it will end. All her privilege won't help. And even if she knew what was coming, what would it matter? She would do it anyway.

. . .

Laura begins here. With Kate. Last year, on a summer Wednesday night in June. Everything before that night feels loose and unbuilt, fogged up by unimportance. There were the tragedies: the death of her father and the soggy, alcoholic dissolution of her mother and then when Laura came into the money, the society columnists, the clothes and parties. She knows how to play the heiress. It is instinct bred in the bone but it is being rather than living. Before Kate, Laura hadn't articulated the difference.

Isolation is strapped to the back of inherited money. The society columns don't mention that, but Laura knew it was coming. What else to do? She *is* different; money pads everything, all the sharp edges of getting through a day, a life, are wrapped in cotton and hustled out. Life is muffled in a downy egg of comfort. It's hard to breathe in a small space. So, she breaks away from the choreography. She tosses out the familiar steps and improvises. She sells the big stone house on Fifth Avenue, the one her mother meant her to pass down to her children. The custom-built Aeolian organ has to be dismantled and leaves the house in chunks wrapped in beige dust bags; she sells the marble statues and heavy gilt mirrors. The crystal chandeliers stay with the house. Laura will not need them in her new Fifth Avenue apartment, high floor, duplex, light. She takes the El Grecos to hang in her study, and the Titian for the hall. No one believed she would sell the enormous house, but she did.

Her friends talk about her, not in groups but in discreet pairs. They tell each other they are worried about Laura's peculiar behavior but really, they are relishing the delicious, unifying recognition that Laura has ruined her prospects. Nothing binds like gossip. These friends talk of dear Laura and how they miss her but as one social body, they take a step back, careful not to muddy their court pumps in their friend's murky new life. The invitations dry up like old fruit and it is the end of the busy evenings of supper parties for Laura Harding and the end of the proposals. Rich with time and choice, Laura takes acting lessons and engages Mrs. Robinson-Duff, the famous voice coach and the rumors rise to a roar. Laura does not care. She wants to go on the stage. Helen Hayes, the Gish sisters, they all studied with Mrs. Robinson-Duff. Laura learns to speak from her diaphragm.

She auditions for parts, Broadway, off Broadway, summer stock, touring. Directors often bring her in for callbacks. Laura knows which cuts suit her frame and she buys the best. She is neat, well packaged, and her voice is mellow and rich with rolled consonants and the crystal diction that speaks of privilege. Her studio photographs do not do her justice. Her grace overcomes her fleshy back and plate round face. Her carriage makes her prettier than she is.

At an audition, when everyone is late and wet because of the rainstorm except Laura who is warm, dry, and punctual, she happens to tell a woman in an outdated felt hat that she has never taken a taxi. She has always had a driver—at that moment, he is waiting outside, smoking a cigarette under a storefront awning near her Silver Cloud Rolls—even in the rain, he will not smoke in the car. The woman has spent that morning carefully re-stitching the edge of her felt hat, trying to breathe verve into the thin cloth before she walked the thirty-six blocks to the audition. The sleet came down gray and slushy but she saved herself the subway fare. The woman gapes. Laura quickly realizes her error and leaves the audition. It is late 1930, forecasters say this depression could last as long as another year, and Laura cannot try to take a job away from a woman who needs the money. The woman in the felt hat turns to two other women waiting to audition.

"She's called Laura Harding," says an actress in a gray suit. She is too young for the role but she has borrowed the suit from her mother to try to look older.

"She has *never* taken a taxi," says the woman in the felt hat.

"Never taken the subway either," says another actress with over-plucked eyebrows.

"She's the American Express heiress," says the gray suit. She works part time sweeping up hair in a beauty salon and reads the society pages.

"I heard she won't marry," says the over-plucked eyebrows.

"I bet no one *wants* to marry her," says the gray suit. "Did you hear that voice? Rolling her r's like she's French and everyone knows she's from Park Avenue."

The woman in the felt hat thinks Laura seemed nice but does not say so; it is easier to dislike her; solidarity feels good.

Some gossip reaches Laura. She tries not to let the inaccuracies annoy her: Fifth Avenue, not Park Avenue, and American Express hardly makes the family any money. The wealth came when her Great-grandfather Cooke financed the Civil War. Wartime is when real money is made. All robber baron daughters know this. Some rumors rot away and other, more lurid stories take their place, but eventually, they all become background noise. Laura stops hearing them, like cicadas, or traffic.

When the rumors bleed into print, she does not correct them—it seems petty. Laura is used to being noticed, not for beauty, for money. Money has its own centrifugal force. And it makes people lie. She has learned how to steer the conversation away when she feels the approach, usually from slick young men whose businesses have gone bust or who have gambled themselves out of their family estate and are living at their club. First, they try to light a flirtation, then they offer dinner, dancing and when all that fails, they bring the conversation around to their current predicament—always temporary, always someone else's fault. People are unsubtle when they ask for cash. It is not as though these men would mind having to marry Laura. But their motives are not what they say they are. She can always tell.

Before Kate, Laura's life was orderly, neatly boxed. The family tragedies were unhappy but they did not break her down from the inside. Her mother had approved of Laura's cold, heavy core. Mrs. Harding believed that grief was a private business and not something to perform in public. By the end, Mrs. Harding was mostly drunk and never went out in public. Laura has nothing to perform. These griefs do not tear her seams. Instead, it is joy that breaks her open. Kate will rip her down to the studs.

The beginning. The mosquitoes are thick that summer. Clouds of them sweep through the playhouse in the Berkshires. Laura will remember the show; she will keep the program, printed on cheap paper. The weight of that slip of paper can sink an ocean. Kate won't know she keeps it. Kate won't remember the name of the play but she will remember this night.

After the show, when they have propped open the back door so they can smoke out in the blue night air, Kate pulls on a man's fisherman sweater, it is too big so she pins it in back with a large safety pin. Laura watches as Kate reaches her arms back and pins it blind, grabbing fistfuls of wool with her long hands. That is it.

Until then, Laura has kept her distance. She had heard that Kate is married and has seen the tasteful bouquets in the dressing room. *For Kate, from Luddy*. Not imaginative but consistent. The play is called *Caroline*. Weak script and only twenty-five dollars a week. Laura often forgets to pick up her check. Kate is friendly to the others in the cast but she can be spiky too. The cast is wary of her. Catch her in the wrong mood and her temper can switch you like a tail. A moat of space opens up around Kate. To them, Kate feels risky, like half-thawed lake ice.

Laura watches Kate rehearse a scene. It is the way she holds herself; everyone watches even though they pretend not to. Even in New England, Kate's voice sounds affected and she can always turn a head. The second lead actress running lines in the wings, the light men, up on the ladders, focusing their spots, the doorman counting receipts, they all turn to look when Kate Hepburn speaks. With clear bones and hooded eyes, Kate is boyish, scrubbed clean, and painfully beautiful, but not for me Laura tells herself, until a blue night in June.

The inns are full and so they are both staying at the Reverend Bradley's New England farmhouse. White clapboard, black shutters, and a loose third step up to the porch. The screen door bangs if you don't close it gently. Reverend Bradley and his wife go to bed at nine. Kate and Laura finish after eleven. It has been a good enough evening: fine show, average audience, but that part of the night is not memorable. On the wooden porch, Laura and Kate drink iced tea and in low voices talk about the script, about the costumes, and about the affair between the director and the ingénue who is too ripe to play an ingénue and too young to be sleeping with the director. They like her; they see her; they want to help. Four in the morning. They try not to wake the reverend and his wife.

Kate leans back on the porch step. It is a bright night but Laura does not talk about the stars—that would be a cliché and Kate would hate that, so she says nothing. Kate looks up, her head tipped back, and the silence quivers and draws bow tight. Neck arched, chin lifted, Kate lets her mouth fall open a little. Later, Laura will tell her it is her best angle. It isn't, but Laura is sentimental.

Laura hates decisive moments. Her instinct is not to act but to react. Her armies know how to defend but not to charge. In finishing school, dancing mistresses in high-necked blouses poleaxed the last of Laura's hidden wildness. All that learned timidity is ruthlessly spoon-fed into the bloodstream of girls like her. It is an artificial weakness, pounded in over time. Laura is trying to undo it.

Sitting on the stage in rehearsal, in the dressing rooms, walking home, Laura has tried to be near Kate. Sometimes they touch. Nothing overt, just small brushes, Laura is not trying to make something happen but just to connect. Connection is not enough.

This night, Laura chooses boldness. Subtlety can be mistaken for friendship. Turning, facing, reaching out to cup that small skull, Laura waits, beat after beat, offering Kate the chance to refuse, to stop it. Laura holds her nerve until Kate's breath shallows and breaks. Laura's kiss, the first frontier crossing, is limber, hesitant. But she gets it wrong. Kate does not want to be loved carefully; trepidation bores her. Kate wants to rip the roof off the world. Gently as if she is carrying a bird's nest, Kate holds Laura's hand. She kisses the part where the thick palm flesh meets the skin. And then she bites, hard. If it is not going to start an earthquake in the blood, why bother? Laura is shaken, unseated and then she surrenders. Laura's neck pinks with shame and hope. Kate meets Laura's gaze, and without hesitating, reaches under her skirt, running her cool fingers up the seam of Laura's nylon until she reaches her clammy thigh. Laura's stomach tightens. This is real. She is already thinking of how she will treasure these moments later. Kate's mouth is hard. Kate is looking for something. Laura's jaw aches and her neck twists; she wants Kate to open her up and climb in.

And so, it is Kate who advances and Laura hurries ahead to dismantle all her borders. Laura feels colonized and new.

Later, Kate laughs and calls Laura's first kiss bloodless. But there is joy in the teasing, there is possession and Laura's world empties of everyone but Kate.

KATE

NEW YORK CITY

She has stayed too long at Laura's and is late but she still has to have a cold shower at home. She rinses away the oily film of sex that Laura's bed has left on her skin. She is not hiding the affair from Luddy because she does not need to. He never asks. It is not *not* allowed in their relationship. They are making it up as they go, Kate tells herself. She knows that *she* is making it up and Luddy is going along but she tries not to think about it. Kate closes her eyes, tasting the water as it slides off in sheets. One can never have too many cold showers, her father always says. Kate tries to live by what Dr. Hepburn says. She has no teammate in her family now; is not neatly paired as the others are, so she has thrown her lot in with her parents. They are happy to have her.

Luddy is already at his office, selling insurance in a gentleman's firm on Vanderbilt Avenue. Kate approves of men who work and so he works. It is midmorning when Kate ties a scarf around her red hair and knots it tight under her chin. She does not want to arrive at Fenwick looking like something that has been to sea. Although, she knows she looks her best by the sea. Wind roughed cheeks against a kingfisher blue water. By the sea or in the sea rather than *on* the sea. Salted air agrees with her, but the open ocean makes her vomit.

She has not seen Luddy in three days. They keep missing each other. Not that she is trying very hard to run into him. She thinks of this as his apartment now, even though her things are everywhere. She does not like to be a person who uses people. The conversation in her head follows a worn track. To stay is to take advantage but to leave would hurt him more. She looks around the apartment, imagining packing crates, movers. What is hers and what is his; books, photographs, china. She imagines telling him she is going, that their life together has finished, but that would mean upending the whole setup and the thought makes her feel adrift and exhausted. Luddy is family, everyone says so, but Kate knows that family can be lost. If she leaves, she will have to move home. That is the part that feels like failure.

LUDDY
NEW YORK CITY

Last year, Kate and Luddy took a ship called the *Bermuda*, to Bermuda. It put her off at the time. But it was her honeymoon and she had said once that she wanted to see the Caribbean and Luddy was determined to give her what she wanted. Even then, she walked on him. Didn't even take her shoes off. She thinks he loves her too much and it makes him weak. That easy capitulation. Spoils the heart and makes it lazy. Luddy knows he is a man who ought to be loved hard but he makes excuses for Kate. *She is young. She needs time to settle.* Anything to avoid the obvious. His method works and she has stayed. Kindness, cut with gentle persistence, can knock a person flat. Sometimes, when he ferries a pair of gloves over to her at Laura's, or meets her with an umbrella outside the theater when rain melts the city, he knows that Kate sees him, really sees him, his unselfishness, his cultivated habit of loving her. And he does. He is built of Kate now.

In these moments, Kate does see him. She resolves to do better; she will pay more attention; she will not be impatient; she will kiss him hello; she will sleep at home. It never lasts. But Luddy's kindness is built like a shire horse. He has mostly guessed about Laura but he will not let himself be certain, not absolutely. Kate sleeping with a woman is different from her sleeping with a man. Isn't it? He has slept with men and so believes he can judge. Luddy rarely has more than two drinks, but when he has three and his hairline starts to sweat, he unwraps the problem gently, careful not to disturb the furniture so he can exit as cleanly as he entered. It is not the sex with Laura that bothers him, but the desire, and of course, the love. He can see Kate already loves Laura even if she can't. He is discreet and he is loyal. He tells no one. It will pass. As long as they are married, she is still his.

. . .

Luddy tries not to but he waits, hoping Kate will decide to live as other married couples do even though she never has. Why would she start now? It has become her habit, the not loving back. Luddy tells himself he is used to it but Kate knows it hurts him. Sometime she will set aside time to try it, try to reorganize her heart and really love him, won't she? She never does. But there is life between them. They share the small intimacies of marriage: shirts picked up from the cleaners, telephone bills paid, plumbing fixed, sometimes brushing their teeth side by side in the bathroom mirror. He loves the ordinariness of it. There is something between them, many somethings, and it is not enough. But Luddy is tenacious. He is framed with that East Coast determination, pilgrim grit, Kate calls it, but things won't change until he changes them, so he has decided to act.

Last week, they ate lunch at the Broadmoor Pharmacy, Kate had the afternoon free and did not have to be at the theater until five. Kate chewed her food. She picks up her sandwiches and never cuts them into small triangles, Luddy likes that about her. She is most attractive when she is most herself. They sat at the counter, always the same two seats on the end farthest from the door. Luddy told her that he has decided to give up the apartment and rent a house.

"But you love the apartment?" Kate said, turning in her high swivel chair to look at him.

The lunch counter was empty apart from a mother and daughter eating cherry pie after a morning of shopping.

"I do love it," Luddy said, "but I have taken a house. It will be better for us." He folded the napkin in his lap into a square.

"You already did it?" Kate said. "Before asking me." He could see she was jolted.

"The agent showed it to me yesterday, before it went on the market, and I knew it was right for you. I am sorry I didn't ask you first. If you hate this house, we can keep the apartment."

"*Which* house is it, exactly?"

"A flat front brownstone in Turtle Bay between Second and Third, beautiful gardens in the back. Please Kate, see it before you decide to hate it?"

KATE

NEW YORK CITY

The house knows they are watching. Kate can feel it. She looks over at Luddy, the way a stranger would. He has gone soft around the middle but his suit is beautifully cut. She knows they walk together like friends not lovers. The house, number 244, is narrow hipped and elegant. Kate and Luddy stand on the sidewalk. He points up at the windows, leaves his arm hitched in the air as he talks about furniture, plumbing and paint.

"The living room would be there. We could take the front bedroom above, or you could take it as an office?" He waits for Kate to answer but she doesn't. Her head is tipped back and she is looking up at the house. He cannot tell what she is thinking.

Kate likes it more than she wants to admit. She likes the way this block was built with restraint and proportion. *Number 244*. A solid number, not showy and not small. This house is not the biggest, nor the smartest nor the smallest on the block. Good. This house keeps its secrets. *Turtle Bay, on the East Side of New York*. She imagines saying it when people ask where she lives. She wants to show Laura.

Luddy is still talking.

"There are two small guest rooms at the top. We could always convert one or both if we need to?" He waits. Nothing. He has been saying things like this recently. Hints that swing in mid-air like a rung bell. Kate has been ignoring them.

Kate and Luddy come back the next day. They stand on the sidewalk, looking up. This time Luddy says nothing.

She can see that this house does not boast about its tumbling gardens or puff out its chest with a bay window. It is the set of a house that matters to her, the character. Can she find one as fine in California? One that will suit her as well? Connecticut houses are born grouchy and then they weather and grow crotchety as they age. Houses on this eastern, river edged side of Manhattan, grow vain. They wear their window boxes and wrought iron jewelry with a tidy smugness that Kate dislikes. This house does none of that. It's plucky and gets on with things. Luddy is right. It is her house. That he would know it when he saw it moves her deeply. She takes his hand but does not look at him. He stands a little taller.

LOS ANGELES

MAY 1932

Are we losing her? No? Maybe. The house is a draw, there is no denying it. There is a life waiting in New York. She can see her way ahead there, something new for her. Usually, she is worrying she is in the wrong place, wearing the wrong shoes. She's good at hiding it. All that bravado, no one would guess. But, we do. We know when someone is pretending. It's our business.

A future in New York. A family. The house listens. Is it a when or an if? It has been a long time since the house has held children.

Luddy does not push for an answer. Poor man. Lost the momentum of the scene. But Luddy is interested only in her, her in her entirety. It is rare for someone to not want to change someone else. Whatever she likes, he will like and what she wants, he will choose to want. Is that weakness? We can't tell. We don't grow these kinds of people on this coast.

Kate is half listening. She is imagining herself opening the front door, banging on the light switch without looking. The way you do at home.

The house is relieved she has come. It has been waiting for her. But we have houses out here. Low, Spanish houses with shade and tile.

Fine. We will wait. We are good at that.

There are many ways to play Luddy. Pathetic? Lovesick? Manipulative? Passive? But, no, you're right, people are never one thing.

Humans are ill mixed and lumpy with all that wanting and trying. Luddy is secretive and he hides his possessiveness well. Kate is different. She wears her skeleton on the outside.

He can hire painters and plumbers and do it all the way she likes but we are going to split her down the middle regardless. You want to be a star? You have to live in the sky.

Anyway, Kate could never stay and be with someone who will stay and be with her back. She has no template for that.

KATE

NEW YORK CITY

It is all arranged and she is leaving town soon but first, Kate comes back to see her house. *Her* house. She has a key now. She and Luddy have gone over the blueprints. He wants to install a ground floor bathroom, he knows his father-in-law, the surgical urologist, will hate any house without one, and so they will not officially move in for a few months. Kate tumbles the key and turns the smooth brass of the front doorknob. After she finishes her first picture, she will come home to this house. The thought settles something in her although when she imagines herself living here, it is alone, or with Laura rather than with Luddy. But, now, whatever happens out there, she has a place to come back to.

Kate will not be in New York for the move. Her life is already facing west. They are arranging it now—the men in beige slacks and the women in back offices who arrange things. RKO has been on the phone to Leland Hayward and Myron Selznick, her agents. Her *agents*. She signed the representation papers last month. She signed the deal with RKO yesterday. A good pen, a thick stripe of ink and she belongs to RKO Radio Pictures. Leland Hayward was in the office. He goes back and forth between the coasts but his partner, Myron Selznick, only works out of Hollywood. Agency, studio, contracts, loan-outs. It is a confusing web of ownership and Kate insists on understanding it. She demands Leland explain it until she does.

With his Princeton degree and sailing shoes and Jazz Age Brylcreem, Leland Hayward looks like the East Coast boys she knows from college. Nothing like the slick-palmed Hollywood agents she has heard about. And he came recommended by a friend. Philip Barry is a playwright Kate knows from her days as an understudy. They would often sit backstage together during his play, *Holiday*, and watch the lead actress who was never ill. At the time, Kate did not know it was unusual for the playwright to come in to watch the show backstage after opening night; even more unusual to watch with the understudy. It is Philip Barry who suggests his friend the agent Leland Hayward come and meet Kate after the show.

"She's a bit East Coast horsey and a little thorny but there is no one like her," he tells Leland.

Leland offers to represent her that night.

Philip Barry looks it over, tells her it is a good contract and that Leland is brilliant. He also tells her that the right offer will come, the right part, right price, right director, right film—wait for it. They thought that director, John Ford, wanted to screen test her but he changed his mind. She read about him in *Photoplay,* liked the sound of his no nonsense directing and the look of his square chin and rough hands. She was disappointed when Leland said Ford had decided not to test her. "Hold out and wait," Leland tells her. *Keep your nerve,* she tells herself. But the offers have not come and now Leland prefers she hold out and wait for the right part in California.

It's time. She leaves a note for Luddy by the tulips on the hall table and takes his car. Cars do not matter to her, any one will do.

One day, when Philip Barry writes a play for her, he will use that line. She climbs into Luddy's grass green Alfa Romeo. When she crosses the narrow bridge to Fenwick, the enclave of summer cottages on the hump of land sticking out into the sea, she feels the peace of being at home. Time to tell her parents she means to go to Hollywood.

Driving clears her head. She tries to memorize the shape of the Connecticut coastline. By summer, the ocean will be on her left when she drives north. She wants to tell her parents at Fenwick. Bad news is easier by the sea. Laura will travel out to Hollywood with her, stay with her, live with her and then at some undefined moment when the adventure ends, bring her home. Leland has made it clear that arriving with a husband is not an option. Starlets do not have husbands. They do not sleep with women either but Leland doesn't have to know everything.

Laura. She has promised to be discreet but Kate knows it will not be easy for her. Kate is relieved Laura will be there to make sure she wears the right shoes and eats enough breakfast. That will reassure Mother and Dad, even though it shouldn't. Laura is the threat they fear but they cannot see it.

LAURA

NEW YORK CITY

Laura sits on the edge of her tub and watches while Kate packs. It is only a few things, toothbrush, tooth powder, hairbrush, aspirin, washcloth, Ivory soap. Things that Laura has loved seeing on her bathroom shelf. Having them here in her apartment has anchored Laura, they promised Kate would come back. *She is only going to Fenwick,* Laura thinks, running her fingers over the empty shelf.

When Kate goes downstairs Laura reaches into her open bag, takes back the hairbrush and tucks it into a drawer. It smells of Kate.

KATE

NEW YORK CITY

Kate plans to be in two places at once. She convinces herself she can do it. Pack a suitcase of summer clothes and live a life in California and then, pull on her winter coat and return to life with Luddy in New York. She has decided to paint the whole Turtle Bay house white and has given Luddy careful instructions about curtains. She does not care much about furniture and will pick some up from the attic at Fenwick. He writes it all down and asks the right questions. White white or off white? Off white with a tinge of blue? White white. Clean slate.

Kate speaks to him about the plans and the paint and the move. She speaks as though she will live there.

LUDDY

NEW YORK CITY

MAY 1932

The doorman hands him the telegram. From Kate's agent. Luddy has met Leland Hayward twice and tries not to like him but does anyway. Luddy brings the telegram up with the post and then sits at the hall table to telephone Kate at Fenwick. Some of him is genuinely excited for her. Eleven rings before she picks up. Ten people in that house and no one bothers to answer the telephone. The telephone is not important to the Hepburns.

"Kate? My darling you did it." Luddy reads out the telegram, rushing; the staccato words stick together like sweaty palms. He is pleased to be the one to give her the news; it gives him a stake in the adventure. Kate whoops and the younger Hepburns come running. Without ringing off she tells them: the screen test that she thought was a bust, wasn't and RKO Pictures have made an offer.

"*A Bill of Divorcement* starring John Barrymore," Luddy says.

"*John Barrymore,*" Kate repeats. Even her brother Bob, who is only interested in organic chemistry, has heard of him. She will play Barrymore's daughter, *Sydney Fairfield.*

Luddy hears the Hepburns scatter to go and tell other Hepburns.

KATE

FENWICK, CONNECTICUT

"Sydney Fairfield." Kate rolls the name over her tongue. It is hilly and sweet. She is still holding the telephone and Luddy waits, listening to her happiness.

There is some objection but her parents take it well enough. Her father might even be pleased, but first he has to rattle the air.

"And with your education," her father says, shucking off his shoes. "You can be anything you want to be and this is what you choose?" Without waiting for her answer, he goes up to have a bath. Like Kate, water is his answer to most things. Really, he is not angry, nor surprised. He already knows that it will be Bob who follows him into medicine. He can see that Kate does not have the patience nor the interest in other people. And though he will not admit it, there is some glamour to her acting life. Flashy and vulgar but magical too; and now she will go to Hollywood.

She knows her father will come around. Dr. Hepburn loves movies. He still calls them "the pictures" and Kate has seen his profile when he watches the screen. Absorbed and wondrous, he offers himself up.

Her mother betrays a snap of disappointment and then recovers. She wants her daughters to keep moving *forward*. Forward is where everything happens.

Kate sits on the damp grass, looks at the water and thinks about the fame, the money. They have met her price. Fifteen hundred a week—a fortune. Luddy has offered to backstop her, she knows her father would too, but now she won't need them. The whole country is going broke and she will be making fifteen hundred a week. Kate lets herself think about the breadlines, the newsreels, the photographs of people living in boxcars and cooking by the side of the road surrounded by dust bowl hollow children, the politicians shouting about the country's smashed-open heart—the great upheaval of people she does not know and will not meet. Kate is a boomerang; human, and reliably selfish, her thoughts return to her own life. She breathes in her good luck. Acknowledging good fortune is important to her. She hates ingratitude; it is lazy. She watches Long Island Sound, imagines the other, bluer ocean, cameras, palm trees, picture magazines, and the ranks of credits filing up the screen.

She may not meet the people on the breadlines, but by god, she will entertain them.

LUDDY

FENWICK, CONNECTICUT

Luddy arrives at Fenwick the next afternoon. Before putting down his bag, he gives Kate the telegram. He can see she thinks he is taking it all very well and she likes him better for it. He never suggests he should come along.

"Just find a house with shade, a deep bath and a telephone," he says. Luddy accepts that Laura will live with Kate. Yes, there is love between Kate and Laura, but he believes it is an unsexy, non-threatening love, schoolgirlish and soft. Luddy also knows that if he tries to separate Kate from this new love, she will fight and grip and tear flesh before letting it go. Losing something will only make Kate want it more. He is Kate's husband. Their legal bond steadies him when he is afraid.

Kate is speaking about the trip; she is using the plural. "Our luggage, our tickets, our sleeping compartments." Is it deliberate? Luddy will not mention it. After all, he is here at Fenwick and Laura is in the city. He will not wrinkle their visit with a fight.

"And if you finish in time, we can still sail to Europe in September, before it gets too rough," he says, halving the "our."

"And if we don't finish in time?" Kate challenges, lifting her bony jaw.

"If you don't, I can rebook," he teases. "I am sure there will be steerage bunks available."

It is an old joke between them. Kate and Luddy have always traveled third class to Europe. Kate is seasick every time they cross the Atlantic regardless of season. "Why pay more to be sick in first?" she says. Luddy would prefer first but he would prefer to please Kate more.

Luddy puts his bags in the guest bedroom across the hall from Kate's room. It is expected. The maid has put fresh sheets on the guest bed, a stack of towels on the chair and set a jug of daisies, cut this morning, on the nightstand. Everyone at Fenwick likes Luddy. Kate sits on the bed and they talk while he unpacks. Neither one asks the questions that would cloud the air between them. Luddy keeps the marriage light. Any weight and he knows Kate will run.

In her way, she is loyal. They file joint taxes, sign both of their names on Christmas cards. She stays. It is enough for him. Luddy tries to imagine life without Kate, probing, exploring the thought the way a tongue rubs over a rotting tooth, but the pain is too nervy and rich and he retreats. There is no life without Kate.

Time to swim. They throw striped bathing towels over their shoulders, as she has always done. Kate bolts down the green lawn. Luddy races her to the floating dock. He knows she loves to hear the second footsteps behind her when she runs.

LOS ANGELES
MAY 1932

We've been studying her. Kate and the Hepburns who surround her. She is not as she appears. The lioness stance and upright boldness is performance, habit. Kate is afraid of getting it wrong, of giving herself away. It is not money that she wants to signal. Money is considered vulgar in her family—but don't marry anyone without it. Although, of course, it is partly money—that need to show that it is there but unimportant. As if the money is so inconsequential, she may have forgotten about it. With her mother's family, it is genuine. With her father's, it isn't. Never was. In the early years of her parents' marriage, her father watched the way that his wife's wealthy relations fearlessly wore old clothes and kept faded chintz armchairs until the stuffing poked out. And then they still kept them. He studied their unconscious inattention. His wife watched him watching them but she could not help. It was not something she could teach.

And, it is not class that Kate wants to signal, although it is partly class. Early in his marriage, her father tried to learn that too. His in-laws, the old money, New England Houghtons curled away from him when he tried too hard. They cringed if he mentioned heirlooms or inheritance tax. They understood the difference between trying and being. In the end, Dr. Hepburn turned on them, those Houghtons of New England. He claimed that privilege encouraged laziness.

"Achievement is the only true worth," he still says at extended family gatherings.

His wife wishes he wouldn't say that. The argument does not hold up with her family who have pedigree, achievement *and* a New England self-discipline. But she doesn't stop him. Kit Hepburn is loyal and knows her husband must break her old monied family down into bites he can chew.

Even now, Dr. Hepburn is sure his wife's family laugh about him, snickering that their Kit could have married better. He is right. They do. But it is not the poverty that bothers them; it's the trying. Their Kit's husband got that wrong. Dr. Hepburn refers to his family's home in Virginia as a "farm" thinking he is conjuring a gentleman's horse farm but his wife's New England family are not fooled. They see his small dirt road roots and hear the hard Virginia twang. Horse farm Virginians sound soft. The Virginia Hepburns sound like tin and sweat. But the Houghtons are salty New England liberals and not snobs; they think he should be proud of his blood. It is his bald aspiration they dislike, and the ungenerous way he rules his family. "Our Kit deserves better," they say to one another.

Kate and Tom were born before their father earned professional clout, before he moved to the bigger office on the second floor of the hospital. They caught that knack of wanting from him. Kate still breathes in the uncertainty her father has learned to cover up. When Tom began his new school, he worried about the right way to walk, to smoke, to swear, to eat. He took extra care to disguise these fears at home. Their father was always looking for weakness, kicking the tires of his eldest son to make sure he would run. Eventually, something would set him off and the air around their father would snap with irritation. Better to hide anything that was not clad in steel. The only person Tom could trust with his fears was Kate.

KATE

FENWICK, CONNECTICUT

Now that it is happening, Kate thinks about how to do it. Lying in the bathtub, she tries to imagine her days. Is acting for a camera harder than acting for an audience? The picture magazines and publicity shots. Will they want her to do all that? Will someone tell her how to stand, to smile or not? Laura will be there. Kate doesn't care if people find out about her lover. Loving women is obvious. Shouldn't everyone? Women are curved to fit, sexy, cultured, artful, interesting and so much easier than men. Men compete, exhausting. Or worse, don't compete, dull.

When Kate is using her body, running, swimming, she forgets to worry and slides into herself. Her body reconfigures. It sweats and squats and cracks its ankles. Her body says damn everyone else, it knows who she is. She wishes there were days when she could not care if there is spinach in her teeth or sweat behind her knees. A day when she could not carry an extra set of drawers in her bag in case the ones she is wearing dampen and stick. But her confidence is fickle. It left her in that attic room when she was un-doubled.

LUDDY

FENWICK, CONNECTICUT

Luddy waits, hoping to be useful, needed. Kate knows Luddy is pretending of course, pretending to love her less. His mother cannot bear this marriage. "If you can call it a marriage," she says. But, Luddy will not imagine life without Kate, or without the Hepburns. They are family, what would happen to his life with them if he were not married to Kate? Pull the pin and the grenade explodes.

Luddy takes his camera out of its bag and cleans the lens with the soft cloth he keeps in the front pocket. His role in the family is to take the photographs. No one else wants to.

KATE

FENWICK, CONNECTICUT

Laura telephones. Kate takes it in the upstairs hall, leaning back in the rattan chair with her feet resting up on the telephone table. Her mother hates it when she sits like this.

"And a car and driver?" Laura asks, checking items off her list.

"Yes, a car and driver and an allowance to rent a house too," Kate says.

Broad figures are not enough for Laura. She wants the fine print. Kate can hear her curving over the telephone, the pearl handled one on her desk; it is too early for Laura to be in bed. Kate loves that Laura is disciplined that way. Kate listens. Laura's voice is breathy, she is tucking the receiver under her chin while she writes down the numbers. There will be lipstick on the white mouthpiece. Kate knows Laura will wipe it with a linen handkerchief afterward.

Kate listens but doesn't. Warm from the sun and the bath, tired, she flexes her feet in a long, shaky cat stretch and pushes her mind toward Fenwick things. In the morning, her father has promised her a golf game. Where are the course shoes that Marion borrowed? Laura keeps talking.

Laura says she doesn't believe the money will be enough. It is 1932; does Laura not read newspapers? Any money is enough. But Kate knows that Laura needs to feel useful and what Laura can always bring to a situation is more money.

Laura rattles off the list of appointments she will make for Kate next week: Monday: hairdresser. Tuesday: fitting. Wednesday: Mrs. Robinson-Duff to work on her voice. Laura felt important when she called to ask Mrs. Robinson-Duff to squeeze in a lesson for Kate.

"No," Kate says. There are microphones in Hollywood. "I could whisper and they would hear me."

LAURA

NEW YORK CITY

JULY 1932

They are going away together. There is no invitation, it is assumed. The way it was assumed that Kate would stay with her when Luddy went away on business. The two rail tickets are mailed to Laura's Fifth Avenue apartment. Kate must have given this as her home address. Kate has the tickets but Laura keeps the envelope. She hoards these throwaway moments of assumption. While Kate is at Fenwick with Luddy, Laura rehearses their new life. They will find a house together, sleep together, eat together. Laura will buy heirloom tomatoes because Kate likes them. Kate will call and let her know when she is going to be late for dinner. Laura wants to hold on to the person she is right now. This is the beginning.

The porter wheels the luggage on ahead of her. The *Super Chief*. Carriage 7, Compartment 3. Private drawing room plus two Pullman sleepers: chocolate boxes, jigsawed together. Laura knows that Kate will feel ashamed of the opulence when the porter brings in her bags, in the way that people from the professional classes do. Laura does read the papers. She knows this "depression" is sinking the country. Kate will be embarrassed and think that in a whole year, the porter will make less than the price of these tickets. Laura will think, how would it help that porter if they traveled third?

Kate will be late. She always is. It is part of her carelessness. Laura enjoys it. Laura enjoys most things about Kate. Laura waits on the platform while the uniformed porter loads her cases onto the train. He is smallish, wiry and sweaty but not unpleasantly so. Laura Harding gives him a six-dollar tip. Showy and vulgar but what does that matter to him? She wants everyone to be happy today. The adventure is beginning.

. . .

Ocean to ocean, ninety-six hours. In a pair of men's trousers, shirt-sleeves rolled to the elbows, Kate refuses to dress for the dining car. "Why bother when we can eat here and be comfortable?" So, they eat alone in their private padded drawing room. Laura, her expensive wardrobe tailored to her neat, cello curves, dresses only for Kate.

"No hat," Kate says, dropping into the wingback chair and hooking her long foot under the stool. "I like you better without a hat."

It is a metal filing. Snapping up from the hot rails. When Kate pulls down the gummy window to see the last scattered lumps of Chicago, it lodges in her eye. The silver steel tube rattles across the vast flat states in the July sun. The low hanging heat smothers the air. Laura does her best to be entertaining. Kate does her best not to complain. With long spoons, they eat Italian ices to keep cool. Kate rubs her eye and tries to stop and then rubs her eye some more. By the time they arrive in California, her eyelid is veined, striped angry pink. Laura suggests face powder. Kate only believes in soap.

Leland has sent a wire. He and the director will meet them at the station in Pasadena and drive them to the studio.

"'Leland is bringing George Cukor, the director,'" Laura reads.

"Cukor?" Kate says.

"Cu— sounds like 'cucumber' apparently." Laura and Leland are Upper East Side friends. Three years ago, he was head of the stag line for most of the season. They come from the same pearly hoops of old wealth. No way in except birth. Leland Hayward is the grandson of a U.S. senator, son of a war hero and the stepson of the woman who traded her Fifth Avenue mansion to Cartier for a string of matched pearls. He is also Hollywood's newest power broker. Leland orders his clothes from London, drinks from a heavy cut crystal tumbler, wears Belgian linen underwear and smells of bay rum aftershave. A telephone is always brought to his table at Chasen's on Beverly Boulevard so that he can conduct business over lunch. Laura has not seen this yet but when she does she will tell him that it's vulgar. But away from New York, Leland does not care about Laura's opinion anymore—only Kate's. Laura will need to find a way to show she has currency in California.

Kate is the point of everything. She is both battleground and prize. Laura Harding has time on her hands and does not want it to show. She doesn't really want to leave New York, where she knows exactly what to do and who to be.

But Laura will have new importance now. The kind that comes from being the closest person to someone everyone wants to be close to. Together, Laura and Leland will launch Kate Hepburn.

PART TWO

THE SET

She is half Botticelli page and half bobbed hair bandit.
She is the find of the year.

—*The New Yorker,* October 1932

CARY
BRISTOL, ENGLAND
1900

Before you met him, before America, before he was an acrobat and he became what he became, he was here. In this river port city, where he was born the son of a woman who regretted her marriage to a man who was unhappy. This part matters but no one will remember this part later, the river port city, the vanished mother, the rough, open voweled accent like all the other knee socked boys. He will change his voice later, melt it down and hammer it flat, curving the liquid sound to what he thinks is an upper-class lilt but isn't. By the time he knows better, it is too late and the voice is famous. He will keep it; it works: unhurried and lifted with irony, his voice will place him nowhere. He will sound more affected than English. Soon, he will change his name. Two beats, one beat, it will stamp the same cadence as his old name. And with the name, this first part will be sloughed off and left to rust. But first, he begins here with Elsie and Elias at 15 Hughenden Road.

. . .

Elias takes her to another doctor. Dr. Ware: a storkish man with thinning hair and a dirty surgery near the Horfield Depot. The seven-minute appointment is blunt and uncomplicated.

The prescription: have another baby.

"It will restore the balance," Dr. Ware says. Elias agrees. It is what Elias has been saying for four months and nineteen days. Since it happened.

But the doctor is wrong. Elias is wrong.

Elsie is sure but her conviction will not rise to the surface. Instead, it sinks through the porous bone to the greasy marrow where it snakes along the veined meat.

She knows what they do not.

You cannot replace what cannot be replaced.

. . .

Elsie gives in. Her walls crack and then cave. She dusts out the nursery and hangs thicker curtains. Another winter birth. Another New Year's son. Archie. This time, she will be vigilant.

. . .

She keeps him in dresses until he is four. They are expensive, more than the family can afford. Elias complains that he looks like a girl. But Elsie disagrees. To her, he looks like her baby. She wraps him up. Scarves, hats, gloves always, and never out after dark. She washes his hands herself when they come inside. Forty rinses with strong soap, scooping the dirt from under the nails. Outside must stay outside. Outside is where the danger comes from. The windows never open and the back garden overgrows with neglect. Elias thinks it makes them look poor but does not say so to Elsie. She would only say that is because they *are* poor. "Marry down" is her phrase. She has married down.

The boy is not allowed to run in the street as other boys do. Elsie will not permit it. Instead, he is home, with her, where he is safe.

. . .

It starts when Archie is six. The questions, the shouting, his father disappearing for days and returning smelling of violet candy.

"Careful son," his father says, sitting at the kitchen table, "marriage can pull you under." Elias ruffs up his hair but Archie pulls away. His mother does not like it when his hair is untidy. Archie does not like it when his father drinks.

Elsie doesn't guess he has another family. A woman yes, but not a family. She will not learn this for years.

. . .

The boy is nine when she disappears.

"A trip to the seaside," Elias says. "It will do her good."

"Mother always takes me with her when she goes to the sea," Archie says. But Elias is already drunk.

Archie accepts it, the way children do. Summer ends and winter comes. Do mothers stay at the seaside in winter? His father never mentions her anymore and gets angry when Archie asks about her. She must be dead, Archie decides, using a child's logic. The pain is deep but the wound is clean. He takes the pain in small bites, chews it up patiently, consistently, digesting the grief. These things must be worked on. The boy has a natural aptitude for pain. At the end of the year, they move in with an aunt. After that, his father rarely comes home.

Archie starts running. He is tall for his age and naturally athletic. At first he runs at night, flying down Campbell Street when no one can see him. The danger, the promised unraveling does not happen. He only washes his hands twice now when he comes inside but is still careful to button his pajamas up to the neck to keep the outside out. He tries jumping, rolling, shouting, spinning. He flings his small rubbery body down a grassy hill. Bruises but no breaks. He is built like other boys after all. Movement, the blood and bones bending in air, brings a feeling of wildness; it is what he lives for.

On a Thursday, after school, he goes to the Hippodrome theater on St Augustine's Parade. He takes a job as a callboy, fetching the performers to the stage. His aunt would give him pocket money but he prefers to earn his own. He loves the Hippodrome, the greasepaint and garish faces, the threadbare costumes, the stretchy bodies and electric lights. With his slim, graceful feet, dark good looks and cleft chin, the managers notice him right away. He has the kind of face you want to watch, a laugh you want to hear again, and the easy charm of a ringmaster. They teach him to be a performer.

Five years later, when Bob Pender calls for acrobats to train and then travel as a troupe to America, Archie volunteers. By now, he can sing, dance, juggle and is fearless when it comes to learning new tricks. He picks up the trapeze in an afternoon. Years later, he is still able to do backflips at parties. They sail in 1920. On the gray morning the boat pulls out of the harbor, Archie does not know that his mother is sleeping less than a mile away from the port. She is in her room in the asylum for the insane where Elias put her years ago. Her upkeep costs Elias four shillings a week. He could pay more, find somewhere better, where the walls are not damp and the food is warm, but he has a new family to support.

. . .

When the tour is over and the Pender troupe returns to England, Archie stays in New York. He likes the wide spaces of America, the surging hum and common desire for *more*. He will act. He is good at pretending. When he finds his way to Hollywood, they will change his name to Cary Grant.

KATE

PASADENA

JULY 1932

An hour outside of Pasadena, she changes into the new suit. Laura chose it so Kate feels safe wearing it, appropriate. Her palms are beaded wet and her eye is still seeping. The train heaves into the station and exhales its passengers. Out the gritty window is California. They are here. Kate looks for the car.

"He'll drive a Packard," Kate guesses.

"No, it will be a Rolls or a Hispano Suiza," Laura says.

Laura is right. A long-nosed Rolls is parked beyond the small fence. "Leland is flashy but predictable."

A small thing but it annoys Kate to be wrong. Laura never gets the details wrong. But with Laura, there is nothing to discover. Peel back her plump skin and she is platinum straight to the bone. Kate isn't. Kate is nervous. Does she have that fresh off the bus look that all untried actresses are said to have? Her new shoes are pinching. She does not know the rules of this place, and she hates that.

"You look beautiful," Laura says.

"Anxious, puffy and sweaty."

"Regal," Laura says, adjusting the tilt of Kate's hat. "And not alone."

Kate loves that Laura knows she never wanted to arrive in this town alone. Kate loves that Laura never made her spell it out.

"Shoulders down, don't crack your knuckles," Laura says. "Here they come. Fifteen hundred a week."

Kate wipes her palms on her new skirt.

They climb down to the platform. The porter is unloading their cases. Porters can sense Laura coming. She lifts her head and they appear. It is not the sort of thing a person can learn. Laura looks them in the eye when she tips. Kate likes that about her. Kate straightens her skirt, it is itchy and hot already.

Pasadena Station has a frontier atmosphere. Outside, distant hills surround them like the rim of a baking bowl. The air is big, sky is big, uncluttered by tall buildings or elm trees. Leland and another man, heavy glasses, doughy face, step forward. George Cukor—*Cu, like cucumber.* The car has no roof. Kate pulls her hat lower to protect her eye.

Forward. The only direction worth a damn.

She is mostly silent in the car. Leland and Laura, in the front seat, speak about mutual friends and coming out parties, but in the back seat, George and Kate are awkward with each other. George looks at her in open appraisal. It is not critical, but it is not discreet either. It is not the way that men look at her in Connecticut.

"Mr. Cukor?" Kate says, pointing to her eye. If she calls attention to it, she will not need to feel embarrassed. She just has to get there first. "There is something in my eye. If you could telephone a doctor?"

"What is the matter with it?" George asks. He speaks in a carefully modulated voice, as though he is cultivating a particular but unspecified dialect. He is already impressed with Laura's shoes and Kate's diction and is trying to bump up his accent and curate his lexicon but Kate does not know this yet.

"As I just said, there is something in my eye," Kate says.

"We're here," Leland interrupts, turning the car onto a broad empty street.

It's a warehouse, Kate thinks, when she sees RKO Studios. Boxy and stucco, it is not the Art Deco, sequined building she expects. Instead, it looks industrial, like a place where newspapers are printed. Eventually, she will appreciate the spare utility, but now she is looking for glamour. She is a tourist here. Until now Los

Angeles has kept faith with her Technicolor postcard imagination. The sentry rows of palm trees, the clean streets, the curvy, silver cars, the bleaching light.

They park and enter through the metal doors. Laura stops her, looks her over, hat, skirt, teeth. Yes.

It is later, as she is leaving and on her way to the eye doctor, that Kate will see the modern diamonds over the studio's door, the stylish lettering and the subtle limestone tile. Beyond the office are the back lot, the commissary, the fake storefronts and paper-thin towns. It's raining in the Wild West on Soundstage 6.

HOWARD

BEL-AIR COUNTRY CLUB

Howard is golfing when Kate Hepburn arrives in Hollywood. He plays to a three handicap and gets irritated if he scores above par. He holds several course records but has asked the management to scratch his name from their books. Howard Hughes is a private man.

Howard was in a bad mood even before he pulled up at the course. It is not just that Billie Dove didn't answer her telephone this morning. It's *Scarface*. Everyone talked about his new film all spring. The trades, the fan magazines, everyone. But the numbers were terrible. Why didn't people go? Noah brought the final breakdowns to the house that morning. Noah Dietrich is the chief executive officer of Hughes Tool Company and Hughes Aircraft Company and even Hughes Film but for Howard, Noah is the man who can make things happen, fast.

"They did go and see it, *here,*" Noah stopped. Obfuscating with Howard can backfire. Square up and shoot straight. "Yes. It was banned in states like Ohio, Kansas, Maryland, and that hurt the numbers." Noah tilted his face up so his voice would carry to Howard's good ear. "And then, cities like Detroit and Chicago wouldn't even run it." Howard was not listening. Noah was saying things he already knew.

"Even after Hawks reshot the goddamn ending." Howard set the papers back down on the desk. "It was good. I know, it was good." He reached for his hat and golf bag, slinging his clubs onto his shoulder. "We'll try again."

Now, Howard is on the golf course and he is concentrating. He believes in doing things wholly, without reservation. He meant to become an excellent golfer, the way he meant to become an exceptional airman; he learned from the best, practiced, got it wrong, corrected, practiced some more. There is no point in doing something just to be as good as everyone else.

IRENE
RKO STUDIOS

There was a fight over the air conditioner. Last month, before they were available in department stores, David ordered his secretary, Marcella Rabwin—she is thinking of changing her last name to Robin, birdlike, elegant—to find a man who knew a man and buy one for his studio office and a duplicate for their bedroom at home. The cost is shocking when Irene adds up the figures, plus the spike in the monthly electricity bill, but David insists. It is the new thing so he has to have it. Irene is miserable when David overspends. She offered him a deal: presents or gambling but not both. Irene is eight months pregnant with their first child this baked clay July. David chose presents, but of course he doesn't expect to keep to the bargain. In his mind, his wife should enjoy being spoiled with gifts, flowers, furs, houses. But she doesn't. She prefers economy and peace. But the air conditioner is a gift and so, the teams from Schultz and Sherman come and install the large metal boxes in the wood framed windows.

"Striking" is the word people use to describe Irene Mayer Selznick. She hates it. She knows it really means not beautiful. But child-woman small, with tiny feet and neat dark hair, she leaves an impression of controlled elegance and ripe intellect. When you know her better, she exudes strength and joy—never extravagance. Her father, the studio mogul, Louis B. Mayer, head of MGM, does not believe in unnecessary expenditures and while they were growing up he insisted Irene and her sister Edie wear their coats and shoes until they wore out. The family had moved from the East Coast, and Louis B. and his wife Margaret were determined their daughters stay uncorrupted by gilded Hollywood. Irene understands the difference between need and want.

Her husband David is an exaggerated man: loud, expansive, and excitable. He chews through life with flashing teeth. Irene is the steady eye of their storm. They were married two years ago at the Mayers' white stucco home in Santa Monica. The guest list was small as the town was still reeling from her sister Edie's lavish wedding the month before. Getting dressed in her childhood bedroom and meeting her father at the foot of the stairs, Irene carried white lilies and wore antique lace. For her, the marriage was the point, not the wedding. Her father wants David to return to MGM to work for him, but David has struck out on his own and taken over RKO Pictures. While David is reckless and broad, Irene is nerved with diamond hard resolve. Together, they are determined to be successful and to do it without help. In David's mind, if they accept help, it is not their success at all.

Irene is standing near the new air conditioner when the trio, Katharine Hepburn, Laura Harding, and Leland Hayward, walk into David's office. George Cukor is a few paces behind. Her husband, David O. Selznick, stands up but hesitates, does not reach out his large, ham pink hand. The O does not stand for anything. He just prefers the cadence. No one moves. Hepburn's eye is red and weeping. David has always been terrified by infection. Irene steps forward.

Katharine Hepburn, tight jawed and racehorse slim, leads the charge. Her back is whipping post straight and her hands ride easily in her pockets. Leland makes the introductions.

"How do you do, I have something in my eye."

Kate's voice. Catching like a barn door, her voice is a firing piston, a steely husk of rubble and energy. The words are ordinary but her tone challenges.

Irene watches. She can see that David is appalled by Kate's appearance. He does not like freckles. Kate's skin is not the uniform cream sheet it looked on the screen test, but a mass of saffron dots. Her red hair is scraped back, her skull is bony and small. The planes of her face read differently in person. The monochrome screen test blurred her into prettiness, which is wrong, Irene can see. She is something more than pretty. Kate is aristocratic but not decorative, and worse, she does not exhibit gratitude. Irene takes her in: High-necked Elizabeth Hawes shirtwaist, the jacket and matching skirt, this season, but too warm for Los Angeles and out of keeping with other, lusher, starlets. No jewelry, no powder, no curves, opening the doors herself, Kate is unapologetic. In Irene's experience, it is always safer to apologize to David. It saves time.

Kate is a declarative sentence: Here I am. Irene shakes her hand. Kate's grip is dry and strong.

"I have something in my eye," Kate says again but is interrupted by the costume designer who brings in the designs for Kate to look over. French, and cigarette thin, Josette De Lima spreads her broad pieces of meshy artist's paper out on the table. The ink swept sketches are showmanship. The designs were made up into finished pieces to fit Kate's measurements weeks ago and are already on the lot.

A beat. And another.

"But they are *wrong*," Kate says, without looking up from the designs. "They are *all* wrong." She doesn't hurry through the architecture of the sentence but squats in its gutter like a bullfrog.

Silence.

David sputters. Josette De Lima takes an elegant French step back from this turbulent woman. George Cukor cocks his head to the side and pushes his glasses up his fleshy slope of nose, evaluating her mettle. Laura and Leland do not move to rescue Kate. They know she does not need it.

"They are *what*?" David Selznick asks.

"*Wrong*," Kate repeats.

Kate's phrase is spare and airtight. And, she is right. The clothes *are* wrong. Irene knows it and should have spoken up before. The role is Sydney Fairfield: young, well connected, old money. And such a woman would not wear these clothes. They are too gaudy, too new. The most expensive cuts are always the simplest and never look freshly bought. This is the secret the fashion magazines never give away.

Irene joins the table and stands between Laura and Kate. Agreement folds through them, buttery and warm.

Kate speaks again. Louder. "Did you hear me? They are wrong." In her vaguely affected, East Coast voice it sounds like "hee-ah me" and she pronounces all the letters in "w-r-o-n-g" sending the g to swing in mid-air like a bell.

The battle lines knife the air and the fruit falls into quarters. The room subdivides and reassembles. Irene, Kate and Laura. The three women do not voice their unity. They do not have to. Irene's blood surges, tangy with iron. Power. She often disagrees with her husband, but she never uses Kate's bold, unfettered phrasing. Life with David would stall and fall out of the sky if she did.

David regroups. "And the clothes you are wearing now," he asks Kate, "what do you think of them?"

He has misjudged. Confrontation does not frighten Kate.

"I think they are very fine," Kate says, pushing out each round word in a rowboat. Irene has heard this mid-Atlantic accent before but it is usually reserved for press interviews. Have elocution lessons given Kate this strange hybrid accent? Some words are clipped and others stretch out for grassy miles. Irene listens. Not an unpleasant voice, but not a comfortable one either.

Everyone is looking at Kate.

David lets out a short laugh but no one laughs with him. "Fifteen hundred a week!" he finally says to Leland, apropos of nothing.

Leland does not respond. It is a huge fee for an untried starlet. But the contracts are signed, and photography begins on Thursday. They are bulletproof. Irene looks over at the agent. Leland must have been careful to negotiate the contract before introducing David to Kate.

"Do you know the designs of Gabrielle Chanel?" Kate directs the question at David but then turns to Irene. One look at Irene. "Of course, you do." Kate turns back to David. "See? *She* understands." Kate says it as though it is a complete thought.

"Yes, I do like Chanel," Irene says, "beautiful lines."

David huffs and looks at Irene as though she is betraying him. He sits. He is not going to pay for a new wardrobe for this picture.

Irene crests with pride for Kate. She does not know this woman, but in this moment, she commits to knowing her. A bolt slides into place. They will be friends. Irene is right, and thirty years from now they will still be friends.

"I suppose the costumes are finished?" Laura asks Josette. "Too late to change?"

"Too late," says Josette. She turns to George. "Fittings begin on Wednesday, just as you asked?"

"You did everything right, Miss De Lima, it is just that now that we have met Miss Hepburn . . ." George lets the sentence fade. He can see that they are right and Kate would be better in Chanel or Schiaparelli. He grew up in New York City and reads the glossy magazines. He knows what a woman like this would wear and should have caught the mistake earlier.

"Spilt milk," Kate says, loudly. Kate has moved on.

Irene watches—it is her specialty. Watching, smoothing over and covering up, the holy trinity. David likes her to be there to meet the new stars. He wants her opinion in this, in everything, he says. Irene's pedigree makes her opinion valuable. But now, Irene is partisan. She roots for Kate; her flags rise on the mast. And she foresees trouble. Kate is table hard, where other actresses have the softness of a shelled pea. There is no give here. Kate strides in, stretches out her hand and speaks first—like a man. In a man, David would admire the forthrightness, but in a woman, it turns over the air like fresh earth and makes everything loose and unfamiliar.

Someday, David Selznick will acknowledge Kate's nerve and pluck, but not yet. Irene Mayer Selznick recognizes it at once.

LOS ANGELES

JULY 1932

We seduce Kate. It is easy. An assistant director takes her on a tour of the lot. She doesn't know enough to recognize the slight. Her director, George Cukor, is not free just now. He and David Selznick are having an argument in a second-floor office. David shouts, calling Kate a plucked stork and George, who never yells, yells back. The errand boy is listening on the other side of the door, remembering, so he can tell others later. Information is currency on a lot. Marcella Rabwin is pretending she can't hear them. Irene arrives with Leland Hayward and the argument is shelved until after the camera tests. George goes to find the head of makeup. There is a lot riding on these tests.

Out in the great warehouse soundstages, Kate is breathing it in. The twenty-two-year-old assistant director does not know what not to tell a new star. This is his first tour. So, he tells her everything: contracts, dressing rooms, loan-outs, cabling, microphones, wind machines, the directors to stay away from, the actors who wear hair pieces and the editors who will only use your good side. All this is against protocol—stars are easier to manage if they don't know anything—but he is young and showing off. He takes her over to the stables where the western horses sleep. Their trainer, who orders their feed from Kentucky, wears handmade English field boots and has told no one that she grew up the daughter of a circus bareback rider in Kansas.

They walk through the rectangular stucco buildings and the assistant director spills out all he knows. Kate listens, full of wonder. It is the puppet strings that make the place magical for her, not the puppet show. The mechanics. Clip the film here and the fumbled line disappears. Tilt the light this way, the sun sets and the day slides behind you. Hide a microphone here and a whispered love scene will boom out in the movie theaters. Choose the right script and the woman morphs from ingénue to aviatrix to lover to dancer. And the studios decide it all.

"Even the gossip," the assistant director tells her. "They make a star—the look, the character, even the boyfriends, the backstory, the life—and then they leak it all to the press. They hold photo shoots on the back lot early on Saturday mornings when no one is here."

"So, when I read *Photoplay* and think Greta Garbo is mysterious, it is because . . ."

"Because Louis B. Mayer and Irving Thalberg over at MGM had a meeting and decided she would be mysterious." The assistant director lowers his voice. The twenty-two-year-old assistant director knows he should not be talking about Garbo.

Even now, when Kate is so green, the idea that men, any men, meet and decide who an actress can or will be, rankles. "Well, with that voice, mystery was their best bet," Kate says.

The assistant director reappraises her. She could do well in this town.

Of course, she loves it. A place where life can be designed, shot, and reshot? Where wrongs are righted and lives are scripted? Where character traits are adopted and discarded? Where the story happens in three acts and all is resolved by the end credits? Where the weather rolls in on great trucks and lighting can reverse the hours? Where she is no one's sister or daughter or wife unless the script says so? Where Miss Hepburn is at the center of it all. Yes. Life is not indelible here. She closes her eyes and tries to share the moment with him. Did he know all this before her? Is it why Tom wanted to write for the movies? Is it why he wanted them to live out here? She will live here for both of them.

LAURA
RKO STUDIOS

Laura pulls up and parks, cranking the emergency brake. The hill is steep but the street is a good one. Names are important. Coldwater Canyon. Chilly, clean. Kate says that her father insisted all the kids swim in the icy sound to wake themselves up—to pound in the living, he said. Kate keeps up the habit in the chilly hotel pool and sometimes, the ocean. Laura is sure Kate will like this name.

It is the eighteenth house Laura has seen and they are bumping together in her mind, rubber cars at a fair. The first one in Hancock Park is out. She originally liked its East Coast shape and butler's pantry but Kate snorted when she saw the photograph. "It's a fake. What does California know about a saltbox colonial?" Laura crosses Hancock Park off the list.

Laura looks for houses that know themselves. Irene gave her the name of a good broker and he is taking her through the Los Angeles enclaves one by one. He offered to drive but Laura refused. She wants to learn the city and if she can drive Kate, it means another reason to go to the set. Laura needs to be necessary. Three more houses on the list and Laura's feet hurt. The heat expands the joints and the air sucks the moisture from her skin here. She feels puffy and her face powder has rutted. She wants to go back to the hotel. She's not used to California. The hot cicada air and flashy cars are exhausting.

She knows it when she sees it and only spends a few minutes inside the house. She does not need more. She checks for basics. Kitchen, living room, bedrooms, bathrooms, bathtub. She turns on the bathroom taps to make sure the water runs clear and fast. A board creaks in the upstairs hallway. A homey sound. Yes. This is it. Creamy and low, with European casement windows, raw beams,

Spanish tile roof and lime washed brick walls in the living room. The house hugs the sloping garden.

. . .

Laura knows she was not born for this; to spend days caring for the small details of someone else's life, but she cannot stop herself. This feeling of being necessary is addictive. On that first morning, she brought an extra umbrella for Kate in case it rained. When the rain started, Laura felt a jolt of relevance.

This morning, she is alone. Kate left for the studio before seven. Laura feels snapping licks of disenchantment, but she doesn't let them catch. All new lives are an adjustment. At the end of the day, when Kate telephones to tell her what time she will finish, Laura surges with the tidal pull of importance and the feeling of rightness returns. The feeling of usefulness. Usefulness is the daily bread she feeds her relationship with Kate. Love is one thing, sex another, but everything dies without bread.

KATE

RKO STUDIOS

"Egg?" she asks.

"Egg shampoo. Every day." George repeats. He is looking down at Kate who is lying with her head in the enamel shampoo bowl. "And then an olive oil rinse at the ends. The cut is good but the hair—hay, dirt dry. And the skin," he says, leaning down to look. "More luster, less freckles. I want a dewy base and then some shine at the temples. Here and here. The lights will pick it up. Don't worry about her mouth too much. Work with the eyes and the bones." He isn't speaking to Kate.

Nancy, the small, efficient hair and makeup assistant, takes it all down in a leather notebook. The shampoo girl gets to work.

George circles Kate, examining her hands and fingernails. "Manicure and pedicure, *today* and steam every day plus a massage. Send Laurent to her house."

"I take *cold* baths," Kate says. It seems important to tell him this. "Dad insists on *cold* baths. Good for body and spirit."

"Yes," George says, "but you can tell *Dad* that the egg won't come out of your hair unless you use *hot* water."

"Mr. Cukor says you are not to look yet." Nancy is drying Kate's hair with a towel. Her hands are strong and her nails are trimmed to uniform pink crescents. "When we're done, you go to wardrobe and then Soundstage 9 for camera tests." Nancy's sentences are tucked in at the corners like hospital sheets and they discourage a response. She seats Kate in a makeup chair that faces a wall rather than a mirror and begins smearing something from an oval jar over her face. It smells of cold roses.

"I don't wear makeup," Kate says. "Nothing matches my skin. Looks awful."

Nancy does not answer.

The dress, a fluted, white satin column, has a high slim waist and a filmy, single accordion ruff over each shoulder. The wardrobe mistress helps her and it swings down over Kate's frame. It was not in the original sketches. Nancy powders Kate's arms and neck.

They are all there. Seated in folding chairs on a concrete floor. They do not stand when she comes in, she doesn't merit it yet. George, Leland, David Selznick and a clutch of men she does not recognize: a united landmass of studio people are waiting. Kate is separate, moored offshore. Only Irene comes over and squeezes her hand for luck. Kate is surprised to see her. Irene is enormously pregnant and looks like a peach about to split open but no one makes reference to it. "I asked Laura to come." Irene speaks quietly, in the voice of a friend. There, by the door, near the upright piano, Laura has slipped into the room. Kate turns, swishing the fluted white dress. Laura approves. Bolstered, Kate turns to the men.

George introduces her to Sid Hickox, the photographer and Mr. Clark, the art director. There are other men too, all in shirtsleeves and beige slacks. One does music, one does something with sound and two are writers. She forgets their names. It all happens fast.

They rehearse—George insists on rehearsal. David Manners, gentle and attractive in a forgettable way, reads with her.

"You'll be on the upper level," George says, explaining the shot. "The camera will be set high and will sweep down into the room and search for something. It is a party. Beautiful women, beautiful men. Champagne. White tie. Music. Dancing. But the camera will keep searching. Until it finds you. Begin."

. . .

They settle down to watch the rushes. Beige slacks step over the long cables and group together as the crew set up the projector, aim it at a white wall. On other days George will watch alone in the screening room but today, David Selznick has invited everyone to watch the first day's photography together. He wants to see what his fifteen hundred a week has bought and he wants it to be public. Billie Burke and David Manners push through the big soundstage doors. John Barrymore comes in and sits in the director's chair. John Barrymore is the kind of star who can sit wherever he likes. Kate still feels as though she is looking at a movie screen and not a real man when she sees him. David Manners and Barrymore have been kind the few times Kate has met them. Billie Burke is not warm. Leland says this is her first talking picture and she is nervous.

But Kate knows that that is not it. Billie Burke does not like her, drops her sleepy fawn eyes and looks away rather than speak to the new actress. But today, Billie is fox bright. She has come to see Kate fail.

Irene and Laura stand with Kate to one side. Kate leans back into Laura, just enough to feel her there. Leland stands with Selznick who is dictating a memo to his secretary while they wait. Kate will get used to Selznick's memos, everyone does. George sits on a lighting crate at the back. He has bet the house on Kate. That she will be beautiful enough, good enough, that she will have that thing that no one can describe but can recognize. The whirring noise and it begins: the party, not tinny and cheap as it had felt when they filmed it, but noisy in the way that parties are, with champagne and dancing and rain running down the windows. The camera is alive; it is the audience. Their arms waltzing, their feet running up the stairs. George is right. The camera is restless, searching. Until it finds her.

Her. Clear and glowing. Light skimmed from water.

Real beauty—Kate had not expected that. She peels away from Laura, stands up straight, quite still. Watching. She has always been happy living in her body in real life, enjoyed the boyish hang of her clothes, her uncurving lines, but she is uncomfortable with photographs. She does not recognize herself in stills. So far, her experience of living in her face, moving in her body, is never reflected back in the camera. Instead, an ill-fitting, mechanical poise coats her skin, stretching to contain the scrubby, skinned knee girl inside. She is ungraceful in photographs. But now, watching these images move across the screen, Kate feels a bone crack of recognition. George has caught it, the loose, arm swinging feeling of being Kate.

Just a brief scene but it is enough. The men in shirtsleeves and beige slacks nod and talk.

"She speaks too fast."

"Why is she frowning?"

"She can't be up lit."

"But she's got it."

The camera loves her. They all agree. Her face is tidal, shifting, as the camera runs over her carved angles. She has no bad side and her terrain keeps changing. She is alive on film. George comes to stand beside her. "Give?" he asks as though they have been wrestling.

"Give," she answers. "Forever and ever, give."

"You'll do it Kate," Irene says, still watching the screen. "You are going to really do it."

Kate does not ask what she means.

IRENE

BEVERLY HILLS

Irene is not like others in this town. She has no origin story of coming to Hollywood and making it. No train ticket or boarding house room key or postcard sent to parents back home. Her family is here. This town is home. True, the family moved from the East Coast when she was young but no one ever remembers that the Mayers are originally from Massachusetts. Her father, Louis B. Mayer, has headed up MGM since she was nine so as far as anyone is concerned, Irene was born into this world. Not that she saw much of it growing up. Her parents kept her and her sister Edie well away from the moving picture business. Louis B. did not want his daughters to get ideas about meeting actors or working outside the home. But Irene never wanted to work in the movies. Although people say she has a keen eye for talent and a gift for spotting a good script, Irene does not like the movie business much. She prefers the theater. Someday, when she is unmarried again, she will find and produce the great plays of the age.

Her parents were appalled when she wanted to marry David Selznick. They saw him as an up-and-coming producer with eyes bigger than his wallet. "He is nothing like you," her parents said. They were right. Apart from being in love, nothing about Irene Mayer and David Selznick made sense. He was loud and showy, and she was restrained, discreet. He was climbing to the top and she was born there.

Her parents said no. But Irene is tough and gets her way when she wants something badly enough. She held firm; David Selznick was the man she wanted. She would consider no one else. Edie was unsurprised but Irene's certainty unsettled her parents. So far, Margaret and Louis B. Mayer had had the final word on Irene's life. Education, hobbies, hemlines, social connections. Margaret and Louis B. were in agreement about everything to do with their daughters. In school, they wanted them to study hard and go to bed early. After graduating, they wanted them to stay home and be helpful rather than attend college. And, absolutely, no bobbed hair or short skirts. What happens on the studio lots and in the fan magazines is for other people. "Ladies do not become *actresses*," Margaret has always told her daughters.

And then Irene met David Selznick. He is someone who lives by his own set of ethics but no rules. A man who believes in enthusiasm rather than decorum. David is more: more stories, more curiosity, more affection. His world is big and he has plans for it to grow bigger. He is unafraid to be wrong if it means that the eventual outcome will be right. He is fearless in that way. Being wrong does not diminish David Selznick. It is one step closer to being great. And, David Selznick is someone interested in making *great* art. When they first met, he spoke of telling *important* stories, provoking profound feeling in his audiences.

"I want to reach in and grab them by the heart muscle and squeeze it blue," he said.

He spoke about film in a way Irene had never heard. He believes what she privately believes, that people are always looking for their own lives, whether in film or novels or art. It only matters if it is about *you*, who you are or were or will be.

"Yes!" David said. "Pictures only work if the audience comes away thinking about themselves, *their* lives, *their* choices. If it is not about them, why would the story stay with them when they leave the movie house? Hell, if it doesn't stay with them, what are we doing?"

Irene felt a ripple of thrill. She had never heard anyone speak of movies in this way before. It made her father's talk of account ledgers and budgets and margins feel small and crass.

Irving Thalberg, Louis B.'s right hand man at MGM, saw Irene speaking to David Selznick in the studio parking lot one Monday in April. He was surprised to see her, as Louis B.'s daughters were rarely on the lot. And this Irene; a woman tilted forward, animated, sweaty, was not an Irene he had seen before. She was not afraid when she saw Irving standing by the soundstage door. She knew he would not tell her father. Irving Thalberg never looked for trouble. It was not his way.

Irene waited for David to climb into his car and pull away. Irving waited, without hurrying her.

"I know he's not who they want for me," Irene said, opting for bluntness. She spoke in the abbreviated shorthand of family friends.

"Is he who you want?" Irving asked.

She appreciated the way he didn't pretend not to know what he knew or see what he saw.

"Yes. He is who I want. Who I will *always* want." Irene stopped. Words like "always" were difficult when speaking to Irving. Doctors had predicted that with his bad heart, Irving would never live to be twenty. He was thirty-two now.

"And?"

"And, everyone is telling me to leave it, to stay away from David," Irene said.

"Everyone told Norma to stay away from me," Irving answered in his steady voice. Irving's strength lies in his refusal to give too much of himself away. His dealings with the world are streamlined, efficient. He does not spend energy anywhere unimportant. Irene was surprised to hear his wife's name. Irving rarely mentioned his health or his marriage. This conversation was something new.

"My wife refused to listen to anyone; she married me anyway." His voice was freighted by years of medical certainty.

"But, you and Norma are so happy?" Irene blurted out. Everyone could see that Irving Thalberg, boy wonder, and lovely Norma Shearer were one of Hollywood's happiest couples.

"Yes. We are happy now. But will she always be? Will she regret it one day?"

"No one is guaranteed anything when they get married I suppose," Irene said.

"No," Irving answered. "No one is guaranteed anything."

. . .

"What if he just wants her to get to me?" Louis B. asked his wife, Margaret.

"*Never* say that to Irene," Margaret said.

. . .

First her mother agreed, and then her father relented. At least he is Jewish, they said. They were mystified that Irving Thalberg, one of the only people at MGM who really knew the Mayer daughters, was for the engagement.

"How is this not an awful match?" Louis B. asked him. "Talk to her Irving, she will listen if it comes from you." Louis B. did not need to flesh out the sentiment. Advice about living means more when it comes from the dying.

Irving sidestepped. "See how she changes when she talks about him?" Irving said. "She becomes more."

"More what?" Louis B. asked. "Stubborn?" He was annoyed and had hoped Irving would talk sense to his daughter, help her see that this match would make her unhappy.

"More Irene," Irving said.

. . .

The Mayers struck a deal. Irene could marry David Selznick *if* she waited for her sister Edie to get married first. Irene dedicated herself fully to the task of finding a man for her sister.

. . .

Irene was not sure Bill Goetz would be right for Edie but she introduced them anyway. Irene was dealing in volume. The more introductions, the more chances at getting it right. If her parents' traditions dictated the older sister had to marry before the younger, fine, but Irene felt that older sister had better get married in a hurry. Irene guessed right. Bill suited Edie. He was a producer at Fox and successful but not yet overly successful. He was easy tempered and genuinely kind, someone everyone liked and felt they knew, even when they didn't. Edie and Bill's interests lined up too. He liked art and could see that Edie had a good eye and a strong sense of her own taste. He liked that she liked what she liked. Bill also liked the way Edie did not pretend. Her family was famous and that was fine with her. It was fine with him too.

In that wet March of 1930, Edie and Bill married at the Biltmore Hotel. *The New York Times* reported that covers were laid for six hundred and crowds waited out front from dawn to see the stars arrive. Louis B. did not enjoy the day. Not that he disliked Bill, he liked him well enough, but he knew once Edie was married, Irene's wedding would not be far behind.

. . .

A month later, Irene and David married in a simple family ceremony in the Mayers' living room.

"But how will it look?" her father said. "Edie had a wedding this town will remember for years. And now this nothing wedding?"

"Exactly," Irene said. "I should think we're doing this town a favor. Imagine if they had to stump up the cash for a second wedding gift? They would go broke."

LOS ANGELES

JULY 1932

Beauty on film is one thing. That's just good bones, the right angles, and a good photographer. *Acting* on film is tougher, but Kate is determined. We respect that. And these farmhand hours agree with her. Up at dawn, shoot, work hard, learn everything, sleep when it's over. She is green as all hell and she knows it but George and Laura will help her hide most of that. She keeps her head down too, shuts up, watches. She is good at imitation, can even do a passable Garbo. You wouldn't guess that skill, would you? One day she will be branded as fiercely unique, but that has not happened yet. Here in her early days, she is still an imitation.

. . .

Back East, in the stock theaters, our Kate made a mess of everything. Said the wrong thing to the wrong person, or did the wrong thing to the wrong person. Yelled at a director when he tried to direct her, refused to wear that or say this, and spent all her time talking to the crew instead of the cast. She was fired from most every show at least once. By the time she got to Broadway, she was more careful. She learned from that slick, smart East Coast playwright, Philip Barry, the one who can write women who are sometimes unlikable but win you in the end, the one who will write a part for Kate one day. She and Philip Barry watched the lead actress, Hope Williams, from the shadowed wings when Kate understudied her in *Holiday*. A good play but will be a better film. Philip Barry is arrogant but a good person to know. They say he spent the summer on the Riviera in '27 with Scott and Zelda Fitzgerald, Cole and Linda Porter and that whole drunken, literate crowd and he has never recovered. Sick with a crawling envy, he only wants to write about that world of careless money he is so desperate to join. On *Holiday*, he insisted the producer cast Kate because he was sure she came from that closed, East Coast sphere of horses and handed-down furniture. The producer refused. Kate was awful in the audition and he didn't want her ruining his show. Producer and playwright compromised; Kate would understudy, Hope would star. "For god's sake, don't get sick," the producer told Hope.

But Kate was trying by then. She asked good questions. She watched. She saw that Hope never charged the stage but let it come to her. "The stage is a wild, untrusting dog," Hope told her once, "waiting for you to make a misstep."

"And then what happens?" Kate asked.

"It tears your throat out and then gets bored and looks for someone else to bite."

The boredom scared Kate more than the bite. Still does. Smart girl.

The stage offered Kate a challenge: beat me and they will love you. Lose, and they will howl for your blood. Hope Williams, boyish, girlish, limber, and spare, knew that. She was talented, should have gone farther. From Hope Kate learned the trick of not hiding her magical androgyny.

Kate did not just watch Hope, she studied her. The lift of her chin, her closed mouth. Kate pulled open Hope's sexiness, reducing the pixie charm to wire and springs. In New York, Kate practiced, in rehearsal, in life: the glide, the light neck, the low, steady voice and quiet hands. Hope never moved unless it bought her something.

"Movement costs the actress," Hope said, as Kate breathed in her damp soapy skin. Hope washed off all of the stage makeup before she left the theater. She liked to go home looking like herself.

"Costs her what?"

Hope wouldn't say.

Kate spent a lot of time trying not to fall in love with Hope Williams.

One night, as she was coming offstage, Hope leaned down to whisper something to Kate. Six curtain calls and Hope's hairline was sweating. Philip asked Kate what she had said, but Kate would not repeat it.

Later, in bed with Laura, Kate told her about the whisper and the sweaty hairline.

"And so, what did she say?"

Kate hesitated, long enough for Laura to worry.

She said, "Spend yourself carefully, Kate. Be scarce and make them earn it."

Even now, Laura cannot bear it when Kate speaks Hope's name.

The only time Kate went on for Hope, Philip Barry came to watch. The star wasn't really unwell. Hope and Philip Barry thought Kate had worked hard and should have a chance to go on before the run ended. It was a mid-week matinee so didn't matter much. When Kate came offstage, he was waiting, leaning against a lighting crate.

"Good?" Kate asked. She needed to hear it aloud.

"Good," Philip Barry said.

"Good," Kate said and hurried down the hall to her dressing room.

Philip was annoyed. Was that it? He had hoped Kate would be so grateful that she might invite him out to Fenwick. He had heard the stories about Kate's summer home in Connecticut. The sound, the eccentric family. He wanted to see it, but flushed and excited, Kate said nothing about an invitation as she packed up to go home after the performance. Philip Barry would nurse a grudge for a while and then get over it and revert to well concealed envy. It was his resting pulse and the source of his best writing but Kate did not see that yet.

Kate used to feel that envy with Laura. Less since they came west. Some of it was Laura's wealth but more than that, it was the *name*. Laura Harding would always be *someone*. Kate wants to be someone but so far, she still has no idea who to be.

KATE

RKO STUDIOS

First day of filming. Lighting crates with *A Bill of Divorcement* stenciled in red are stacked outside the soundstage. They are for the afternoon scenes and the crew are loading them in. Barrymore gums up his big scene and quietly asks George if he can retake. He nails it. Kate pretends she did not hear him ask. Nancy in makeup says Barrymore wants to get it right for *Kate*. Barrymore is a leader; it catches on. Now, *everyone* is pulling for her, they all want her to be good. She is trying. Getting it wrong feels awful when everyone is rooting for her. George can see that Irene Selznick is right. Kate is something new. Not boy, not girl and not moving to please anyone else, self-possession when she walks. And so earnest.

But, for now, when she speaks, the illusion cracks open and shatters on the floor. She works on it.

Even David Selznick is coming around. Kate's new shorter hair helps. It is down now, not school marm tight. Not too short, that wouldn't work for this. Sydney Fairfield. She is free but not wild. Good role for anyone, great role to turn a nobody into a somebody. And Kate can already see that on a set, you are only safe when you're a somebody. George asks Selznick to come to the set on days when Barrymore is thundering through his big scenes. He wants Selznick to see that he is getting his money's worth. Selznick wants George to wrap up these scenes fast. Barrymore's salary is the most expensive on the lot.

Selznick has not heard Kate's dialogue yet. Her voice is raspy on the edges and runny in the middle. She doesn't have it. She asks Billie Burke for advice.

"Fight hard, win the stage," Billie says, turning from the chair in her dressing room. Billie's scenes are not until this afternoon; she is there early because she wants to watch her competition. She does not invite Kate to sit down.

"Stage?"

"Even a Hollywood soundstage is a stage, Kate. Don't fool yourself into thinking it isn't."

"Shakespeare," Kate says.

"Shakespeare. And get yourself a personality, find it, keep it. Do it fast. This ingénue phase doesn't last long. The whole thing doesn't last long."

Kate doesn't ask her what she means. Everyone says Billie Burke is getting too old for this. Billie is in her forties but looks early thirties at most. Too old for what?

. . .

When Kate got fired from her early jobs in New York, it was with good reason. She was terrible and she behaved badly. Then she found her tempo, learned to hold the drum-tight silence long enough to make them crave her voice. Why can't she do it here?

The big scene. Rolling:

Him: "My wife's not my wife, she's my daughter." John Barrymore is heavier and washed out compared to his heroic silent movie days but his rich, textured voice curves the words with wonder, loss and sex. It's hard to tell he's drunk.

Kate: "You're forgetting it's been years and years." Off key. Flat. The man holding the boom microphone looks away.

George clears his throat and calls, "Cut." They are into overtime now. Barrymore lights a cigarette. The crew reset. They know they will have to go again.

LOS ANGELES

JULY 1932

We watch Kate stand very still, appalled that she is causing this extra activity. She can hear the mistake but can't fix it.

Reset. Lighting. Sound check. We see Barrymore take his place, adjust his raincoat and slick back his hair. He adjusts his crotch too. He thinks no one can see but of course, everyone can see. George Cukor waits until the soundstage settles, and the actors are ready. He is good with actors.

"Action!"

Oh, we see, it is the reunion scene: the seeds of all the trouble and low built insanity. It's a good script. A man spends his life in an asylum and does not recognize his daughter when he gets out. Fair enough. But now the daughter knows. Madness runs wild in the family blood. She won't escape—her life, her lover, the hoped-for children, all forfeit.

Kate knows about that resolve. Suicide lives in her family blood too. That deep gut drive to stand too near the platform edge when the express train passes. She has lived this. Why can't she play it?

GEORGE

RKO STUDIOS

"Cut!" George Cukor pulls her aside. They know each other now. Kate calls him "Gor-udge" in her New England Hepburn diction, dividing his name into sludgy hunks. George calls her accent "mid-Atlantic"—not midway down the Eastern seaboard, but halfway to Britain. George means it as a compliment and lately, he has been subtly trimming his loose Lower East Side vowels to match hers. The crew snickers at Kate's pronunciation at first but now they don't hear it. It is just how she speaks; part of her, just like the cold cheese sandwiches and milk she has for lunch every day. A man usually has to be besotted with her before Kate can trust him, but not George. She is trusting him with all her weight. The devotion is mutual.

It is late on this Tuesday afternoon and George sits next to her on the window seat. The propman looks at his watch. Twenty minutes over. George does not look at his watch. It would only spook her, but he can feel that the day has run long. David Selznick will send a memo. George has stopped reading them; whatever it is, another will come along in a minute. Selznick himself can never be on time for a meeting but he hates for the shooting schedule to go over. More money out of the stretched budget, but there's no use in rushing her is there? In forty pages, she is meant to sit on this window seat and tell David Manners that her mad blood is too dangerous and she cannot marry him. None of that will work unless she nails this scene.

George speaks quietly, shifting so his back is to the tired crew.

"Kate, try the scene as if you don't know what he will say next." George has a knack for distilling the problem. Dividing the failure from the failed. Kate is playing the whole scene as if she already knows the ending; she has to discover it.

"She is just realizing that this family trait will change the course of her life, stuff up everything she ever wanted."

She is listening, she is with him.

"This line sets it up. The payoff is later. The fact that she will have to live her whole life without the person she loves best in the world. Do you see? How would that feeling begin? Let it happen, let it land on you. Don't know what you don't know."

Good advice. Trouble is, she does know. She learned a long time ago.

LAURA

RKO STUDIOS

AUGUST 1932

Laura comes to the lot every day now. Kate has fallen hard for California, although she will deny it later. Laura does not let on that she finds this state hot, brash and uncultured. She wants to show she is game and has even bought an old Ford pickup. She drives over to the lot with Kate's lunch. Kate's driver, Louis Prysing, stays at the house and eats chicken salad sandwiches at the kitchen table with his wife, Ragnhild, who is the cook. Kate loves their operatic names. Laura loves that they never comment on the sleeping arrangements at the house.

When the first assistant director calls lunch, Laura and Kate climb up onto the flat bed of Laura's truck and unwrap their sandwiches. They wear floppy sunhats and eat with their legs swinging down. Laura is never late. She knows it's important to be consistent. Laura is the place where Kate is safe. The crew can see that Miss Harding is important to Miss Hepburn. Scenes go more smoothly when Laura is there. Fewer resets, fewer takes and they get home earlier. They have seen stars ask for some strange things. One will want the exact same lunch brought every day. Apples sliced the same way, milk poured just to the same line, fork placed at the same angle. Others want their coaches, dialect, dancing, fencing, whatever. Tedious business as the coaches all want lunch as well. Miss Harding brings her own lunch.

The crew keep a chair ready for her. Miss Harding is gracious, polite and never gets in the way. She rubs Kate's shoulders in between takes, runs lines with her, goes to meetings for her. By now, anyone who wants to speak to Kate alone must be approved by Laura first, which annoys Leland but Laura knows it makes Kate feel safe to have a buffer. Laura can read a room and is never wrong about people.

The house is coming together. Laura's bedroom is done—bamboo shoot green and gold. Kate's is finished in boat fresh blue and white. It feels like Tom's seaside room at Fenwick, before it was washed clean of Tom.

Laura's sheets are satin. Kate brings her pillow tucked in a white cotton pillowcase to Laura's bed with her. She cannot sleep on slippery sheets but they are fun for not sleeping. Often, they eat sandwiches at midnight, sitting at the kitchen table, bare feet on the red tiled floor, and by quarter to five in the morning, the day starts over again. Kate stays until Laura's breath sinks into her chest and then she pads down the hall. Kate likes to wake up in her own room.

Laura sits at the back of the screening room, six rows behind Selznick, George Cukor and Sid Hickox, the photographer. She watches the rushes and then, once they're home, she coaches Kate. Small adjustments, inflections. "Lower your voice. Slow down. Come out of your nose. Relax your throat. *Slow down*. Breathe. Wait." All the things Mrs. Robinson-Duff taught them, all the things that women of Laura's world do without thinking. Laura repeats what George has said. Change the inflection. Think. Feel. Live as the character. How does heartbreak sound?

Kate tries the line. "*Oh* Kit don't." Nasal.

"Oh *Kit* don't." Whiny.

"Come to bed," Laura says. They are getting nowhere.

. . .

Laura can see what Kate needs to do, can hear the right inflection in her head. She has learned not to flinch when a take goes wrong. Her face gives nothing away. In the beginning, Kate turned to look at Laura after each take; she looks at George now. It's natural, isn't it? He is her director. It still makes Laura dislike George.

Laura finds other ways to be useful. She schedules all of Kate's appointments, not only the social visits but the doctor and dentist and beauty appointments as well. The costume, hair, and makeup departments call Laura to arrange fitting and lighting tests. Only Leland refuses to book through Laura. He is irritated by the way that Laura is always there, on set. He told Kate he hates the way that Laura carries a notebook and takes down everything George says so that the two of them can digest the notes together at home. He wishes he had thought to do it. Kate told Laura right after he said it, worried that Laura should, "give Leland room," whatever that means. Who cares? Leland is from Laura's life before, the life of white tie and museum benefit galas. Laura sees that Leland no longer brings his wife to parties when he knows Kate will be there.

Laura is not jealous of Kate's success; she has shed the skin of wanting to be a star. Now that she is out here, she can see that it is not for her. Laura knows the camera does not love her. Her face isn't built for it. She looks doughy on film. She has stopped auditioning. This kind of earned fame is too small, she sees that now. Laura prefers the fame she was born with. She is not chasing Hollywood for herself anymore; her ambition is only for Kate.

IRENE

BEVERLY HILLS

"Kate is awful, and not even interesting awful. Just awful, awful," David says, sitting down hard on Irene's side of the bed. "Are you even awake?" he asks. It is after two A.M.

"Yes, I am." Irene sits up slowly. She wasn't and will not be able to get back to sleep. She'd had no idea that pregnancy went on so long.

"What if she can't ever do it?" David asks, his voice nursery small. "She looks different, good really, once you get used to her. The way the light hits her is . . . something George said. And George is right. She's not like anyone else. But then, the cameras roll and she *can't* do it."

"She can. Trust George, trust yourself."

"I trust you," David says, leaning against his wife.

"Then trust me. She can do it," Irene says. "Come to bed."

Some of David's early requests were unspoken: that Irene remain as slender as possible for as long as possible, that she always love him best, and that the baby be a boy. Some requests are explicit. David asks Irene to promise they will go to New York right after the baby is born. Not because he wants to go to the city, but because he wants to know he can still have her to himself. Irene knows David will feel more a part of fatherhood if he is there at the start. She extracts a promise of her own: He must be in the delivery room.

"So I can meet him first?" he asks her.

"So, you can meet *the baby* first." Irene is unwilling to commit to the sex. If she does and is wrong, David will feel betrayed as if she has backed out of a promise.

CARY
SANTA MONICA
AUGUST 1932

Frank Horn is sweating in his light wool suit. "It is just not smart, Cary. You can't do it," he says hopping up to sit on the Formica countertop. Cary Grant is leaning against the sink, not sweating. Unless he is doing his daily calisthenics, Cary rarely sweats. He thrives in the heat, the California sun and after running every morning on the beach and then kicking through the cold surf, his skin has turned nut brown. He chooses pale shirts and bright red neckerchiefs to set it off. His teeth are white. Cary has a perfect eye and knows what suits his narrow-shouldered frame. Someday it will be written into his Paramount contracts that he will wear his own clothes.

Cary and Frank are in an empty house by the beach. The kitchen floor smells of Clorox. This room is an unforgiving, hard white: kitchen, walls, tile: the sediments of color are scooped out and the pigment is reduced to light. Light is the religion of this house. But that is not what Frank wants to talk about.

"You just can't *live* here," Frank repeats.

"Sure, I can. Look at this place, right on the sand," Cary says.

"I mean, you can't live here *with* Randolph," Frank says. Frank has heard the rumors that Cary lived with a man in New York.

"Ah, but could I afford this on my own?" Cary waves his arm at the great sheet of windows that wrap the seafront side of the house. "No."

"No, you couldn't," Frank agrees. Already Cary's secretary, he has also taken over Cary's bookkeeping until he can hire a good accountant, although it seems redundant. Cary is meticulous about his finances. "How much is this place? Can you even manage your half? How much is Randolph paying?"

"Nine hundred and sixty. And Howard staked him the deposit last month," Cary says as he folds the rental agreement into neat thirds and replaces it in the envelope. Frank knows that Cary will label and file the document today.

"Howard Hughes gave him the deposit? Why?" Frank knows that Randolph is on a leading man contract now and besides that, he comes from old Virginia tobacco money. Unlike Cary, Randolph Scott does not have to work if he doesn't want to.

"Howard is like that. They are old family friends," Cary says as if this explains everything. He moves to the window. Beyond, the light flashes and white foams on thick green curls of seawater. "I was born near water," Cary says, facing the salt-sprayed glass. Frank waits for him to go on but he doesn't. Cary turns back to Frank, "I'll take the room down the hall, Randolph wants the one by the pool. And we'll turn the downstairs bedroom into a gym."

"Cary, think about this," Frank says, jumping down from the counter. "You and Randolph, living here, together? People will talk."

"Yes, Frank, but people will always talk."

Frank is gone and Cary and Randolph have spread out a picnic dinner on the floor of their new house. Their voices echo, elastic and thin, the way voices do in a room without furniture.

"She would have loved this," Cary says, facing the ocean. The water is silver now, darkening to gunmetal.

"She liked the sea?" Randolph asks, regretting the words even as he speaks them. He knows Cary's mother went to the seaside one day and never returned. But nothing between them is forbidden. Nothing too delicate to be voiced.

"I think so," Cary says, his voice warm with memory. "She must have liked the sea."

. . .

"We're going to call the house Bachelor Hall. Catchy, right?" Ben Schulberg doesn't wait for Cary to answer. "The publicity team came up with it. We have to get out in front, show there's nothing to hide. And we're shooting for a spread in *Life* and maybe another in *House & Garden* once we get a decorator in there. You need a decorator; don't argue." Ben Schulberg, the general manager of Paramount, hunches like a walnut shell over his desk and scratches an item off his list. Schulberg lives his life by lists.

"Yes, I heard. Decorator is booked for tomorrow and the photographers are coming on Thursday. Beach shots only until the house is finished, apparently," Cary says, shifting in his chair and recrossing his trousered legs. Cary has found a tailor on Wilshire who measures him three times a month and cuts his clothes exactly as he likes them. Cary doesn't bother to smooth the edge off his tone. He is annoyed. He resents being summoned to the studio to discuss his living arrangements. They called Randolph in this morning to have the same conversation. He wants to refuse the decorator.

"We need girls, Cary, parties, photographs, get yourself talked about. We have three guys from the publicity department on it already."

"You want me to get my private life *into* the papers?" Cary said, his hammered accent flattening the words. The southwest of England still flecks his speech when he is irritated. "I can do that." Picking up his hat and beautifully cut coat, he leaves the office, pulling the door gently closed behind him. Cary Grant is not the sort of man to slam doors.

KATE

COLDWATER CANYON

The dinner went on too long and the straps from her shoes have left red welts. Leland gave them a lift back to the house and would not stop talking about how important these dinners are. Laura asked him in for a drink. Annoying. Kate wants him to go home.

As soon as she is successful enough, she will stop wearing heels. Not that she doesn't like how heels look on other women. Laura was breathtaking tonight in that silver dress. Sat at opposite ends of the table, Kate was able to watch Laura, to miss her. She can only feel value when it is almost out of reach. She can hear Laura running a bath and goes up to shut off the tap. She wants Laura to get a little dirtier before she gets clean.

HOWARD

HANCOCK PARK

Howard Hughes has heard of her by now. Most people in the business have. Soon, her name will turn up in the fan magazines and younger actresses will talk about dying their hair dark red, but not yet. Howard has also seen her name on the course records at the Wilshire Country Club. He saw her on the course once. He is playing the back nine, and she is two holes ahead of him. He likes that she doesn't wait for Ladies' Day. He catches up and watches from the trees as she lines up the shot. She doesn't hesitate. She moves into her stance, her body fluid from long practice. She follows through like a windmill. He is impressed. She has a good swing.

He wishes Billie Dove played, but his lover thinks swinging a club is ungraceful.

LOS ANGELES

AUGUST 1932

Only Billie Dove knows this will be her last picture. She has not told anyone. Not MGM, not Irving Thalberg, not even her lover, Howard Hughes. Someone should have told her that MGM was making the picture with Hearst's money. She would have turned it down. Irving Thalberg would have told her, he is decent that way, but he didn't know. Louis B. Mayer did not tell him. But, everyone in this town knows that William Randolph Hearst will cut a film to ribbons before he lets another actress overshadow his love, Marion Davies. Most powerful newspaperman in the world and they have been an item for more than a decade but Hearst is forever courting Marion Davies.

It is too bad about this picture. Billie Dove wasn't cast as the villain. She is too young for that. She and Marion were meant to star together. But the producers have gone behind Billie's back, rewritten, reshot, used a body double, and now she *is* the villain. It is over. You do not come back from being the villain. No way back to leading lady after playing the baddie. So Billie Dove has decided to get married, and then right away, to have a baby. She has not picked the groom yet but she will. The baby part is essential. Once a star has a baby, she's out. It is an iron rule. A mother can never be desirable. It's a graceful exit.

This morning, quietly, with no fuss, while Howard's house on Muirfield Road is empty, Billie Dove is packing it in and leaving Hollywood. If Howard wants to marry her, it must be now. But he won't. Billie knows that already. It would be too easy. Howard cannot respect anything that comes easily. She will move her things out before he comes home from the golf course. More elegant to have it over and done.

IRENE

BEVERLY HILLS

AUGUST 1932

It comes down to brute force in the end; Irene pushing, the doctor, pulling, soaked towels on the hospital tile floor. Irene's sister Edie waits in the hall. The baby is a boy and David is there. It is only after Irene is stitched up and asleep, after the baby is fed, foot printed, and taken down the hall to the nursery that David, his brother Myron and brother-in-law Bill leave the mingled herd of Mayers and Selznicks in the waiting room, the two families who have become grandparents together tonight, and go out into the dry California neon dark. They are going to the Clover Club on Sunset.

Irene's father, Louis B. Mayer, gives them a disapproving look as they leave. Louis B. is a powerful man in this town, but he is at a loss with David. Already, he wants to knock his son-in-law's teeth out. What kind of man leaves his wife and new son? David would say, "The kind of man who needs to celebrate!" Louis B. Mayer does not think much of the way his son-in-law celebrates. David is sure Irene will understand. He has never met such a capable, steady woman as his wife. He is confident that having a baby will not change that.

The back room at the Clover Club is smoky and cramped. The higher the stakes, the smaller the room. Myron Selznick never bets big, he doesn't see the point. David is bored until the stakes become ruinous. "Why bet if you're not prepared to risk it all?" he says. Once he bets, more than he can bear to lose, the adrenaline thrashes and David crackles with life. David's brother-in-law Bill Goetz, a good husband but an unimaginative film producer, gives the impression of betting more than he actually does. Bill's wife, Edie, Irene's sister, is still at the hospital so Bill is free to stay out all night but he won't. He will want to get back to Edie.

"David," Myron cautions, but he recognizes his brother's mood and stops. Myron had hoped tonight would be remembered for Irene's new baby but, if David loses this pile, this, this will be what they talk about tomorrow.

Twinning uppers with booze, David loops higher. He tells himself that losing doesn't get him down, only boredom. David is up on the night until three A.M., but as always, he stays at the table too long—stays until he loses. David is always more interested in what he can't do than what he can.

"Without risk there is no progress," he tells Myron. "Without progress, there is no *life*!" He is yelling now. Myron has heard these arguments before: David cannot leave the table when there is the possibility of *more*. Myron has left his car at the hospital. Bill calls a taxicab. It is time to go home.

David never wins at Gin, but he still believes that Gin is his game. He pays Bill with a promissory note. David will not tell

Irene how much he loses, it is not a number he can say out loud, and what if she brings it up with Edie, or worse, her father? Irene is loyal but tonight's losses are extreme. David is sure his promissory notes have paid for Bill and Edie's new swimming pool, so, perhaps it is a good thing? In any case, why distress Irene on such a happy day? Nothing can tear down his Benzedrine-fueled, screaming joy. Nothing except tragedy, *catastrophe.*

When David returns to the hospital, hungover, unshaven, and late, he uncovers the terrible truth, the horror that no one else can see. He thunders down the white linoleum hallways to break the news to Irene. He wakes her roughly. She sees the Benzedrine frenzy, smells the scotch. Her first thought is to hide him, get him home and cleaned up before anyone can see him this way. Her father, Louis B., already suspects. He and his wife talk about it late at night when the servants have gone to bed, but do not mention it to Irene. They are not that kind of family. Irene tries to soothe David; makes the shushing noises she will soon use to quiet her baby. David will not be calmed. He is ridged in fury. He tells her in a rush, a lash, a nonsense bolt of words shot from a canon: their baby has been stolen.

"No. I want the police in here *now,*" he shouts down the long quiet hall. "What are they doing that could be more important?" he yells at the orderlies. He will not stop or sit. Everyone is awake now. The head obstetrician has been called and is on his way. The orderlies have called in the hospital security guard, a small, paunchy, unarmed man called Ed who wishes he were not on duty tonight. He too is following David down the white tiled corridor. They are all sizing up David. He is a big man and will be difficult to remove.

The policeman comes to Irene's room. David is still searching the wards, trailed by orderlies in white shoes.

"Mrs. Selznick?" Officer Kaplan hesitates in the doorway, embarrassed to be intruding on a brand-new mother. He and his wife have a four-month-old girl.

"It's all right," Irene says, and the policeman steps into the room. He is aware of his dark boots and unwashed hands. He takes out his notebook.

"You don't need that," Irene says. "My husband is mistaken. I apologize for the disturbance he is causing."

"Mistaken? Your son is not missing?"

"My son is sleeping down the hall. Two maternity nurses and my sister are watching him. Second door on the right. His blanket is tagged Selznick, his measurements match the ones they took last night exactly, and, I know my son."

"Your husband . . ."

"Is under a great deal of strain," Irene says, dignified, loyal.

The policeman goes to see the baby and then leaves. He will fill out his report at the station. Families should be alone at this time.

Four hours and nothing Irene can say will change his mind. Crazed, David calls in the hospital administrator, all the obstetricians, the head maternity nurse—sleeping hard after her twelve-hour shift, and woken after only two hours. "There has been a switch!" David shrieks. He will not stand for it. He will close down this hospital! Their baby, the baby Irene gave birth to, is not this baby tagged "Selznick" and swaddled in the sky-blue blanket. Take it away! This baby is foreign, alien, inferior to the perfect infant he met last night. Someone has made off with their better baby and there will be hell to pay. All the overhead lights are turned on and the nurses apologize to the raw new mothers on the ward. But everyone has heard by now that it is David O. Selznick, son-in-law of Louis B. Mayer who is making this racket. There is only one industry in this town, and no one complains.

Irene is appalled by the display. Her steady need to contain, to cope, keeps her voice level, which only infuriates David. He rails at her, "What kind of a mother are you that you do not fight for your child?" The nurses turn away and leave with the baby.

At the edge of Irene's calm is a band of outrage, a hot ring around cold Saturn. David has made this day about him, not them, and he has demoted her new, beloved baby to an inferior replacement, a second choice. He has absolved himself of this baby. This child's failures will not be David's failures. Irene burns down her frustration until it is a soft pile of ash. Six more hours, a search of the entire hospital (all the clean linen is tossed into heaps on the floor and must be rewashed), an exact matching of the tiny footprint taken last night, and David *might* concede that this is his baby. He is coming down. Anyway, he says, "I am used to this baby now. No point in turning him in for another one who might be worse." The orderlies, both failed actors, remember every word so they can repeat it later.

. . .

Calmer, drinking coffee by the window, David has come back to himself. Bill and Myron walked the corridors with him for hours, while Edie sat in the hard hospital chair beside Irene. At one point, Edie suggested they call their parents. Louis B. and Margaret Mayer are both notoriously private. There will be conversations about airing dirty laundry. Margaret Mayer finds it to be a crass phrase but an effective one. Edie waits, it is Irene's choice.

"The newspapers," is all Irene says and Edie nods. Irene wants to keep the circle small, but she knows it's too late for that; the noise, the nurses, the other mothers and beyond that, Edie, who will tell their parents everything. Irene knows that Edie is enjoying this. Not on the surface, not in a way she would admit, but somehow, Irene's failure is Edie's success. It is how they are.

Irene is right; it is too late. The gossip is zipping up and down the wards. An orthopedic surgeon tells the head of pediatrics that David shook the baby. A janitor tells an ambulance driver that David threatened Irene. A ward nurse tells an operating room nurse that there has been a kidnapping. The hospital administrator has had to call a general staff meeting to warn them all not to call the newspapers. The Mayers are generous patrons of the hospital. One of the failed actor orderlies auditioned at MGM nine times and never got a callback before his agent dropped him. He calls *The Star* anonymously from the payphone at the diner on the corner. The reporter writes down the tip in her spiral notebook but she wants to move up to cover Hollywood features. She tears out the page and throws it away. She will call David Selznick's office in the morning to tell them he owes her.

It is over. David is embarrassed about his behavior last night but will not admit it to Irene. So, he picks a different fight.

"But you agreed to call him Jeffrey?" Irene repeats.

"What kind of a name is Jeffrey? It sounds like a medieval knight in a B grade picture—a non-speaking role," David says. He is still pacing the floor, careful not to knock over any of the standing flower arrangements.

"It is the name we chose," she says. "I suggested it and you agreed."

"I don't remember that."

Irene understands him but wishes she didn't. She does not want to help him out of his embarrassment but knows she will. They are a family now. Irene is tired and wants to sleep. Watching him thread through the bouquets of flowers, she reminds herself to make a list of who sent what so she can send out thank you notes. She will not give up on the name but she will not fight for it right now. She will do it when she wakes up.

Eventually, Marcella Rabwin arrives at the hospital. Irene knew it would happen. David has already spent three hours dictating memos over the telephone this morning. Marcella brings small blue booties. Blue. No label; she knit them herself. Irene is touched by the thought. Are there pink booties somewhere? Or did she just know? Marcella is the kind of woman who knows things. Marcella also brings the Dictaphone but David doesn't use it. Why use the machine when Marcella is here? Marcella has asked her neighbor to feed her cats and has packed lunch and dinner. She knows she is not going home.

LAURA

COLDWATER CANYON

Laura listens to Kate's end of the phone call. She hears Kate's easy laughter and feels her guts twist, curving like a garden hose. She pretends to read while she listens, trying to work out who is on the line. Call times, marks, rehearsal, script pages: has to be George. Again. Laura doesn't mind if it's Luddy. She is used to that.

Kate calls Luddy, every morning after breakfast before she leaves for the studio. Luddy never schedules meetings between nine and eleven A.M. now; he does not want to miss the call. Their conversations always follow the same template: the house in New York, the furniture, the paint, the plumbing, her dinner, his dinner, her bath, her sleep, have a good day on the set darling. And Kate calls her family on Sundays, talks to all of them. Their conversations ricochet from tennis to books to politics to golf to medicine. This one has an exam, that one just removed a gallbladder. Everyone interrupts everyone, except when Dr. Hepburn is speaking. Interruptions annoy him. Mrs. Hepburn asks about everything but Hollywood and the younger sisters ask about nothing but Hollywood. At the end, they always send their love to Laura and she sends her love back. While Kate is on the telephone, Laura stays close. She wants to be there when it's time to send love to the Hepburns. They are her in-laws aren't they? Although they do not know it.

Now, there is no schedule at all and the phone rings all the time: dinner invitations, publicity people, the studio, scheduling changes, script changes, Leland, Irene. Often, George calls at night to make sure Kate made it home safely and the two of them talk for over an hour. After spending all day together. Laura tries to understand. The shooting schedule is short and there is not always time to talk through everything on set. Kate lies on the floor of the hallway and rests her feet up on the wall while Laura waits and dinner gets cold. Some nights, Leland Hayward calls or worse, stops by. And now, he pops over on the weekends. Kate will come down from her bath or in from the pool, wrapped in her terry-cloth bathrobe with the faded candy stripes to find Leland lazing on the sofa or nosing through the bookshelves. When Kate flops into a chair beside him, he will suggest a drive or golf or tennis or flying, and Laura feels their day drift away from her. She feels pushed out of the center when Leland is there.

Laura shows none of this to Kate who would only feel trapped and not sympathetic. To Kate, if you want to be in the center, you had better be damned well interesting enough to hold on to your place. Instead, Laura asks Ragnhild to make extra food for friends who might come by. Kate is delighted by Laura's thoughtfulness and Laura moves to the center again.

LOS ANGELES
AUGUST 1932

Changes are coming. The six decide to meet at Cocoanut Grove. Neutral ground. There's a private room and the staff are discreet. Each studio head takes a turn to speak, equality is important in this room. They must present a united front and have to fall into line before the state congressional hearings.

Louis B. Mayer is irritated. They are here to talk about the censorship problem and he wants to get on with it. His son-in-law David is talking now: about the Hays Office, ratings and autonomy. A stricter Production Code of Ethics could mean more regulation. *Undue exposure. Sex hygiene. Perversion.* Louis B. stops listening. As if MGM would ever make a film that crossed these lines. David Selznick is still talking, now about their common goals and shared endeavor, their artistic freedom. His elbows are on the table; his phrases are reduced to bursts of hot breath. No substance. No character. Louis B. is angry. He knows his son-in-law owes money all over town.

Irene and the baby come home from the hospital today and Louis B. wants to be there with his wife when she arrives. *Someone* should be there. David has hardly mentioned the baby. He just keeps talking about Irene's recovery, as if she has been ill rather than pregnant.

Louis B. watches his son-in-law. He likes David's work. The man makes excellent pictures, brings them in on time and on budget and he respects that. He wants David back at MGM where he can get a better view of things, keep an eye on the finances. Louis B. believes family should work together, sail under one flag. And if David is back at MGM, Louis B. can make sure Irene gets what she needs. He and his wife speak about how to give money to Irene.

Edie accepts it, builds a beautiful home and is grateful, but Irene? No. His wife has told him that Irene is worried about the cost of the private room at the hospital. Louis B. blames David.

KATE

RKO STUDIOS

"Again!" George calls and the actors reset.

It has been going well, Barrymore is remembering his lines. The mood is relaxed and George is happy that David Selznick is not on the lot today. There is a note clipped to his script: a reminder to send Irene camellias and messenger his gift, a custom carriage robe, over to the house on Rexford. The cast also prefer it when David is not there. David has already sent a dozen memos today. George is ignoring them. Marcella Rabwin opens the soundstage door and leaves the memos with the prop man who drops them into an unlabeled box. No one can keep up with Selznick's memos. They have grown worse since the baby. The prop man has heard a rumor that when Mrs. Selznick wants to teach her husband a lesson, she makes him read his memos out loud. It's probably not true; it doesn't sound like Mrs. Selznick. The prop man sits on a lighting crate and returns to his crime novel. Miss Hepburn has been through the scene three times and has not got it right yet. They won't need him for a while.

Kate is strung tight with tension. She tries the line the way she practiced this morning in the bathroom mirror, the way she and George spoke about before. The same goddamn heartbreak line. It falls flat, she can see it in George's expression. The words are worn out, they've lost their properties and are reduced to wet clicks of tongue against teeth. Kate hates the line and wants to cut it.

"Kate," George says, taking her to one side. "I can't ask the writer to cut it. It's the whole point of the film." He stops, worried that if he highlights the drama, she will try to do the next take *dramatically*. New stars can be so literal. He does not want her to wear the pain of the scene on the outside. The audience must just catch a quick glimpse of how it lives *inside* her. It's what will make them feel they know her; if they think they can see something in her that others cannot see. It will make her theirs.

"Kate, you are *acting* the words. Think. Imagine this moment; imagine you are right now realizing that you cannot marry the man you love, cannot have the children you crave."

Does she crave children? She has always assumed they will arrive, on time and neatly packaged so as to not upend her life, the way they never upended her mother's. *Crave?* That is a strong word.

"Kate, imagine that you will never have any other family but this one, the one you were born with and so will be alone for always. Say it as if you *feel* it but do not want to *show* it, as if it's something you dread."

Feel it. *Alone for always*. He wants her to open the door and invite that time back in. Kate considers the words. It is a skeletal line with nowhere to hide. Feeling it means finding it, letting it find her; as if that feeling does not know where she lives. Kate stops, steadies. She needs to be good at this. Fine. How *does* heartbreak sound? Not like this, not the way she has been trying it, with the emotion bald and front-loaded. Real heartbreak is noiseless. It is named. The names you never speak aloud.

She tries it again.

"We can't push the scene Kate," George says, sounding genuinely sorry. "We have to get it tonight. We'll photograph the other close-ups now. Go home for an hour, stop thinking, have dinner with Laura and we can start again."

"I'm getting worse, that's what you mean," Kate says, sitting down so that Nancy can wrap her hair in a net. Nancy knows that she will most likely have to start from scratch with Kate's hair when she comes back from dinner but the net may help some. Kate doesn't bother to ask if they can soften the words. George is fanatical about staying true to the text. "Don't lie to me, Gor-udge. I know when I'm goddamn awful."

"You are not *awful*," George says carefully, "but you *are* getting farther from it. You're getting impersonal. Haven't you had your heart broken?" George's question is seamed with wonder. An undamaged heart is something that George cannot fathom; his own bulges with scar tissue. "Kate, find something, do something, anything that will bring you closer, help you connect to the words. The line has to be *yours*."

Laura, standing in the door of the makeup room, waits for them to finish and then drives Kate home.

LAURA

COLDWATER CANYON

They eat in the kitchen, at the pine table. Over cold cheese sandwiches and milk, Laura brings up the family: Mrs. Hepburn's uncle and Dr. Hepburn's brothers. Laura says she has heard a rumor. Really, she heard about Kate's family from Leland. He takes care to research his clients. Laura hears Kate's blurry hot rush of defense, but Laura is not attacking but waiting, surrendering and open-faced and Kate cannot respond in anger to a question asked with such unrelenting tenderness.

KATE

COLDWATER CANYON

Kate speaks about her family's dead in small, oval phrases. But not about Tom, never about Tom—she keeps him safe, cocooned in his white attic room. Kate's voice is tight but level and the stories, metallic and hard won, shudder from disuse. The Hepburns do not speak of these people; Kate says she no longer remembers why.

Laura is patient and waits to catch the words with gentle arms.

"So many," Laura says, when Kate has finished. "On both sides." Laura is dissolved, her edges ragged. She had not expected so much self-inflicted death.

"Yes. So many," Kate repeats, her voice sounding like her voice again.

"How?" Laura asks.

How. People always want to know how they did it. What does it matter? Is one way better than another? Easier? Is automobile exhaust less messy than a gun? Choking better than a slug of bullet? Drowning better than jumping? Either way, the end is the same. People just decide a thing and get on with it. Once the decision is made, they are gone already. *How* only matters to the people who have to clean up.

GEORGE

RKO STUDIOS

"Once more," George says, his voice low.

The scene resets. The grips and prop people move quietly, tilting a light, replacing a handkerchief, understanding that something important is happening.

Kate has got it and George does not want to crack the dense air around her. She has done it, he thinks. She has found a way to be someone else. The cameras roll forward. Kate and David Manners begin the scene again.

She will make it. George knows it when he sees it.

LOS ANGELES

AUGUST 1932

Selznick still says she is ugly. He tells Irving Thalberg at MGM that she has an ugly mouth. Irving has seen her screen test and tells him he's wrong. Irene tells him that on film, Kate reads differently. Her steep reef of cheek, ledge of jaw? She will be beautiful, Irene says. Just wait. Irene knows, Kate is something new. Not pretty, not trying to please you, there is no softness, no give. She is utterly herself. Don't look too closely. Kate's face can unravel, especially when she is concentrating and her lips press straight. Bogart will eventually call it her schoolmistress look, but that is not until they shoot a film on a river in Africa.

She has it. Not all the time, but most. We see that it can be easy now, the equilibrium, the loose-jointed fluency. Something has broken open, some road unblocked. She can shove her hands into the dirt and pull up the roots of the thing. She'd missed it before, had it wrong. She doesn't need to play someone else. It's an easy mistake; the language can trip you up, make you look for another you, but there is no one else. It's a magic trick, a hoax. The woman is not sawn in half. The white rabbit was already in the top hat. She only needs to play herself—more of herself than she would willingly give away.

There used to be another her.

Kate remembers the conversations they used to have; his idea that it was better to be the words than the mouth; her idea that fame would protect her. But then, she had not understood the cost, the self-invasion. We never want them to know the price up front.

KATE

RKO STUDIOS

Kate wants to move fast. She comes in early, reads off-camera lines for the other actors during their close ups, stays to finish the scene, even when the camera is not on her. Selznick lets one of the stand-ins go. Why pay another person when Kate is willing to do the off-camera lines? The stand-in gets a job at MGM and tells stories in the commissary about this new up-and-coming star. The cast and crew say Kate is generous, professional, a real team player, but that's not it. Kate is just anxious to catch and keep this clicked-into-place feeling. She tries to describe the feeling to her family, to Laura, but can't. They are not on the inside. Magic is not built from parts of speech.

. . .

The big scene, the break up scene. The one where she tells David Manners she will not live her life with him. George has held back from shooting it until now. He must think she is ready. She knows how to do it this time, where to find it. She lands it in three takes.

Later, at home, Laura asks her about Tom. It's different from when Kate offered up her other family, invited Laura in. Kate tells her some, not all. There are small things that Laura seems to guess; the stiff door, the heat. But then, it was an attic, Kate said that, of course it would be hot. Did she mention the door? She does not remember.

CARY

SANTA MONICA

He sees it in *Screen Time*. Right beside a column on the "Six Best Money Stars." That sounds like the six stars who best handle their finances rather than the six stars who bring in the most money. *Screen Time* should hire better writers. But there it is, spelled out in a small, black outlined box. "Mr. Orry Kelly to be the new chief costume designer at Warner Bros." The article says Mr. Kelly is coming straight from Australia but the article is wrong. Orry Kelly is coming right from a damp one-bedroom apartment in Greenwich Village. Cary should know. He left him there when he moved out.

LOS ANGELES

AUGUST 1932

We knew she could do it. She just gets better. Her scenes are clean: Barrymore is experienced, generous, we have not seen him so engaged in years. He is not even drinking now. He concedes the spotlight and Kate is fresh and glorious and each phrase is new. George watches her, relieved. He bet the farm on her. Leland watches her, bewitched. Laura Harding's hand covers her red mouth. This whole town, this whole country, is going to fall in love with the woman she loves. The photographer rolls past cut, he cannot lose a frame of this.

LAURA

COLDWATER CANYON

Since Kate learned to act, the sex has mostly drained off the love, but for Laura, the love is enough. And it's only temporary. It will all go back to how it was when the picture finishes. This is the nearest to real life Laura has ever been; the life she wants and the life she lives are running so close they nearly touch. Kate has not been coming to Laura's room but Laura hopes. Of course she does. Being alive has an addictive quality. But what if this life in Hollywood goes away? The wrong words to the wrong people and this life could vanish for Kate. Would that be so bad?

There are good days to hold on to, important days. The day she filmed the break-up scene and Kate spoke about her brother. That day, when Kate came home, she told Laura everything, the unspeakable history of her family. The railroad tracks and the running engine. Laura knew most of it already. When Leland first told her, she had her lawyers in New York pull the police report. It is public information, she reasoned. She read about the hot attic room, the door, the beams, the way his feet touched the floor. What she read and what Kate told her blend together. Eventually, Laura doesn't remember asking for the police report. Absolution comes easily to her.

Knowing these private Hepburn tragedies makes Laura feel important, their relationship scrubbed clean and newly baptized in intimacy. The day Kate told her about her family, they returned to the set together, and Kate landed her scenes as Laura knew she would. George had drunk three cups of coffee by then, thinking the shoot would take all night. It was over in seven minutes. One take and he had it. Two more for good measure but he didn't need them. Laura felt essential, responsible. You have to earn your keep with Kate.

Laura knows so much that these movie people do not. Things they will never know. It makes Laura feel safer.

KATE

COLDWATER CANYON

And then the cameras stop. They are done for the night. The film is tucked into its canisters and the lids are snapped shut. Actors change their shoes, root in their bags for their glasses. George wipes his face with a blue handkerchief. John Barrymore lights a cigarette. Everyone turns back into themselves. Kate feels that tugging loss, the kind you feel after a dinner party where you have said too much. It's uncomfortable. But she is tough. She sets her teeth and un-grips her hands. The camera has to want you. It's transactional. That's the only way this works. The camera will never want you unless you offer up your secrets. They are the price of doing business. Kate is proud she is able to do it but feels split open and raw.

She wishes she had something to sell besides herself.

PART THREE

RECASTING

HOWARD

PASADENA

SEPTEMBER 1932

In September, the most eligible bachelor in America disappears. He has done it before. His business partner, Noah Dietrich, calls all the usual places: the Muirfield Road house in Los Angeles, the golf course, the airfield, the Hughes Film production office in Culver City, the Ambassador Hotel on Wilshire, even the Yoakum Boulevard house in Houston, but cannot find him. Howard *had* been at the Ambassador Hotel that morning but only for a haircut. The long, sexy hair he wore while directing *Hell's Angels* is shorn off. A regular job needs regular hair.

He pays for the train ticket in cash, stooping down to slide the money under the window. Usually, he charges everything to the Hughes Tool Company in Houston but Noah has made him promise not to until the company finances are back in the black. It is 1932, and like the rest of America, Howard Hughes is going broke.

Howard does not mind the third-class carriage. It's a little dirty, but he is careful not to let his sleeve touch the armrest. It's an adventure. No one recognizes him, but then no one expects the richest man in America to be traveling to Texas in a third-class carriage. He is wearing a shirt he bought that morning from Sears. The label is itchy. He wishes he could tell someone where he is. He wishes he could tell Billie.

He arrives in Fort Worth in time for the interview and presents a Texas driver's license in the name of Charles Howard. He had it run up on Olvera Street last week. He is waved through to the line of applicants.

The other applicants are all about twenty, twenty-two at the most. Howard feels too old at twenty-six. And too tall, at six foot four, but he hunches, collapsing his long, thin frame. Yesterday, his uncut brown hair would have fallen into his eyes but not today.

"Baggage handler, sixty dollars a month," the crisp American Airways man says, offering him the job.

Deaf in one ear, Howard leans forward, struggling to hear. Half lip reading, half guessing, "Yes." Whatever the American Airways man has said, the answer is yes.

The man looks down at Howard's application. "Pilot's license? Do you want to sign up for the commercial pilot training program?"

"Yes." It's what he has come for.

. . .

The 7:30 A.M. from Fort Worth to Cleveland. A Fokker F.VII, six years old and compact but in perfect shape. Eight passengers, one air hostess, the pilot and the co-pilot. Howard checks the bags, stores the bags and then moves up to the cockpit and folds himself into the jump seat. The older, experienced captain narrates the flight and Howard, sitting behind the co-pilot, takes notes. He notes everything, the levers, the switches, lights, the landing gear. When filming *Hell's Angels*, Howard learned military planes. Now he is learning commercial aircraft. He is happy. After the plane lands in Cleveland, while he is meant to eat and rest up before the flight back, Howard asks questions. He speaks to the mechanics, the fuel men, the control tower men, other pilots and the passengers. He is thorough and has already filled two notebooks. He has ideas for how to make the company, the engine, the airports more efficient. Howard likes to get the most out of things.

The captain knows he can already fly. It is the nature of Howard's questions, the specificity, that gives him away. They take him out for a test run. He excels. After his first week, his captain tells him he has the makings of a first-rate commercial pilot. He is a natural in the air. His hands are steady and his instincts are good. Howard is a man who trusts himself, invaluable in a pilot. After his second week, he is promoted to co-pilot. Howard's salary jumps up one hundred dollars a month. He cashes the checks at the Fort Worth National Bank and keeps the money in a drawer in his hotel room under his socks. On his day off, he goes out to the army base at Tarrant Field to watch the planes. He would like to pick up a girl but he's afraid of being recognized.

Noah Dietrich is still looking for him. Today's newspapers are dusty and dry in the sun outside the gate at Muirfield Road. Noah stops by the house, waters the plants, opens the mail. Howard never deals with the post anyway. Noah brings in the papers but he is late today. He was held up at the bank where he was trying to arrange for Howard's soon to be ex-wife to receive her quarterly payment. Her pay out. Pay off. Howard leaves these details to Noah. Howard never loved Ella and so he sees no reason to speak to her. They married young and she was useful to him, until she was not. Billie Dove was different but since she left, Howard refuses to speak of her.

Noah opens the Spanish wooden door. The house is quiet and wears a stale, airless smell. Noah has given the servants a holiday. Howard would not like anyone but Noah in his home when he is not there.

. . .

It is six weeks before Howard is recognized. One of the American Airways officials has seen *Hell's Angels* seven times, has a teenage daughter who reads about Howard Hughes in *Screen Time* and *Pho-*

toplay. American Airways gives Howard a fresh uniform, calls a photographer and the newspapers. Howard feels loyalty to his new company and does as he is asked. He poses in front of the plane, in the cockpit, on the stairway and even moves some baggage so they can snap that too. In the morning, American Airways politely fires him. They tell him how sorry they are, and they mean it. He is the most naturally gifted flier they have ever seen.

LAURA
COLDWATER CANYON

Laura Harding doesn't want to go out tonight. There is a party at the Mocambo. Louis B. Mayer has heard rumors of this new actress at RKO and wants to introduce her to MGM's new leading man. This is how it happens, isn't it? Someone tells someone and that someone tells someone else. And then a groundswell. Is that all it takes? In New York it takes generations.

Kate says there is talk of a loan-out. Laura is not sure Kate knows what a loan-out means. Laura had to ask Leland Hayward what it meant. Leland told her there will be photographers there tonight and Kate is *not* to wear trousers. He said no one will want to hire Kate on "loan" or otherwise if she looks like a man. Do they think Laura is Kate's, what? Assistant? Dresser? Laura sits in one of the deep green Westport chairs and scans the list. The names are familiar, sent over by the studio: men who can escort Kate to dinner parties, film screenings, picnics at the beach, opening night parties: any place where she might be photographed.

The best of them are from George Cukor's crowd, they are more fun. All of them are a bit fruity but the people who buy the fan magazines in small town drugstores don't know that. They rotate—last week, Anderson Lawler took Kate to the premiere of Tallulah

Bankhead and Gary Cooper's new picture and then next week, Billy Haines will take her to the party at the Alhambra. Billy's lover Jimmie Shields will take some other starlet. Once inside, away from photographers, Billy and Jimmie will sit together and eat off each other's plates. The publicity department has stressed that Kate is never to be seen with any one man too often. Except Leland. A star can be seen with her agent anytime. Some men on the list are on the way up and will be stars someday soon and others never quite happened. But they all have money or talent or connection or beauty, the only currencies that count in this town. The men who escort Kate understand the rules—and if they don't Laura explains in short, strong sentences. No groping, no touching except to take her hand and help her out of the car, smile for the flash and that's it.

"If they are shocked, they won't show it," Kate says. "Most of them leave to go and fuck a man after dinner anyway."

Laura is not as bohemian as Kate and is awkward with profanity. She hates sounding prim. Laura chooses a name from the list and rings the studio. The name she chose will be delivered to the house in two hours, dressed in a dinner suit. Laura will go with Carlton Burke, reliable, easy to talk to, handsome enough. The rumor is that he is her beau and Laura is pleased. As rumors go, it's a good one.

It is only four P.M. Laura is already winding into a tight spiral. Her slippery insides twist and wring out. Without consulting Laura, Kate hired Joanna, her dresser from New York, to help Ragnhild manage the house and the clothes and the hair and all of it. Having her in the house makes Laura feel replaced, her advice on hair and skin and clothes no longer necessary. Laura wishes Joanna were not so competent. Joanna has dressed everyone on Broadway and is impressed by no one. And she is tactful. Joanna avoids difficult questions that may lead to messy answers. Laura does not ask Kate why she hired her.

KATE
COLDWATER CANYON

Kate will flirt with men tonight. Laura is fine with it. It happens when they go to parties. Not that flirting with men is forbidden between them. Not even sleeping with men is *really* forbidden. Laura is easy that way. And even if she isn't, Kate is less interested in making Laura comfortable now.

"I am *not* a lesbian," Laura often says to Kate.

"Maybe I am?" Kate says.

But she isn't, not fully, and they both know it.

Kate doesn't care one way or the other what Laura calls herself. Bodies are bodies. Growing up in a medical household has inured Kate to gender.

"Who cares?" Kate says. "Love them, don't love them? Fuck them, don't fuck them. Does it matter what they are called?"

Yes. To Laura it does.

To Laura, lesbians are predatory, aggressive women who cut their hair too short and wear unflattering shoes. Kate wishes Laura wouldn't cringe at the word. It makes her seem provincial. To Kate, there are women, intelligent, sexy women who sometimes sleep with other intelligent, sexy women. Kate's family have endured tougher rumors than people talking about who is sleeping with who.

LAURA
COLDWATER CANYON

Laura is modern, she has tried it with men and found there is not much point. She understands the mechanics, the geometry. It is the awkwardness of the thing she cannot bear. The sex is just a collision of joints and there is nowhere to put her hands. When she is in bed with a man, she feels removed, as if she is on the far side of a street watching someone else's house burn down. But with women, sometimes, there is a faint something. A slice of light under the door. With Kate, life rushes up to meet her, like the ground, like water, and she cannot be anywhere else. Laura's mind returns again and again to those rare, powerless nights with Kate, looking for small, unexplored corners to unwrap and taste. Now, she must be careful and hold back. These days, Kate does not like to be touched. The early passion burned off after a few months, but for Laura, those days still glow red. They are skinless, raw, private and hold more intimacy than Laura has ever known. Those nights were unspeakable and wild, but Laura knows that the memory of them does not shake Kate to the roots of her teeth.

Laura is afraid. What if it is not that she can only love women. What if she can only love Kate.

Dressing for the party, Laura chooses a Vionnet halter neck. She has never worn it and tonight she wants to be someone she has never been. Since coming to Los Angeles, Laura has stopped telling herself that she has just not met a man she liked enough and if she did, she would marry him. She has met every leading man here, and nothing. Even to herself, Laura is not a good liar.

Kate is not lying. She looks at men, flirts with men, and would sleep with a man if she felt like it. She has not promised fidelity to anyone. Laura knows that sometimes Kate wants a roughness, a strong-handedness that she doesn't find with women. Sometimes she does not want to lead. And beyond all that, Kate is still married. Laura pretends not to mind any of this. It's the deal she has made.

"What we have is new . . . not female, not male," Laura tries to explain to Leland after the party. She is still a bit drunk. "What we have is *important*. For Kate, for *me*."

"Whatever it is," Leland says, annoyed, "never tell the press."

LOS ANGELES

SEPTEMBER 1932

In this town, the air is curdled with sex. Here, anything can happen, and anything happens every night. Kate Hepburn is interested in fame but Laura Harding yammers on about sex and love. It is always *love* with Laura. She wants a public connection to Kate and breathes easier when she hears their names spoken as a compound noun. A "pair," Laura says, where Kate cannot hear her. She has gone so far as to call them "an item" to a Canadian actress who was too drunk to hear her. But Laura is careful with the press and there has been nothing in print, nothing that could harm Kate.

Here, the rules are clear—do anything, with anyone, but don't tell anybody who might tell the real world. When Clara Bow told someone who told someone who told a reporter about her open marriage, the prairie-living public never forgave her. Her career was finished. Clara forgot that most basic rule—an actress is always acting. She dropped the script, abandoned the character the studio had tailored for her—these characters are custom-built to appease the people who take out full-page advertisements in newspapers to rage over Hollywood's loose morals.

The studio executives and publicity departments hold meetings in hot California rooms and make decisions: he will be debonair and collect engraved cigarette cases—tell the makeup department to slick his hair down. She will be milk sweet and come from a small farming town—pale lighting for her, no strong shadows on her face. He will be rugged and fond of cattle rustling—find the diction coach, he needs to ditch that Long Island twang. She will be elusive and European—tell them to draw extra arch in her eyebrows and teach her to smoke. They are still working on Kate. So far they have come up with moneyed, New England, sporty and possibly eccentric; it depends on how her role in *Divorcement* goes over. Her easy boy/girl arm-swinging walk is new in movies; the publicity office hopes it is a gamble that will pay off.

The press are in on the secrets, of course they are; they go to the parties and know who is sleeping with who, who is married for real or for show, who likes boys or girls or boys pretending to be girls, who likes handcuffs and who likes Griffith Park after dark, who likes pills and who likes booze, who turns tricks when the roles dry up, who is cheating on who and who makes filthy long-distance calls. They go to the dinners on Cordell Drive and know that Billy Haines quit MGM because the studio asked him to stop sleeping with Jimmie Shields. Billy chose Jimmie and a real life together. Now, Billy is a top interior designer and the studio heads all want him to do up their beach houses. Six spreads in *House & Garden* last year alone. He prefers designing to acting. He plays himself now. Good that he got out when he did; the public scrutiny is coming into focus now. 1930's America wants its stars at best married, at worst, clean, virginal, living the wholesome lives they wish they could lead. Soon, America will want them to sleep in twin beds onscreen. Even the suggestion of sex will send the country howling.

The press also know the dirty, sexy difference between publicity stills and real life, but as long as the studios feed them enough choice cuts of manufactured gossip, they are respectful and steer clear of the damaging stuff. The press feed off these golden geese just like the rest of the town.

Until the damaging stuff is too juicy not to print.

CARY

SANTA MONICA

Frank Horn is driving Cary and Randolph home from a lunch party at the Selznicks' beach house. The press do not dare follow stars to the Selznicks'. Last year, a photographer managed to snap a picture of Irene and her sister, Edie, from the beach. Louis B. Mayer threatened to permanently deny all press access to any paper that ran it. The man never sold a photograph again.

Cary and Randolph are talking about producers. Ben Schulberg from Paramount was agitated at lunch, talking about marriage again. "There was another movie theater boycott in Ohio this week. We need a Hollywood wedding. A big one. *Someone* must *want* to get married," Schulberg said, balling up his napkin.

"It used to be that stars were more popular if they were single," Pandro Berman, Selznick's number two producer at RKO said.

"Yes," Schulberg agreed, pleased to have the support. "Now, there are campaigns in the Midwest to ban pictures because of the stories they hear. Sex and drugs and god knows what. What we need is a wholesome news story, a Midwest friendly news story, but look at you all," he said, gesturing to the guests gathered around the table. Kate, Laura, George, Tallulah, Cary, Randolph, "No weddings anywhere."

"*We're* married," David Selznick said, standing to refill Irene's glass.

"Marriage would get horribly in the way of sex, don't you think?" Tallulah said and everyone laughed, except Schulberg. They all know that marriage and sex are two different arrangements.

The party ended early. Everyone was surprised the Selznicks were hosting a party so soon after the baby.

"Why does it bother the studios so much?" Cary asks.

"Because it bothers the ticket-buying public so much," Randolph answers. "Church groups are taking out advertisements to tell us how immoral we are."

"The studios are not helping themselves," Frank says without taking his eyes off the road. "Look at *Divorcement*. Sexy script with an unmarried star, unmarried director. It's a risk for RKO. Same thing happening at Paramount. Schulberg is sure the country is starting to notice."

"Notice that George Cukor is unmarried?"

"Notice that unmarried people are making racy pictures about unmarried people."

"The country is worrying about how to *eat*," Cary says. Unlike Randolph and Frank, Cary knows what it is to be poor.

"Being hungry never stopped anyone from having opinions," Frank says. Frank has put in an offer on a small but elegant house down the road from George Cukor on Cordell Drive. He worries the purchase may be a mistake. Scandal can tank property prices.

. . .

An article appears in the *Los Angeles Times*. Laura is called Kate's "companion" and the studio is furious. Cary Grant and Randolph Scott read the article at their beach house that Friday morning. Randolph reads it first while Cary is on the telephone buying shares of First Atlantic Telecom. Without comment, he hands his lover the newspaper. They debate calling Kate in support but decide not to. They have met her at parties and with Irene but this article is too close to the electric nerve. They do not call. They decide they do not know her well enough.

IRENE

BEVERLY HILLS

Irene reads the article over breakfast and then throws it away. The shower is running upstairs. David will hear all about it when he gets to the lot anyway. Irene would rather have a quiet morning and Jeffrey is sleeping in his basket. She has finally stopped bleeding and almost feels able to sit on the white sofa. She will call Laura when David leaves.

On the telephone, Laura is less friendly than Irene expects. Laura thanks her but does not need "condolences" as she phrases it. Irene is stung. She lives her life terrified of mis-stepping and hates getting it wrong. Laura shows a hardness Irene had not seen before; but then Laura is a woman used to getting her way. Irene will be more careful of Laura in future.

David does hear about it on the lot. And then Irene hears about it after dinner.

"Does this woman want Kate to ditch the protocol? The whole mimeographed backstory, everything the publicity team has cooked up for *Divorcement*?"

Irene wishes he would not talk so loudly. It is ten P.M. and she does not want Jeffrey to wake up until David is asleep. At the lunch party, Irene heard from Tallulah who heard from someone, a someone who might have made it up, that Laura has been complaining about the studio-ordered dates. Whatever the story, Irene can see that Laura wants to arrive at parties and openings on Kate's arm. But, even for Hollywood, it is a half step too far and no one would like it—not the studio, not David, not the town. And not Kate.

KATE

COLDWATER CANYON

Irene is right. Kate doesn't like it. Laura helped her get settled out here, but Kate wishes she'd had the courage to come on her own. Laura is now a liability. Drinking too much, saying too much. Is it intentional? Is Laura a threat? It is never articulated, but Kate can feel a danger in the way Laura complains if Kate talks for too long to any one person, man or woman.

. . .

Kate hates it when they fight. She doesn't mind the shouting, but she hates the lying that comes afterward. The pretense that pads the argument. Laura's flat, small smiles in public after the tears and slammed doors at home. Lying can rust out a love affair. They fight less often now. Because Kate loves Laura less now. It feels like there's less to love. Kate sleeps in her own bed. She prefers it but selfishly, when she misses Laura's warm feet on her legs and her light, wet snore, Kate will go and slip into Laura's bed for an hour or so in the middle of the night. But she will not sleep in Laura's room. It would be giving up ground, something Kate does not like to do.

Leland has told her she must do something about the rumors. She asked him not to speak to Laura; she would do it herself. But then she put it aside for another day and didn't do it. Why make *this* day or *this* day or the next day unpleasant?

LELAND

RKO STUDIOS

When Leland stops by the studio to show Kate the newest copy of *Screen Time*, she is in the makeup chair brushing her teeth. He opens the page to an early press article on the cast of *Divorcement*.

"'Katharine Hepburn and her *companion* Laura Harding,'" he reads out to her.

"What's wrong with it?" Kate asks, after spitting out the baking soda foam. The studio want her teeth whiter and Nancy brings Kate a toothbrush and a baking powder solution after every cup of coffee.

"Kate, they are calling Laura your *lover*. And this is a *national* paper." Leland sits down heavily in the chair beside her.

"It's just a fan magazine," Kate says, her voice muffled as she wipes her mouth with a towel.

"Exactly! A fan magazine! And now the fans will think you have a lover. A woman lover."

"Can't we just tell them I'm married?"

"My god. That's worse. Kate, you cannot be married and you *cannot* have Laura as your lover. If you're married, then where *is* he? You're out here alone and so have deserted your husband and are sleeping with Laura? That would end it all."

"You want Luddy to come out here?"

"I want Luddy to not exist. He is not famous and not in this business. He is *no one*. And you left him behind and are living with a woman? No."

"Everyone we know is married *and* has a lover, or has a husband and a boyfriend *and* a lover, or a husband *and* a girlfriend *and* a lover. This town doesn't care who gets in my bed." Kate flicks the copy of *Screen Time* back toward Leland.

"*This* town does not care but *those* towns out there, the ones with Mr. and Mrs. Picture Goer, *they* care."

As much as she wants Laura to go, she does not like to feel pushed and she does not like change. "George, Jimmy, Tallulah, Cary? This is the *one* place where no one cares. I won't tell her to go. If they want me, they will accept her. And they do *want* me."

"Not yet they don't. Kate, you are not anybody until the picture opens. The studio can just tear you down, toss you away and create someone else." Leland tells himself his motives are good, he is doing this for Kate's good.

"But in this town . . ."

"This town is changing Kate," he interrupts. It is unlike him to be rude but he has to make her see. "The Production Code is becoming serious. You can't get away with this sort of thing anymore." And under his breath, "The country is in a bad mood and is starting to notice that we live differently."

"Why should they give a damn about how we live," Kate says. It is not a question. "What does it matter to them anyhow? They don't know me?"

"They buy the tickets, Kate," Leland repeats. "And if all this goes the way you hope, they *will* think they know you. That is the point. Whichever you they can find."

KATE

COLDWATER CANYON

Kate reads the article when Leland goes. It is not the innuendo that bothers her but the food. Laura has talked to the press about "Katharine Hepburn's favorite foods." It is the implication that Laura knows *all* about Kate Hepburn that she can't stand.

No one is the expert on Kate but Kate. Laura is here for fun. Her life does not depend upon this. Kate's does.

LAURA

COLDWATER CANYON

Leland comes over to the house to talk to Laura while Kate is shooting. Laura sends Joanna and Ragnhild to the market. The driver, Louis, understands that Miss Harding would like to be alone with her guest and goes out to the driveway to polish the car. Leland sits on the low white sofa. Outside, Louis can hear their voices rising. He knew this trouble was coming.

Inside, Leland is getting exasperated. "It is just for a few months Laura!" Leland lowers his voice, reins in his anger. He is a man of restraint. "We've asked you to be discreet and you won't. In the paper. 'Companion.' *Again*."

"A *local* paper," Laura says.

"You are missing the point! Bigger papers will pick it up."

"*You* are missing the point!" Laura shouts. She and Leland know each other well enough now to shed politeness.

"It would be one thing if it stayed *in town*, but it is getting out, and if Kate becomes a star, they will use it."

Laura floods with anger. He has to understand. She cannot lose this chance to have a real life. "We are doing this *on purpose*, Leland. We are doing something important, Kate and I. Don't you see that? And it is more important than being a *film star*!"

"There it is," Leland says. "That disdain. I knew it was there. It must be exhausting, all that pretending."

LELAND
COLDWATER CANYON

Finally. She has said it out loud. That the whole industry of this town doesn't matter.

"You can *do something*, Laura," Leland says quietly. "You just can't do it *and* keep Kate. Kate *wants* to be a film star. It is maybe the only thing she truly wants. Everything else is a game."

Laura sits, boneless; she is unused to blunt honesty. Money usually shields people like her from hearing what they do not want to hear. But, he has said it, sober and in daylight. She can pretend to be outraged but it must be something she already knows.

"I want . . . I . . ." Laura does not finish.

"You want *her*," Leland says. "All of her." He has made his point, said the things that cannot be unsaid. Now, he can offer kindness, revert to being the Leland he is when he is with her. Leland must spend his life being one step ahead. He is a different somebody with everybody who matters.

"You want to be happy," he says, dropping into an armchair. "But you will *ruin* her, Laura." Leland warms his words with sympathy. It is genuine. He knows what it is to want Kate. "You will ruin her before the film ever opens. And then what? Do you think she will love you?"

CARY
SANTA MONICA
SEPTEMBER 1932

They drive an hour out of town to the Cinemaland Theatre in Arcadia. The picture is seventy-two minutes long including credits and they watch it twice. Randolph goes back out to the box office to buy another pair of tickets. They saw the official premiere at the Alhambra a week ago but were sitting four rows apart surrounded by studio people. They tell each other they want to see it again in a real theater with a real audience. Really, they want to be alone in the dark to see themselves together on the screen. The theater is largely empty. They can hold hands.

Hot Saturday is a mediocre script adapted from a mediocre novel but it was a leading man contract for Cary. And he is starring with Randolph. Cary is distracted by the cut of his suit. The jacket bags. White suits must be cut even better than gray suits. He told the director the costume department needed a better tailor.

It is dark when he and Randolph leave the theater through the velvet doors. Cary, cheek to cheek with Nancy Carroll, is not smiling in the enormous poster which is framed in the Cinemaland lobby. The director wanted him chiseled and serious and Cary thinks he looks uncomfortable. But Randolph is right. That doesn't matter. Stacked alongside the image are their names: Cary Grant, Nancy Carroll, Randolph Scott. They both wish they were listed in alphabetical order.

LAURA

COLDWATER CANYON

Nine P.M. And Kate has not called. Leland must have driven straight back to the studio when he left the house. Kate will have heard it all by now. Laura should pack and just go. In New York she can have more life than these small humiliating days strung together. She can be more, wield more, but going means she will lose Kate entirely. Kate is not one to be alone. She lets the thought come into focus. She had told Leland, "*We* are doing something important," but is Kate part of that pronoun? No. Kate is doing something else.

One A.M. Laura hears the front door open, hears the heavy sweep of it shutting, hears the creaky board in the hallway, hears the shower running. Down the hall, Kate switches off the bathroom light and Laura hears the click of Kate's bedroom door closing behind her. They are starting to end. Laura had thought maybe Kate did not see it, did not mean it; maybe she was not paying attention. Now, Laura is sure. All this week, Kate has been either distracted or absent. Three nights in a row Kate has forgotten to telephone to let her know that she will not be home for dinner. Laura does not delude herself that the filming must be running late or that Kate needed to stay after shooting to meet with George, but her honesty does not go beyond that. She is not ready for the next part.

Laura is practical. If she can hold on until they finish filming this damn movie, things could change, will change. This artificial family of cast and crew will disband and Kate will see that they are not real. She will come back. They will go east where these people have no footing. They will go back to themselves.

GEORGE

RKO STUDIOS

George watches her between takes. The set of her, the carriage. He has heard she comes from aristocratic stock. There are rumors about her family: shipping magnates, captains of industry, senators and Swiss finishing schools. Some of it must be true, he thinks. You do not speak that way if you come from nowhere. George took French classes last year and now sprinkles phrases like *mise en scène* into his conversations.

This picture has the makings of a hit. He is protective of Kate and urges her to speak to Leland *now* about upcoming scripts.

"Don't wait until *Divorcement* comes out," he says when she comes to sit beside him on a lighting crate. The lead photographer is changing lenses.

But she doesn't understand. She has learned so much so fast but no one really understands fame until it happens.

KATE
RKO STUDIOS

She is no longer treated as a newcomer; they no longer speak quietly and explain things slowly. But they do talk about her. Kate can hear them: the director, the cameraman, George and Leland Hayward. The lighting, the angles, the shadows. Kate loves the moment they switch on the lights. Great silver cups of bright spill over her shoulders and run down her arms, pulling blood to the skin, making her alive. It washes her clean, just like a good shower. They all agree, the camera loves her. If the camera is in the right mood and senses a competent hand at the helm, her face will oblige and become something indelible, memorable. Kate is not afraid to be photographed. Luddy took excellent photographs of her—ripe, clear nudes. She has forgotten where she put them.

"Do you want her sitting? Too stiff?" the lead photographer asks George.

"She has to stand," David Selznick calls out. He spends whole days on set now, irritating George and dictating memos to Marcella Rabwin. He told George Kate's broomstick posture is not sexy when she sits, but grudgingly now he can see that when she stands, one foot forward, hips angled just so, she may not be beautiful but Irene is right and she makes a breathtaking photograph.

"Here," George says. "Twist your leg out, tilt the hip, there."

Kate can always trust George. He is family now.

Kate stands and a prop man comes and repositions the chair on its mark.

The sound and lighting men huddle and point in a way they would never do at a melted center starlet. Kate is in her huntress stance, rail slim and strong. She enjoys these photography sessions now. Flanking her are John Barrymore, older than his pinup heyday, his skin paunchy and lived in but the wardrobe girls still suck in their stomachs when he walks by, and on the other side, David Manners, diluted and thin. The marrow of the scene flows to Kate. Her Connecticut Hepburn diction rings out like a church bell.

But she is changeable. Without warning she shifts, softens, unzips her teeth. She has learned to do this now. The tension in the room flexes and falls slack. Sound men who have been holding their breath without knowing it exhale and stretch out the knotty kinks in their necks.

The camera is an instrument of translation, attuned to her like a lover. They have come to an agreement, the camera and Kate. When she lets her shoulders slide down her back and drops her weight into one hip, she can feel her body shed its protective boyishness. Nothing overt but suddenly there is rise and dip. Kate becomes flirtatious. It is tinny and shrill but effective. It is a deliberate lessening and it makes all the men in the room feel more sure footed. They never sense the trick. The hunter wolf in the hunted sheepskin. The men do not understand how it happens. But watch, already she does.

LELAND

RKO STUDIOS

"George insists you have to talk to David Selznick about scripts *now*," Kate says, her voice muffled by a towel. Even if she is going straight home, Kate refuses to leave the lot in makeup.

"He's right. I will." He was already planning to speak to Selznick and has just been waiting for him to catch the building excitement around Kate.

"When?" she asks, folding and hanging the towel up on the rack.

"Soon." Leland likes that Kate never leaves a mess in her dressing room for someone else to clean up.

CARY

SANTA MONICA

"He won't be there tomorrow. Why would a head wardrobe designer go to a screen test?" Cary says.

"To get a look at my ex-lover's new lover? I would."

"Does it make a difference?" Cary asks, dropping his legs into the water. The sun is high over the pool and he shades his eyes to look at Randolph.

"That you loved him or that he has moved here?" Randolph asks. He is dry and sitting under the striped umbrella. He does not want to be sunburned for his test at Warner Bros. tomorrow.

"That I didn't tell you about him before."

"I trust you. When things are important, you'll tell me."

KATE
RKO STUDIOS

She hungers for the moments when George is pleased and Barrymore stays on to watch after his scenes are finished. She can feel them all pulling for her and it makes her feel strong. When the working day ends and she leaves the lot, she is impatient to start the next day so she can go back. She is not thinking about life at home because it's not the life she is really leading. Kate can only lead one life at a time.

Please make me stand out. Make them like me, love me, going round her head like a toy train while she waits for them to set up the shot. It is more important than who she loves or who she refuses to love. All that is secondary. She knows that only the apex predator is safe in this town. Everyone else is in the food chain.

LOS ANGELES
SEPTEMBER 1932

We knew it was coming. The verbs of falling in so often lead to the verbs of falling out, especially here. Out there, splitting up, divorce even, is a black mark against you, but not here. Here, everyone understands recasting. Laura is tougher than we knew. That grifter, robber baron blood is still in there. We are impressed. We do not usually misjudge and almost never underestimate. It is too soon to tell but we can see that Laura is willing to hold on, to sink into Kate until her fingernails bleed. And she is unafraid of looking foolish. She doesn't need anything from this town. That makes her dangerous.

She still brings Kate coffee every morning after her cold shower but even this habit will chafe soon. Chains chain you even sweetened with milk and sugar. Hayward was right, she should have left with grace. Grit we have seen before, but grace is rarer on this coast.

When Kate is on the lot, she is thinking about trying to do well, act well in the next scene and the next. Cukor's approval, Barrymore's, Leland's, Selznick's, Irene's, she is driving herself hard. She had decided to become *someone*.

IRENE
BEVERLY HILLS

Fifteen months. When he goes over to her father at MGM, and Irene already knows he will, that is how long David will have been at RKO. Right now, he has the job he has always wanted. His own studio. Irene is sure RKO has no idea that David will not renew his contract in November. RKO is thrumming with new blood, handpicked by David. Why leave? David has just contracted this new man, Fred Astaire, a dancer. David says he is a bit short, a bit bald and his trousers are hemmed so high they are belted at his rib cage. His ankles hang out of the cuffs, but all that vanishes when he begins to dance. Will he be able to take a risk on someone like that at MGM? No. Irene already knows the answer. Why do it? Why trade a job he loves for one he will hate?

Money. That's why.

There is already tension in the house. It's worse since the baby. David is gambling, staying out. He is losing, coming home angry or fervent but never happy. He is losing money just when they need to be extra careful. In the morning, he is himself again, and Irene has to listen to his contrition. He feels terrible, weeps and promises it will never happen again but he does not change. Irene knows this cycle. Yes, she's constantly worrying about how to pay the grocer and the tailor in the same month but she is accustomed to the juggling now. It is just life with David and will happen whatever job he has.

Her problem is different. David does not touch Jeffrey. He does not like the baby.

"We'll have lots to talk about when he's older," David tells Irene.

RANDOLPH

WARNER BROS. STUDIO

Of course, he isn't there. Randolph should have spent the time rehearsing his lines for the test rather than rehearsing what he would say if he met the designer. He flubs the test. It's fine. This is the one studio where he does not want to work.

LELAND

HOLLYWOOD

A release date has been set and Leland and the publicity team are busy clamping down the lids on Kate's secrets: Luddy, the secret husband, Laura, the secret live-in lover, and the bohemian Hepburns, her radical, free-thinking, sexual disease-obsessed, birth control-advocating parents.

Leland shares an office with his business partner, Myron Selznick, David's brother, the one who doesn't gamble. Leland does most of his business at Chasen's anyway.

This morning, he is in his office where a conversation is happening. There are three of them. Leland, Myron and the head publicist from RKO Studios.

"Dollars to donuts the papers won't find out," the publicist says.

It irritates Leland when people say things they don't mean.

"Christ," Leland says. "Venereal disease and abortion. Kate could not have worse parents."

"She could," Myron says. "She could have parents who talk to the press."

LAURA

RKO STUDIOS

Laura is watching Kate film and thinking what it would be like to burn it all to the ground. If she is not ever going to be Kate's equal, why not break it? Laura is getting to know people in this town. No one gets to Kate without getting past her, but Leland is right; for Laura, these are not people who count.

Sometimes, when she is at a party or the hairdresser, she wants to say something shocking, something private and declarative about Kate. She could. Has Leland thought of that?

LOS ANGELES

SEPTEMBER 1932

George Cukor, David Selznick, the studio, they have all bet on Kate. They are sure they can manage it. They discuss the problem away from Kate. Irene tells George Cukor not to worry, that Leland and the studio will disappear the husband, water the lover down to friendship, and pull a new Kate Hepburn out of a hat, a fresh virgin ingénue, the way they always do. Irene speaks with compassion. She understands what it is to disappear.

The movie machinery hums. The publicists are hard at work building a fake history. They have been hinting in the press that

Kate is the daughter of a wealthy industrialist, one of the Manhattan Hepburns, who don't exist. Kate's great uncle *was* a wealthy industrialist. He was a Houghton, the one who owned Corning Glass. But he killed himself, as Houghtons do. Suicide is the democratic siren song crouching in their bloodlines. Leland and Laura keep that secret too. Suicide does not sell tickets.

HOWARD

HANCOCK PARK

Howard has seen her at the Ambassador Hotel and once at the Garden of Allah, where the night clerk, the one who brought him his coat last week, will be murdered in less than a decade. He sees her red hair and sometimes he can hear her. Her angular voice cuts across the soundless air of his bad side, reaching his good ear better than most. He hopes her producers don't try to break the spine of that voice and make it sound like everyone else. He watches her on the night of the RKO party at the Cocoanut Grove. She wears a silver dress. She kicks off her shoes and drops her legs into the fountain. She has already decided to become a person in this town who can do things like that. He likes that about her.

Howard's divorce from Ella has been finalized. The divorce negotiations were longer than the marriage. Ella drove hard terms, but Howard can respect that. He doesn't care about the money but she has stipulated that he is not allowed to direct another film for ten years. She wants her alimony and does not want to risk him losing all the money again the way he did on *Hell's Angels*. Fine, Howard will find other things to do. He is more interested in flying these days anyway.

Billie left with nothing but grace, and Howard finds that harder to forget.

KATE
RKO STUDIOS

Leland is on the lot, waiting for her. George walks her to her dressing room. He has no formal notes anymore. They do it differently now. Together. Would it be better if she said it this way? Or this way? Stand here, or here? Try everything! George changed tack after the night they filmed the break-up scene. Kate is free to try anything as long as she does not change the script. George has a granite respect for writers and won't change a line without dragging the writer across town to approve it while the whole set waits. It's expensive and drives Selznick mad. But, whatever they are doing is working. Barrymore offers Kate advice, tips to charm the camera. Cheat your hips this way, lift your chin, close your lips when you have no lines. She is a game kid and he likes her. He wants her to be good at this.

And now, she *is* good. The crew has seen this before. Either an actor arrives knowing how to do this, knowing it without worrying about how, or they have to learn. Learning is harder. The crew have seen a new actor or actress fumble and shrink, unable to drive the scene. Everyone waits to see if they will find the nerve to be someone they have never been and storm the camera, find a character where they can be bold and potent. Often they don't find it and the editors cut around the weakness, clipping lines into a new cadence to create what was never there. The crew watch Kate follow the path only a few others have found before her. She does not bend herself into a new shape, the camera bends to her. They watch her decide to become herself.

Now Kate throws blue fire in each take. They just filmed what George describes as "her" scene. Kate is not sure why this scene is so important. It is a moment where she does nothing but walk across a room swinging her arms and then flop down in front of the fireplace. "Do it the way you would do it at home," George says. George has been over to the house at Coldwater Canyon. He telephoned the writer last week and asked him to add in this scene. There are no words, only stage directions. He wants a shot of Kate being Kate.

Everyone on the soundstage sensed that something important was happening. Actors came out of their dressing rooms and the prop men stopped to watch; even the wardrobe lady took the pins out of her mouth.

At the back, the soundstage doors opened and banged shut. The outside warning light was on. Normally that kind of disruption would irritate Kate, but she was concentrating too hard to notice. Nine takes. And George never called cut. He just let the scene loop round and round while the expensive film ran. Selznick watched from his chair near the camera and did not object. He could also see that something important was happening.

Her dressing room is crowded. When she gets it right, everyone shoves in.

"You were wonderful darling," Leland says, kissing her cheek. George's eyebrow lifts. Last month, when she could not get it right, Kate was not Leland Hayward's darling.

"Did you want something?" Kate asks, reaching around to unzip her dress. Elsie, Kate's on-set dresser, hurries in to take over. Miss Hepburn tears her costumes when she tries to get them off herself.

"Just wanted to tell you that you're wonderful," Leland says.

"You said that already," Kate says. She knows that Leland only came in as they were finishing up and did not see much. "What else?"

"Isn't that enough?" Leland asks.

George sits down. This is not what Leland is here to tell her. Kate waits.

Leland has his audience. "*Divorcement* will preview in Santa Barbara in October," he says.

"Santa Barbara!" George whoops. Only a film predicted to be a smash will preview in Santa Barbara. It is too close to Hollywood to screen a flop.

"When?" Kate asks, breathless. "When did they decide this?"

"Just now. Selznick was considering Fresno but then he saw that scene. He called me at Chasen's and told me to run over here after the first take."

"That scene," George says, "is where the world will meet Kate Hepburn."

"I am taking you out to celebrate," Leland says in Kate's ear.

George stands at the heavy soundstage doors and watches them walk off the lot. Nothing else to do; they did not invite him to go.

LELAND

RKO STUDIOS

Leland is ready for the day to be over and it is only three o'clock. He had been to a meeting with the head of MGM that morning and after talking about golf, the weather, and four loan-outs, Louis B. Mayer asked him, straight, "Is Kate Hepburn . . ." and he left the sentence swinging in midair. Is Kate Hepburn what? Tall? Direct? Married? Living with a woman? Ambitious? What? Leland did not rush to fill the blank, and the two men sat in the awkwardness of a room where everyone knows what everyone knows but no one will say it aloud. Mr. Mayer is a family man and does his best not to know about any "irregularities," his wife's term. It does not help that George Cukor and his bohemian circle of friends call themselves the Irregulars.

Louis B. Mayer broke the silence. "I have heard wonderful things about Kate from my daughter, Irene."

"Yes, they are terrific friends. Irene had the whole cast of *Divorcement* over for a dinner party the week after filming began. So kind." Leland left the sentence there, waiting to see what Louis B. would say.

"Yes, David and Irene love to entertain. I was going to ask Irving to have a word with my son-in-law about a loan-out but—" He stopped when he reached the delicate terrain. Leland waited for him to finish. Louis B. was building up a head of steam. "But then I saw that article. I may not know *all* that young Hollywood is up to but I am not an idiot. And neither are the people out there who buy the tickets. She wears trousers and lives with a woman, for god's sake."

"Kate's family are East Coast. Moneyed, protective. Her family would rather she did not live alone and so Laura is here. Did you know she is the American Express heiress?"

"And Kate's husband?" Louis B. refused to be distracted.

"The husband is regrettable. They were young. She's going to go to Mexico. Quickie divorce."

"When?"

"Soon, tickets are bought. They will sail from New York and then fly from Havana," Leland said. He is not sure Mayer believed him. He will ask Irene to have a word with her father. To back him up. And he will have to tell his office to buy some air tickets to Mexico.

IRENE
BEVERLY HILLS

How long is it meant to hurt like this? She still feels split open, as if too much air is getting in. And the dampness. Not quite blood, just pinkish and thick. It is hot in town but Irene wears heavy woolen skirts. More fabric between her and the world. Bending down to get Jeffrey makes it worse; she needs to run to the powder room and check to make sure she's not leaking. If David were a different husband, he would spare her the trouble. If David were a different husband, he would reach down into the Moses basket and pick up his son.

CARY
SANTA MONICA

Four years and three months before Cary finishes his contract with Paramount. A war picture and *two* Mae West films all in the next year. Ben Schulberg gave him the scripts this morning. Cary said he wanted a leading man role in a comedy or at least a serious role playing a serious person in a drama. Instead, he will be a punching bag and a wartime sidekick. No wit. No gravitas. And all in ill-fitting clothes. He is going to insist on bringing in his own tailor. The head of wardrobe won't like it and Mae West won't like it but he will pay for it himself. Cary knows exactly how he should look and what suits his frame. Of course he does. Orry taught him.

KATE

COLDWATER CANYON

Now it has really started: press leaks, rumors.

Last week, at an opening party Laura got drunk, messy drunk. She was feeling ignored and tried to kiss Kate in front of a reporter, a young and hungry reporter. The journalist walked away but Selznick had heard about it by morning. RKO paid the man off but the story got out. It did not change things exactly, but it has made people look harder.

Kate does not want to be romantically linked to anyone, not in public. She wants to be known for herself and not for who shares her bed. Even Luddy. She bristles when he refers to her as his wife. It is not that she's against marriage. Kate knows a wife can be strong. A wife can hold the electrical charge in a pair. Look at Irene. Irene is cored with slender rods of iron. Look at Kate's own mother, a suffragette who is scheduled to appear before Congress to speak about birth control. But Laura is not that sort of person. She is known for what she did not earn.

Kate is proud of Luddy for *not* coming to California. Luddy. His pliable generosity gives him strength, and an elastic power. How can Kate walk away from a man who gives so much and asks so little?

LOS ANGELES

SEPTEMBER 1932

And what is she doing during this time? This woman people are talking about? This unborn star? She is trying to get ahead, to be better than all the other nascent stars. She has realized that saying no makes her different.

"No, I will not sit for the photograph."

"No, I will not wear a dress."

"No, I will not be like all the others just off the bus."

But the "no" does not get her very far. She doesn't have any power yet. She has not been part of something that has done something. And so, Kate has to do it. Whatever it is—wear a dress to this opening, smile for this photograph as if she has a secret. Even when she is yelling and saying she won't. That part is theater. And she knows when she's doing it, whatever it is, the photograph, the dress, the opening, it is not for the studio or Selznick or Leland. It is for all the people out there, the ones who have never heard of her. Kate looks at people on the street, the man crossing the road by the studio gate, the woman with a yellow Labrador, the delivery boy from the greengrocer, bringing fruit to the commissary. People she will never see again. She wants them to know her, to go home and tell their friends, their husbands, their children, "I saw her. I saw Kate Hepburn today."

KATE

COLDWATER CANYON

Kate is good at detaching. The more distance she gains, the more she dislikes herself for ever needing Laura, for needing anyone. *Was* she clinging? Did anyone notice? She feels self-contempt.

The more distance she gains, the more she also dislikes Laura. Her calm, her acceptance. Kate makes herself believe this sea change is Laura's fault. "Fight for something if you really want it, dammit." But Laura does not fight; she does not realize she needs to. It is unwinnable anyway. Kate knows that. If Laura fights, Kate will despise her for hanging on; if she accepts the reality, Kate will hate her complacency. It is not Laura who is fighting, pushing, changing. It is Kate. Needing someone is dangerous, someone who can always leave.

LAURA

HOLLYWOOD HILLS

Leland does it on a Wednesday, in George Cukor's terraced garden. She hates that he does it in public. George is up in the house, organizing chicken salad sandwiches and she and Leland are sitting on the patio in the shade. Both of them are watching the swimmer. Kate is doing laps, striping the pool with a slim ruffled wake. They always watch Kate.

"Give me six months, Laura. Just until we get Kate up and running," Leland says.

Kate cannot hear him. Rhythmic and even, her triangle of white arm breaks the water's surface and her head swings up for air. Kate never looks more at ease than when she is in water. Laura waits a long time before speaking. They have time; Kate's not called to set until three.

"Up and running? You make her sound like an airplane or an automobile," Laura says, leaning back on a striped canvas chair, trying to hold her composure. "Something mechanical with an engine."

Still watching Kate slice through the water, Leland answers, "What makes you think she isn't?"

Leland sells it hard. He makes leaving town sound chivalrous, loving. He uses clumsy metaphors designed to shame.

"Help me raise her up. She needs you."

The image is ridiculous, and Laura thinks less of Leland for using it. Kate needs no one to raise her up, doesn't Leland know his client?

"She needs me to be here, with her." Laura knows she makes Kate a better actress and she is not afraid of Leland. Any Fifth Avenue supper party and Leland would be a nobody.

"What Kate doesn't need are rumors," Leland says. "And the rumors are all about you." Leland's ace.

"And the publicity department?" she says. "If they're worried, why don't they do something?"

"Laura, this *is* them doing something. That's why I'm here."

They both know the truth will get out. Rumors are airborne and lethal. Someone will tell someone who will tell someone who matters. And then they will pull Kate down, especially if Kate is a success.

"Do you want to bring her down with something *you* have said?"

Not *because of you*. She could have lived with that. But because of what she has said.

Laura is quiet, feeling real fear for the first time since Leland began speaking.

Leland presses his advantage. "As much as they love to birth a star, they love to smash one more. And now Kate is vulnerable. *You* have made her vulnerable." Leland decides to finish the kill. "She needs you to get the hell out of town and stop saying things you know goddamn well you shouldn't."

He has said it out loud. In New York, no one would be so tactless. Beaten, Laura nods. This is the argument that matters.

Leland leans forward and yells. "Kate! She said yes!"

Kate pulls up, punching out of the water. Laura is rattled; they've talked about this? Has Kate been waiting?

"Yes, to what?" Kate asks, swimming to the side, shaking the water from her face.

Damn you; you know very well what. Laura is surprised by her own vehemence. Her anger has never been directed at Kate before and it makes Laura feel powerful. Kate shakes her head like that when she gets out of a cold shower too. The way a dog shakes.

"Yes to going back to New York," Leland says.

Kate is breezy and unfazed. "Oh, that. Good." Laura recognizes this Kate. Now that the hard part is over, she is light, free, and prepared to be generous. "Maybe you could come to Europe next month with Luddy and me?" Kate pulls off her bathing cap and turns to Leland. "That would be all right, wouldn't it?"

"Kate. For god 's sake," Leland says, but he's not angry.

That is the wonder of this woman. Laura watches Leland watch Kate. Perverse, obtuse, relentless and often selfish, but singular. In all this town, there is only one of her.

KATE

COLDWATER CANYON

Laura books onto the *Super Chief* and is gone the next day. Kate is impressed by her speed, but it is too late. Laura should have left earlier. Kate would have missed her. Kate is sure she would like Laura more if there was more chase, more threat and danger, more that was *mean* in their relationship. She is wrong, but she doesn't know that now. Kate does not realize it's possible to value something that values you back.

The house is different without Laura, and Kate is not sure how to be there in the daytime. She tells herself it's because she's not working as much now that most of her scenes are shot, but that's not it. It is because her days were entirely managed by Laura. Without noticing, Kate stopped making all the small decisions in her life. She can hear Joanna and Ragnhild downstairs now. They sound easy, comfortable, as though they are used to having the kitchen to themselves. She runs a bath. Everything resets with water.

. . .

She has dinner alone with Leland. He drops by, as he always does, but now they are a twosome and the air has changed. He flies them up the coast and they watch the sun sink from the air. They can't hear each other over the engine but Kate prefers it that way.

LOS ANGELES
SEPTEMBER 1932

Three days overschedule. Selznick does not want to move the release date back. Pay the crew time and a half; keep the actors awake. Finish. Selznick, who is never on time for dinner, hates to bring a picture in late. Cukor, who is never late for dinner, hates to rush the actors. Barrymore is due to start photography on his new picture on Monday. Selznick is on set every day now, wild with Benzedrine, the man never sleeps. The crew know he would rather be here than home. He can also be found at The Beverly Hills Hotel, that pink pastry of a heartbreaker. Cheaters always book in there.

CARY

SANTA MONICA

The new bed fits. Cary and Randolph have been worrying about it. Frank Horn has already spoken to the best architect in Santa Monica in case they needed to move the wall. It's important. Cary's new custom bed is more than a bed. With built-in shelving, lights, a portable desk and telephone table, it is also a home office. When the reporter from *Modern Screen* came with a photographer, Cary showed them the bed but did not allow them to photograph it. Instead, the photographer shot Cary and Randolph in a series of happy domestic poses: reading in the living room, dipping in the pool, running on the beach, lifting weights on the sand, drying the dishes. Young and lean with pinup looks, the two men gleam with health. Frank Horn objected when the reporter suggested that Cary put on an apron in the kitchen shots but no one listened to him. All their lives, they will treasure these photographs, despite the rumors they ignite.

. . .

"Girls, Cary. There were supposed to be *girls*." Ben Schulberg's copy of the article is crumpled and coffee stained.

"There weren't any girls at the house that day, Ben," Cary says easily. "If you wanted girls, you should have sent some."

"All right. Next time, I'll send girls." Schulberg writes it down on his list.

"He'll do it, you know," Cary says, dropping his legs into the pool and tipping his face up to the sun. "Schulberg is a bulldog when he gets an idea. He'll send them, great herds of them."

"So, he'll send them," Randolph says, swimming to the side.

"We will be cordial, take them to dinner, make sure we get photographed, and then we'll come home. Together."

Randolph reaches up and Cary slides into the cold pool. Randolph's fingertips are ridged and pale from the water. Cary's skin is still sun hot. Their bodies jigsaw together, sharing the warmth.

They don't speak any more about Schulberg and his lists. These lovers have that rare ability to hold rich silence, gently, dearly, between them. They understand how lucky they are. A phone rings inside the house. Both men wait, listen.

"Yours," Cary says.

Randolph pulls away and swings himself out of the pool in one quick movement. Cary, left in the water, watches him, halved and listening. The two men have separate telephone lines. As they both spend the mornings speaking with their business managers, buying and selling shares, it makes things easier. Their answering service does not realize the wires lead to the same address.

KATE

RKO STUDIOS

It ends abruptly. Out of sequence. Before lunch on a Friday. George Cukor gives a small speech while the prop men pull down the set and load it onto trucks. It will be stored under *Interior/Staircase* in Shed 8. The shot list is complete; the canisters are snapped shut. The lights switch off and the cables are rolled up into great hoops of black rubber. The routine is broken, the actors shake off the characters, and the crystal hard bubble splits open. They will not see each other tomorrow. It turns out they are not a family but separate people who will go back to separate lives. Kate can already feel the difference in the group. The currency is lost and the familiarity is an effort now. It was based on something that is no longer there. The bonds are stale. She knows this exact combination of people will not come together again. Even when they hug each other hard and promise they will.

. . .

Two o'clock on a Tuesday afternoon and Kate has nowhere to be. She is homesick for the set. She has already been swimming and played three sets of tennis. Under a jacaranda tree at the club, Kate sits on a broad, green and white striped sun lounger. Leland is late. Kate orders lemonade. She has been forgetting to wear a hat and tawny freckles stretch across the bridge of her nose. She has been playing often. Harvey, the tennis pro, makes time for her whenever she appears. He has a waiting list but she no longer has to make an appointment. People do things like that for Kate. She is not lonely, not exactly, but restless. She wants the next thing to happen now. The thing just out of reach is always better, isn't it? Must be.

LOS ANGELES

SEPTEMBER 1932

They run out of time and never quite develop a persona for her but the exposure is coming anyway. Articles have run in the trades, a spread is planned in *Photoplay* and there are already billboards in New York, Connecticut and San Francisco. Soon she will be on the sides of New York buses and her college friends will stop and point. Her early East Coast actor friends will swear they are still in touch with her and drop her name in conversation.

Her face is a familiar one here: at the club, at the parties, in this town, in this America. She dines at El Coyote, at Perino's, at the Brown Derby and is part of the envied set who spend Sundays at Cukor's house on Cordell Drive in the Hollywood Hills. It feels like their clubhouse. She has stopped wearing a bathing suit when she swims in his pool. Later, when she cultivates outsider-hood, she will deny this time ever happened, the time of belonging to a group, a town, this time of kinship here. But it did happen. At all the best parties, just outside the photo's frame, there she is.

. . .

The studios are worried. The producers have talked to the agents and now the agents are worried. The parties, the drinking, the sex: men and men, women and men, women and men and then women. And if it gets out? The press are young tigers, jumping through flaming hoops, tame, as long as they are fed. But when they don't like their dinner? They will roar and they will bite. Secrets are a rotten business. The studios clean house. Unmade stars and the ones on one-year contracts, if they have messy lives, they're out. Older stars, the ones who used to be worth the trouble in the silent days but have not made the jump to talking pictures are also out. Studios will be careful who they sign from now on.

Only the three men in the upstairs RKO publicity office know that Kate has a husband in New York and a lover who just vacated the house on Coldwater Canyon. The boldest of the three has made inquiries; there are four towns in Mexico where Miss Hepburn can get a divorce in twenty-four hours. And then the marriage can disappear. Mrs. Ludlow Ogden Smith? Never happened.

KATE

HOLLYWOOD HILLS

Bathed, fresh, trousered, she walks the pale sidewalk under the big ball of California sun. No one walks in Hollywood, but she does. Or bicycles. She prefers it to driving. She has been walking three miles a day since they finished last week. Not *finished,* she thinks, *wrapped.* Some Hollywood words are still coppery and new in her mouth. Others slide out on rails: assistant director (AD), trailer, lot, commissary, grip, wardrobe, contract, loan-out, soundstage, shot. After the filming come a gift and a party. Hollywood rituals.

She swings her arms. Her muscles stretch, elastic. There are moments when she feels part of this sun-bleached city. There is a tightness in the air around her. It is about to happen, about to break, the summer storm that will split open the ash white sky.

They have picked her next three films. Everyone agrees. Strong women, that will be her thing.

. . .

There is a party tonight. Kate arrives at six. George has invited her for six so she arrives at six. Best to be the first to arrive and the first to leave.

The music spills from the open windows and slips down the curved driveway. The taxi pulls up in front of the lit-up house on Cordell Drive but the taxi driver is not interested in these shiny people. He doesn't go to the pictures. Fancy people with problems that resolve by the credits. The taxi driver has a family to take care of. He knows there are sixty, a hundred, two hundred waiting men who would take his job and do it just as well. The whole country is afraid and these movie people worry about all the wrong things. Careless people, living careless lives. But the skinny woman with the sharp jaw asks his name when she gets into his cab, and it becomes harder to dislike her. His voice cracks from disuse when he answers. You can go ten hours without speaking in this job. The cab stops and he pulls the brake. She remembers, calls him "Mr. Arberry." This woman looks him straight in the eye, thanks him and gives him a good tip. The taxi driver sits straighter in his seat. He will remember her.

Billy Haines is telling audition stories, and Kate is laughing. George is laughing too but more because his guests are. Audition stories make him sad. He is a snob socially but that is an abstraction; really, he hates disappointing people. Even after four years in Hollywood, George wants everyone on the lot to like him. But that doesn't mean he will invite them to his home. The men and women scattered around his oval living room are selected with care. They are smooth, glassy, but you need more than beauty to gain entrance to this house. George enjoys wit, subtlety, beauty, naturally, but above all that, class. Manners matter to him. Anyone who does not send a thank you card is never invited back. He cannot bear dullness or crassness. This is not the South or the East Coast where the right family will launch you into the room no matter how terribly you bore people once you get there. This is the frontier, the wild and glorious West Coast, where you have to earn it.

Kate warms to the room slowly, a slim flame breathing in the oxygen, expanding. Her back is tight, and her stomach is hurting; she is hoping it won't rumble. She should have eaten before she left the house. Leland appears beside her, smelling of aftershave and scotch. Garbo is not here yet. George has told her that when Garbo arrives, she keeps away from the thick of the guests and instead pulls the room to her, spinning it like a cyclone. Garbo still makes Kate feel gauche. It is not her beauty, but the way people talk about her talent, their lack of cynicism, their reverence. Garbo is never a joke. Kate grinds with envy. She wants to hear her own name spoken that way. Kate says this to no one. Leland understands it without her telling him.

Laura once said Garbo's eyebrows are over-plucked and that she heard Garbo eats only yeast and spinach to keep her figure. Laura.

The party feels more and less dangerous without Laura. Kate feels alone but she does not churn with the constant tide of strain she felt when Laura was at the parties. Laura could always say the wrong something to the wrong someone.

As the world out there gets more precarious, the world in here gets cattier. Who will feed whom to the lions first? Do they talk about her? What would they say? Controlling? Headstrong? Argumentative? Fine. All her abrasive faults are true—of course they are. They are deliberate. It is who she decided to be years ago. There is no one in the foxhole with her, and no cavalry is coming; she must always attack. Shoulders back, chin lifted, Kate laughs loudly at Leland's story that is more mean than funny. Kate secretly worries that she is the bore—every party has one. Bores will out eventually, her father says.

George comes to find her. He is attentive, calls her "dear" and seats her to his right, next to the new man, Cary Grant, who came with Tallulah and upset George's numbers. But Cary Grant makes you feel like you are at the best party in town and so he is already welcome everywhere. He is one of those people who can pull an evening tight and make it happen. Plus, he can do backflips. George says last week Tallulah dared him and he flipped clear across the room and then sat down and never mentioned it again.

After a sit-down supper for thirty, (thirty-one, including Cary) in the long dining room, the rest of the guests arrive and the party starts. Kate and George go out to the garden, leaving the crowd behind. Kate is not in the mood for glitter and wants the ease of being alone with a friend. George points out the changes he is making to the house, the roofline, the windows, the shrubs, the pebbled walk and terraced hill. He wants Kate to like it. He is building three cottages on the property, one for her if she ever needs it (he means it and she will take him up on it one day). Their friendship is load bearing, built to last. A door opens and the noise of the party slips out.

"People ask if they can bring people. I say yes and now look." George and Kate are sitting under the walnut tree and the night feels like satin.

"Here they come. Goddamn." Kate can swear in front of George.

A party will always chase the most interesting people, or at least the people who most want to speak alone. Spilling down the shadow lawn, under strings of fairy lights, men in black tie—white tie is saved for premieres—and women in narrow satin dresses. Their host is in the garden so the garden is now fair game. Tallulah comes and sits too close to Kate. Kate stands. She has already refused Tallulah twice. It annoys Kate and embarrasses George. George is discreet and meets men in Griffith Park. Sometimes, George goes with Billy Haines and Anderson Lawler to look for rough young men to love in the dark, but only after the parties. Tallulah does not interest Kate but there are others who do. Men, women, she is prowling for them all. Kate wishes she had arrived in this town earlier. She wishes Laura had gone home sooner. Variety suits her.

Kate kicks off her shoes and digs her toes into the spongy turf. Her feet hurt. She has reached the point where she feels like she has nothing left to say and wants to go home. Someone sits beside her on the stone bench and hands her a drink. It is the new man, Cary Grant. The cocktail is in a heavy tumbler, one of George's good ones from the library. The liquid is dark and sliced with a lemon. No ice, but the glass is cold.

"What is it?"

"A *Sazerac*, from New Orleans, invented by a Creole apothecary. You are meant to drink it in an egg cup but George's whiskey glass is better."

"And what's in it?" Kate usually drinks only champagne at parties, she likes to keep her head clear.

"Rye, bitters, sugar, you can use Herbsaint or even absinthe but I make it with pastis. George thought you might like it."

"George made it?"

"I made one for George and he wanted you to try it and so I made one for you."

"Because?"

"Because he is our host and he asked me to."

Kate and Cary have spoken at lunch parties and dinner parties and premieres but never alone. He is different without a crowd. Kate can see why everyone wants to know him. Easy, charming, urbane and gracious, he makes conversation easy.

"He brought out his good glasses. Rare. Means he likes you," she says.

"George did that for *you*. He clearly adores you."

"Who adores you?" Tallulah asks, sitting down on the other side of Kate.

"Everyone, obviously," Cary answers and then changes the conversation.

Kate likes that Cary does not invite Tallulah into their moment.

The garden is noisy with party guests now. Kate goes back up to the house. A tall man Kate has not met has called her a cab.

"You looked like you were ready to leave," he says. "Are you?" He is direct, unusual in this town where everyone is trying to be liked.

"You were watching?"

"You're the new kid. Everyone is watching."

The man is familiar and not. Tall, he is built like her father. The man does not introduce himself. He assumes she knows who he is. She does. He is the director, John Ford.

LOS ANGELES
SEPTEMBER 1932

The shouting is over and now the three men are talking in Selznick's office. They agree; they have a smash with *Bill of Divorcement*. The early in-house test screenings have been a huge success and they open in Santa Barbara in a few weeks. Kate is the scene-stealer and Hayward has ensured she has a good billing. Hayward says Billie Burke is nearly finished. She has reached some unseen frontier where a woman's career on film ends. But they are wrong. All children will grow up knowing her. Three days of filming in Technicolor Oz, fifty studio dwarves, big pink dress, tall crown, a wand and she will forever be the Good Witch of the North.

Selznick sent the memo to Marcella Rabwin. Kate will get a proper launch: three good parts. Selznick worries these parts are not what the country wants right now. They are women who go too far, are too raw, too unbridled, but George Cukor and Irene understand that Kate is something new. It is in the way she walks, half boy, half girl. If you are very lucky in Hollywood, this is how it happens. George wants to direct. He should. He says he can get the very best out of Kate. He can pull a performance from her no one else can find. He can set her on fire.

These pictures will be bold but not sexy. They all know that these are the last sweet days of this private, sex-soaked Hollywood. All the rumors about the stricter Production Code and morality standards speak of the end of something. The Hays Office has now stipulated that onscreen married couples must only kiss on the cheek. Three of Paramount's scripts have been rejected this month, all for lewdness. Mae West has just arrived in Hollywood after a smash run on Broadway. The Hays Office has decided Miss West is a threat to family decency but she squeaks past them on brassy courage alone.

GEORGE

HOLLYWOOD HILLS

John Ford calls George the day after the party. He wants her telephone number. George hedges. Ford is famously Catholic and married to a woman who is not afraid to make a scene or call the press. She has done it before. It never stops him. Hard-living, hard-drinking, Ford belongs to a different crowd; mostly Irish, charming as hell when the evening starts, drunk and difficult by the time it ends.

"George, I want to *work* with her," Ford says. "Picture about pilots. Adventure, romance. Good part. We start next month."

"I can give you her agent, Leland Hayward's number?" George does not even want to do that but he is no good at saying no to powerful men.

"Why would I want that sop's number? I want to speak to Kate Hepburn. I saw her, up close, spoke to her, at *your* house. She has something. You saw it? I heard you saw it before Selznick did. I see it too and I want it."

George gives him Leland's number.

KATE

COLDWATER CANYON

Kate tells no one her real reason for wanting to be in Europe when *Divorcement* opens. If she were here, she would have to go to the premiere, and she would have to watch the film while others are watching her. She doesn't think about whether or not she likes herself onscreen. She just knows she cannot be exposed that way in front of people. The better she gets, the more private it feels. The dread lies somewhere between superstition and self-doubt and she does not want to investigate where. What if it goes badly? What if no one laughs or cares? No. She will go to Europe as planned and put as much distance as she can between herself and the people who will pay to watch her pretend to be someone else.

. . .

Time to go. East, to New York, to her husband. Husband. The word sits awkwardly in her mouth. After her morning phone call, Kate mostly forgets about him. It is a surprise to her when she sees her wedding ring in her jewelry box. It all feels like it happened to someone else, a long time ago. She tries to remember why she did it, but none of the reasons seem plausible now. But, that is just the *marriage*. Luddy, the man, is family, and the Hepburn dinner table would look wrong without him. That table is real life—a fishing line, it yanks her back, pulling her out of the silver-finned city.

LELAND

COLDWATER CANYON

Leland tries to talk her out of going to Europe with Luddy. His reasons are professional, in her own best interest. Aren't they? He tells her that *Bill of Divorcement* is set to be a hit and the press will come for her. He can see she doesn't know what he means. How is there so much she doesn't know? It exasperates him. It endears her. She cannot be in Europe with a *husband* no one has heard of if she wants to be a star. She can either show up with the husband and *be* married or she can fake it and *get* married, but she can't do this in-between nonsense. Leland goes out of his way not to say Luddy's name.

Leland takes her flying on a hot September day. He is also a natural flier. The last time he saw Howard Hughes they spent two hours talking about flat rivets. Hughes is a foot taller, richer and far more famous; Leland would rather Kate not meet him. He would also rather she never see Howard pilot a plane. His takeoff is too clean, too elegant. Leland does not want her to watch other men fly. He wants her to see him roar to life in the air. Flying is the point of everything for Leland. He tells himself that he bears Hollywood only so that he can do it but it is not true. Hollywood power feeds his hungriest beasts.

Leland's Waco plane is painted buttercup yellow. Kate is not fearless, but she wants to be. He loves to watch her overcome her hesitation and decide to be brave. She will always choose to do rather than not do. Life is for living she tells him. But it scares her, the raw risk of launching yourself into the sky, trusting your life to a tin tube and cloth wings. He feels protective when they fly. On the ground, she never needs him, or anybody.

They land outside of Santa Barbara, leave their goggles in the plane and, giddy with air and height, wander down into the small town for lunch.

"Selznick signed your new deal," he says once they've sat down. It's a restaurant with sandy picnic tables by the beach, the sort of place that would only be open in the summer if it were on an East Coast boardwalk. But it is here, in California, and it is open all year round. "The next picture, plus the bonus, you will be up to four thousand a week."

"Four?" He can see the number surprises her.

"As much as the big stars. More than the directors."

Kate is happy. And Laura is not here to puncture the number, comparing it to her millions and leaving it flat on the side of the road. *Four* would never impress a woman like Laura.

"Four. Plus, as you asked, they will allow you to go to New York to do theater and," he says, "they *cannot* fire you without a reason." Leland watches to see her reaction. She has not been here long enough to understand the significance. Only the very biggest stars are shielded from dismissal, the others all build their lives on the rocky floodplain.

"We were at his house in Malibu on Saturday, and he didn't mention any of this," Kate says.

"Of course not," Leland says. "You never bargain with the star."

LOS ANGELES

SEPTEMBER 1932

Leland waits until Kate is on the train back East before he returns Ford's call. It annoys the director.

"Booked," Leland says. "Booked for her next four films." The fourth, *Little Women* with George Cukor directing, is not confirmed yet but Leland doesn't want Ford to know that.

"*Divorcement* is not even out yet and Selznick is betting that hard?"

"She's that good."

Ford hangs up. Contracts can be broken. He will wait until Katharine Hepburn comes back to Hollywood.

KATE

HOTEL GEORGE V, PARIS

OCTOBER 1932

"Speak up will you?" Kate says into the black enamel telephone. "We're listening." Kate sits at the desk and Luddy stands beside her.

"*Variety* is calling you a *smash*!" Leland is shouting now. "The film is a *hit*! Audiences love you, critics love you. Get back here!"

Luddy knows not to touch her. A *smash*. She has done it. *Smash*.

Kate feels the word fall over her. She waits for it to make her feel different.

"Kate? *Kate*? Are you listening? Careful at the docks! Photographers will be there!" Leland shouts down the line.

"*Who* will be there?" Kate asks.

"Press!" Midmorning in Paris, middle of the night in California but Leland is still shouting.

Press.

"Photographers?" Kate asks, without artifice. "What about Barrymore and Billie?" Kate is fidgeting, tearing a thick sheet of hotel stationery. The pieces are falling onto Luddy's shoes.

"The press will be after them too," Leland says, "but not the way they'll be after you. They are making *you* the story."

"*Who* is the story? I didn't hear you?" Kate says loudly. But they had both heard him. She just wants to hear it again.

. . .

They leave the hotel early the next morning by the back door. The concierge has already arranged a car plus a taxi to bring the luggage from Paris to the boat in Le Havre. The driver does not speak English. Kate does not risk her rudimentary French. Luddy prefers it quiet anyway.

Leland is right and the press are waiting at the boat. How did they know? Luddy and Kate sit in the taxi and watch as the photographers with their rumpled suits, hatbands and boxy cameras loiter around the gangplank. One has lost interest and is flirting with a pretty French passenger but the other four are looking for Kate. Kate is sure she can outsmart them. It is a game and competition quickens her pulse. She prances in her starting gate.

Luddy gets out. The press don't know to look for him yet. The steward checks his papers. Mr. Ludlow Ogden Smith traveling to New York with his wife.

. . .

Only one photographer is actually aboard the ship and he cannot find Kate. He is annoyed. He convinced his boss to book the passage so he could get the first shot of her. The rumor is that she's on board but no one has seen her. The photographer has three more days to find her.

Leland booked Kate and Luddy into a first-class cabin suite. It is smaller and toward the bow but was the last one available. The photographer asks every member of the crew but no luck. Kate, as always, is seasick and does not leave her cabin. The purser arranges to have all their meals brought to them and the waitstaff and crew do not give them away. Luddy tips well.

Luddy has friends on board. No one is looking for him so he wanders around as himself. The Seaworths are traveling home from their tour of the Loire Valley and the Haverbacks are returning following their daughter's wedding. Luddy is a good listener. It saves him the trouble of cooking up good conversation.

The press are there, waiting when they dock in New York. Luddy walks off the boat and hails an anonymous taxi. Kate wears a new Schiaparelli suit she bought in Paris and disembarks alone. She waves but it makes her feel silly so she stops. The photographers' shutters click. It sounds like walnuts cracking. One reporter asks to see the ship's manifest but the purser, who feels a sense of allegiance to Mr. Ogden Smith and his wife, refuses.

. . .

Kate and Luddy go home to the brownstone on East Forty-ninth Street as if they live there. There are ladders and drop cloths and boxes of tools. Kate and Luddy talk about paint and plumbing and water pressure. Luddy sleeps upstairs in an attic bedroom. Kate's bedroom overlooks the garden. She can feel the tug of a life here. But Leland has a rail ticket waiting and two days later, Kate boards the *Super Chief* to Pasadena. Luddy goes back to work in his downtown office. Kate has left instructions for the tile in the new downstairs bathroom. The house is nearly ready.

LAURA

NEW YORK CITY

It's in the papers. They docked this morning in New York Harbor. The papers say that *Kate* has docked. No one knows she is not traveling alone. The photographs are good. Kate remembered to angle toward the lens the way Laura showed her. That small moment gives Laura a sense of ownership.

At the hairdresser, at dinner parties, Laura wants to drop Kate's name into conversations, just to have the feel of the letters in her mouth, but she doesn't. It is not the thing in her New York to care about film stars and she is trying to show Kate she can be discreet.

. . .

On the third day, Laura goes to the house in Turtle Bay, even though she said she wouldn't. The squirming feeling of knowing Kate is here propels her, and with all the press for *Divorcement*, who knows how long she will stay on the East Coast?

Luddy opens the door and leads her up to Kate in the newly painted sitting room. They talk about the boat. Who was on board? The Haverbacks? The Vanderbilts? Kate is uninterested.

"I was busy sicking up my breakfast," Kate says. "Why would I care?"

Laura cannot find a subject that will hold Kate's attention. She is not current. How did that happen so quickly? It has only been a few weeks but they are talking like other people. Kate and Luddy are speaking in the fragmented shorthand of a broken-in couple. It hurts.

Laura sees the ticket on the hall table. Kate is leaving on the *Super Chief* at five o'clock. Four months ago, Kate had never crossed the country on a train and Laura had to show her where to find the dining car and how to turn on the shower.

In the apartment on Fifth Avenue, Laura is packing a bag. One P.M. Four hours to go. Should she? Or she could go with nothing and send for her things? Or buy new things. Who cares? She just wants to be there. But Kate has not asked her to come back to California and Leland only booked one train ticket. Without ever speaking of it, they have dissolved.

Laura is alone in the tall broken-toothed city. In Midtown it is getting hard to look up and find the blue.

LUDDY

NEW YORK CITY

Luddy cannot find space in himself to feel sorry for Laura but he feels something else, an uncomfortable kinship. Laura is the only other person who knows what it is to lose the love of this impossible woman. All that wanting. He understands it. But he knows Kate cannot bear someone wanting her openly, it reminds her of when she wanted someone she could not have.

Now, Laura is making things worse. Showing up at the train station to see her off. Poor taste. No matter the crime, with Kate, it is always up to the victim to buck up and get on with it. Being hurt is no reason for acting hurt.

LELAND

COLDWATER CANYON

Flowers arrive at the Coldwater Canyon house. White orchids. She looks, no note. She won't find it. The note is crumpled in Leland's pocket. He went out to accept the delivery from the flower van when Kate was in the shower.

Let's meet?
—JF

Leland does not want Kate to meet John Ford. He tells himself it is because Ford would want to put her in a western or an adventure film, where she would be diminished. She would play the hand wringing girlfriend opposite Duke Wayne or that young, barrel-chested genius Spencer Tracy. He would take her career in another direction. But that's not it. Really, it's because that crowd are charismatic as all hell. Men's men, and Kate would like them.

PART FOUR

QUICK CHANGE

KATE

COLDWATER CANYON

DECEMBER 1932

Kate rolls over. Leland is already awake. Kate has never had a lover who is a morning person. Luddy only woke up early to please her and Laura would have slept all day if she could. Kate shovels Laura, and that dreadful afternoon at the brownstone, from her mind. Laura was waiting for an invitation. To where? Back here? To visit? To *live*? No. She will not give in to all that wanting. Laura will be fine. It is always possible to live without.

"Coffee?" Leland says from the wide mahogany bed. Kate knows he rose earlier to make it. He is a thoughtful man when he remembers to be.

"Take me flying," Kate says.

"Ha!" Leland laughs. "You only want to go flying because up there we can't talk."

"I don't *want* to talk," Kate says. "I want to *fly*." Kate goes into the small bathroom and shuts the door. She can hear Leland getting dressed. He doesn't like to speak about anything that matters until he is dressed. Kate's family could walk naked from the sea up to the house shouting good morning to the neighbors. Leland cannot meet her eyes when he is undressed while standing up. Leland keeps a full wardrobe here, in this small apartment. He keeps the apartment so that he can meet her.

On the sink is a new blue toothbrush. Leland must have bought it. Does he have a whole box of them somewhere? Kate keeps forgetting hers. She can't bear to start the day with grubby teeth; still the fact of it bothers her. It reeks of possession.

"And what if *I* want to talk?" Leland asks through the door. He must be dressed now. Pocket square, Brylcreem, even on a Saturday.

"Too bad," Kate calls out. She does not want to talk about what Leland wants to talk about.

Kate does not want to divorce Luddy and she does not want Leland to divorce his wife.

Now that *Divorcement* is a hit, Kate is a name but she doesn't receive sacks of love letters and marriage proposals as other new actresses do. George says she is going to be a thinking woman's woman, whatever that means. There are approaches. Some successful, some not. Tallulah's friend, Iris; Jane Loring, that brilliant film editor with the black rimmed glasses; David Manners, and Leland. George says there are others but will not say who.

And Laura. Kate knows that Laura is rotted through with hurt; she has seen photographs in the society pages, Laura's skin tugged down with disappointment. She does not let herself think about it. Leland also is looking anxious recently. She tries to ignore it. Leland is a distraction, a flat place to catch her breath. It almost began before they left for Europe but Kate put him off. She was not ready for it to start yet.

The before-part, where nothing is ruined and everything is possible? That is Kate's favorite part, but it never lasts long. It began when Kate returned to Hollywood. The details of Leland's seduction were predictable. His hand on her leg at dinner, his mouth on her neck when he drove her home. All pedestrian. She had expected something more imaginative from him and the excitement seeped away. Not all at once, it was a slow leak. But when he takes her flying, he is different. Possessed by a milky calm, he is afraid of nothing. And she likes being off the ground—the air and the silence. In the plane, they are perfect together and she can feel everything that she cannot feel on the ground. She tells herself it is because she likes watching him do something he loves but that is not it. It is something less generous. In those rushing blue moments, he does not need her.

CARY

SANTA MONICA

FEBRUARY 1933

He meets her in front of the Brown Derby on Wilshire. He is not supposed to be there. He had planned to go home to the beach house after the party but it got late and Randolph does not like to drive after drinking champagne so they are staying in the Hollywood apartment. Cary enjoys the throwaway luxury of having two homes. Randolph thinks nothing of it. It was the premiere of *Blonde Venus* and everyone wanted to talk to Cary Grant. The studio sent a starlet, Jeanine something, but Cary only agreed to go if he could bring Randolph. It is his first hit and he needed Randolph with him for it to feel real. Good things can crumble to powder if Randolph isn't there. The velvet ropes held back the crowds; the photographers' cameras flashed white, the lights swung and crossed overhead. Cary stepped out of the limousine first, followed by Jeanine the starlet, followed by Randolph, climbing out of the long car like an extra syllable. But Cary believes that things that are awkward will become normal if you insist long enough. In the end, the columns do not mention Randolph. The reporters all write that Howard Hughes was at the premiere. Nothing sells papers faster than stories about Howard.

It is after two in the morning and Cary and Randolph sit in the center booth at the Brown Derby and order Reuben sandwiches and coleslaw. The party follows them. The Brown Derby sends out more champagne.

Cary goes outside to get the car while Randolph pays the bill. Virginia Cherrill is standing alone, smoking, being herself. Cary will see her play many people, but this first night, her shoes pinch and she is too tired to pretend to be someone else. She is small-framed and blond with thick lashed crescent eyes, shaped like sunrise. Her mouth is small and curvy. She is prettier when she doesn't smile. Her teeth do not photograph well. Cary has heard about her: that Charlie Chaplin went crazy for her, that she is a friend of Marion Davies and so is often a guest at William Randolph Hearst's fairy tale castle at San Simeon, that Ziegfeld wanted her and she said no, that MGM wanted her but lost out to Fox, that Louella Parsons says she is the most beautiful woman in Hollywood. He does what he never does and walks up to her. Cary can do this, he can make people feel good, feel seen. Usually, he saves this skill for the camera.

She writes the telephone number on a white card. She does not use his pen, she has her own, pulls it out of her evening bag and leans on the hood of a car to write. He is worried she will get grime on her dress. Cary looks. It is a Hollywood exchange. She says she lives with her mother. Not Chaplin then. He's heard rumors. By the time Randolph joins them, the white card is in Cary's breast pocket and Virginia's date has brought his car around.

. . .

Cary is walking to the set of the new Mae West picture. Mae West has been spreading the story that she saw him on the lot, put him in her picture. Fiction. They met at the Friday night fights once he had already been cast. It's the second week of filming and everyone can see they work well together. His reserve grounds her blowsy charm, pinning down her wit like a stake anchoring a circus tent. Cary does not like her much but a good part of that is jealousy. Mae West is getting rich off this picture. Again. She is the writer and star and she's a skilled negotiator—she held out for a good contract. Cary feels undersold when he learns what she's making.

Mae West has given herself the best lines. Anyone would. In the script, he sets up the pins and she knocks them down in one sharp swipe. It doesn't leave him with enough to do and so Cary repositions. He doesn't quite change the text but he doesn't play the part as she wrote it. It is his phrasing, his stillness. His performance is small and tight and it resets the physics between them. He pulls back and she steps forward to fill the space—she must chase *him*. Cary has figured it out: it is better to be the pursued rather than the pursuer. The audience think just a little bit less of the pursuer, just a little bit more of the pursued. This will become his signature stance. By 1955, audiences will expect Grace Kelly to chase him across the French Riviera in an ice gray Sunbeam Alpine convertible. It will feel plausible.

Walking across the bright pavement, Cary is thinking about Virginia Cherrill. They have been out four times now: two lunches, a dinner at the Cocoanut Grove and the opening for the new Garbo picture. It's not that she is a woman. That has happened before, not often, two, maybe three times. It's the urgency he feels that is unusual. He wanted to telephone her that first night, the next morning—the hours felt fizzy and incomplete until he called her. When he telephoned, her directness was unexpected. Yes, she would meet him for lunch. Yes, she could do it today.

They met at Musso and Frank's, sat in one of the cracked brown leather booths. Reporters arrived. Someone must have called the papers, a busboy, the bartender.

"Photographers. Schulberg will be pleased," Cary said, pointing to the men in brown jackets peering through the front window.

"Schulberg wants to see you photographed with women? Or with *me*?" she asked, delicately wiping her mouth. She ordered the roast beef but would not take another bite now that there were cameras.

"With you," Cary said, reaching for her hand, and lying. "They are all so happy about you."

. . .

He is right. Schulberg is delighted when he sees the photographs and the suggestive headlines. Schulberg puts in the call to Louella Parsons himself. She leads with it. Now everyone is watching Cary Grant and Virginia Cherrill.

The paper lies open on the kitchen table, the page turned to Louella's article. Cary does not bring it up. Neither does Randolph. Cary cooks breakfast, crisping the mushrooms the way Randolph loves. He does it automatically. His thoughts are elsewhere.

. . .

Walking in the hot morning air, Cary is thinking about his dates with Virginia; how many? Six? Eight? All in three weeks. The colors smear and the edges grow wide and soft; he cannot remember what they talked about. Where did she order the chicken? Where did she drink pink champagne? What did he say when he dropped her at her apartment on Melrose? What did she say when he introduced her to Irene Dunne at the Ambassador Hotel? Where did she catch the heel of her shoe on the doorsill? It doesn't matter. What matters, is that each time, Virginia Cherrill agrees to the next time. Cary knows he is the pursuer but he doesn't care.

LOS ANGELES

MARCH 1933

Cary Grant and Randolph Scott are watching the photo shoot from their kitchen window. It is cold on the beach and empty for a

Saturday morning except for the photographers, makeup team and the two stars. It is their friends, Joel McCrea from Paramount and Kate Hepburn. McCrea waits until the cameras are set up before he takes off his shirt. Kate wears a striped sweater and shorts over her swimsuit but still rubs her arms to keep warm. Publicity teams always prefer winter for beach shoots. Less busy, better light, plus, actors work fast when they're cold.

Cary and Randolph agree that Kate and Joel are well matched, believable romantic leads. They are making each other laugh, easier to get good photographs that way. Teeth, real smiles. Kate and Joel huddle together under a striped towel between setups. Randolph has heard the rumors about Laura. He looks at Cary who knows Kate better.

"*Men*?" He doesn't need to say more.

"Sometimes, I think. Depends on the man apparently."

"I thought women."

"Same goes for women."

Randolph understands. The same can be said of Cary.

The photographs are good. Kate and Joel lying on a beach blanket, Kate and Joel peeking over a wall. These are publicity shots for a film that won't happen. Paramount is asking too much for the loan-out and RKO won't agree. Too bad, they would spark together onscreen. Cary and Randolph bring out blankets and mugs of hot coffee.

By the time Leland Hayward arrives, the photographers are packing up the last of their equipment and Kate and Joel are gone.

"In there," the makeup woman points to Cary and Randolph's house.

Leland goes around to the front door. He knows the house. Two rising stars from the Paramount stable live here. He can hear bolts of laughter, deep and from the belly. It's all of them. He leaves without knocking.

HOWARD
HANCOCK PARK

Howard Hughes does not like to employ people who lie. But in Noah Dietrich's case, he makes an exception. Noah is indispensable. What Howard wants Noah buys. Today, Howard wants to buy a plane.

"Sikorsky. Announced it today. Did you know?"

"Howard, we have to get Hughes Tool back in the black. Things are bad. We laid off a *quarter* of the workers, the bottom dropped out of the oil market! Haven't you seen the papers?" Noah lowers his voice. He doesn't want to sound as though he is accusing Howard of being ill informed, even though he is.

"I did *see* the papers," Howard says, holding up a page of *The New York Times*. "And I *saw* that Sikorsky is coming out with a new amphibian for Pan Am and we *need* it! You usually know months before they announce. Now, did you know?"

"Howard, I am telling you that your employees lost their jobs, their pensions, their homes and you are worrying about buying a *plane*?" Noah stops, grips his anger with both hands, pressing it flat into something he can store. Insinuation. This is as far as he goes. It is their waltz, Noah and Howard, circling in perfect time, the same steps, same rules. Howard will never fire Noah as long as Noah can pull down the sky when Howard asks for it. Noah will never leave Howard as long as he feels indispensable. Noah tells himself that Howard is not like other people. Howard has never had to worry about how to pay for rent or food or gas or taxes. Those are other people's problems. Noah likes that he is no longer one of the other people.

KATE
COLDWATER CANYON
APRIL 1933

The phone is ringing again but Kate does not look up. She is slicing bread for toast, her knife rhythmic and heavy. It will be Luddy, it will be Leland, it will be RKO. She doesn't want to speak to any of them. What would she say? The knife slides through the dense, spongy loaf. She has been feeling off lately and all she wants to eat is bread.

The goddamn article is in the morning paper. She does not say straight out that Kate is married but next time she will unless they can trade her something better. Louella does not bluff. She means what she says. It is her way. Leland leaves early for the studio. He has a meeting with George and Selznick so they can "put their heads together" as he phrases it. What can they do? Louella has more arrows in her quiver. She knows about Laura as well as Luddy, not that there is anything to know anymore but what there is, or *was*, will not help matters. And then there is Leland. Louella knows Leland keeps spare shirts at her house. And that is enough to put the rest together. She may even know about the small apartment in Laurel Canyon. Laura, Luddy, Leland. All Kate's problems begin with L.

Dinner is cold and sticky. Kate is sorry Ragnhild went to the trouble; she has to ask her to stop trying. All she can eat is bread and milk. The phone has stopped ringing. The East Coast is asleep. Luddy has had a telephone installed by the bed in his house so he can wake if she calls him late. Kate finds it endearing.

Kate leaves the food on the table. She has hired a woman who comes in to help Ragnhild and Joanna with the cooking and cleaning. Leland hired her. "And, we will hire a secretary for bookkeeping," he tells Kate. "Everything Laura did." Kate knows it's his way of keeping Laura away, but it is difficult to say no when so many need work. "*Everything* Laura did?" Kate teases. Leland can get twitchy when talking about Kate and Laura in bed.

Tonight, Kate has sent everyone away. If her soft, round world is going to split open, she wants to be alone when it happens. Kate switches off the lights and goes upstairs.

"Selznick gave her an exclusive with Connie Bennett and I gave her Clark Gable," Leland says, rolling his head back and stretching out his shoulders. He looks worn and the skin under his eyes is baggy and saddlebag creased in the morning light. He did not sleep well.

"Both?" Kate asks, cracking eggs into a blue bowl. She keeps up the egg shampoos at home now.

"I was worried she would ask for Gary Cooper and I knew Paramount would never agree. Louella is relentless and her threats are never empty."

"Let her publish and be damned," Kate says. She is irritated. Why should the public care about her private life? But she knows they do, and she wants them to care. She would be crushed if they didn't.

"You will not be able to make another picture if your *husband* gets into the papers," he says. "A wife who came to Hollywood, deserted her husband and lied about it? No. And then you"—he pauses, either for effect or out of exhaustion, Kate can't tell—"would have to go back to your old life. Do you want to go back to being Mrs. Ludlow Ogden Smith?"

"Mrs. S. Ogden Ludlow," Kate says, tipping the shells into the sink. "He called this morning, early." She doesn't turn around. "When he read the article, he went straight down to the registry office and changed his name. If Louella Parsons looks for Mr. Ludlow Ogden Smith, she will find no one there.

LOS ANGELES

MAY 1933

We are discreet, civilized. We understand how these things are done. Cary and Randolph are uncomfortable. Their neat square of life has been stretched into a thin-skinned triangle. Reservations for three. Invitations for three. Hollywood hosts spread the word. It is now Cary Grant plus two. No one is shocked. These are the last sexy days of old Hollywood. Some are curious about the details of Cary and Virginia and Randolph. How does it work? Where do they sleep? Some are fascinated by the inevitability of pain and watch to see who will get hurt. Some say it will be Virginia but most who know them say it will be Randolph. Some, those who know them best, phrase it in the past tense, as though it has already happened. It has.

Cary still hopes he can pull it off; love Virginia when he is with her and then come home to the steady heartbeat of his life with Randolph. It is selfish and Cary does not think it through carefully. He does not have time. Virginia is popular, flirtatious and poised for flight. Richer, more handsome, more successful men will get her if he lets her go. And so, he chases Virginia and tells himself Randolph will understand.

The gossip writers notice the triangle but Paramount is good at distraction. Cary and Virginia are offered up and the press, that many-mouthed public animal, bites greedily, grinding bone, teeth and muscle until the juice runs down its chin.

KATE

BEVERLY HILLS

Lies bother Kate. Kate knows Leland is married, but it is something she has chosen not to think about. She tells herself that what he says is true: emotionally, sexually, his marriage is over. Infidelity doesn't bother her much but lying doesn't sit well. And everyone is lying. She met Leland's wife Lola at a party at the Cocoanut Grove and was unimpressed. She is not much of anything, she tells Irene. They are sitting by the pool at Irene and David's beach house.

"She must be fascinating. They divorced and then Leland remarried her," Irene says.

"She is not an actress, not a writer, not an editor. Doesn't she want to *do* something?"

"She was a debutante," Irene says, turning toward the house, listening for the baby.

"That's something?" Kate says.

"And a wife," Irene turns back to face her.

Kate doesn't answer. Irene is a wife. Kate is a wife.

"You can never know what goes on in someone else's marriage," Irene says.

Kate knows Irene is talking about herself. She sees the strain when David walks into the room.

Kate sometimes forgets she is also married. She has told Luddy about Leland, or at least has hinted enough for him to guess. But, he doesn't guess and instead changes the subject. Kate doesn't think of them as married like that anymore. Luddy tells her he has taken an apartment that backs up to the house in Turtle Bay. "Better to have a separate address. Just in case they find me again," he said last night on the phone. The Thirty-ninth Street apartment, the house, and now an apartment on East Forty-eighth. He would buy up all of Manhattan to keep the press away from her.

. . .

Laura calls from New York. Sometimes late, sometimes drunk. Laura doesn't care about keeping Kate safe from the press.

LOS ANGELES

MAY 1933

Did you see that? She signed the contract for *Morning Glory* without reading the whole script. She says she finished, but we know she lied. Good for her to grab it. She is learning how this town works. A story will grow that Kate saw it on Pandro Berman's desk and convinced him to dump Connie Bennett and give it to her. Fiction. That never happened. But the story will stick and will become part of Kate's anarchic mythology. It irritates Connie Bennett, who never even read the script. Pandro always meant it for Kate. It is a bold part and he knew it would suit her. His first big picture as studio head.

They mean to move fast. They want to shoot it in eighteen days, edit it in twenty, in time for a summer release. Kate knows the schedule is tight and is worried her luck won't hold but it all unfurls like a ribbon. She gives a fast, clean performance, one take, one take, glove tight. She is serious about this business now. No distractions. She refuses to see Leland while they are shooting and will not pick up the phone for Laura or anyone else. She gets superstitious too. She eats the same small breakfast, lunch and dinner for all of the eighteen days. Her stomach has been unpredictable and she doesn't want to risk anything that will not agree with her.

Her cheeks hollow but that only makes her photograph better. George Cukor is worried about her but he can see that she's holding her breath, willing this film to go well. George has an early draft of *Little Women* he wants to talk through with her. But, he will have to wait. He knows she will be a perfect Jo March but there will be no talking to her about any other scripts until filming is over. Good for her. She will win an Oscar for this picture.

Enjoy it now. These things don't last.

. . .

Did you think he forgot about her? The charming director with the charming friends? He didn't. He is waiting. John Ford does not ask people twice. George Cukor said she has signed on to four films. He is counting.

CARY

THE BEVERLY HILLS HOTEL

Randolph stays at the beach house, Cary stays in town. The two men talk on the phone every morning but Cary no longer calls to say good night. He is afraid he will call one night and Randolph will not be alone. Cary knows it is hypocritical but hypocrisy does not unravel his fear. Randolph tells himself that if Cary calls, he will not pick up and some nights he deliberately leaves the receiver in the living room off the hook, but he knows it's too late to play hard to get. Randolph finally asks Howard, who tells him yes, Cary is sleeping alone and he always drops Virginia home by eleven. Howard thinks he is being reassuring but Randolph wishes he had not asked. It would be better if she stayed the night with Cary in their bungalow. Now, Randolph knows. Virginia Cherrill is holding out for a proposal.

LOS ANGELES
AUGUST 1933

Irene is right. The press are more mean-spirited now. Everyone is mean in 1933; mean or exhausted. The days when the press could be entertained with a rosy hint of a love affair or a photograph of a starlet pulling malteds at the soda fountain are gone. They need something hard and bright that will sell. Something exclusive. The studio press offices still grind out mimeographs, hawking potted biographies on sheer pink paper. The press leave them, coffee stained and crumpled, in their cars and on the pale concrete pavement. They are not worth reading. Official stories do not interest them anymore. Now they trade only in gold.

CARY
SANTA MONICA

They have to talk about it. Cary has begun to feel sneaky and he hates it. There has always been a spring water clarity between them. They agree: trust must be absolute. They cannot help the inequality. To Cary, there is Randolph and then everyone else in the world. To Randolph, there is only Cary.

Cary must begin it. He has brought this complication into their lives. It is his responsibility. The morning is pale blue and the air is cool, fogged with salt. The Pacific curls and groans onto the yellow sand. Cary watches; Randolph is on the phone. Their oil stock has gone up. Howard said it would. Cary looks around the room, feels the weight of their joint life, the mingled books, the dishes they chose together, the two desks, two phones, two phone lines, the calendar on the kitchen wall marking filming starts and wrap parties and a snapshot of the Halloween barbecue they hosted in matching circus strongman costumes. Cary closes his eyes and treasures the peace he is about to smash. He waits for Randolph to finish his phone call.

"How can you say nothing will change?" Randolph asks. "Things have already changed." He is sitting at his desk, looking down at his notebook, still adding up the column of the morning's figures. He knows the sums will come out wrong and he will have to do it again but he can't stop—it is better than doing nothing and leaving his mind wide open to his lover's crashing words.

"Why should anything change?" Cary asks, his tone easy. "Schulberg is always telling us to have girls around."

"For the *papers*. For *show*," Randolph says, standing. He is not prepared to have this conversation in his bathrobe. He does not need to explain what Cary already understands. The conversation is finished.

Whatever the terms, Randolph will agree. Life is not life without Cary.

Later, before bed.

"Is this important, Cary?"

"I think so."

There is more. Randolph waits for him to finish.

"I would not do this to you if it weren't."

"Marriage?" Randolph asks. "Have you asked her?"

"With a girl like her, it has to be marriage." Cary has not thought beyond the competition, winning the prize. He can only pursue.

"So, you've asked her. When? How?"

"Small," Cary says. "Soon."

"And this house?" Randolph asks.

"This is our house," Cary says. It has never occurred to him to give it up.

PART FIVE

CUT

IRENE

BEVERLY HILLS

DECEMBER 1933

Cary and Irene are sitting in the kitchen, avoiding the party. Cary has become one of Irene's favorites.

"The note in the margin was 'NTS,' '*Not* the Selznicks,'" Irene says without laughing. "That means they want to place people anywhere except with us."

"They gave you an acronym?" Cary says. "How glamorous." Since being with Virginia, he has smoothed out his voice; it is pudding soft.

"It is *not* glamorous," Irene says, pouring the coffee into two thick-handled mugs. "People must be miserable working here."

It is two A.M. and there are fourteen people in her backyard, and a mountain of dishes still to clean. *Of course* people hate working here.

Randolph is reading the paper in Irene's living room, Cary pours another mug of coffee and brings it to him. Irene has asked the housekeeper to put fresh sheets on the guest bed for them. Virginia has gone home.

"But you already knew they were miserable working here, darling," Cary says, sitting down again. He does not usually drink coffee at night but he means to be out late this evening.

"I didn't know they were *that* miserable."

"Irene, more than a quarter of the country is out of work and they quit their jobs." Cary leaves it there. Everyone reads about the breadlines, the Hoovervilles, the great dusty migration toward the hope of jobs and a new life on the bright blue and yellow California coast. He doesn't need to say more.

Irene has no idea where Cary comes from, who his people are. She had assumed he came from money, but now, she's not sure. His voice takes on a nerved steeliness when he speaks of the Hoovervilles. His accent is mid-Atlantic, unplaceable. That is how it is here—everyone reinvents. All she does know is that Cary has married and still loves the man in the next room. She remembers the first night she met Randolph. It was at their Halloween party and they were dressed in matching strongman costumes. That fits, she thinks. This is the circus.

KATE

HARTFORD, CONNECTICUT

This house is good for Christmas. The fir, the holly, the gables. The Connecticut snow ices the house in white. Kate relishes these East Coast things. Wood smoke burns the cold air and the walls smell of nutmeg even though Fanny finished the baking yesterday. Fanny has her own house now. The Hepburns helped her buy it as soon as they could afford it. She still takes the 36 bus every morning to Bloomfield Avenue. Kate has collected a book of autographs to give to her for Christmas. Leland said it was in poor taste but Kate doesn't care. She is willing to have less taste to make her family happy.

Kit Hepburn does not ask about the work, only about the weather, the politics and the availability of birth control. She is giving a speech with Mrs. Sanger to Congress next year on the subject and is interested in the opinion of Californian women. Her father waits until they are alone. Everyone else has left the table and are playing charades in the living room. He asks her about her life: the films, the actors, the stories and the sound of the rolling cameras. She stalls. More than insider gossip, she wants to tell him what it is like to live in Los Angeles in 1933—the buoyant, lawless freedom, and the selves she has found there, but it doesn't feel like something she can explain. Her Hollywood would get lost in the telling. Annoyed, he drops it. Later, he snaps at her in front of her sisters. The reason is minor, made up. He just needs her to be smaller.

The Hepburn siblings are noisy. Marion and Peg want to hear everything. Has she met Greta Garbo? Marlene Dietrich? Bette Davis? Are Howard Hughes and Billie Dove really over? Did Tallulah Bankhead fall in love with Gary Cooper? Is Leslie Howard really English? Is that all Irene Dunne's own hair? Dick and Bob ask about the cars. Kate goes to bed early.

Luddy is here. It was not discussed beforehand. The assumptions are binding and comforting at once. Kate sits on his lap on Christmas morning and he winds up the ribbon after she tears through the paper. He gives her a Brownie camera. She gives him an antique pen. They know each other and each gift is perfect. He sleeps in his usual room across the hall but most nights, late, she crosses into his bed. Kate has grown accustomed to warmth, to breath in the bed. Leland calls in the afternoons but no one notices. He is her agent.

The food is too rich. Kate asks Fanny for boiled chicken and white bread. Pale food cures everything. Marion and Peg look at each other. They have heard about Hollywood diets and have noticed Kate's hollowed out clavicles and bony knees. Her father disapproves, sends the food back to Fanny in the kitchen.

"This is not a restaurant," he tells Kate.

At three A.M., Luddy rubs her back as she curls over, his hand running over her walnut shell spine. He lifts her off her childhood bed. Stays with her on the floor. The stiff carpet leaves marks on her face. The next night, they sleep on the cool white bathroom tile. Luddy brings a pillow from the bed, a tartan blanket and a large mixing bowl. He looks for a bucket but cannot find one.

On the fourth night, Luddy brings her father. Her father calls his hospital. The surgical team assemble in fifteen minutes.

It isn't the food.

LOS ANGELES
HARTFORD HOSPITAL
DECEMBER 1933

Kate will never remember this part. The surgery takes nine hours, four more than he expected. Hartford's best anesthesiologist runs the red lights and arrives just after midnight. The junior surgeon was already at the hospital. Dr. Hepburn kisses his wife, signs the release, and scrubs up. Just as when she was in college and he removed her appendix, Dr. Hepburn does not trust his daughter to another surgeon. He will open her himself.

A nurse adjusts Dr. Hepburn's glasses, resettling them on his nose. Kate is not Kate but, "the patient" or "her." She is on the table, draped in a white sheet. The junior surgeon stands on one side, Dr. Hepburn on the other. The anesthesiologist sits by her head. He does not look up from the gauges in front of him. Together they form a triangle around her. The surgical tools are lined up on the metal tray. Dr. Hepburn is particular about his tools. The nurses discussed it beforehand. Surgical patients are always undressed and gowned, but it is his daughter. Does that change it? No, she is a surgical patient. They follow the rules.

The first hour. Three white circles of clinical light and the brush of steel on steel. The soft give of metal pushing through skin. He is lead surgeon, and so decisions are his to make. There are choices, it is more complex than they thought. It has spread, crawling over her uterus and ovaries like ivy punctuated by muscle bound fibroids.

The second hour. They try the newer, subtotal procedure. Dr. Hepburn is less familiar with the new method. There is always more to cut away. Just like any other patient. Health is sovereign. Organs, tubing, like fibrous plants, nesting cups, rooted by a stem. Slice the stem and the bulb will come away.

The fifth hour. The older procedure is radical but tidy: the heavy center, the connecting web, all out, leaving the cavity neat and hollow. The subtotal procedure is messy, risky, and requires careful calculation, discussion. The junior surgeon squeezes the clamp, the nurse holds the sponge, the anesthesiologist watches the canisters.

The seventh hour.

"Is it possible to leave some ovary there," the junior surgeon points. He is new to the hospital, to the profession, and hesitant to offer suggestions.

"Risky," Dr. Hepburn says. "Pressure?"

"Steady but low," the anesthesiologist answers.

He works quickly, consults no one and cleans her out.

The ninth hour. He closes her himself. He takes time to keep the stitches small and tight. He has always prided himself on his stitches. The anesthesiologist watches the gauges, wishing the surgeons would hurry.

Only after the procedure, once the blood on his hands slides down into the drain and the small, heavy organs lie on the tray, does he recognize that it is his daughter's blood. He will ask her mother to tell her. Kate is a sensible girl. Why keep some if you can't use it?

Dr. Hepburn washes his hands again and fills out the order to send samples down to pathology.

Luddy is in the hallway, beyond the white swinging doors. As her husband, he is her next of kin but no one consults him and her father signs the paperwork. There are no chairs so Luddy paces. This hallway is not for visitors and family are asked to wait in the waiting room but no one asks him to leave. He is Dr. Hepburn's son-in-law.

Should he telephone her mother? Laura? Is he bargaining? Laura could leave Manhattan in the gray dark and catch the 5:12 A.M. from Grand Central. Would Kate want her here? No. And Kate will not remember this part.

Hepburn children are scattered around the hospital. Dick is asleep across several chairs. Bob, now in his first year of medical school, is in his father's second floor office, studying for an exam on the functions of the spleen. He is trying to think like a doctor would, to separate the problem from the person. It is not his sister in that brightly lit room but tunnels of tissue funneling into spongy, wet organs. Marion is fifteen. She sits alone on the linoleum floor outside the operating room. When she found small bursts of rusty blood in her white underpants just before Christmas, she was calm. She was not like the other girls in her class who shrieked and panicked. Her parents had talked to her about things like this and she had always known it would happen. But now, sitting in the cold white hospital corridor, she is sure she never wants it to happen again.

Dr. Hepburn washes the flecks of blood from his glasses and drives home. He reviews his decisions, critically, counting them like a rosary. Yes. He was right. He will not risk his daughter. The junior surgeon has a healthy two-year-old at home and does not know what he knows.

Without all, what good is some? Parts do not function without the whole. Why hold on to what is already dead. Or almost dead, or could be dead? Best to prepare for the worst. Just like any other patient, he tells himself.

His wife will understand. They have learned their lesson. They will not lose another child.

. . .

The patient is in the recovery suite. The doctor has gone home. His wife is already running him a bath. The nurses talk quietly as they clean up the leavings of surgery. Doctors drop sponges on the floor. It is not their job to care where they land.

"Did they speak about it beforehand?"

"She was unconscious when they brought her in."

"How old is she?"

"*Modern Screen* says she's twenty-four."

"Twenty-four."

HOWARD

MINES FIELD AIRPORT

Glenn Odekirk, Richard Palmer and Howard Hughes are at the airfield talking about flight. They are building the fastest plane ever to slide through the air. Faster than sound. It sounds absurd but they are serious. Faster than sound was Howard's instruction. Palmer, a brilliant Caltech graduate and Odekirk—"Ode"—an engineer who has been with Howard since *Hell's Angels*, are going to make it happen. She will be "sleek, light, fast, perfect," Howard says, looking down at the drawings. For Howard, planes, like ships, are the bodies that carry you. They are always *she*.

. . .

Howard is drunk. *Picturegoer* lies open on the desk. In the photograph, the newly married couple lean toward one another. The woman is smiling in the way she does when she thinks no one is photographing her. Howard has heard of the man but never met him. The pair look happy, complete. Howard wishes someone had warned him not to look. But who would do that? Not Noah. That would be an overstep. Billie would have warned him. But, right now, Billie Dove is on her honeymoon in Yuma, Arizona with her new oil tycoon husband. It says so, right there in the caption.

KATE

HARTFORD, CONNECTICUT

The day after. The mother tells her daughter in a spare, fast sentence, stripped of pity and remorse. Those sentiments weaken and do no good. "Ovary, uterus." The vocabulary is familiar. Kit Hepburn works with Margaret Sanger and is not afraid of these words. This is her lexicon.

Her mother walks around the white hospital room, straightening what is already tidy. It makes Kate dizzy to watch.

"If there is no infection, the doctor says the wound should heal clean and the scar will be discreet. It will fade and won't show."

The doctor.

Kit Hepburn cannot tell if her daughter is listening.

Kate's insides feel sloshy with liquid; the back of her head feels open, spread out and weighted, rooted into the mattress. She hears her mother's voice but how can any of what she is saying matter? Kate is never going to get up from this bed again.

. . .

Kate asks a nurse, the one who clucks when she turns her over to sponge her back and tucks the blankets in tight, the way Kate likes. Kate listens, trying to line the words up into phrases that make sense. It is too hard. She closes her eyes, stealing a few more minutes to be the person she was. When you do not know, it has not happened yet.

Kate asks for another blanket. She needs the heaviness, the division of space, somewhere neutral to rest her hands. The junior surgeon and the hospitalist have been to see her.

She tries to imagine what is gone; now, she runs her hands down the bony slopes of her hipbones avoiding the sewn-together skin.

. . .

Her father comes and stands by the side of the bed. He uses medical language, metallic, antiseptic. Because his wife has asked, he is willing to do this once, and then they will not speak of it again. He genuinely does not understand Kit's anger. He has saved their daughter. How can that be wrong?

He asks a junior doctor to check his daughter's stitches. It feels too personal for him to do it himself.

. . .

These days are hazy and out of focus. They move her to the convalescent ward. She doesn't move around as much as she should.

She gets stiff, old. It will take months to stretch out after all this stillness, they tell her. Mostly, she is left alone, folded into the rhythms of the hospital. She tries, but cannot bear to touch it. Not yet.

. . .

Kate hates the stale Christmas hospital decorations, the browning wreaths and the sagging evergreen. She is uncomfortable, her body does not fit together well, it is too tight and her stomach has ballooned in the cradle between her ribs and her hip bones. She looks like she is something she will never be.

. . .

Her father is irritated. His wife should feel grateful to him for taking such care.

"I will not take risks with my family," he says to his son, Bob. Bob understands. He is old enough to remember.

Family, the core of everything that matters. But, Bob is not thinking like a doctor or a brother this Christmas, but as a man who is thinking of proposing to the woman he loves. A man who wants to become a father one day. His sister's blood, that specific alchemy of Kate-ness, will stop with her; she can never share it with someone else and make someone new.

. . .

It hurts like hell. The borders of her incision wound are puckered and sewn up tight with black thread, like a basted and stuffed hen. But the scar does not fade as it should. Day after day, it stays an angry red ridge that has knitted together but will not blend with the neighbor skin.

They want her to eat; she can't. She is already full.

. . .

The junior surgeon comes to see her.

"Your father took such time with your stitches. It is a beautiful incision."

Kate does not want to hear that again. Wounds are not beautiful; they are scabbed and ugly. She cannot think about her father. She pushes away the image of the nurse adjusting his glasses on his nose so that he can see better, tilting the big light so he can get on with the delicate needlework of sewing his daughter. She tries to keep her mind out of that well lit room. She cannot renegotiate the decisions. This will be the only blood family she will ever have, and she does not want to start an unraveling that she will never be able to fix.

January in Connecticut. She tries to remember warmth.

. . .

Her brother Bob removes the stitches after the holiday decorations come down. He has been able to stitch and unstitch wounds since he was twelve. Bob looks at the unthreaded, thick raised skin and pronounces it "Excellent." What else is there to say?

He does not tell his sister that he is engaged.

. . .

Another week of healing and her skin itches with growth. She is carrying more body and less body than she is used to. She waits for the nurses to leave and then pulls back the gauze bandage and runs her hand over the ridges of the wound. She knows that under the healing is an absence. Nothing there, an empty cavity full of space. She wants to stick a pin through the tight balloon skin and hear the bang when it pops.

. . .

Home. She is told to stretch. She does. It becomes a habit she will keep for a lifetime. She hears the chime of breakfast dishes but she does not go downstairs. The ground floor is full of noise, banging doors, ringing phones and people.

Her mother asks Fanny to stop bringing Kate breakfast upstairs. "Kate must *walk,*" she says.

Kate doesn't mind. She isn't hungry.

"It's time," her mother says.

"Is it?" Kate always answers. "Doesn't feel like it." *Time for what?*

There is no anger in her, nor even regret. Just space where feeling should be.

GEORGE
HOLLYWOOD HILLS
JANUARY 1934

George telephones the Hepburn house. Kate has been nominated for Best Actress for *Morning Glory*. It is the sixth year of the Academy Awards and everybody wants one. He expected a whooping phone call from Kate after the announcement but none came. He leaves a message with one of the sisters. How many are there? Two? Three? He will ask Kate when she returns his call.

KIT HEPBURN
HARTFORD, CONNECTICUT

Acceptance came too soon, her mother tells her father. Kate should have been angry, railed, screamed. Kit herself still struggles to accept it, but no one needs to know that. Who would it help? It cannot be undone. When her husband climbs into bed at night she still coils away from him. She is still too angry to even pretend to be asleep.

. . .

"Kate?" Peg knocks lightly. "Do you have time to help me with my French lesson?"

It is a ridiculous question, Peg knows, Kate has nothing but time.

Mrs. Hepburn rarely speaks about Kate's "*condition,*" as she calls it, to her younger daughters. And they do not ask. It's not so much the surgery that bothers them, the children of a surgeon, they are able to separate the person from the procedure and dissolve all the terror into practicalities with a sterilized magic. It is the change in their sister that frightens them. She is no longer there. The four siblings go into town to see her movie. It is playing at the Colonial on Farmington Avenue. On the screen they watch her, alive, animated. At home, she is blank.

Peg waits in the doorway.

"Tomorrow?" Kate says. "I have too much to do today."

Kate is sitting in the chair next to the window. Peg doesn't notice that the mirror is gone. Kate asked Luddy to take it down and put it in the attic. There is a rectangular patch of darker wallpaper over the dresser.

"Yes, tomorrow," Peg says. Tomorrow she'll try again.

. . .

Kit Hepburn makes a decision. If Kate is still here in the spring, she will take her to Fenwick. Her daughter will heal faster by the sea. Kate is nominated for an Academy Award. That agent keeps calling to ask Kate if she will attend. But her daughter doesn't care and has asked the agent to RSVP no for the ceremony.

Tomorrow, Kit Hepburn will call the New York telephone number she has carried in her pocket for two months. The exchange for the Fifth Avenue apartment of the person who in all the world, loves Kate the most.

LUDDY

HARTFORD, CONNECTICUT

FEBRUARY 1934

Luddy helps Peg with her French and Marion with her grammar. He has not returned to New York. Does he still have a job there? No one thinks to ask.

Before Kate was discharged, Dr. Hepburn spoke to him about the surgery. Did he feel he owed Kate's husband an explanation?

"Adoption is always possible," Dr. Hepburn said. The words sounded rehearsed. They were. The surgeon was uncharacteristically forthcoming. Dr. Hepburn finds it easier to talk to men.

Luddy did not say that he would speak to Kate about it. Both men knew that he wouldn't.

. . .

When Leland Hayward, the agent, calls from Los Angeles, Peg hands the phone to Luddy. Her sister is still not accepting telephone calls.

Luddy hears what the man has to say. The message from the director is still scratched out on the notepad.

LAURA
HARTFORD, CONNECTICUT

She speaks to everyone in the house before going up to Kate's room. She has never been to Kate's Hartford home. It's ordinary and does not have the faded, old money grandeur of the summer-house by the sea.

The Hepburn children hug Laura as if she were a family friend. It makes her feel important. Peg tells her that Luddy spent the morning on the telephone. Marion tells her he pulled the telephone into the dining room and closed the door. He never does that, they say.

Luddy catches her before she goes up the stairs to Kate's room.

He asks for her help. He has made all the arrangements.

. . .

"Pack," Laura says, throwing Kate's empty travel case onto the bed.

"For what?" Kate does not open her eyes.

"Mexico." Laura keeps her voice steady and low, as if she is trying to calm a wild animal. "Leland called. The press know you're married. It's time."

"Leland called you?"

"No, called here. Luddy answered. I was still on the train." Laura wishes Leland had called her. She'd found the best hotels and lawyers in Mexico long ago.

"Do they know about the other thing?"

"No. No one knows."

. . .

"Luddy made the bookings," Laura says, showing Kate the tickets. Passage next week to Havana and then on by plane to Mérida, Mexico.

"Luddy? Arranged his own divorce? How like him," Kate says.

Laura can see that Kate feels such affection for him, this gentle, unobtrusive man who is nobly doing what is best for her. Even when it means letting her go. Annoying.

Even now, Laura knows that Kate does not understand the man she married.

"Yes. I had it all planned out last year," Laura says, straightening the bed covers. "We were going to stay in a beautiful hotel. I don't know what this one will be like." She cannot keep the spite from her voice. Because she does know. Luddy has chosen the prettiest hotel in Mexico.

Kate doesn't answer. She's like this now. Laura wishes she would hold up her end of the conversation.

"Kate? Do you want to just take a few cases or do you want your steamer trunk?"

"No, Laura," Kate says. "I am not going to Mexico."

"The man arranges for you to break his heart in splendid style and you won't even go?"

"I do not need to go to Mexico now," Kate says.

And then Laura understands. Kate means to stay here, in this ordinary, suffocating house and be almost married to this lump of man rather than get back to work, make pictures, and be alive in the world.

Laura had not realized she could feel such contempt for Kate.

LOS ANGELES

MARCH 1934

Cary will pick up the wedding photos from the printer on Thursday. At the wedding breakfast, Tallulah drank too much and kept calling Randolph Cary's "best man." Irene left early to check on the baby and of course, David stayed to the end. David even helped the caterers stack the chairs when it was over. Howard Hughes made a toast. He doesn't like to speak publicly, but he does it for Cary.

Leland sent a note with Kate's regrets and congratulations. He spent too much on the gift. He signed the card from both of them.

It didn't work. People still talked. Jimmie Shields told Pandro Berman, now head of production at RKO, it was measles. Pandro Berman repeated it to Randolph, who was too unhappy to care. Ben Schulberg heard from someone who heard from someone, that it was TB. Tallulah said it was a Swiss clinic, "To deal with a pregnancy of course."

Leland, you didn't think of that, did you? Now, you can't think of anything else.

Was it yours?

No, Leland. It was no one's.

IRENE
BEVERLY HILLS
APRIL 1934

It is a rare rainy Tuesday and Irene is upstairs, in her son's room, thinking about divorce. Divorce does not happen in her family. Marriages may be rocky but the rocks never shatter. She has a cousin who lived apart from her husband one spring and the whole family talked about it for years. Her father knows that something is wrong in Irene's marriage but has no idea how much trouble he has caused. When she tried to talk to him, he brushed her off and told her that David was doing "splendidly" at work, fitting right in at

MGM, and that she should buy the new Frigidaire like her sister's. Irene left his office shaking with anger but she still kissed and hugged him goodbye. Irene does not know how to cause a scene.

Life with David is not possible at the moment. He works until late and then goes out: cocktails, stars, over-budget pictures that must be finished, meetings, more drinks, night shoots, dinners, and then poker. He cannot keep away from it. David comes home, eyes shot through with Benzedrine and smelling of Arpege or Shalimar. And on the weekends he throws parties. At first, it was grief. His father died last year and his father had been everything to David. But now, it's life. It's habit.

Irving Thalberg has come back to work but does not want to take on too much. Only a handful of people know how sick he really is and Louis B. does not want it to get out. His wife, beautiful Norma Shearer, has lavender crescents under her eyes. She has given up acting. People who do not know think it's because she is pregnant. Louis B. tries to take pressure off Irving by promoting David. And so, David is mired deeper in a company he does not love. Irene shakes the idea away and thinks about something Kate asked her last spring. Why does she think of her husband's happiness more often than her own?

. . .

David does not want to talk about work; instead, he wants to throw a party; he wants people around at all hours. Music, tennis, dancing, champagne! Often, ten or fifteen people will appear on a Saturday morning expecting a house party. She can hear David on the patio telling guests that of course Irene is expecting them, even though she isn't, and how throwing a party together is as easy as breathing for her. Irene spends her time apologizing to her housekeeper and scraping extra money together to keep her cook from walking out. She refuses to accept money from her father and refuses to buy the Frigidaire.

But that is just life with David and not why she is thinking about divorce. Her reasons are primal. How does she stay married to a man who doesn't like his own baby? Her baby. Not a baby. Jeffrey is nearly two now. He chats happily with her but with David, his speech slows, stumbles and falls away. Irene recognized the symptoms immediately. Last summer, Jeffrey was pointing to cars as they went by. "Blue! Green!" and then David joined them. "R-r-r-r-r-r," Jeffrey said, sliding over the letter. The apple red car waited at the light, turned the corner, and drove away. "R-r-r-r-r," Jeffrey tried to grizzle out the word. Irene scooped him up, his thin shoulder blades spread open like wings as he wrapped his arms around her and she tucked his soft baby head under her chin. Years of speech therapy to cure her own stammer and she still avoids the letter r.

"*Red*, Jeffrey. Come on now," David said.

Stop, she does not say. David will not hear the word "stop."

Sometimes, Irene feels sure that David will adjust, grow comfortable with his son, and sometimes, he does. Sometimes, he will point out sailboats or tell him stories from the set that Jeffrey can't understand. These are the days, walking down Santa Monica Pier, or by the reservoir, when they feel like a family. Irene sees other people watching them. She wants to ask, *Do we look relaxed? Do we look young and happy*? Don't envy us. We are pretending. *Screenland* did an interview with David last month and called the Selznicks "Hollywood royalty." David brought the piece home to show her. Irene read it sitting on the white living room sofa. David was on the phone and Jeffrey's alphabet blocks were on the floor. He screamed at Jeffrey when he tripped over them. No one knows what happens in other people's families.

It happens again; David speaks over Jeffrey, trying to reach Irene.

All David wants is Irene. Jeffrey has learned not to seek out his father. It is not that David does not love his son; it is that he loves his wife more. Now, Irene wants another baby, company for Jeffrey, but David is adamant. He says one is bad enough. Irene flinches as though she has been hit.

KATE

FENWICK, CONNECTICUT

MAY 1934

Luddy has been let go from his job at the insurance agency on Vanderbilt Avenue. Kate sees the letter by chance. In the pile of post there is also a notice that the rent on his apartment is late. She knows he has paid for the rent on her townhouse in Turtle Bay a year in advance.

Kate is disgusted with herself. Luddy has made it easy for her to behave badly and she has been a pig to hold on to him for so long. From the moment she arrived in California, she knew she would never go back, but she let Luddy wait and then she moved into the beautiful renovated house on East Forty-ninth and he moved into the flat that backed up to her garden, just to be near in case she needed him. He waited, all that time, never complaining, just in case she changed her mind and decided to love him. And he paid for it, all of it. Kate is horrified that she had never thought to be horrified before. She will make it up to him. She will phone the bank in the morning and pay it all back. Luddy has never given any indication that things are difficult. He is just there, hand outstretched with whatever she needs.

And now this. This thing that has happened that is not to be mentioned. He is supporting her through that too. Is Luddy paying the rent on the house in California? Must be paying Louis and

Ragnhild? She certainly isn't. Or is Laura? Kate has lost track of the details. California feels far away and part of a long ago person. But she is sure Luddy has kept it all together for her. He is like that. Luddy has been there, discreet, tactful, with an impeccable sense of privacy. He knew to put the gold statuette the Academy sent in a drawer in Marion's room. He knows when to leave the room to make space for Laura, when to leave Kate to be alone. Laura does not have the same sense of timing. Laura tries to tell her that this procedure—Kate wishes she would not call it that—does not affect *them*. Laura tells Kate how they will be happy, they will do up the California house, Kate will be a star, they will have freedom, they will *not* have children and they will do it all *together*. Kate is revolted by Laura's soft, persistent pressure. She cringes when Laura says it doesn't matter.

Luddy tries only once to convince her. He puts down his book on a rainy afternoon and takes her hand. He tells her that it makes no difference to him. He does not mention that her father spoke of adoption or that he has put their names down on the list of a private agency just in case. He tells her that all he wants is her.

He nearly had her. She is drawing warmth and belonging from being inside a marriage, even a marriage as unconventional as theirs. But then he spoke of wanting her, and she could hear all the unsaid conversations to come. If he wants her, someday, he will want more of her, and there can never be more.

Her brothers and sisters do not remember it but her parents do. They know this silent, absent Kate; they recognize her from before. This time she is not up trees or on her bike. She has disappeared into her own room instead. Dr. and Mrs. Hepburn talk quietly in the study. They decide they will just act as if it did not happen and go on as before. It was a *medical* decision, Dr. Hepburn asserts again. Mrs. Hepburn tightens her jaw. She has said it all, that there were other choices, other procedures; he storms away each time she says it. She knows that one day he could march off and not come back, or worse. She thinks of his brothers, their son, the pistol in the locked bottom drawer. He is absolute in his beliefs. Dr. Hepburn will not have his medical decisions questioned.

"What Kate needs to know is that there was no other choice," Mrs. Hepburn says, watching the door even though she knows Kate will not come down.

"No, what she needs to know is that I, as her surgeon, as well as her father, made the *best* choice."

"No," Kit Hepburn says. "That is what *you* want her to know."

Her family lives by the principle of speaking one's mind—only not about things that cannot be solved. Kate remembers from before; her parents are right and you can't bring back things that are gone. Not speaking of it is fine with Kate. She does not want to know about the circumstances, the details. It's over, isn't it? Clean, finished. She has to get on with the business of being a different person.

Luddy understands her, just sits beside her and reads without talking. She watches his familiar profile, legs crossed, head bent close to the page. Yes, he is family, no matter what. But they would only ever be two, and that is a couple, not a family, isn't it? Luddy deserves better, more. He should be remarried by now, to someone who wants to be married to him. Is she leading him on? Of course she is. She is letting him wait for someone who does not exist. She will telephone Laura and go to Mexico; she cannot quite bear to travel alone. And then she will go back to California and earn all she needs to repay him and then some. It's time to do something good for him.

LAURA

HOTEL ITZA

MÉRIDA, MEXICO

AUGUST 1934

Laura finds the porters and the car; she gives the driver directions in Spanish. Kate looks up, surprised, and Laura feels herself become valuable. Of course she speaks French and only a bit of Spanish and so was mostly just speaking French with a Spanish accent but the porter and driver seem to understand and Kate doesn't notice the difference. Travel is Laura's element, born of years of practice. Nothing frightens her and her ease speaks of money. Laura knows all this is appealing to Kate but tries to pretend she doesn't.

Don't push too hard. Don't ask too much. Laura sits, in the shade of her room. Just be there, calm and useful, and wait.

KATE

HOTEL ITZA

MÉRIDA, MEXICO

The heat wakes her up. New smells, pink buildings, red flowers, poverty. Kate pretends she remembers how to be alive. Laura waits for the right time to talk about the surgery, the scar, the divorce, anything real, but Kate is not interested. She only wants to be exactly where she is and forget the rest. The owner of the café recognizes her but pretends he doesn't. The hotels order the glossy magazines. He brings fresh flowers to their table and offers them champagne. Kate is not irritated by the attention, she is warmed. The next day, he tells her that he will keep the best table empty all day in case they want to come back. Kate tells Laura they should go there for dinner. Their first dinner out. Kate is getting ready to pretend to be Katharine Hepburn again.

LAURA
HOTEL ITZA
MÉRIDA, MEXICO

Damn. A reporter from the Associated Press was waiting for them at the hotel. Laura kicks off her shoes and sits down heavily on the bed. She feels responsible. Did she tell too many people that she was going to Mexico with Kate? Did those people tell other people who told the press? The reporter said he was tipped off by the owner of the café in Mérida.

KATE
MÉRIDA, MEXICO

The paperwork is quick, the paragraphs brief. The lawyer, Mr. Francisco Acevedo Guillermo, is soft spoken, elegant and unrushed. Kate likes him immediately. Sitting in his cool, shuttered office, he points to the pages she needs to sign. Luddy's sloping signature is above hers. She can tell he used his best fountain pen. Mr. Francisco Acevedo Guillermo walks her across the street to the small, run down clerk's office, checking the street to make sure there are no reporters. Kate does not want a repeat of yesterday. Laura must have told someone.

In the clerk's office, Mr. Guillermo apologizes that the room is so hot and that there are no chairs. He waits outside until the clerk has stamped and filed each paper. Kate stands and waits in the hot room. She stretches her arms up and swings her torso from side to side, alarming the short, bald clerk. It has become a habit of hers. Her skin itches and she still feels the pull of the long removed stitches.

Their marriage is over in an afternoon. Kate waits to feel sorry, or sad, but the feeling doesn't come. She only feels grateful. She tells herself she is gifting Luddy his freedom. Now, he can find someone to love, but really, she does not expect him to stop loving her.

LELAND
COLDWATER CANYON
SEPTEMBER 1934

"Because we decided not to sail. It was not a *holiday*, Leland," Kate says, sliding off her sandals. She seems edgy and uncomfortable to be back here.

"Kate, there were openings, press ops, the *Oscars*, and you were *nowhere*!" She expects him to make her a star but a star out of what? You have to *give* the press something.

"Yes, I was nowhere," Kate says, unconcerned. "Nowhere you need to worry about. Why are you so het up anyway? It's my career that's tanking, not yours."

"Kate," he says, exasperated. "My career will go down with yours. That is how this business works."

"Kate," he says, softer now, "why didn't you cable from Mexico? Or return my calls in New York or Fenwick?" Leland asks, hating himself for asking. "I haven't heard from you for months." They are sitting on the bench by the door. Kate's house has four bedrooms, a patio, garden and a pool and somehow they always end up sitting on this bench outside the front door. Leland worries it is because she does not want him to come any farther into her house, but he flattens that idea and folds it away.

"I called you from Connecticut."

"Twice, and then you put bloody Laura on the phone."

Kate stretches her arms over her head. Is her back hurting her? Tallulah must be wrong. She looks the same. Thinner, if anything.

Kate has stopped listening to Leland; she can do that now. She doesn't want to hear what he will say next so she won't.

"What would I have told you on the telephone then that I couldn't tell you now?" she says. "Anyway, you're the one who said I had to go to Mexico."

"Kate, you have been gone for *ten* months, people are talking."

"Talking about?"

"Anything, everything! Are you ill? Did you panic? Are you really cut out to do this?"

"So, fear, sickness, ineptitude, incompetence—anything else they are suspecting me of?"

"*Ten* months, Kate, you know what they're thinking." He cannot look at her as he says it. He did not want to ask her like this.

"Are they thinking it or saying it? Or are *you* thinking it?"

"Of course, I don't think it. That would mean it was mine, *is* mine?" He is waiting for her to correct him, interrupt him. She doesn't. "The press won't print it but the gossip is that there is a secret baby hidden away back East."

"Hidden away. No, Leland, there is no one hidden away."

Later, they sit by the pool. He watches her, the ginger movements, the stretching, but he cannot ask her again. She is not swimming. And she always swims.

"Did you get it? You could at least tell me that?" Leland asks, sitting on the edge, swishing his foot in the cold water.

"The divorce? Yes, I told you I did."

"I want to hear it again," Leland says.

"I got it. It was in a grubby little county clerk's office from a nice man with a sweaty forehead." She takes off her sandal, rolls up her pant leg and drops her leg into the water.

"Do you want to get in? I'll swim with you?" Leland never swims. Once dressed for the day, he doesn't like to get undressed again.

She ignores him.

"Luddy is a saint to put up with me. Do you know he paid for the whole thing? Even surprised Laura and me with champagne and strawberries in our room on the morning before we left Mérida."

Our room. Kate is needling him, looking to see if he noticed. But Leland is not worried about Laura. To him, Luddy is the threat that matters.

KATE

COLDWATER CANYON

Leland always worries about the wrong thing. She hadn't noticed before how obvious he is.

"Luddy was *there*?" Leland asks. "Only Luddy could turn a Mexican divorce into a way to get you back."

Leland's jealousy is reserved for men. It irritates Kate. She thinks of Laura, of the sweat-damp days when they stayed in the square, white bed, hiding from the heat of the Mexican afternoon. Kate's jaw softens and her shoulders slide down her spine. Laura would never miss a pronoun. She would never be that careless. But Laura is in New York, exactly where Kate wants her to be. Mexico was a time out of life and Kate does not want the twoness to creep back.

Leland is still talking, sailing on, propelled by puffs of indignation.

"No, Luddy wasn't *there*," Kate finally interrupts. "He must have telephoned the hotel to make the arrangements. Thoughtful of him. I'll have to give him something extra special when I go home for Christmas this year." She is prodding him again. Why is she hurting him? She doesn't know, but she knows she cannot stop. Leland's mouth hangs open. Kate pushes harder. "And, Luddy *will* be there for Christmas this year. Husband or not, Luddy is family."

Leland has already booked his tickets to Mexico. He has not told Kate that he is divorcing too.

CARY

SANTA MONICA

Pulling into the studio, Cary is annoyed. Drivel. All of it. All four pictures Paramount has assigned him in the last six months. No, not drivel. It is not even that the scripts were bad. They were just not *good*. And Cary wants to be in films that are excellent. No actor, no performance, can elevate a mediocre script. Two years left on his contract. And then he *could* forge his own way. No contract to any one studio, a free agent. It's dangerous. Studios will always prefer an actor from their own stable.

He and Randolph ran the figures this morning and with income from their investments, Randolph thinks Cary could just about afford to wait for the right script. But it's dicey. The talk of renewal will start next year. Cary will give no indication that he is reconsidering his contract. He will even give the papers to his lawyers to look over. But if he doesn't sign or if he buys it out? He could choose his own scripts, his own terms. Cary has two years to become indispensable. He will not talk to Virginia about this. She is not always discreet.

KATE

COLDWATER CANYON

Kate had meant to wash out the clothes she wore in Mexico herself. The sweat in the armpits of her shirts feels shameful, private, but recently, it is hard to do things that could be done later.

Twelve days in Mexico. Laura had wanted to come back to Los Angeles with her but Kate had told her no, not yet. "When *is* yet?" Laura asked. Yet is just not now. Laura knows too much and would tell people. She can bear Laura's indiscretions about lovers, sex even, but not about this. Not about the stitches and the emptied middle. But, without hope, Laura can be dangerous. Kate understands that now.

What Kate needs is to work.

PART SIX

THE PLOT

Katharine Hepburn is the handsomest boy of the season.

—*New York Herald Tribune,* December 1935

CARY

SANTA MONICA

DECEMBER 1934

Most married couples live alone. A couple is by definition *two.* Cary accepts that. In their new house in Brentwood, he and Virginia live alone as a couple. But the Santa Monica beach house is in both his and Randolph's name. It is Cary's signature address. His mail goes there. He tells her that it's a compromise. He tells Randolph he will never let go of the house. They are also a couple, a two.

Cary and Virginia are arguing again.

"Right now, Randolph pays the bills. All of them! The electricity, the water? Randolph pays it all. I *have* to pay my share." Cary is scrupulous about fairness. And debt. Cary does not permit debt. He will repay Randolph, deducting the percentage of time he has not consumed the utilities.

"He can pay it all!" Virginia says. "You don't live there. You live *here.*" She is exasperated. Why is she explaining what he should already know?

"But it's ours. Mine and his. We have to share the cost."

"Yours and his? Why should anything be yours and his? He is not in this marriage!"

She is wearing the pink nightgown. The one he bought her for their honeymoon. She is in bed, and he is stalling. He knows she is waiting but he is still putting ornaments on the tree. She was furious when she found out there were other ornaments, on *another* tree. He has said he was too tired four nights running. He cannot refuse her again.

How does he tell her that he wants her to touch him this way, love him this way? How does he tell her he wants her to love him like a man?

KATE

BEVERLY HILLS

DECEMBER 1934

She has to tell someone. Her parents pretend it never happened and when Laura calls she is clumsy and alludes to it as though it is a conspiracy binding them together. Anyway, impossible to speak about it on the telephone. The local exchange can listen in. So, she tells Irene. They are sitting on patio chairs in the Selznicks' garden. At first, Irene says nothing. Irene is not the sort of woman to clutter up the air with words that make noise but do not matter, nor does she say things that are obvious.

"And now, are you well? Has it cured you?"

Kate is surprised. She always thinks of what she has lost rather than gained.

"Yes, the organs are gone, so the problem is gone."

Irene nods.

"Aren't you going to ask me about adoption? About that part of life that will never happen?"

"If you're going to adopt, you will adopt. You know the facts. What would I have to offer?"

"You're a mother."

"Yes, and I know how *I* would feel if I were to adopt. But I'm not you." Irene breaks off.

Kate waits, but Irene is quiet.

"You never say any more than you need to," Kate says. "It's marvelous."

"I stammered for years. I was lucky if I could say anything at all." Irene is surprised she has admitted this. She rarely mentions her stammering.

"Is that why you don't mind silence?"

"It is why I don't mind silence."

The two women sit on the patio. It is good to sit and be quiet with someone who knows.

IRENE

BEVERLY HILLS

Good things do not have the staying power of bad things. Bad things have weight and gravity, while good things float up and away.

"I have tried to buy her contract twice!" David shouts from the bathroom, where he is crashing around, knocking things out of the medicine cabinet. "My own brother is one of her agents, all the gossip about her is bad and I *still* can't get her."

She hears the clink of medicine bottles. He will say he is looking for headache tablets but Irene knows he is looking for Benzedrine. He won't find it, because it is gone. She threw it all away yesterday, after she found Jeffrey on the kitchen floor playing with an open Benzedrine inhaler.

"She would be perfect for *Dark Victory*," he says, still rummaging.

"Whose contract?" Irene asks over the noise. She is reading and hasn't been paying attention to what he's shouting.

"Kate Hepburn's, of course," David says. The words are muffled by foaming tooth powder but Irene understands him in the way that longtime couples do.

"The talk about her is bad?"

"Oh, you know, that she's not up to it, that she is sleeping with everyone, that she has a secret baby stashed somewhere—that kind of thing."

Irene turns out the light. She doesn't want to hear what people are saying.

. . .

She is buttering toast when David walks in waving the paper.

"Why doesn't someone talk to Pandro? He can't even manage the press. Did you see what they wrote about her?"

Of course, Irene has seen what they wrote. By now, everyone will have seen.

"They found the husband," David says.

"Ex-husband."

"And they wrote about it! Swine. How can Pandro allow this? How can he make these *blunders*? Kate left the divorce too late."

Irene is relieved. There are worse things they could write.

LELAND

HOLLYWOOD HILLS

JANUARY 1935

This is absurd. His relationship with Kate is many things but it is no longer a love affair. It has been months. Kate has not asked him to stay over once since her divorce in the summer. She has not touched him, not even looked at him properly. And, she clearly does not want him to touch her. Just because she is not with anyone else doesn't mean she is still with him. Leland knows there is something wrong with her. Of course there is, everyone knows. She is not swimming in George's heated pool, not golfing, not even walking much. She is rake thin and she is either shooting a picture or she stays home in that damned house doing God knows what and is always doing that weird stretching.

What was it? What kept her home all that time? Cancer? Good god, venereal disease? It's her father's field—natural that she would be treated at home? Or is it true? Ten months. If he could just marry her, if they could be officially, legally bound, then she would tell him. Whatever it was, he tells himself he would understand.

. . .

He asked again. Seriously, on one knee, with the ring he bought months ago. And she laughed and told him to get up. He feels silly, exposed. They should be closer after her divorce but no, she ignores him. She flinched when he reached to hold her wrist to keep her from stumbling this morning. Hell, most days, when he walks in, she doesn't even ask him to sit down. He has clothes upstairs in the drawers. His toothbrush and tooth powder are still in the bathroom. He has a shoehorn by the door. Weren't they close to marriage? Enough of this. He pours himself a drink and sits down anyway. Is it because the press found the husband and all they do is fire questions at her about goddamn Luddy? Has Kate soured on marriage altogether?

Leland is surprised. Kate has not answered the press, not snapped. No acerbic Hepburn reply. She takes the insult, absorbs it like a punch. Leland doesn't know how to deal with this new undefended Kate.

She's holding a script she is not reading. It's one he asked her to look at, the new George Stevens picture. But she has made no headway since the last time he saw her holding that script a week ago. Is it regret over the divorce? Since becoming a better actress, she's harder to read. Is she thinking of that goddamned rubber husband she can't shake even after she divorced him? Right now, goddamn Luddy is at Fenwick, that family fortress, on a skiing trip with the younger Hepburns; Leland can't keep track of their names. Why doesn't that man get on with his own life? Leland wouldn't hang on like that. When the time comes, he will cut ties and go. But when is that time? With Kate like this, it is impossible to know.

Whenever that time does come, he will have to sever professional ties as well, or at least loosen them. Best to face it. Leland is no longer her agent, not really, and not her fiancé. She never said yes and not saying no is not the same thing. He is something else now, something in between and it won't work. His impulse with Kate is to commit, fully. He decided to become her agent after seeing her for five minutes onstage. He decided to marry her after he watched a scene where she dropped onto a sofa without saying a word. And now, Leland must be her fiancé if he is to stick around. It's why he is such a good airman. He is decisive. He takes pride in his ability to choose. He is angry and maybe even a little out of love with her, but that is not enough for him to let go of her. Leland hates to lose.

Leland's wife, Lola, believes in being decisive too. If she is not a wife in life, she won't be a wife on paper. She filed for divorce. *Again.* And then beat him to Mexico. She is not afraid. This will be the last time.

Leland feels weakened. To have neither of them was the thing he most wanted to avoid. But he knows there is no way back to his marriage. Lola will never believe him again.

. . .

They drive to the studio together from the house on Coldwater Canyon. Kate closes her eyes when he takes a corner on West Jefferson too fast. He bristles. She used to like the danger of riding in his little MG K-type. He had it sent from London. He loves that the steering wheel is on the right.

KATE

RKO STUDIOS

The three men in shirtsleeves are sitting behind typewriters when Kate and Leland come into the RKO press office. It is too hot for jackets. Leland wants to remove his but is afraid he has sweat through his shirt. On the table is a tall stack of papers. They sit down and get to work. Two hours later, there are two stacks: yes and no. Press releases, photography sessions, ribbon cuttings, parties. Her calendar fills. When they finish, Kate is ready to be presented to the town again, officially unmarried. It never happened. She can say that to the reporters and mean it now. But, it's pointless. The press knows it all already, Luddy, the Mexican divorce and maybe even Laura, but Leland says they have been bought off. The scene is rehearsed. Everyone knows their lines. Why go through all of this?

Pandro wants to see them. Kate, Leland and the three-man publicity team file into his big, upstairs office. The one that used to belong to David Selznick.

"No ineligible men," Pandro tells her. "We can't have any skeletons, Kate," he says, looking pointedly at the publicity team who nod in agreement. They understand their job. They will horse trade with the press until Katharine Hepburn is rebuilt as a virginal ingénue.

"Everyone has skeletons," Kate answers, folding her hands together in her lap.

Good god. Why say that to a studio head? Does she care if her career goes away? Yes. Yes, she does. She will never have a family. She must build a life of something. Time to get on with it.

HOWARD

MINES FIELD AIRPORT

FEBRUARY 1935

Howard is flying. And thinking. He has seen her again; she was at the airfield last week with that agent, Leland Hayward. Hayward is a good pilot but too small and neat for Howard to really trust him as an airman. Howard watched as Leland handed Kate her helmet and goggles. No one helped her into the plane. She climbed up herself.

Howard banks low, checking the gauges automatically. When it is a time trial or he is testing new equipment, his attention narrows, closing in on the problem like a microscope. Today, Howard is flying, to not be on the ground. He wants to meet her. He decides that the first time was just rehearsal. It was not memorable. It was too loud in the Mocambo and even though she is tall, he couldn't hear her. He is always at a disadvantage when the room is loud. She would not accept a drink and refused to sit at his table. She left with George Cukor, a man who owes him nothing. Cary knows her but says she is not interested and advises Howard not to pursue. Cary is a man who doesn't lie, embellish or ever tell Howard what he wants to hear, but Howard is a man who ignores what he doesn't want to hear.

The next time he meets Kate must be accidental, important and casual all at once. He has been tracking her press: the secret husband, the Mexican divorce, the mystery disappearance. There are rumors that she had a love affair, a nervous breakdown, a child. Howard believes none of it but is pleased that she is less popular than she was the first time they met. It makes it easier for him; like stalking an animal that has been wounded. He checks the gauges on the board, looks at the levels again and makes automatic adjustments. He could ask Noah to arrange a meeting, but that would cheapen the evening, and he wants this next moment of collision to hold its value. Anyway, Noah can do many things but Howard does not trust him to outmaneuver a woman like Kate Hepburn.

LELAND

HOLLYWOOD HILLS

He has reached the moment he knew was coming. When he dropped her home after flying, she hardly looked at him. What has happened to her? He can't ask her again. Leland is tired of chasing, of waiting. He is ready to be happy, partnered. Enough. Leland decides he will invite that young actress, Margaret Sullavan, to dinner. She has a pixie delicacy and an irritating voice but she will be a distraction from Kate.

LOS ANGELES

FEBRUARY 1935

Sometimes the wrong people end up in a room together. George Cukor wasn't to know that back in New York, Cary used to sleep with the new head costume designer at Warner Bros. He wasn't to know that Cary and his wife have not spoken in nine days. He wasn't to know that Randolph and Orry Kelly have never met.

Randolph can speak to anyone. He is known for it. Hostesses

put him next to their most awkward guests because he can always find something to talk about, some common interest. Sitting at George's table, between Kate Hepburn and Tallulah, Randolph has run out of things to say. He is aware of Cary at the other end of the table. Randolph watches as Orry Kelly pours just the right amount of milk for Cary's coffee. In the mornings, Cary drinks it black but in the evenings, he likes a splash of milk.

"His ex?" Kate asks, apropos of nothing.

"You can tell?"

"Your face gives it away."

"I'm usually better at hiding it."

Across the table, Cary's wife is watching Randolph watch Cary. Like Kate, Virginia can recognize possession.

After dinner Orry finds Randolph in the garden, offers him a cigarette.

"She's gone home," he says, as if they were already in the midst of a conversation.

"She?" He knows exactly who he's referring to. Randolph accepts the cigarette. Smoking helps when he is nervous. He came outside to avoid this man his lover loved.

"Yes, *she*. The wife."

"Virginia."

"Yes, Virginia. Mrs. Grant. Not that I think she'll be Mrs. Grant for long."

Randolph is uncomfortable. He doesn't want to discuss Cary. Not with this man.

"The position is already filled, you see," Orry continues.

"What position?"

"Of being Mrs. Grant, the person who loves Mr. Grant."

"I do love him."

"Yes, and he loves you."

And then Randolph sees it. This man is being kind. He understands better than anyone in the world what it is to be in love with Cary Grant.

KATE

HOLLYWOOD HILLS

APRIL 1935

Kate has rolled the script up into her bag. George Cukor has not been offered director, but she needs to know what he thinks. She has finally finished the script. It has brought her a feeling of purpose, of doing. This character, this *Alice*, she is someone Kate can understand, she is someone who has lost everything. It is a grown-up part, more than Jo in *Little Women*, more than Eva Lovelace in *Morning Glory*. She knows she is ready to do this part well. A different George, George Stevens, will direct and already Kate dislikes him. Is it because he is the wrong George? Maybe. Some people tell her this picture will ruin her career; some say the opposite. Kate doesn't trust her judgment anymore. Not that the studio gives her much choice in her movies anyway. She needs to ask someone she does trust.

. . .

"Hallo, Gor-udge!" Kate calls, marching up the walk. This is what she does when she arrives at Cordell Drive now. Fair warning to anyone lurking within. She is hungry and goes round to the kitchen entrance. Opening the cupboards, she finds flour, chocolate and sugar. She opens the icebox for milk and butter. It is a good day for brownies.

"You've turned the oven on?" George asks, swinging through the door from the formal dining room. "It's blazing today. After my next hit, I am going to get one of those air coolers that Irene has in her bedroom."

Everything in this town happens after the next hit.

"David had one at RKO," Kate says, rooting in the drawer for a wooden spoon. "I don't think Pandro knows how to turn it on."

"Poor Pandro," George says. Pandro is that rare man who can produce flops and remain likable. "Is this it?" George asks, taking the roll of script out of Kate's bag. "*Alice Adams*. Titles like that never work."

"You are only saying that because George Stevens is directing and not you. The brownies will be ready in forty minutes. Read."

While he reads, she dips her legs in the pool. She is not ready to swim, not yet, but loves the cradling give of water. She could swim, not naked, as she used to, but in a bathing suit, no one would know. George wouldn't ask but he would notice and worry. She never wears a suit in his pool. Better to wait. The scar has faded to pale red and will go white sometime next year. Kate still gets dressed in the dark.

GEORGE

HOLLYWOOD HILLS

The brownies are too cooked but will soften with ice cream. They eat them on the terrace under a striped awning. He reads quickly and closely but he knows from her opening entrance on page six that it's good. Good words, good characters, good story. He is annoyed he was not asked to direct. And the last scene. It is extraordinary.

"Do it," George says, pulling his hat lower. Even at five o'clock, the sun is still strong.

"She is the right part for me, isn't she?" Kate asks. "Alice."

George doesn't ask why she has come to him about this role rather than Leland. He has heard the rumors and is glad it has ended between them. Leland likes the parts of Kate that he likes, loves even, but not the whole of her. George hopes the breakup will stick. Kate is changed since she came back. George does not pry. He trusts her to tell him whatever she wants to tell him, when she wants to tell him. He knows she cherishes that trust and he will not break it. But she is so thin, and she is not swimming.

"Yes, she is right for you." He loves the way Kate talks about her characters as though they are women you might take dancing. "Alice is lovable," George says, "and you can *make* her real, that is what matters. Do it."

"I will." Kate speaks with confidence. She sees it, then. She recognizes to play Alice will take guts. George squeezes her hand for courage.

. . .

John Ford calls George again. He could call her agent but he hears that Kate Hepburn and Cukor are inseparable.

"She is going to play Alice Adams. That's *five,* George. Hayward said she was booked for four."

"She *was* booked for four but then some things had to get moved around." Kate has not told George why she was gone for so long but she has almost told him.

"Mexico, I heard. I don't care about the gossip. I want her in my picture."

"Which picture?" George can't remember what Ford is about to shoot.

"Any picture. I'll build it around her."

George gives him Myron Selznick's number. He knows Leland is not handling her bookings now.

HOWARD
MINES FIELD AIRPORT
MAY 1935

"She is about to start filming *Alice Adams* over at RKO," Cary says, closing the car door. They are back at the airfield. "End of this month. But you already knew that, didn't you?"

Howard doesn't answer. Yes, he already knew that. He was only asking so that he could feel the sensation of her name in his mouth. Sometimes, he shouts her name into the blue air when he is flying alone. He has had other love affairs recently, and the long end of his romance with Billie Dove has been in the papers but things that are ending don't hold his attention. Beginnings interest him. And Kate is not like anyone else; he is sure they could have more than a beginning. Each time they have spoken, her directness made him feel calm, safe.

"I have been thinking I should buy RKO," Howard says. He hasn't been thinking about it at all until this moment but now he's said it, it sounds like a sensible idea. "Pandro Berman is making a hash of it over there and I'm sure they are in the red. I could pick it up cheap."

"You aren't allowed to make pictures right now," Cary says. "Wasn't that in your divorce settlement? Anyway, there are easier ways to talk to Kate." Sometimes, Cary is still thrown by the sheer scale of Howard's wealth. Howard thinks of buying a studio or plane or company the way Cary thinks about buying shoes. Cary looks down. His shoes are handmade now. Italian. It is not enough.

"True. That is my newest, there." Howard points at a sleek silver-blue plane. "I am calling it, *The Racer.* H-1 for short. The new flush-to-the-skin rivets reduce air resistance and the covered monocoque with stressed outer sheeting shaved twenty-six minutes off my flight time coast to coast." He turns to see if Cary looks impressed. He knows it would be better if he could look surreptitiously, but Howard is not like that. Anyway, he needs to see people's lips move to understand them. There is no point in subtlety. But Howard is not really here to talk about aircraft. "Who else is in this picture with her?"

"This is the one with the hydraulic landing equipment?" Cary asks, reaching up to touch the nose of the plane. "It tucks up?"

Howard likes that Cary asks good questions. Some men talk just for the sake of furnishing the silence, taking up space. Cary doesn't do that. "Yes, we lift the wheels eight minutes after taking off, and they sit here." He points to the underside of the aircraft. "All planes will do it eventually. Stupid not to. The air-drag on all that machinery hanging down is just not worth it."

"H-1. *H* for Hughes?"

"*H* for Hughes." Howard turns away from the plane. "Are you going to tell me?"

"Tell you who is in the picture with her?" Cary understands his friend. Howard doesn't let things go. He is binary; there is no gray. "No one is in it with her. No one who matters anyway."

"Fred MacMurray matters," Howard says. He has already asked around and has the cast list on a sheet of mint green paper on his desk.

"Yes, but not to Kate. Fred's engaged to be married next year." Cary is not surprised that he already knows the cast list. He appreciates Howard's thoroughness.

KATE

RKO STUDIOS

Leland is not there on the first day of filming. She knew he wouldn't be but she is still surprised. He does not sit in on the table read as he usually does and there are no flowers sent to her dressing room. It hurts. She can't say it doesn't. But, not like the other hurt, the one pressing against the buttons of her trousers. Leland is a cozy habit she has to give up. What Leland said is right, isn't it? They had to move forward or back. They could not stay where they were.

And now, they are somewhere new. She has used him; she knows that, and he knows too; it makes her insides tilt and churn to think of it. It is not that she dislikes herself for behaving badly, but she cannot bear the feeling of being caught out. She hadn't expected him to hold her accountable for her poor conduct, or to be decisive and really leave her. Years of slack from Laura and Luddy have made her lazy. She works to ignore the desire to call him, to try to hook him back to her, and disrupt his new life. She does not want him to have a new life. She wants him to be here in his old life, at the table read, sending flowers to her dressing room, missing her, wanting her. Starting a film without him makes her feel small and she hates that feeling.

Worse, now he can no longer help steer her career. Myron, always in the background before, will be her agent now. But Myron is less comfortable, less reassuring. He doesn't send flowers on a first day nor sit in on the table reads. His job is not to make her feel safe in the world, only to make her safe on paper. Myron gambles with her career in private, his job is not to protect her, only to protect what she can earn. Myron does not ride out ahead of her to check the road for bandits.

No. Leland helped her this far and that has to be enough. And she should follow his advice even now they are over. Laura and Luddy. Leland was right; they are people she cannot afford to lean on anymore. Kate knows there's no room for them now if she is going to live in this more scrutinized town. And the end of this thing with Leland did not cause scandal. Leland left her life without an argument or even a discussion. He had the telephone company disconnect the telephone by the bed while she was at the studio and slipped her key through her letterbox. That surprised her. Why wasn't he heartbroken? Leland proposed, didn't he? Or did he just talk about proposing? She cannot really remember. Aren't they the same thing?

Now Leland has met Margaret Sullavan and Kate has heard he's happy. Kate watches their love affair unfold, wishing it would stop, come to a fiery public end. It's not envy that propels her but something else; something even less honorable. She doesn't want him but she still wants him to want her. It is petty and wrong and she will not admit it to anyone. Leland has found something real and he is moving forward to grab it; she recognizes his quick surety. Kate has forgotten how to love like that.

LOS ANGELES
MAY 1935

Everyone says Katharine Hepburn is leaving Leland Hayward. They are wrong. He left her weeks ago. Kind of him to let the story stand, to play the jilted lover. Maybe it's financial. She is still on the books of his agency and studios pay less for jilted lovers. They are downgraded goods.

So Leland Hayward has found someone new. He has, and yes, it is something real, but soon the talk will move on and the town will look away. Happiness is uninteresting unless it is contrasted with unhappiness. The *have* is only compelling because there is also the *have not*. Now they are watching Kate. It is her turn to find someone. And she is looking, every day, sizing people up. She will not be alone when Leland is happy. She is competitive that way.

Why does Kate invite her? There have been other people, other women, other men, since Laura. You don't need to haul someone in from the East Coast to not be alone. It's something smaller, meaner but more understandably human. You know what it is. We have all done it.

LAURA

THE BEVERLY HILLS HOTEL

AUGUST 1935

She could have stayed home. Luddy stayed home. Why does she still compare herself to him? He still lives in that apartment behind her Manhattan house, he still spends weekends at Fenwick, and he is her *ex*-husband. Pathetic. She shouldn't have come, or at least, not so easily. She should have said no, hedged, made Kate ask her again. She could have just read about it all in *Screen Time*. Why did she travel all the way out here? Because Kate asked and that faint tug on the air between them was enough to pull her to this lightweight, salt dry coast. But, she will not share a house with Kate. Not now, when she doesn't know if Leland still sleeps there. The columns say he is happy dating that Margaret Sullavan, the one with the irritating voice. But papers get it wrong and anyway, if he is happy with someone else, Kate will certainly try to yank him back to her. Laura understands this woman she loves.

Laura checks into the pink hotel with the white sugar writing and ice blue pool. She has reserved a bungalow. They are homier. Randolph and Cary keep the next bungalow over. The Beverly Hills Hotel understands that sometimes, a movie star cannot go home to his wife.

. . .

A fourth night in the bungalow. Laura has hung her dresses in the closet and knows the bellmen by name. If Kate asks her, Laura will move back to the house. Cary says that Leland is not staying there. Leland and Lola have divorced for the second time and she has heard that Leland is seen all over town with Margaret Sullavan. Kate says Leland is ready to stop looking.

The premiere. Laura sprays scent on her wrist and smooths down her dress. Cream, cinched at the waist with a narrow black belt, very modern, very East Coast. She bought it at Bendel's in New York. She wants to stand out against the starlets.

. . .

She's not sure what she was expecting, but not this painful delicacy. *Alice Adams* is a good film and that director pulled something raw and alive from Kate. The scene that everyone said Kate railed against, the one where she had to face the window and cry, was perfect. Cary has told her that Kate wanted to do the scene differently and argued with the director in front of the cast and crew, but he wouldn't back down. Laura knows that losing a public battle is exactly what would make Kate able to cry. It would make the scene real for her. The director called for the scene to be shot again with the shock of the argument still ringing on the set, and it worked.

Cary tells Laura she's right. That is the take they used. "Quickly," the director had said under his breath to the photographer. He caught it on film—Kate humiliated. Kate called Laura after the scene. That's when Kate asked her to come out to Los Angeles for the opening.

. . .

"That blasted scene." Kate lays her head down in Laura's lap; Laura begins kneading the spot in Kate's shoulder that gives her trouble, instinctively seeking to comfort Kate's body. "It was a good scene and I was wrong."

"You wanted to cry on the bed?"

"I wanted to sob with my face stuffed into the goddamn pillow, and he said no. He saw it differently. No noisy weeping, just silent tears in front of a window."

"It's beautiful," Laura says, still massaging Kate's shoulder.

"There was a showdown in front of everyone and I lost. As I should have; I was plain wrong. Best to just say it, but my god did he let me have it."

"You hate being wrong, but you hate being in a bad picture more." Laura traces the bones of Kate's skull. Who else has touched Kate's face since she's been gone? Who has slept next to her, kissed her, bought her presents, made her toast, driven up the coast sitting in her passenger seat? Whose bathing suit hangs in the pool house and shoes are in the mudroom?

"Is that who they want me to be?" Kate asks. She has not moved her head from Laura's lap.

"Who wants you to be whom?"

"Them, out there, is that the person they want me to be? Fragile, sniveling and weeping in the rain by a window and then rescued by a rich man?"

"The scene was more than that," Laura says. She worries if Kate gets agitated, she will get up and start pacing and this moment will end.

"I won't do that again. I need more punch and grist." Kate does not get up and pace but tucks her head deeper into Laura.

"They like seeing you feel," Laura says, touching the knobbly bone at the base of Kate's neck. She knows this bone. It is where Kate's spine begins its long march down the body Laura loves.

"I always feel," Kate says, stiffening.

"Of course, *you* feel, but you don't break open onscreen." Or offscreen anymore, really, Laura wants to add but doesn't. This moment is delicate. "They want to see that you're like them?"

"They want to see me fall, you mean?" Kate says, ducking away from Laura and unfolding her long body. "And I won't."

. . .

Laura remembers it all. There is a board in the upstairs hallway in the Coldwater Canyon house that yawns when you step on it. Halfway down the upstairs hallway, near the door to Laura's room. That soft groan of out of joint wood would wake her instantly. Laura hears it as Kate returned to the bed with a tray of sandwiches and milk. Kate's kisses are hard; her mouth bruises, the way it used to. She is unapologetic, the way she was before they ever came west. Laura's jawbone will be sore tomorrow. It's the price of doing business, Kate used to say, before they left New York. Laura hated when the soreness wore off.

Tonight, Kate asks Laura to "keep her eyes open while they fuck." Laura shivers when Kate uses this pungent word. She asks Kate to say it to her again.

"Why fumble around with your eyes shut?" Kate says instead. "Why pretend it's not happening? If you are going to do it, get on with it."

Laura remembers the way it felt in the bed on Fifth Avenue. Laura knew Kate wanted to consume her, use her up. In those weeks, Kate would have eaten Laura whole, bones and teeth if she could. Laura remembers the nights when it was the two of them, alone in the world, on the wide, rumpled bed. There was tenderness and a delicate truth that bloomed like blown glass. They would stay on the bed, their bare feet dusting the floor. Until they got hungry and Laura made them cheese sandwiches. They ate them together on the white sheets.

. . .

She wishes they were staying home, together, alone. She had suggested they light the fire and play backgammon but Kate only laughed. Kate takes these press parties seriously now. Laura is glad she bought the dress. Dark green satin and cut just low enough in the back with a high curved waist that flatters her figure. Laura can hear Kate's shower running down the hall. They have reverted to the old language of the house. Kate's room, Laura's room, their bed. Kate has not asked her to move back in but neither of them has spoken of Laura leaving. Laura is hopeful. She waits until the last moment before putting on the dress. She does not want it to wrinkle.

. . .

How can she have been so stupid. She'd drunk too much last night. Drinking has become a habit since she left Los Angeles, since before she left Los Angeles, if she is honest. She hadn't planned it. It had just happened. It was loud and the nobody reporter from the nobody paper asked who she was for the third time. It just slipped out. It *did* just slip out, didn't it? Lying has also become a habit since she left Los Angeles. She didn't know the nobody would tell Louella Parsons. Did she?

KATE

THE BEVERLY HILLS HOTEL

It's a twenty-seven-minute drive. The new traffic lights make everything take longer. Kate is furious. The column in the paper this morning. Leland was right. Cary was right. Everyone was right. She should never have let her come back. "Husband." Laura is not her *husband* and how dare she tell the press she is. Kate had not understood before. If she is bigger; Laura is smaller. And Laura was not raised to be smaller. Kate will give nothing away, and she will be more careful in future. She just needs to get Laura away from her, fast, with minimum melodrama.

Kate will not be near anyone who wants her to be smaller. Her work is who she is now.

LAURA

THE BEVERLY HILLS HOTEL

They sit in the automobile without speaking. Kate is dropping her back at the hotel, where Laura will *not* make a scene. It is Sunday, Louis Prysing's day off. Kate is scrupulous about respecting her staff's time. Laura sits up straight, clenching her toes inside her court shoes. There will be no kiss, no pretense at the end this time. Kate will not even cut the engine. They will leave each other with the motor running.

Laura will not ask Kate to come and see her off at the train platform in Pasadena tomorrow. That part of them is over for now. Laura will go back to New York and wait; she is used to waiting. Laura watches Kate's hawkish profile. The cords are standing out on her long neck. Kate is usually so careful to relax her neck and hide that infrastructure. This cannot be the end. It's never the end with them, not if Laura waits long enough. Something will happen. She is sure Kate will do something terrible eventually, some public blunder, and then she will need Laura again. Laura no longer bothers to lie to herself and pretend she is finished with Kate Hepburn.

LELAND

THE BEVERLY HILLS HOTEL

He sees Laura standing in the drive of the hotel. The porters are tripping over themselves to get to her. Laura tips well. Was that Kate dropping her off? She must be in a hurry to get somewhere to leave Laura in the roadway like that. Leland trains his brain to not ask itself where Kate is hurrying off to. Laura, *again*. He warned Kate she would fumble and say something stupid, and now, she has. Of course she has. "Husband," good God. It was in Louella's column this morning. There will be no stopping the rumors now. Not his problem. But Kate is still at his agency. Isn't he partially responsible? No, he has handed her off to Myron. Good luck to him. Like everyone else in the country, stars are disposable now. The public is no longer in the mood for Hollywood's problems.

Kate doesn't protect herself, does not watch where she is going, never has. She just thunders off in a direction until she rams into something tougher than her. It is hard for Leland to break the habit of watching out for her. He goes inside to find Margaret.

KATE

BEVERLY HILLS

Kate does not look in the rearview mirror. She does not want to see Laura watching the car pull away. It will just annoy her. Kate is agitated, irritated. Leland was right; Laura does not want real success for Kate. How could she when she'd go and say something like that? "Husband." Even Luddy never used that word until he was her *ex*-husband. She wants to call Leland, just to tell him he was right, but that is not really why she would be calling. She can't quite believe that lie. She would be calling to try to tug him back into her orbit and away from goddamn Margaret Sullavan, of course she would. Not forever, just for now when she feels let down, when she wants someone familiar.

She doesn't ring him. She will not like herself tomorrow if she does.

When the mind is restless, tire the body. Something her family believes. Kate means to play golf or tennis every day until her new picture starts shooting. She has not moved her body enough since last year. Being gaunt and wan worked for *Alice Adams* but it won't work for her next picture, and she wants this next picture to be a smash.

After the success of *Alice Adams*, Pandro says he trusts her and will let her make what she likes. He says she has earned it. Fine. *Alice Adams* was an uncomfortable film to make. She felt raw, exposed in that last scene. For the premiere, she stayed in her seat until the lights dimmed and then slipped out to the lobby of the theater. She could not watch herself in that role. Now, she can make what she likes, with whom she likes. George has told her that the director John Ford wants her but she puts off telephoning him. She wants to shoot the script George found, called *Sylvia Scarlett.* It's a big part. George wants her and says he is casting the male lead now. She is sure this picture will keep her on top. She will spend most of the picture playing a woman who is playing a man. Good. She is not much of a woman anymore anyway.

GEORGE

HOLLYWOOD HILLS

Yes. They are a solid pair. He wanted to be sure before he asked Paramount for Cary. It will be a quick shoot but the dialogue in this picture goes like lightning. He needs believable leads. George is pleased. He sits back on his sun lounger as the two of them sit forward and discuss politics. George has seen Cary and Kate speak together at dinner parties at the Selznicks' and here at Cordell Drive but that is not the same as seeing them get along in broad daylight with no music and champagne. But George was right, they work. Clickity-clack. The conversation snaps back and forth: European politics, sea sickness, exercise, the studio system. These two can talk about anything.

"And Myron Selznick is your agent now?" Cary asks.

"It was too awkward with Leland," Kate says. George is surprised she refers to their relationship. Usually, she avoids it. "How much longer on your deal with Paramount?"

"One more year."

"And then? Will you renew?"

"Oh, I'm sure I will."

It's the "oh" that gives him away. The three of them laugh, really laugh, at all that does not need to be said. Because Kate and George understand immediately. Cary Grant has decided to become a free agent.

LELAND

HOLLYWOOD

SEPTEMBER 1935

"How could you let her make this picture?" Leland is trying not to yell. Myron doesn't like it. Kate is his client now. "You could have just said no."

Myron doesn't bother answering. Leland knows better than anyone that saying no to Kate Hepburn is not always possible.

Leland closes his office door. He should never have seen the memo. Kate is not his client. But it was addressed to both of them.

"RKO wants to know why we are refusing the commission," Leland says. "I did not know we *were* refusing the commission on this picture. The script is that awful?"

Myron hasn't told him, not about the commission nor the script.

Myron tries to mention Kate Hepburn to Leland as little as possible.

"They have called twice today and want to know why," Myron says, not answering Leland's question.

"Pandro wants to know or RKO wants to know?" Leland asks.

"Their lawyers," Myron says, sitting down heavily. "I took our names off the contract entirely."

Leland is surprised. It is a drastic move. "Does she know you did that?"

"She will if she reads the contract."

"So, she negotiated the terms herself?"

"Nothing to negotiate. Private deal with Pandro," Myron says. "For a studio head, he is a terrible negotiator. He met her new quote, standard concessions."

"Have *you* read the contract?" Leland asks.

"I heard. And yes. The script is *problematic*. She is dressed as a man for most of the picture."

"A wig or . . . ?" Leland leaves the sentence hanging.

"Kate wants to do it. George says they will wait and cut it once her early scenes are wrapped." Myron hands Leland the shooting schedule from RKO. "George thinks it will be like when she cut off her hair for *Little Women*."

"It won't."

KATE

HOLLYWOOD HILLS

"We need the audience to love this picture, for it to carry them through to a *big* feeling," Kate says. "Comedy or tragedy, it doesn't matter as long as they get to a big feeling; nothing forgettable."

She has used that phrase several times. A big feeling. She is sure Cary and George know what she means. They are sitting in the shade on George's terrace, drinking lemonade and talking about the script.

"Exactly," George says. "Something *bold*, well made. When money is this tight, an audience doesn't need to spend their pennies on anything mediocre."

"Yes," says Kate. "Bold, *provocative*."

"Are bold and provocative the same thing?" Cary asks.

"Of course, they are," Kate says without really considering it. "How can something be bold if it doesn't also make you think? What would be the point in that?"

CARY

SANTA MONICA

Cary is crying. But only because he thinks he should be. He is performing, even though no one is watching. He goes to the mirror to watch his eyes fill up and spill over, watching makes it more real. It counts more if it's real, doesn't it?

"You've called her four times already, Cary. Clearly, Virginia does not wish to answer the telephone," Randolph says with a pen in his mouth. Randolph always does the Sunday crossword with a pen. Cary does it in pencil.

"Why doesn't her mother pick up?" Cary asks. "She doesn't know it's me?"

"Every time you fight, Virginia goes to her mother's. I am *sure* she knows it's you."

"This is more than a fight."

LOS ANGELES
OCTOBER 1935

She does it the day they finish the early scenes, the ones where she is a woman, playing a woman. Doesn't tell anyone she's going, not even George. Walks right into the Grand Prix Barbershop on North Vine just before closing and asks for Clark Gable's cut. Longer on top, waved over and short on the sides, plenty of Brylcreem. The shop is empty. The barber hesitates and then cuts. When she is gone he sweeps the long red strands from the floor and throws them away.

HOWARD
TRANCAS BEACH, CALIFORNIA

Howard Hughes lands his plane on a strip of wild beach, in the middle of the take. The cinematographer is so surprised when he sees the aircraft cross the shot he forgets to stop the film. An expensive mistake. As promised, Howard has come to visit Cary Grant.

The day Cary first told Howard about the picture, Cary called his part, "dynamic and exciting," but Howard doesn't remember if he described the plot. They were with Randolph, on the back deck at the beach house when Cary told Howard he had accepted the part. "This picture is something fresh and *new*; smugglers and artists—bold doers who are *doing* something rather than waiting for something to be done *to* them, but it's a risky script."

Howard only cared that Katharine Hepburn would star. He was pleased Cary would be the other lead. Nothing to worry about with Cary. And with Cary in the cast, Howard would have an excuse to see her.

"And you are sure they'll make it? George has a budget approved?" Howard still thinks like a director even though he has had to stop directing, but Howard is more interested in flying these days anyway.

Cary was certain the picture would go ahead. "Yes," he said, "he has a good budget, and it's fully cast. I was the last principal to sign on."

Howard likes that Cary is smart, he pushes hard for good roles with good contracts. Howard is the one who suggested that Cary insist on wardrobe approval and the right to use his own tailor. Howard hates the idea of wearing someone else's clothes.

Cary likes the way that Howard roots for Kate even though he doesn't know her yet. Howard thinks that onscreen she is magnificent and he wants the world to agree with him. Randolph hopes Howard would feel the same way if he was sleeping with Kate Hepburn.

"Pandro Berman is no dummy," Howard said, pulling his chair into the shade. "After the money *Alice Adams* made, RKO ought to give her a blank check and let her make whatever she wants."

"Oh, oh no," Cary said, "George Cukor had to fight the studio to get this script approved."

"*Alice Adams* is going to win everything this year; it's going to clean up," Howard said. "Best Picture, Best Director, Best *Actress*, the works."

"Yes, *Alice Adams* is a hit. Lucky, as no one can afford a flop these days," Cary said.

"As a director, I think I could have survived any flop," Howard said.

"Howard, the country is broke," Randolph said. "People get angry if they pay their money to see a bad picture. These things matter more now."

"This film will work," Cary said. "It has to."

KATE

TRANCAS BEACH, CALIFORNIA

By the time Howard Hughes lands his plane in the middle of the shot, Kate is already in a foul mood. George Cukor and the whole of the cast and crew have come up here to shoot *Sylvia Scarlett,* they are three scenes in and the crew isn't laughing, not even on the first take. And this morning, George told her that Leland and Myron are refusing to take a percentage of her fee on this picture.

"But you are my agent?" Kate says, when she telephones Myron's office.

"Not for this picture."

She doesn't telephone Leland.

Kate is livid when she sees that it is Howard Hughes who is piloting this incongruous airplane. All morning, Kate has been looking for a reason to be furious. Now she has one. George Cukor is too surprised to be angry and calls for the crew to break for lunch.

Only Cary and George know that it's not just that Myron and Leland took their names off the contract and refused the fee. Kate is rattled by the photo spread that ran in *Modern Screen* today. Photographs of Leland and Margaret Sullavan walking together on the Santa Monica pier, holding ice cream cones, shielding their eyes from the sun. They look happy, the photographs seem unforced. *Engaged*? the headline reads.

CARY

TRANCAS BEACH, CALIFORNIA

Cary tries to wave Howard off, shouting that he needs to park his great big plane elsewhere. Howard cannot hear him. Cary knows

Howard thinks the sound of an airplane engine is beautiful, powerful, but Cary wishes he would turn it off. When Howard finally cuts the motor and climbs out of the egg-shaped cockpit, he is faced with a clutch of angry film crew. Cary can see that Howard is hurt but is trying to hide it. Cary watches, wishing he could pull Howard aside and explain. It's not him, it is not even the interruption or the plane. It is just the wrong day.

As promised, Howard has flown his newest, fastest plane to impress Kate. He has not considered how noisy it will be. But then, Howard is half deaf and so noise is different for him. Cary waits for him on the ground, Kate stands beside him, dressed in a man's suit. It is good material, tailored beautifully. Her short hair sharpens her features. Long hair seems silly on her now. Howard jumps down.

Cary steers Howard away from Kate, away from the crowd, toward the dunes.

"Wait," Cary says before Howard can speak. Howard has trouble gauging volume, and Cary does not want to be overheard.

"You *said* you would help me meet her again," Howard says.

"I said I would help you meet her again *soon*. Not *now*."

"Why not now?"

"Howard, we talked about helping you meet her again, but I assumed you meant *after* this picture. When the filming is done." Cary waves at the cameras dotted around the silver plane like tent pegs. "Does this look done?"

Kate, George and the film crew are now sitting on the picnic blankets spread over the sand on the other side of the plane that Howard refuses to move. They are eating sandwiches wrapped in checkered paper. Can they hear?

"You did not specify *not now*," Howard says. "Anyway, I am here, she is here, so why *not* now?" He lowers his voice. "What? Too loud?"

"No, you are not too loud." Howard never refers to his deafness and it is only recently that Cary has realized how often Howard is reading lips. Cary is moved that Howard would mention it. Cary sits on the slope of sand dune. Howard drops down beside him.

Cary tries again, gentler. "Howard, it is the wrong time because we were filming a scene. And you have parked a bloody great plane in the middle of the shot? How would you have felt if someone landed a plane on your set when you were directing?"

"My film was about . . ."

"Yes. About airplanes. People landed planes on your set all day long." Cary understands that Howard is not being funny or even difficult, just literal.

"This is not the easiest shoot and Kate was in the middle of a good take. She is annoyed and it does *not* look as though she wants to talk to you now." Cary doesn't explain the photo spread. There is no whispering with Howard and Cary knows Kate would not want him shouting about that. "At least move the plane and then we can talk."

HOWARD

TRANCAS BEACH, CALIFORNIA

Howard watches her film all day. He watches her as he would if he were directing the scenes himself. He sees her snap from Kate, focused, diligent actress, concentrating on her upcoming scene, into a cagey street boy from another era and then, when George calls cut, she switches back again. He watches the set of her teeth, her long neck and loose stride; her lean geometry. He sees that the boy is crouching there when she plays the woman and the woman is there in the light grace when she plays the boy. He sees that she has rolled up a sock and stuffed it down her trousers. It only makes him like her more.

"Explain the plot once more?" Howard asks Cary before he climbs back into his plane. He is stalling and does not want to leave without talking to her.

Cary goes through it again but gets knotted up in the chronology of the storyline and gives up. He says that *Sylvia Scarlett* is hard to explain. Howard asks for a copy of the script so he can read it himself. Really, he wants to read the lines she is learning by heart.

"Maybe if I fly back up next week?" Howard says. "I'll park down the coast and drive up?" The idea of not knowing the next time he will see her bothers him more than he'd realized. And there is something compelling, addictive about being on a film set. The togetherness, the made-up, thrown together feeling of family. He's missed it. He also has a few ideas about George's wide shots. They're too loose and he's not waiting for the right sky.

CARY

SANTA MONICA

They are sitting on the back porch, looking at the sea. Randolph brings out thick wool blankets to pull over their knees.

"She *will* meet you again but not now." Cary knows that some things have to be spelled out for Howard.

"But it *was* romantic," Howard says. "That is categorical. Irrefutable."

"I am refuting it," Cary says.

"I flew my most beautiful plane," Howard says, as if that wins the argument.

"Wait until the filming is done and then show her your beautiful plane." Cary says. "Timing is everything in romance, and sometimes, even good timing is not enough to save it."

Some things Howard understands immediately. Howard reaches out to squeeze his friend's shoulder. It is rare that Howard touches other men. He knows it's over between Cary and Virginia. He's heard that she has already been out with one of the studio heads over at MGM.

"Divorce. My god, I hated it," Howard says simply.

"Yes," Cary agrees. "I hate it." What else is there to say?

HOWARD

BEL-AIR COUNTRY CLUB

Howard disregards Cary's advice and tries to see her again. A week later she is golfing on her day off and he pulls the same trick. He lands his plane right on the fairway. She ignores him and plays through. He admires her for it. Billie would have shrieked if an airplane landed near her but Kate just kept lining up her shot. The golf club management is furious and the plane has to be disassembled and carted off to the nearest airfield. The golf club sends a bill for resodding the lawn. When it arrives Howard hands it to Noah without opening it.

CARY

SANTA MONICA

"And she didn't say anything?" Randolph asks.

"Nothing. Pointedly, she said nothing."

"That sounds like Kate," Randolph says.

"Does it?" Howard asks.

Cary forgets. Howard has *seen* Kate often but has hardly spoken to her. How like Howard to be so decisive on the back of so little. When he says this to Randolph later, Randolph doesn't answer, waiting for Cary to hear himself. It's not only Howard who makes enormous decisions based on slender instinct.

"Landing your big, noisy plane in the middle of her day a *second* time? Kate would ignore you on principle for that," Cary says. He has seen Howard pursue women before and he has never seen him fail. But he knows Kate, and pressure makes her angry.

"It was the H-1 Racer."

"Why did you think it would be different this time?" Cary asks him, shifting his chair to block the sun for Randolph. They are sitting together on the deck at the Santa Monica house. Cary and Randolph have fallen back into the ease of the long-married. That Cary's divorce is dragging on is not something they discuss.

"She wasn't working," Howard says. "I wasn't inconveniencing anyone. And your film is almost wrapped?"

"Most likely you were inconveniencing everyone and almost wrapped is not wrapped," Cary says.

"And wrapped is definitely not released," Randolph says.

"She is jittery about this one," Cary says, closing his eyes against the sun. "Give her room."

"She may be right to be jittery about this one," Howard says. It's true. The talk around town is not good. But the talk can be wrong? Howard is not critical, only concerned. He does not want this woman to fail.

"This script *is* a risk," Cary says. But it's not his risk. He knows he is safe. His lines are good. His role is good—clean and legible, and he is good in it. Cary has learned how to choose well.

"She makes a beautiful boy," Howard says.

"She is a beautiful boy," Randolph says.

"Yes," Howard says. "I will wait."

KATE

COLDWATER CANYON

NOVEMBER 1935

Is she pretending? Are they *all* pretending the picture is good?

"They'll laugh when they see the *whole* film," George reassures her. "Right now, there is no *context*."

But they don't. They do not laugh at all.

. . .

George calls her the morning after the test screening. The studio is recutting the ending and trimming the middle but he already knows it won't help.

"And they are releasing it after Christmas?" Kate says. Smaller audiences, lower expectations. After Christmas is better.

"Or on Christmas? The dates are fluid. But that means you have some time before it comes out. Line up your next project *now*."

"Next project? What director would hire me now?"

"I know there is one director who wants you."

HOWARD

HANCOCK PARK

Wait. As if waiting is natural, easy. Waiting makes Howard feel powerless, and that is something he cannot bear. So, he'll do the opposite and do something he can do well, better than anyone. He will do something strong and big. He will go back to what he was doing before he was landing on golf courses to impress this woman. He will fly his new H-1 Racer and break the world record for air speed.

PART SEVEN

RETURNS

Katharine Hepburn. Ha, ha, ha!

—Edwin Schallert, *The Los Angeles Times*

LOS ANGELES
JANUARY 1936

In the end, RKO pulls the picture but they are not quick enough. Should have done it sooner. Or, really, they should have sent it out far and wide and pushed this lazy country to get on with it. "Adapt or die." Darwin never actually said that, but he should have; it's a good line. Hollywood is following a different Darwinian phrase, the one we all know. And the fittest who will survive these days are the ones who abide by the damned Production Code. *Sylvia Scarlett* is everything the Production Code fanatics rail against. Sex, gender swapping, con artistry, the lot.

Cary Grant is so upset by the public revulsion of the film that he offers to do another picture for Cukor without salary. Cary can offer anything he likes. He is a free agent; he's bought out his studio contract, and can choose for himself now. He selects his wardrobe now too. Picks the very best and then gets to keep the clothes.

Smart man; good with money. He does currency investment too, did you know? Cary bought six thousand yen before breakfast. He never talks about it except with Randolph. He is salting away enough cash so that he can walk away if he wants to. Cary knows the world will always want someone who can just walk away.

Unlike Kate, who is contracted and trapped, tossed right into the mouth of their dislike. She is bitten and chewed up by the public as the press snarl at her. Her boy is too good, too real, too beautiful. Her girl who is a boy is desirable. Lean, arrogant and sexy, a surefire way to make the country angry. Kate is shocked by the venom. She genuinely does not understand. We do. It is her ease that unsettles people. You see it? There is no giggle, no wink to the camera to let the audience know that the ingénue is still in there, untainted and finding all this dress-up a bit ridiculous. No, Kate Hepburn plays for keeps and the country can't see it yet, but she is glorious. She feels their dislike. She feels them turn on her. This is a company town. To be popular here, you must be popular out there. The press lead the charge. It is viral. Meanness is easy to catch when everyone has it. Ticket sales for *Sylvia Scarlett* are rock bottom, yet ask anyone and they've seen it. Ask anyone and they have *plenty* to say about it. Critics are ruthless. They call her rude, haughty, and odd. Kate is a star they enjoy pulling to pieces. We are not surprised. We knew they would do it the moment they got the chance. Their love was not a generous love. It was envious. Of course it was. Her originality is not put on for show; it was not for them. It is the ordinary that is pretend with her.

George Cukor will be all right. Directors can survive these kinds of things. Yes, he skated near the edge of the goddamn Production Code but clever George, he signed a brand spanking new seven-picture contract at MGM before *Sylvia Scarlett* flopped. Selznick thinks he lured George over to MGM with the promise of bigger budgets, better writers and wider releases. Irene knows that these are not the reasons George signed. She knows that George is not always as confident as he seems. He needs the feeling of family, of a pack, of working with trusted friends where he will never feel foolish. Smart Irene. She knows George Cukor has missed the safety of working with David Selznick. George can relax with Selznick at the helm. Good or bad, Selznick will always stand out in front of a film, flat footed and square to the wind, sheltering the cast and crew behind him. He will take it all on the chin to protect his people and his picture. Irene loves that about him, but she cannot convince him that she herself does not need shielding. Marriage is not a film set.

David Selznick has made promises. Scripts he will commission, contracts he will buy out. George is still hoping Selznick will bring

Kate over to MGM as promised, when she finishes her RKO contract. But that was before *Sylvia Scarlett*.

. . .

There's Laura, on the white sofa in her Upper East Side apartment. Is she happy Kate has fallen? Yes. She is a human. Laura reads the reviews and hopes Kate will call. Laura will pretend she has been busy and not yet seen the notices. Really, she goes to the library to read *all* the reviews in *all* the papers. Did you see? She tore away a sheet from the copy of *The Philadelphia Inquirer* and slipped it into her bag. It is the page with the photograph of Kate in a suit, full-mouthed and unsmiling.

. . .

The Hartford Courant runs a story using the photograph of Kate dressed as a boy—hair cropped and slicked, her angular face a downward triangle. The Hepburns decide that they all love Kate's short hair. They are loyal. Mrs. Hepburn says she has never seen her daughter look more like herself. Dr. Hepburn sees the article open on the kitchen table and starts to say that Kate has gone too far but his wife cuts him off. She will not hear it. Not when her daughter is in trouble.

. . .

Howard goes to the late showing at the Los Feliz Theatre to see it. He goes alone. He has been at the airfield and smells of fuel. No one recognizes him. He goes back the next day to see it again.

. . .

And Kate? She is trussed up in a corset playing Mary Queen of Scots for John Ford on the back lot at RKO. Not the script he would have chosen for her but the studio wanted it and he wanted her. They needed her covered-up, wigged, feminized. Did they even read the script or just skip to the big finish? A public head chopping for Kate Hepburn. Maybe that will appease them.

IRENE

BEVERLY HILLS

Irene and David are at home in the sunken living room when they read the newspapers. David folds the paper in two and does not pass it to Irene.

"As bad as that?" Irene says.

David doesn't answer her question, which answers her question. He cannot bear to admit the fall of anyone he has championed. And my god did he champion Kate.

"Now what?" Irene asks.

"Her next one has to be a smash. There is no other way. Pandro says they're nearly wrapped. John Ford is directing. Could go either way, but she has to change," David says. "She has to agree to be less."

"Less what?" Irene asks.

"Less everything, less Kate."

Irene knows Kate was less for so long when she came back from Mexico. *Sylvia Scarlett* was her choice; Kate believed in it. Kate was the engine. It brought her to life. Irene does not want her friend to be less. She understands how life shrinks when one agrees to hide.

LELAND
NEW YORK CITY

Leland Hayward is in New York, buying passage on the *Bremen*. He was going to sail on the *Europa* but the *Bremen* has faster mail service. It does not leave for Europe until the last week of June but the first-class state rooms sell out quickly. Margaret wants a suite with a terrace for their honeymoon tour and he wants to get this marriage right.

The women in front of him are talking about *Sylvia Scarlett*. "Her hair, her walk, that bulge."

Have they even *seen* it? Leland knows it opened in three theaters in New York and closed again in forty-eight hours with hardly any ticket sales. No. *No one* saw it.

Kate. She has done everything Leland told her not to do, including work with John Ford. *Mary of Scotland* of all things. As if chucking her into a huge skirt and whacking off her head will help.

Things are only getting worse. All the rumors are back: stories about Laura, about the secret, abandoned husband, even about their so called engagement, and now rumors of an affair with the married director. Leland put in a call to Myron this afternoon. It's still morning on the other coast. Myron can steer her through this nightmare. Myron is steady, relentless and crackerjack savvy. He will pull Kate through, if she will let him. Leland tells himself he can't do it anymore; really, he will not do it anymore. There is a difference. But is it graceless of him to walk away now? Leland is angry. Not only that she wouldn't marry him, but that she stopped listening to him. He was her agent but he couldn't stop her. Kate had this unhappy, hungry country on her side and then she took all that success, her Oscar for *Morning Glory*, *Divorcement, Little Women*, *Alice Adams*, all that goodwill, and squandered it doing exactly as she pleased. She did it her own damned way, the way she does everything. That woman can hold her nerve like no one else, he'll say that. Leland is half impressed.

No matter what, Leland Hayward knows he needs to feel less of everything about Kate Hepburn. It is Margaret who matters now.

LOS ANGELES
JANUARY 1936

Leland is right. The studio does not know what to do with her. No one wants to cast her and no one wants to loan her out. She's dead storage. It is not just that her picture flopped. Studios have mopped up careers after a flop before. It is Kate. Her career is dying of terrible rumors: Hepburn is really a man, a boy, a boy dressed as a girl dressed as a boy. She is a woman who wants to be a man. She sleeps with women while dressed as a man, she sleeps with men while dressed as a man. It would be easier for them all if she weren't so damned attractive as a man. Onscreen she doesn't smile, isn't sad, isn't wistful, strides around with confidence and a downturned mouth and still, it is impossible to look away. And, those bones. Were they always there, coursing down her face? She cut off her hair and looks better, more like herself. That's not supposed to happen. It is the moment when the heroine unpins her hair and it falls softly around her face that your heart is meant to lurch for her, that is when she becomes the beauty she was all along. Not this confusing beauty that is not beautiful.

That film. Is it good? What a question. No? Yes? Does it matter? Cary Grant was good. He plays a swindler, but a lovable one. He is a man playing a man and reassures the audience. Katharine Hepburn does not reassure. Even on the posters she is asking too much. The way she looks right at you, unnerving. She is daring you. The audience do not want to be dared. They want to be comforted, excited to an extent, naturally—but not like this, not in a way that makes them ashamed. It does not even look like she has to try in this film. Doesn't look like acting. That's the arrow that kills her. Was that a bulge in her trousers? Did you see it too? No one says it but everyone thinks it. It is where everyone was looking. We cannot help her. The press have turned on her. Katharine Hepburn has made herself unlikable and there is no cure for that here.

KATE

RKO STUDIOS

It was a while before she learned to sit down in the whole rig but she has the knack of it now. If she sinks to the ground and lets the thing puddle around her, she can do it. The voice is harder and she doesn't quite have it, but the history is wrong and the script is not up to scratch, so what does it matter? The more shots of her they cut the better. At least it's quick. Twenty-four day shoot cut down from thirty-six. For a period drama? But Ford will only do one take, two at the most. Ford. *Sean.* She remembers him from the night of that party. But she was a different person then.

They had a rocky start. He wanted to know where she had been for ten months, what had gone wrong. Came right out and asked her after the table read.

"Why would I tell you that?" she said, too shocked to be angry.

"You're going to tell *someone*. Why not me?"

You're going to tell someone. No. She isn't. Irene knows, her family know and that is enough.

"You do not know me at all."

"No. But, I'm going to."

The ten months. It feels like the whole town wants to know where she was, what happened, why she won't swim, but he is the only one who asked her straight out. First she hedged and then she dug in and it turned into something else. Now, will to will, they go at it. He yells and she yells. At first the stakes were high but now it's fun. As long as the camera isn't rolling. When he is the director and she is the star, they take it seriously. They focus and work hard. But the rest of the time? They trade insults. About anything. The lights, the lines, her hat, her hair, his gut. All of it. They are alive in each other's company.

LOS ANGELES

JANUARY 1936

Mary of Scotland. Ford would have quit the production but for her. Hard to do a film when everyone knows the ending.

She calls him *Sean*. It is what his grandmother called him. He was sure it would be an on-set romance—he has one on most pictures—but it's something else now, something finer. At first, he didn't think it was fine. He thought it was aggravating. He pouted, he sulked, he refused to watch the dailies. Absurd to see this great bear of a man sulking because his lead actress will not tell him something he wants to know. But, she can manage him. She has experience maneuvering men like him.

KATE

RKO STUDIOS

Mary. The script is riddled with the name. It's on a sign pinned to her dressing room door, her costume rack, her wig table. It's in the title, it's everywhere. The director should be saying it hundreds of times a day. It is also his wife's name. John Ford calls her character

The Queen. Kate calls her *Mary*, just to see what will happen. It is her safeguard reminding her he belongs to someone else.

GEORGE
RKO STUDIOS
FEBRUARY 1936

George comes to the RKO lot to watch the filming. He is surprised by the yelling.

"Is it always like this?"

"No," Kate says, "sometimes it's better. Sometimes we throw things."

George telephones Leland in New York.

"Should I worry about her? It's not a Kate I know."

"Worry about her? Why? She can hold her own."

"But is it healthy? All that shouting?" George asks.

"I think Kate has been wanting to scream for months."

KATE
RKO STUDIOS

On the last day of filming, the canisters snap shut and then the cast and crew eat together at a long table in the sun. On film sets, Ford usually eats in his private room. Rumor has it that he drinks and naps in there but Kate now knows he never drinks while filming a picture.

"And after filming ends?" she asks him.

"I get some friends together, take out my boat, the *Araner*, sail down to Mexico, stay drunk for a week. We leave tomorrow."

He does not ask her to come. He already knows she would refuse.

IRENE

BEVERLY HILLS

"He wanted me to tell him," Kate says. They are sitting in Irene's sunken living room. John Ford has left on his boat and Kate doesn't want to be alone.

"Tell him where you were?"

"The ten months. And *why* I was where I was."

"He said that?"

"No," Kate says, "but it would have been the next question."

"And now? He no longer wants to know?"

"Now, he likes me for not telling him. And I liked him for not asking me again."

Irene is too subtle a woman to comment on her friend's choice of tense.

CARY

SANTA MONICA

"Do we tell her?" Cary asks. It is one A.M. and Cary and Randolph have just come home from the hospital. "He asked if she knew."

"Tell her that he crashed or that he survived?" Randolph asks.

"Tell her that before he crashed, he broke the world record."

KATE
RKO STUDIOS

She reads it in the morning papers. Seven passes, cutting the flight path in opposite directions. 352.39 miles per hour in the plane he designed. He did it. He crashed the plane on its belly in a sugar beet field but he did it. While she has been worrying about box office numbers and reviews and playing dress-up with someone else's husband, Howard Hughes did something no one on this earth has done before.

LOS ANGELES
APRIL 1936

Mary of Scotland is going to flop. Everyone knows it. The country will not let her have a smash, not anymore. First, they have to punish her. She will do an interview for the *Los Angeles Times*, a one-on-one, toughest interview in town. She is trying to turn it around. Gutsy. That's why she's our girl. The *Los Angeles Times* sends their harshest critic, Edwin Schallert, who has never liked her. He has already spent the morning collecting unfavorable adjectives to describe her.

Kate spends the morning gathering up her courage, determined to show this reporter everything, all her soft human parts. Cary, Irene and George all agree. If he can know you, he will love you. It's the right play if she can win him over but it will not win the country. One interview will not turn them, not yet. And this will hurt.

Edwin sits on the sofa in her Spanish style house. He wonders if he should have taken his shoes off.

She is not the same woman he met before. She does it. She tells him of her fear of failing, her drive to be liked, her fear of boring people, all the reddest meat on the bone. And it works, he sees her, he likes her, but we are right too, it is not enough. The country is not ready to forgive her for being a whole human.

HOWARD

HANCOCK PARK

Howard reads the Schallert interview and feels she is speaking to him alone. Cary told him she will start rehearsals for a play, *Jane Eyre*, on the East Coast sometime in the summer. It will rehearse and preview in Washington, D.C., open in Boston and tour until early next year. She must be desperate to get away from this town. Howard telephones Noah and tells him to telephone Ode. Howard needs a plane. Now.

He calls Cary.

"Wait," Cary says.

"Again, wait. Why?" Howard says.

"Who do you want to talk to when you feel like a failure?"

Howard agrees to wait to approach her until her play opens. But he schedules meetings with the Federal Aviation Commission in Washington, D.C., for August. He tells himself that watching from the audience will be enough.

LOS ANGELES

JUNE 1936

Everyone is happy Kate Hepburn is going East to do a play. No one will hire her here. Nothing else to do. Another classic, another corset.

. . .

We've kept an eye on them, those East Coast Hepburns. Some are in school, some are getting married, getting medical degrees; all predictable. Luddy still comes up to Fenwick for weekends. He is the family photographer, never in the photographs, always behind the lens. It gives him a purpose.

"We were at Fenwick and did not have a chance to see Kate's last picture." That is the Hepburn family's answer when neighbors ask.

"Kate is going into rehearsals for a play. *Jane Eyre*, beautiful adaptation. We are all going up to Boston for the opening," Kit Hepburn tells the postman—the postman will tell the rest of the neighborhood.

Kit Hepburn is proud of her daughter. She went, alone, on the only Saturday *Sylvia Scarlett* played. She had to go to New York to see it, a hard city for her. She was careful to stay uptown. She watched her boy/girl daughter living on the screen. The story did not matter, the man/woman clothes, the dialogue, the nonsense pretending, none of it mattered except her daughter's vitality. Kit Hepburn never takes it for granted that her children are alive.

PART EIGHT

FLIGHT

She is more of an actress now
than she was then.

—Brooks Atkinson,
The New York Times

KATE

WASHINGTON, D.C.

JULY 1936

Why did she think a play would change things? A play will just leave her out there, like rotting fish, stinking in front of people, *all* the time. In front of people is exactly where she does not want to be. She knows what she was thinking—gravitas, courage, get out in front of all this dislike and face them down. But, it's the wrong play. Jane Eyre is not powerful. She's a mess. Rochester has his first mad wife locked up in the attic and holds all the cards. Kate hates him for it. Her skin crawls when they rehearse the scene where she grovels for his love at the end. Meanwhile, the other woman, the one locked upstairs, the one with grit, jumps from the roof. Jane ought to have fired the house, rescued the wife, and pushed Rochester off that roof by the end of Act I.

Rehearsals will end, previews will begin and then the tour, she tells herself. It is *hot.* Why does no one tell you that the nation's capital is in the South? Six weeks of rehearsing. Two articles in the *Post,* both guessing that her Jane will be lukewarm. Amazing what people can write about something they haven't yet seen. And now they have scheduled a tea with President Roosevelt. It's not that she doesn't want to meet him; she does. She thinks he is a marvel. She just does not want to meet him when she's not on top. But then, Roosevelt knows something about bad press.

She will be a better Kate in a new city. She has to keep moving.

LOS ANGELES
AUGUST 1936

It is a full dress rehearsal and the house lights are down. The posters are up, the work tables have been removed from the stalls and the fight coordinator is going home. The first Mrs. Rochester jumps offstage and so all he had to coordinate was a couple of fainting spells, one stumble and an arm catch. The fight call rehearsal was quick. My god, that Kate Hepburn hates stage fainting, the fight coordinator thinks as he waits for the bus.

The fight coordinator does not see the man watching the rehearsals from the very back of the stalls. An usher lets the man in each day. First preview is tomorrow, what harm can it do, the usher thinks. And, it is *Howard Hughes*. The usher will go home and tell his mother that he helped Howard Hughes today.

HOWARD
WASHINGTON, D.C.

She is miserable. He can see that. His first wife, Ella, used to tell him he had no emotion, could not understand emotion. Maybe because he had the lawyers tell her about the divorce rather than telling her himself? Maybe because he cheated and never bothered to hide it? Howard doesn't think much about Ella. She married him for money and money is what she got. Emotion would have cost extra.

He can see that Kate does not want to be there, in those stuffy costumes, under the lights. He can see that she does not want to be anywhere. He knows that feeling. Of wanting to vanish and be seen everywhere, both at once. She is no good in this play, but the tour is long. She'll get better. He leaves through the side door. He wants this woman to like him, and she won't if she knows he has seen her do something badly.

Howard refers to Ella as his first wife because he hopes there will be a second. One who will not start ordering stationery and furniture and automobiles in the name of Mrs. Howard Hughes even before they are married. One who wants to be someone else, a person, rather than just more of him. He met two senators who are hoping Hughes Tool will bid for the military contracts, and he finished his meetings at the Federal Aviation Commission before noon. If he hurries, he can get to the airfield before midnight and be home by morning.

. . .

Howard reads all three articles in the *Post*. The third is better than the other two. Noah knows to clip any articles where her name is mentioned. Cary asked him if he thought it was obsessive, his interest in her. Maybe. But what's the point in things if they're not obsessive? All the things that matter to Howard obsess him, or why would they matter? His films, his friends, his planes, and now, this woman.

She is going to meet the president. Howard has met him. Good man, good company, strong stomach. Funnier than he has to be. No one expects a president to be truly funny.

LOS ANGELES
AUGUST 1936

A book has come out. The book that everyone will read. Hollywood chews its lip. It is too long for a film, too expensive. How can any studio afford to shoot it? It's period, everyone says, with a huge cast. The worst combination. And dangerous. The Civil War?

Touchy subject. How to do it on film? No one can do it safely, convincingly. And who would insure it?

While Hollywood debates, Irene knows to act. She is a fast reader. Over a thousand pages and it takes her two days. The book gets wet as she keeps on reading while Jeffrey is in the bath. Irene wants to be sure. Yes, she's right. She tells him to buy it and he trusts her instincts. The film will be huge, consuming. Irene is built of family patterns and this film will keep her in her marriage. She will get stuck. She still thinks her job is to be dependable when needed. And her husband will need her.

Because David Selznick is going to burn Atlanta.

. . .

Irene calls Cary and she calls George. She sends the novel to them both by courier. She still doubts herself even though she shouldn't. One day she won't, and she will follow her own taste all the way to a playwright named for a Southern state. She will take the playwright to Broadway and join the luminaries, but now she still doubts herself. Cary is only on page 600 but agrees, Selznick should buy the rights to it immediately. George has finished it. If the call comes, would he direct? Would he cast Kate? Would Selznick allow it? George hesitates. Irene knew when she told George and Cary that, even on the East Coast, rumors of this book that will become a film would have reached Kate. When Kate calls long distance to ask about the part, Irene hesitates. She knows this is not her comeback picture. The budget for this film will be enormous and no one would stake that much money on Kate.

HOWARD

BOSTON

OCTOBER 1936

He slips the note under her door. He rewrote it six times in his suite before sealing the envelope. And then he called the bellman to come and empty his trash can. Howard cannot bear the disorder of an unemptied trash can. He flew in last night and is checked into the penthouse suite. Noah spoke to the desk clerk on the telephone; Noah would never book him into anything smaller. They have the fruit and linen Howard likes and the staff have been courteous. The room is not overfull with furniture and the bathroom has brand new towels still in their boxes as Noah requested. Howard likes this hotel. He will come back here.

Her room is three floors down.

KATE

BOSTON

Kate meets him in the lobby. He is where he said he would be, when he said he would be. Points for that. At least it's a change from dinner on a tray in her room. He is taller than she remembers. Six four at least. Damn. She should have worn heels.

"Ready?" Kate wraps her scarf around her neck.

HOWARD

BOSTON

"I'm sorry?" He cannot lip read with the scarf covering her mouth. They are walking toward the restaurant.

"Oh! You're deaf!" Kate says it without hesitation. "I forgot. Cary mentioned that you were deaf."

No one has spoken those words aloud to him since he was a child. When he grew up, he learned that adults say things like that quietly, behind a hand or under the breath. She doesn't.

"Only in one ear," he says, relieved that he can explain and not hide it.

"Which one?"

"The left."

"Then I will always walk on your right," she says, moving to his other side. She pulls the scarf from her mouth, tilts her face up when she speaks and moves her lips deliberately and clearly. How does she know to do that?

They change restaurants. The one she had suggested was too noisy. "Why have the background noise when you can't hear to begin with?" she says.

He is astonished by her lack of tact. Is she rude? Or is he just used to dishonesty disguised as manners? She's different from when he met her in California, disarmed. This woman is never the same person twice.

KATE

BOSTON

They walk the snowy streets until they find somewhere small and empty. Later, both of them will remember the checkered tablecloth, the candles and Chianti bottles. She will remember the way he didn't seem to know what to do with his hands. Lay them on the table, or keep them in his lap? And the first time his mouth widened to let out a real laugh. It makes her feel good to make this man laugh. He tells her later that he will always remember the way she asked if she had something in her teeth, the way she asked the manager to turn down the gramophone and the way her foot tapping made him feel less self-conscious about his own bouncing knee, but neither of them will remember the name of the restaurant.

HOWARD
BOSTON

When he is back in his room, Howard calls Noah. It is one A.M.

"Yes, for the next three months."

"Howard, you have meetings, board meetings, meetings with the aviation commissioner, your aunt's birthday? How can I just cancel everything?"

"I'll do it all on the telephone. Simple, I don't need to be there."

"Howard, your plane is being delivered. Do you want to accept delivery without testing it? Without flying it?"

"Delay the plane."

"You just told them to rush the plane."

"Noah, delay the plane. And get me a better telephone. I don't like using other people's telephones."

KATE
BOSTON

My god. To go through life that way. Not the deafness, the hiding. His deafness makes him dear somehow, tender. Before he'd seemed taciturn, roguish even. She never wanted to admit it but she'd felt an edgy thrill when he had pursued her, a danger that pretended it was not dangerous. When he landed on the golf course she walked back three holes to stand inside the tree line and watch while they disassembled his plane. Before Boston, it was a game. Matched wills, power for power. Now, he is a person, a bit broken, cut down to the size of human frailty. She can't care for him once he's just like her, can she? She feels only protective. Affectionate. But now that she knows he's not someone she can love, the tension has gone slack and it is an easy, platonic, friendly affection. She can only love someone who scares her a little, someone unknowable. Someone who might go away. Anything less chancy and all the feeling goes dormant. How would the relationship end if he's someone who would stay?

. . .

The tour moves fast. Load in. Load out. Each city, a note under the door. A walk, a meal, a slow peeling open of stories and life, but not love.

When he asks her to come up to his penthouse suite, she always says no.

. . .

In each city, she calls Myron. "Anything?"

"Nothing yet," Myron says. "Patience."

"Scarlett?"

"Nationwide search. They haven't found her yet, but Kate?"

"What?"

"She is not for you."

. . .

"Myron says 'patience.'" She flops into an armchair in the hotel bar. "Would you have patience if you were no longer invited to do the thing you love?" She was surprised at first, but it's easy to talk to this man about failure. He flew six hundred flights *before* he broke the world record. Six hundred tries before he did the thing he set out to do. He considers them failures.

It is early, before her show, and the bar is empty. Howard sits in the club chair opposite. "I don't wait to be invited to do the things I love."

"You just go ahead and do them."

"Yes."

"And if you're not allowed?"

Howard looks at her, amused. She already knows the answer but is just waiting for him to say it out loud.

"I do them anyway."

Thinking about it later, Kate is fascinated by the bravado of this man. He is able to lie, right to her face, and make it sound true. She knows about his divorce. Cary told her Ella insisted on the clause. Howard had lost too much money reshooting *Hell's Angels* with sound and Ella knew he would likely go bankrupt if he made another picture. No money, no alimony. And so, Howard no longer makes pictures. Kate admires Ella. It must have taken nerve to add that clause.

CARY

SANTA MONICA

OCTOBER 1936

It is early. Cary and Randolph are still in their dressing gowns when a courier from MGM brings the small brown envelope. A cable from a solicitor firm in Bristol. International telegraph service is expensive. The solicitor firm only uses the important words. "Regret to inform."

Cary's father is dead.

RANDOLPH

SANTA MONICA

In the end, Randolph does what he always does, gives Cary the grace and room to speak when he's ready. With two parents alive on the East Coast, Randolph feels that anything he has to offer will sound hollow and borrowed. He does not know what this feels like. It's two hours before Cary begins to speak. Cary wishes he had gone home to Bristol. Randolph understands why he didn't.

"He came down to the station the day I left. That was the last time I saw him."

"I always thought you ran away to join the circus." Too light? He does not want Cary to think he's speaking frivolously.

"No, my father had to sign the contract with Mr. Pender, to prove I was permitted to go. Mr. Pender was decent that way."

Randolph notices that he does not say that his father was kind to let him go. What kind of father allows his only son to sail away to America with a troupe of acrobats?

"Will you go back now?"

"For the funeral? I could, but the one person I want to see won't be there. And, they will be there, but yes, I will go back."

They. The other family, the new family. Randolph offers to go with him, to make the bookings, arrangements, but Cary says he will make them himself. But, he doesn't. He stalls.

Howard is back in Los Angeles for the day, a flying visit, taking a quick break from chasing Kate Hepburn up and down the East

Coast. Randolph intercepts him at the front door. It is impossible to predict how Howard will respond to news like this and it's better to tell him privately. Howard hears the news and tries to push past to find Cary.

"And?" Randolph says, stopping him.

"And what?"

"And, don't you want to know how he is before you see him?" Randolph says exasperated.

"I know how he is," Howard says.

"You already know how he is," Randolph says. Sometimes Howard's brutal practicality is irritating.

"Of course I know, Randolph. I am orphaned too."

Randolph lets him through.

CARY

SANTA MONICA

Later in the morning, the phone rings. Long distance, from England. Yes, he will accept the charges. A woman is on the line. Cary has never heard this voice before.

"You are sure?" he asks, feeling as though he is on a film set in the midst of a critical scene. Randolph looks up, listening.

"Quite sure, Mr. Leach. But, it has been two months now and payment is overdue. Your father's agreement for this year was one pound a week."

Silence.

"Mr. Leach?"

RANDOLPH

SANTA MONICA

Randolph does the calculations. The *Super Chief* from Pasadena to New York City. Five days on the boat. And then the port, the trains, to the city of his birth and the mother who birthed him. He wants to go alone. Randolph cannot bear that solitude for the man he loves. But then, Cary cultivates aloneness. Most people don't even know he is English. They assume the accent is fake. They are right; it is.

One pound a week.

Was she insane? Is she insane? *Why* is she there? Has she always been there? How is she alive? The voice on the phone sounded quite sane, polite. As if she were talking to a florist or bank teller. Randolph leaned forward so he could hear but stayed where he was. He knew in this moment Cary would not want to be touched.

"May I still call you Archie?" is all she said.

Cary's face, tanned brown in the California sun, was white.

"I am coming. I will book passage and comc now."

She said goodbye and rang off. Abrupt. Cary rang back and the nurse explained. Mrs. Leach was worried about the cost of the call; it was not personal.

It was not until he hung up the receiver that he said the words. "My *mother*." A phrase Cary avoids, always.

One pound a week.

Now, Randolph can hear Cary on the other telephone, booking passage. Lost a parent, gained a parent. Cary will be with his mother by the end of the month.

Howard offers to fly him. No. Cary wants to go alone.

LOS ANGELES

OCTOBER 1936

Few things take us by surprise. This did. She's alive. In a psychiatric institution, Bristol Lunatic Asylum. One mile from the harbor where he sailed away. All this time. While her son changed from boy to man to acrobat to actor. She was alone in that damp room. Does she know her son is a star?

Does she know her son would trade it all just to see her again?

CARY

BRISTOL, ENGLAND

They work together quickly, use both phone lines. Cary books the hotels and Randolph books the train tickets. The funeral is set for the eighteenth. They will wait for him. Randolph will go along but check into The Savoy. He will stay in London and not go on to Bristol. Cary will not allow anyone to go with him to his home city where he was never Cary Grant.

They will be there, his father's other family, the one that his father kept secret until Cary became Cary. Randolph calls the records office in Bristol and makes inquiries. He does it out of love, without Cary asking.

"She has a daughter from a previous marriage and they have a son together. I didn't want you to go home and be surprised," is all he says.

Home? No, not anymore. Archie Leach lived in Bristol.

He doesn't speak to them in the church, but he can see them lining the front pew. A boy and a girl. Eric and Eliza. The boy is soft, small, younger than Cary was at his age. The girl is older, taller, wearing a black velvet hair ribbon. Beside them is a woman in black bombazine; the woman his father called his wife. She isn't. His father only had one wife. The woman is Mrs. Mabel Alice Bass, but she calls herself Mrs. Leach. Cary understands the power of a changed name. He will call her Mrs. Bass. The girl, Eliza, is from Mrs. Mabel Alice's marriage to Mr. Bass, whoever he was. Eric is the son of Elias Leach. John, Archie, Eric. His father had three sons who never knew each other.

In the churchyard, the mourners stand around the rectangular hole and the damp pile of earth while the vicar speaks about dying in the midst of life. Of course one dies in the midst of life. Dying is a binary business. Cary stops listening. The woman in black bombazine who is not his father's wife stands between her two children. Cary watches the way Mrs. Mabel Alice Bass touches them both, cupping a chin, cradling a head. They are easy with her, unafraid. It is love without words. As soon as the coffin is in the ground and the dirt is dropped on top, the vicar closes his prayer book and puts up his umbrella. It is mist not rain, but the vicar hurries back into the church.

The reception is two streets over, in the house Cary has never seen. He had not planned to go but is carried by momentum and curiosity. The herd of mourners bear him along. The house is small but neat. The door is freshly painted and the windows are new. Cary sent money every quarter. Did his father spend it on windows, on velvet hair ribbons? "One pound a week for upkeep," the nurse had said, a pathetic sum, a public hospital.

Inside, framed photographs line the hall. Portraits, snapshots, some blurry. Eric in the family christening robe—the one Cary wore before Eric and John wore before him. Elias Leach cannot hold on to his sons. Cary didn't know his father took photographs. He must have been behind the lens as he is not in any of the frames. And then, as Cary moves into the front room he sees them. Over the fireplace, three large, framed photographs: publicity stills from *She Done Him Wrong* and *Sylvia Scarlett*. His father must have sent for them from America. His father, who had never asked about Cary's films. Cary, who had never asked about his father's new family. Cary sits in the corner armchair and looks up over the mantel. This family sees these stills every day. His father saw them every day. These photographs have been here as they have lived their secret lives he knows nothing about.

Cary feels ill. He has forgotten the bready heaviness of English food, so different from the citrus clarity in California. A bosomy matron brings him a second plate of shepherd's pie he will not eat. He is careful with his figure and does not want to eat any more, or really to be there any longer but it seems a great effort to get through the thicket of bodies to the door. They are crowding in and speaking to him now. The fork and plate of shepherd's pie has broken down some barrier. Cary is surprised by their frank curiosity about his life, by how easily they say his name, by how much they know. Their questions are not what he expects.

"Do you have a swimming pool?"

"Do you drive on the other side?"

"Does Mae West really talk like that?"

"Have you met Greta Garbo?"

"What happened to your accent?"

The boy and the girl and the woman in black bombazine watch from the sofa but do not speak to him. Not yet.

The crowd thins. When Cary is speaking to a loud man about silent pictures, Mrs. Mabel Alice Bass comes and touches his shoulder. He is surprised. He had stopped watching her.

"It's nearly five. You should hurry. Visiting hours end at six."

"Visiting hours?" Cary says. "How would you know about the visiting hours?" He cannot keep the brine from his voice.

"Because I take the children to see her every week."

. . .

It seems everyone in Bristol knows that Archie the acrobat is now Cary the film actor. Cary had written to his father once a month. Diligence has always been his defining characteristic. He never knew that his father had told so many people that his son was an actor, that he had been proud of him. Cary had always assumed that his father was ashamed that his son was gone—gone, never to come back. His father never once asked him about life in California. Elias Leach had asked about Cary's wife, hinted at grandchildren but never asked about the work he did. Cary returned to Bristol expecting to find Archie Leach. He didn't know that while he was gone, the city had claimed Cary Grant, the famous actor, as their native son. He thinks of Randolph, waiting at The Savoy. If they knew all of his life in California, would they still want him?

But they are trying to be kind, to mourn with him. How do they all know his father has died? Men, with dust on their boots, finishing work and spilling out of corner pubs, tap him on the shoulder and give their condolences; the cab driver, the bellboy, the hotel desk clerk all offer their best wishes. Everyone calls him Cary, as though being from this city, they have earned that kind of familiarity. In Hollywood, Cary is safe, he can keep whole tracts of himself in reserve. He is someone new there and can hide in plain sight. America has never met Archie Leach; they cannot know him and so cannot get too close. But here, Cary is unmasked, exposed. Cary has never minded fame the way others have, or said they have. It was not really him who was famous. Here, all of him is a star. Cary wants to stop the two halves of himself from bleeding into each other but the wound is too deep.

As they shake his hand and wave and smile at him, Cary thinks of his mother. *One pound a week.* Did they know? Did they know all that time?

. . .

Only his mother remains remote. Courteous, pleased to see him, as if he has been away on a short trip. He enters her room but does not embrace her. It seems too sudden, too familiar. There are two photographs, in silver frames, on top of the small dresser. One is the familiar photograph of his brother, John, taken at six months old, five months before he died. The other is of young Archie holding a kite. He must have been four or five. Did his father take it? Cary has never seen it before. The room is white, spare. He had spoken to the administrators before he left California and had her moved to the best room in the hospital. Seeing the room, he is still shocked by the bareness. She cannot be released until he collects her in person and signs the forms as her nearest relative. Did his father put Cary's name and telephone number on that paperwork? The nurses are sure-handed and gentle with her. With them, Cary sees his mother laugh. The nurses call her Miss Elsie. As if she had never been married. She thanks Cary for the new room.

"I'd never been up to this floor before they moved me here," his mother says.

Cary does not ask where her room was before. He already knows it was on the ground floor where the windows are set high on the wall to prevent escape. Too high to see out.

"Would you like to move to a hotel? I am at The Royal and we can go there, or The Grosvenor or even The Hydro, if it's still good? Wherever you like?"

"We stayed in The Grosvenor in London once. My parents and I. On our way back from Scotland. I was eleven and it was beautiful. It was on Buckingham Palace Road."

"It is still on Buckingham Palace Road. Would you like to go back? I can hire a car and driver this afternoon?"

"Archie, what fun, but I'm afraid"—her hand flies to her hair and her voice drops—"I'm not smart enough at present."

"We'll fix that," Cary goes to look for the nurse.

Before he leaves, he asks the nurse, does his mother know his father has died? Cary had not wanted to mention it in case it would upset her. He is Archie again, the boy who never wants to upset his mother.

"Oh yes, Mrs. Leach came and told her straightaway."

Mrs. Leach.

"And what did she say? Did you hear?"

"I was there, in the room. I often stop in and sit with them when Mrs. Leach visits."

"And? What did she say?"

"Miss Elsie asked to see little Archie."

. . .

Money changes Bristol for Cary. He wires his bank and arranges for his mother to have a good line of credit, not endless, but good. He finds a hairdresser who will go to the hospital and asks the hotel manager to send someone from the best ladies' dress shop. Ever professional, the hotel manager remains expressionless. He knows they do things differently in Hollywood.

When Cary returns to see his mother, she is different, stylish. Her hair is cut and colored and set in a neat chignon. He buys a camera to take her photograph. They go out into the grounds. She is unsteady on her court heels but has insisted on wearing them. She says she wants to be pretty. He arranges for her release. When Mrs. Mabel Alice Bass visits, Cary asks her to help him find his mother a new home. The two women are comfortable together, easy, from long practice.

Mabel calls his mother Mrs. Leach.

His mother calls her Miss Mabel.

Mabel calls him Cary.

His mother calls him Archie.

Cary understands. Names are important.

KATE

DES MOINES, IOWA

DECEMBER 1936

She's improving. It is not the practice that is making her better, it's him. It's knowing he is out there every night, in the dark, watching her. She loathes the role, loathes Jane Eyre. Crawling to goddamn two-timing Mr. Rochester. She tells Howard she would eat Rochester's heart raw if she could. Howard laughs and says he would like to shoot Dennis Hoey, the actor who plays Rochester, if he could.

An usher in Boston told her that each night, at the moment when Dennis Hoey's Rochester kissed Kate, Howard Hughes looked away.

. . .

Someone, a stagehand, a dresser, the doorman, has told the press. Fans crowd into the lobby of the theater and clog up the alleyway at the stage door eager to get a look at America's most glamorous couple. By Chicago they have a police escort. Twelve feet to the car but it is impossible to get through the crush without men in uniform clearing a path. She has not understood real fame until now.

CARY

SANTA MONICA

Neither Cary nor Randolph is shooting today. They read the paper over breakfast. Their friends are on the front page.

"She looks happy," Randolph says, handing the article to Cary.

"He's not looking at the photographer." Howard is wary of reporters. Doesn't like to take his eye off them.

"No. He's looking at her."

They have been staying in more since they returned from England. Everyone understands. The invitations can wait. Right now, Cary just wants to be with Randolph. They will spend the day decorating the tree.

KATE

CHICAGO

She stays the night in his penthouse. No sex. Not yet. But no sleep either. She is too aware of him beside her. His breathing, his warmth. She feels an unbearable safety when she is with him. Would sex change that?

Downstairs, she rumples the sheets on her bed so that housekeeping will think she slept there but why would she stay in her own room when she could be with him?

. . .

Monday, her day off. He wants to take her flying. She wants to stay on the ground where he can hear her. They order in and do the crossword up in his suite. She doesn't bother unmaking her own bed anymore. Everybody knows where she sleeps.

HOWARD
CHICAGO
JANUARY 1937

"The hotel is surrounded. They're waiting outside every entrance," the hotel manager apologizes. "Even the supply doors. Someone told them how you often get away through the kitchen. Not my staff, Miss Hepburn, Mr. Hughes, I assure you." His forehead is seeded with sweat even though it is a bitter winter in the Midwest.

Howard turns to Kate. He cannot hear the hotel manager who is rather short.

Kate tilts her head toward his good ear. He leans toward her. It is fluid, automatic. He relies on her to translate. When she is not with him, he feels a little apprehensive out in public now. Not afraid, exactly, just less attached to the world.

"We're surrounded, buddy," Kate says, speaking up. "It's the Alamo, you and me. Enemy at the gates. How do you want to go out? Guns blazing or in disguise?"

It is a game they play. In each city, each theater, each hotel. Partners, friends, almost lovers but not quite. Eluding the press is their favorite sport. The kisses that feel most alive happen when they have slammed the door on the press.

He waited until she asked him to kiss her. It was important to wait, important for her to want him. He will not tread on any part of her freedom. Her freedom is what he loves best about her.

KATE
CHICAGO

The show is playing to packed houses and they all stand at the end, but they just want to see her with him. She is honest and tells Howard the truth. Embarrassing but she wants them to want to see *her,* just her; photograph her, read about her, the way they used to. He says he understands but really, he doesn't. How could he? He has always been famous.

Kate is anxious to get back to California and wants this tour to be over. Howard talks about his house in Hancock Park. He wants them to live there together. Kate laughs it off. It is too soon for that and it's hard to see what happens next. The rumors about her past are drowned out by the rumors about her present. Reporters and photographers wait by the stage door, shrieking questions as she goes in and out. It annoys her that the articles they write hardly mention that she is an actress, only that she might or might not be engaged to the richest man in America. With all the press coverage, she sometimes forgets that they're not engaged. All this press helps the theaters sell tickets but it doesn't help her get good roles in good pictures with good scripts, and there are two roles she wants, badly. She calls Myron every day.

He tells her that the studio is thrilled she is with Howard Hughes and delighted by the press coverage but does not want her for either picture. They want Irene Dunne to play opposite Cary Grant in the adaptation of *Holiday* and they want Connie Bennett opposite Cary for *Bringing Up Baby*. George Cukor is set to direct one or both pictures depending on the schedules. Myron suggests that if she marries Howard, and RKO had exclusive rights to the photographs, they might cast her? Kate puts the phone down on him. When she calls the next day, Kate tells Myron that she has spoken to George Cukor and Cary, and that they will insist she be cast in the leads. They will insist because she has asked, and she never asks for anything but also because they agree she would be perfect for the parts. *Holiday* has always been hers. She's right. George and Cary insist that only Kate will do for the picture. Cary is a free agent and can always walk away. MGM wants him back and RKO knows it. It is the threat he never needs to articulate. It's a power Kate envies. Cukor says he will not make *Holiday* without her. The script is perfect for Cukor, party scenes, old money New York, all his favorite things.

Casting Kate in *Bringing Up Baby* is tougher but Kate chases it hard. When she feels that Myron is not doing enough, she lobbies RKO herself. As she tells Howard later, what other actress would work with a real leopard?

. . .

He is in the audience every night. It makes it worse when she's onstage and flubs a line. It makes it better when she comes offstage and realizes it doesn't matter. On her days off, they golf or fly depending on the weather. He loves to watch her play golf, she loves to watch him fly. It is the excellence that fascinates them.

By Detroit, she goes to bed with him. Why was she waiting? Their bed becomes a sovereign kingdom. She cannot predict him; he cannot predict her.

They are themselves.

HOWARD

HANCOCK PARK

He flies to New York but doesn't like any of the stones at Harry Winston. They are ordinary. He is tired but staying in New York overnight means another night away from her. So, he directs the driver to take him to the airfield. He pays the local ground crew overtime to get his plane ready and flies to Los Angeles. Before he leaves, he calls Kate and apologizes for missing the show. He means it. He loves to watch her onstage.

Watching the woman he loves doing what she loves and not needing him is exciting.

. . .

He finds it at Brock and Company in Beverly Hills. A heavy emerald-cut emerald. He draws exactly what he wants, two flawless diamonds flanking the center stone and then two smaller diamonds stepping down to the band, completing the symmetry. He wants it ready in a week.

"Diamonds do not have enough personality for her," he tells Cary later. Her hair is red, she needs an emerald."

"But, will she say yes?" Cary asks.

KATE
CHICAGO

He is not here. He left. Flew away with no explanation. He can do that. They are both free. She is surprised by this basic fact. She peeks out from backstage to see the packed house that feels thin and prosaic without him.

HOWARD
HANCOCK PARK

He leaves Cary and Randolph's wanting to reach her, speak to her, to be sure of her. He looks at his watch. She will be coming offstage now, taking off her lipstick now, unpinning her wig now, showering now. He likes knowing her routine.

He calls her. Cary has told him that RKO is still refusing to cast her in these pictures and she is in a foul temper. Ella had never shown her temper while they were married. Her mettle came as a shock once they divorced. Howard is happy to see all of Kate. He likes that he knows that in golf, tennis, badminton and backgammon she is a sore loser, that she gets irritated when he has used all the bath towels, that she tells him loudly that she has to urinate, that she hates radishes and thinks parsley is pointless, that she needs three showers a day to feel clean, that she will tell him when she wants to be left alone, that she lies. It makes her whole. When you're as wealthy as Howard, few people will show you their whole self. The house on South Muirfield Road feels empty without her even though she has never been here. He will sleep for three hours and then fly back to her.

RANDOLPH

SANTA MONICA

It is one A.M. and there is banging on the door. Randolph quickly gets up and puts on his dressing gown. Cary has been unable to sleep well since they returned from England, and Randolph doesn't want the noise to wake him.

"Howard? You were meant to be flying back."

"I am flying back. Plane's ready. I called everyone to the airfield for midnight."

"Sounds expensive. Why aren't you there?"

"I have to ask Cary what he meant."

Randolph understands. After all the articles about women trying to ensnare the most eligible bachelor in America, it has never occurred to Howard that if he were to ask a woman to marry him, she might say no.

"Howard, Cary didn't mean anything by it. It was only a question."

"Does he know something I don't? They're close. I know they talk all the time about this damned casting business. Did she say something?"

Howard is still standing in the doorway. Randolph, who can nearly match his height, is blocking the door.

"Cary is sleeping, Howard. He is finally sleeping."

Howard understands. He is one of the few people who has spoken to Cary about his mother, his father. When Howard's mother died, he could not sleep for two years.

Randolph steps out into the small front patio closing the front door behind him. He does not want Howard in the house. One has to speak so loudly to him and Cary is a light sleeper. The two men sit on the low wall. At this time of night, without the street noise, you can hear the ocean.

"Randy, do you know if she said something to him? I know Cary would tell you."

"No, she hasn't said anything to Cary. Not really. Nothing important."

"What has she said to him that was unimportant?" Howard's voice is rising and Randolph motions for him to quiet.

"Just that she has to *be* someone to be *with* someone." Randolph wishes he had never started this.

"What the hell does that mean? Of course, she *is* someone."

"I would just ask her soon, Howard. Before she comes back here and thinks she is less of a someone than she was."

KATE
CHICAGO

When she comes offstage, she will not ask him where he was, or why he went. And he doesn't say.

"Good show."

"I dropped six lines. The prompt man just told me."

"No one noticed."

"*I* noticed." She is still determined to be good at this.

The press are at every entrance and exit to the theater. Kate complains about the press but secretly, she is reassured by the attention. But yesterday and today not one of the articles in the national papers mention that she is an actress. Not the *Post,* nor the *Times,* nor the *Herald Tribune*, none of them. They call her a "celebrity" but not an actress. It matters. A celebrity who was not born a celebrity can easily become uncelebrated. The people who buy these papers want to see her photographed with America's millionaire, but they do not want to see her in a new picture.

Damn them.

"Where are we?" Howard says, although he knows very well. "Chicago? Last stop on the tour." Subtle, gracious. She knows Howard is leaving it up to her. "Want to blaze the guns?"

"Make them cough up some column inches for me?" Kate says.

"For us," Howard says. "Always plural."

"If *you* were not here, would *they* be here? No. So, how can it be for *us*?"

She hears herself. She sounds angry, she *is* angry. Why is she spending time with this man? It will not help her, only him. Love affairs never help the woman once they're over. When did she become someone who will only do things if it makes others like her? No.

Success is not about having people like her, it's about earning a place that cannot be taken away. She will end it. Even as she makes the decision to end it, she knows she won't do it. He has become important.

It started right away. She had not expected that first kiss to reach into her, to unseat her. She thought she was driving the scene on this flirtation. But, that kiss surprised her; his willingness to follow the tour surprised her. This man is not what she thought. The richest man in the country, the man who has broken the world record for air speed, the man whom the president telephones to talk about combat aviation, this man does not look away when she's speaking, even when someone is trying to get his attention. Leland always had half an ear cocked in case a bigger star came along. He was still doing it, even when he was trying to marry her. Must have been habit. Is it because Howard is reading lips? Is that really it? Or is Howard someone who just knows what he wants and doesn't second guess? That is the habit that is bred to the bone. Howard does not seem to care if she's famous. He only wants it for her because it is what she wants. If she announced that she never wanted to make another picture and just golf all day instead, he says he would be happy for her. But playing golf all day will not make her his equal. It will never work between them if she is anything less than him.

After that first night, Kate made him wait three more shows before she kissed him again. He never mentioned the three days. They were what she needed and so he was happy for her to have them. So much like Luddy, but Howard cannot be pushed this way and that way the way Luddy could, the way Luddy still can. Howard has value and he knows it. He has kept some of himself back, not to keep it away from her but to keep it for himself. She likes that about him. There is a reserve about him that allows her the space to want him, to miss him even when they are in the same room. Missing is a footprint she understands. It reads as love to her.

But they are not in love. Not yet. Kate will not permit it.

LOS ANGELES

JANUARY 1937

The employee is fired and the manager of Brock and Company writes Mr. Hughes a personal note of apology. The manager knows it was one of his people as soon as he sees the article. The measurements, the descriptions, all too precise. Has to be an inside scoop. The 2.67 carat, step cut, rectangular emerald, two 1.20 carat emerald cut flanking diamonds, two .20 carat epaulet cut diamonds. Reporters are waiting in the street when he comes to open the shop the next morning. The manager could retire on what the *Herald Tribune* alone is offering for a photograph. He could do it. The ring is still locked in his personal safe. But, the manager refuses. As he tells his wife later, "What is left if I sell my integrity?"

In the personal safe, the tag on the velvet ring box reads *Mr. H.* The manager had not wanted to take any chances with the client's whole name.

KATE

CHICAGO

Kate reads the article, sitting up in the white hotel bed. She reads it before anyone tells her not to. Did he buy a ring? Design a ring? Is that why he left for New York that morning but ended up in Los Angeles? She knows the jewelry store. It is beautiful, discreet. Tallulah bought herself a diamond bracelet there and then lied and said it was from a Texas oil man. The article runs in the *Herald Tribune*. Will her parents read it? Her siblings? They know the truth. They know she could not possibly marry a man like Howard Hughes. The publicity, the scrutiny, the questions when the years pass and there are no children. She could never marry him, could she? Is she waiting for someone to give her permission?

Kate looks at the clock. It's 3:45 A.M. in California. Too early, even for Cary, who gets up at five to run on the beach. She will call him after breakfast. No, she won't call him. What if he says the story is true? What then? How can she ever marry again? Marriage. Family. Children. The children she will not have. She cannot do that to him. She has not told Howard. Since Irene, she has told no one. She will never be a person in the plural and no one has a right to know why.

HOWARD

CHICAGO

The note from the jewelry store manager is kind but unnecessary. Howard knows he is not the one who spoke to the press. He is sure it was the blond weaselly boy who left fingerprints on the glass of the jewelry case. Dirty people are up to no good.

He denies it when Kate asks. She assumed the rumor was untrue anyway so the subject drops.

"The press will say anything to sell papers," Kate says, ending the conversation.

The next time it comes up, he will ask her if she likes emeralds.

. . .

Howard had not expected the article to make her angry. Annoyed at the intrusion maybe, but not furious. He understands that she prefers her life to remain private. Is she against the whole idea of marriage? Family? Hard for him to tell. She was married before? She kept repeating that it is all "impossible." Did she mean him? Or them? Or marriage? Or the press? Time is passing. Howard wants to have the thing settled.

IRENE

BEVERLY HILLS

Irene is home alone when she reads the article. Jeffrey is at school and David is at the studio. She reads it twice and then shreds the newspaper. As if that will make the article disappear. Speculation that Howard wants to marry Kate is one thing, a ring is something else entirely. A ring implies a future, and a future is what Kate believes she has to forego. She said it, that day they sat in the garden, no matter how many times Irene tried to tell her otherwise. Kate believes her ability to share a future was scooped out along with her womb.

When Kate calls, as Irene knew she would, it's between the matinee and the evening show and they speak in the broken sentences of friends who understand each other.

"You could do it, if you love him enough?" Irene says.

"No, that is what I cannot do to him, if I love him," Kate says.

"Not all men want children, even when they have them," Irene says, but she understands. Why get close enough for it to hurt every day?

HOWARD

CHICAGO

Did he convince her? He can't tell. The situation is new and bewildering for Howard. He has never had to exert such effort to convince a woman that he is *not* proposing. He told her that yes, he was in the shop, even that he picked the stones, but that the stones were meant for a necklace for his aunt's birthday. Ridiculous. His aunt would never wear emeralds. Now, he will have to have an emerald necklace made up for his aunt and sent to her in Texas just in case. He calls Noah and tells him what to order.

PART NINE

POISON

LOS ANGELES
JANUARY 1938

No one says it out loud, but, yes, it's because she's a woman. A man can make six flops in a row and his salary won't budge if he has enough star power. But a woman? No. The public will not forgive Kate for playing a woman playing a beautiful man.

Holiday and *Bringing Up Baby* are good, but they will both flop anyway. Her name on the billing is enough to sink them. Cary Grant is untarnished and his quote goes up by 30 percent.

We never promised this town would be fair.

KATE
HANCOCK PARK

The house is right there, on the eighth hole of the Wilshire Country Club course. She and Howard often take a couple of flashlights and go putting in the moonlight, and when they get home from parties or premieres, they swim. Howard refers to it as "their life." Kate and Howard, Country Mouse and City Mouse. He talks about them in the plural. She doesn't.

The press still chase them. Are they engaged? On the rocks? Secretly married? Everyone wants to know. Kate and Howard read about themselves over breakfast. At Christmas, photographers broke into her house in the canyon. She and Howard were not there, but Kate has not slept in that house since. Casement windows are easy to unlock, the policeman told her.

Now, Howard always wants them to stay at his house, where the security is absolute, and that's fine with Kate as Howard is so often out. She moves Joanna and Ragnhild and Louis over there, and now her house is hollow. At first, Howard wanted to buy a house for them, but she says no. Buying a new house would have put her in his debt. She tells him that this house suits her, less messy to move back to her own house if they end. Kate always thinks about the end. And mostly, his house does suit her. Large, squared off rooms, tall windows, space, and separate wings. They have their own phone lines, do their own work during the day and in the afternoons, meet in the kitchen or on the sofa in the library. Kate reads scripts with her feet tucked under his legs. Howard tells her that he normally cannot bear women's feet near him, but he adores hers. It is the nicest compliment he has ever given her.

Kate is still surprised by how fiercely she wants him.

. . .

He is shouting downstairs. She runs to meet him on the landing. Did she ever run to meet Leland or Luddy?

"Mouse, we have to go now! Now!"

"Now? As in *now,* now?" she teases. Howard is still astonished that she can shower and be ready to leave the house in under ten minutes and is never late. He calls it her greatest achievement. Good god, I hope I do more with my life than that, she always says.

"Yes! Now! We've removed ninety pounds from the plane!"

"Howard, we went to the airfield to see the plane yesterday."

"That was before the ninety pounds!"

Kate pins up her hair with one hand and grabs her sun visor. They go to the airfield.

The plane without the ninety pounds looks the same to her but is clearly wondrous and changed to Howard. *He is really going to do it.* Kate admires the sheer nerve of the thing but does not understand how he *can* do it. The current record for an around the world flight, or series of flights, is 186 hours. Howard says he can fly at a higher altitude and cut the time in half. Even so, how will he stay awake for 93 hours? He has been planning the trip for years. Since he broke the record for speed. She pulls on her sun visor. It is bright at the airfield.

. . .

The next morning they are still talking about flying.

"Now, we will have the room and weight for an engineer as well as a navigator, as long as they are small."

"Are you going to advertise for very short engineers and navigators?" She's not serious but knows he will take her seriously.

"Yes! That's an excellent idea! We must tell Noah. You're brilliant. I love you." Howard picks up the phone on the hall table to dial Noah. He no longer waits for her to say it back. He says he loves her enough for both of them.

. . .

Does she love him? Hard to know when she's not working. The press hardly mention that she is an actress anymore, only that she is the woman Howard Hughes loves. It is not enough. If she is evicted from herself, how can there be enough of her left over to love him?

HOWARD
HANCOCK PARK
MARCH 1938

"Buy it out, just cut the ties," he says as she lines up her shot.

They are golfing on a sunny Wednesday. He would never admit it to her, but he loves that she is not working. The long days of filming for *Holiday* and all the press for the opening night of *Bringing Up Baby* last week meant that they'd hardly spent any time together.

"My contract?"

"Of course, your contract. Cary did it, and he was on top when he did it, must have cost him double."

"And I can buy my contract for peanuts now that I'm at the bottom? Is that it?"

A script, *Mother Carey's Chickens,* had come through that morning. She told Myron to turn it down and didn't bother to read it. They are offering her one fifth the money they offered her for *Bringing Up Baby*.

He knows he is being too blunt but there is no way to back out of the conversation now. "With the scripts they're offering you and the pay? I would hope your contract is cheap."

"And what does that say about me?" Kate says, lowering her club. "What does that say that *you* think about me?" She squares off, speaking loudly up to his good ear.

"I think you're marvelous."

"But you think my contract will be cheap now that I have no future?"

"It's not a bad thing, Kate. It's basic economics, Kate. Buy low, sell high."

KATE

COLDWATER CANYON

Kate is driving up to her house. She needs a night in her own home, even if it will be musty and empty. Joanna, Ragnhild and Louis all offer to come but then as Louis pointed out, who would take care of Mr. Howard? They have become his staff now, a fact that makes Kate feel resentful and petty. Logically she knows he invited her staff into his home and fired his own so *she* would be more comfortable. But Kate is not in the mood for logic.

Buy low. Sell high. The theory is sound but only if there is a realistic expectation of being on top again. She can feel it everywhere, her irrelevance, her unimportance. Being with Howard makes it worse.

IRENE
BEVERLY HILLS
MAY 1938

David and the studio have already settled on Vivien Leigh but they are not going to announce it. Irene wishes they would but David says the "nationwide search" is drawing publicity and he wants to keep the interest going. Irene insists that at least he tell Myron that Kate isn't getting the part. Vivien is unknown, inexpensive and perfect for Scarlett but that does not make it any easier for Kate. Myron says that Kate took the news quietly. Irene is sure Myron has not told her. Taking things quietly is unlike her.

. . .

Irene makes the decision when she is in the bath. Jeffrey is asleep, David is naturally not home, and the house is quiet. As soon as this film is released, and the spotlight shifts again, she is going to leave him. They cannot stop fighting. David thinks every absence, every transgression is excusable because he is doing great things, he is making "the greatest picture ever made." He has had the nerve to call it that. They fight in front of Jeffrey now, something they promised never to do. David storms out but then returns with extravagant gifts they can't afford.

She has contacted a real estate agent in New York. A college friend of Leland's. Once she lets her marriage go, Irene knows she will want to let Los Angeles go too. In New York, she will be someone new. Someone she has been all along. New York will suit her. In New York, no one cares about what happens out here.

She will find great writers. Produce something for the stage. Irene has always preferred plays to films.

. . .

"Of course, you should do it," Irene says, sliding her chair back into the shade.

"Is it even worth it? Buying myself out of a contract will just make it easier for them not to hire me." Kate holds up her hand to shield her eyes. The sun feels good. Freckles don't matter. She isn't filming anything.

"But when they *do* want you again, you will be able to set your own price." Kate reaches out to squeeze Irene's hand. Thanking her for the "when."

KATE

HANCOCK PARK

JUNE 1938

Turning it down was the right thing to do. She will not make a film called *Mother Carey's Chickens* for a fifth of her quoted fee. Third rate. All of it. The script, the director, the cast, the costumer, the photographer. Nobodies.

She telephones Myron to ask what she can make instead. Nothing. There is nothing she has been offered instead.

CARY

SANTA MONICA

"You moved up your flight by two months?" Cary says, reading the announcement in the *Herald Tribune*. He hands the paper back to Howard. How like him not to tell them.

"It's not just to impress her or to get her to go to bed with you, is it?" Randolph asks.

Cary turns to look at his lover. Randolph knows that since late last year, Howard and Kate have practically moved in together. *Of course* they go to bed together. But then, Cary heard from someone who heard from someone that they sleep in separate rooms and she turned down his proposal. But are rumors like that ever true? According to *Photoplay*, they have been married and divorced six times already. He repeated the rumor to Randolph but he never thought Randolph would mention it to Howard. And then Cary understands, and loves his lover for his tact. Randolph is giving Howard a natural opening, a graceful way of hinting that there is a problem and they *can't* go to bed together. It can happen to men. It has happened to Randolph, but only while Cary was with Virginia. It would explain why Howard has stopped talking about Kate.

"There are other reasons to fly around the world, Randy."

"It *would* be impressive to just up and go, though," Cary says.

"It *will* be impressive," Howard says. "If I am going to be an airman rather than a film director, I want to be the best goddamn airman on earth."

"And this would make it official?" Randolph says.

"Yes."

Howard likes things to be official.

. . .

"Don't read them," Randolph says, turning on a light. Cary is sitting in the study, four papers open in front of him. Early reviews for wide release of *Holiday* are terrible. It's Kate. Anything she touches goes sour.

"Could *you* not read them?" Of course not.

Cary is thinking of all the people in Bristol, opening the morning papers and reading about the failure of their native son. He thinks about Mabel Alice and the boy, Eric, his brother. The word "brother" is woolly in his mouth. "Brother" has always meant the first boy, the first edition, the one his mother is sure would have been perfect had he lived.

Cary has bought a house for his mother in a good part of town and engaged a housekeeper, gardener and nurse in a white aproned uniform. It's not that he thinks she needs a nurse but she is used to having one near her. A nurse is a comforting constant for his mother after all this time. Cary already has tickets booked to visit her again just after Christmas. Randolph suggested he bring his mother here but he can't. Elsie Leach would mean inviting Archie Leach into his California life. No. Archie Leach stays in Bristol.

He will call the house in the morning and ask them not to show his mother the newspapers.

HOWARD

SANTA MONICA

Howard likes to eat dinner with Kate but has taken to stopping in at the beach house in the early evenings to see Cary and Randolph for a drink. Good for him to be out of the house much of each day. Kate is leaving for New York in another month. Maybe being comfortable in the house will make her change her mind and stay? He wants Kate to feel happy in his house, and she will only do that if she is there alone most of the time. Howard knows that Kate, like all the best engines or plants, needs just the right conditions to thrive. She needs sunshine and cold water and movement and simple food. His Country Mouse. She teases him for needing none of these things, only airplane machinery, engine manuals and sky. Her City Mouse.

The three men are sitting out on the back deck, facing the ocean. Easier to talk when not looking at each other. These men can talk about almost anything together.

Howard knows Randolph was asking about sex the other day. His decision to stop talking about Kate has nothing to do with sex. Nothing to do with the bed. Howard will just not talk about Kate that way. Other women, in the past when there were other women, maybe, but never Kate. Their bed is a wild and ecstatic world built only for them. Maybe the feeling will dissipate or disappear one day. Until it does, or if it never does, Howard just wants to be near this woman. Talking about it would let other people in.

"This flight is something I have to do," Howard says.

"It's dangerous," Randolph says. "But you know that. What if you fall asleep and go slap bang into a mountain?"

"If I crash into a mountain, it will make more noise than 'slap bang.'"

"Cary, say something," Randolph says. But Howard and Randolph know that Cary goes long periods these days without saying anything. More animated than ever onscreen, Randolph says Cary has adopted a deep quiet at home. Randolph has told Howard that sometimes he goes to watch Cary on set, just to hear him talk. Cary has told Howard that he wishes Randolph could understand that it is nothing to do with him, or with them, that for now, he just needs to be home and still when he is not out there being Cary Grant, but Randolph has parents and so can't understand.

Later, when Cary is in the kitchen, Howard tries to explain to Randolph.

"Cary *has* a parent," Randolph says. "He lost his father but regained his mother. Why would that not make him happy?"

"No. Cary lost twenty years with one parent because the other took her away."

. . .

He will change the route. After months of planning, Howard decides he'll begin and end his round the world flight in New York and not Los Angeles. It will mean hauling the equipment and the ground crew and the spare crew to the other coast and putting them all up while they test engines and the weight. Ode will not like it. He thinks the sky in New York is too cluttered to enjoy flying. Noah is worried about the cost. Howard is resolute. The thing has to begin and end in New York.

It is where Kate will be.

LOS ANGELES
JULY 1938

It's a cheap shot. She doesn't even have a new film out. It is not a particular performance, it is just her. Garbo and Crawford, fine. They can take it. They are powerful old hands and their careers have weathered worse. Even if they never make another picture, the world will not forget Garbo and Crawford. They know how to keep away and wait it out until they're beloved again. But Kate Hepburn? Seems cruel. The Independent Theatre Owners Association meant to wound when they took out a full page in *The Hollywood Reporter* to tell the world that Kate Hepburn is *box office poison.*

KATE

HANCOCK PARK

Kate reads it alone. He leaves her sitting on the sofa in her study, legs tucked under her. Howard understands that she needs to read it the first time in private. On another day, she would love that he understands that about her. Today, she is reading the article. Howard did his best to warn her about what it says before he left for the airfield, but nothing can prepare her for seeing her name, despised in tall, black letters. Despised by people she has never met.

She can hear the telephone ringing. It has been ringing all afternoon, but Kate is still reading the article.

Joanna sticks her head into Kate's study.

"Myron, again," Joanna mouths.

Kate shakes her head no.

Myron, Irene, Cary, Laura, her mother, Luddy, George. No. Kate does not want to speak to anyone.

She is never going to leave this sofa. Waiting for them to take her back will never work. She has to *do* something.

Buy low. Sell high.

Kate stands, stretches her legs and then goes to call Myron. She is going to get out of this town.

. . .

She goes to see Cary on his day off. He is the only one she knows who has done it. Randolph opens the door and takes her down to the pool. Cary is sitting up on a yellow sun lounger, his script for *Gunga Din* open in front of him. The pages are covered in Cary's penciled notes.

"I thought you were off book with that script?" Kate says, dropping into the chair beside him. Kate knows Cary has been preparing for this film for months.

"I switched parts. Have to start all over." He leans across to kiss her cheek.

"Switched parts? With whom?"

"Doug Fairbanks. Now I'm playing Cutter and he gets to marry Joan Fontaine onscreen."

"Yep. They tossed a coin for it," Randolph says, pouring lemonade for Kate. "Now, Cary is the lead."

"The director agreed?"

"The director suggested the coin toss," Cary says. "Last resort, I would have walked."

"No contract. No studio. No agent."

"No contract, no studio, no agent," Cary says, understanding her right away. "He had to negotiate with *me*."

. . .

When Kate tells Myron she wants to buy herself out of her studio contract, he begins speaking of their relationship in the past tense. As if she is buying herself out of his representation as well, but she isn't ready to make that leap. Cary says life is easier once you are a free agent. But Cary is wanted. An unwanted free agent is just an outsider.

She will go home. Howard even says he'll fly her there if she likes. Irene has been talking about New York lately and it has made Kate hungry for her house. She tells George she is going. Not right away, but soon. George wants her to find a script. She has no idea how to do that. Where to look. She will go to New York and watch plays. Actors acting right in front of you, no safety net, no second take, no drops in the eyes to fake the tears. Stage acting is the real thing. Kate only wants to be near real things.

She will hole up in her beautiful city house and figure this thing out. She can't think in this low, flat town where she is not wanted anymore.

HOWARD
HANCOCK PARK

What did Randolph say? "So she will go to bed with you?" He *would* break the record for flying around the globe if it meant she would go to bed with him, and it would be worth it, but thank god, he doesn't have to. Bed is the only place the press can't get at them, which is fine as bed is where they like to be anyway. Even when nights go by and nothing much happens there, they are still bound by that frontier spirit of adventure when they lie down together. Together is where he is happy; it is where he wants to be.

At first, he moved the date up to distract Kate from the national opening for *Holiday*. Now, it is to fix something else. When the Independent Theatre Owners Association take out a full-page advertisement in *The Hollywood Reporter* and call the woman you love *box office poison,* it's time to change the national conversation.

. . .

"Are you moving it up so they will stop writing about me?" Kate asks.

"Beating the World Record for flying around the world just to change the subject?" Howard says. "Who would do that?"

"You. You would do that. You darling crazy man."

"It *will* work, and if not, we'll think of something else," he says, kissing her.

He doesn't notice that she does not answer.

Yes. He would do that. And he will do that. It is not only to stop the press from tearing into her; it's also just to do *something*. Move the air, the rumors, the story. When he comes back from the airfield, she is angled over a notebook, writing something. She does not want to talk about how to fix the problem. He can't be still and do nothing. He has to break the siege. If it will make her think about something else, even if the something else is whether or not he will fall asleep, or run out of oxygen, or if his engine will fail or he will get pulled down by the g-force. Whatever will make her forget these small people and want to live forever in this house, with him, he will do it.

He understands why she takes it hard. She was let down by the people who promised to protect her and back her, always. None of the others on the list are taking it as badly. Garbo shrugged it off and Joan Crawford was just offered a huge loan-out by MGM. But not Kate. *Bringing Up Baby* flopped when it should have hit and *Holiday* is smash material, but the studio has already decided to pull it from most theaters in the South and the Midwest. These pictures are good—really good. Howard can see it. The studios can see it. But, Kate can't.

. . .

The timing is not perfect but it *can* be done. He will make it work. She is scheduled to go back to New York mid-month and his flight is now scheduled for the end of July. Noah and Ode just confirmed with the airfields. Ideally, Howard would have done more test flights and met with the ground crews before announcing, but there is no time. Kate is booked onto The *Super Chief* and he wants to be there when she arrives. He has offered to fly her but she says she is taking too much luggage. Howard has to fly the navigator and engineer, so it saves him a trip, but he would have done it for her. He would have even reinstalled the seats he'd just removed if it would make her more comfortable.

Howard understands packing heavily for a trip; he likes his own things when he travels.

PART TEN

SOMEONE ELSE

KATE

NEW YORK CITY

JULY 1938

He's done it. Howard and his four-man crew, in a Lockheed Model 14 Super Electra. The radio reported that there were some dicey moments but Howard Hughes never lost confidence. What does the radio man know? Howard has just touched down. He told her once that one day, he would die in a plane. "But not this plane," he said when he left her New York brownstone four days ago. The radio man says the ticker tape parade will start before Howard has even left the airfield. Too many people are gathered on the streets already. The police don't want to wait. The radio man doesn't know where Mr. Hughes is going but he's sure that he will arrive at the parade soon.

Kate knows where he's going. He called her from the airfield and is on his way to her, in a car Noah rented. A car that looks like all the other cars. Howard said that first, before he showers or sleeps, he wants to come here, to her brownstone. She is touched that to see her, he will be late for his own parade.

She knows he designed his arrival back in New York to coincide with the nationwide opening of *Holiday*. Extravagant but pointless. It won't help and he doesn't see it. All the noise and celebrity he cooks up only make it worse. He cannot get her out of this mess by being faster, louder, *more*. And, if he could get her out, it wouldn't count. She has to dig her own way. Anyway, how does breaking a world record help her? Yes, it keeps them in the papers but their balance is gone. That force that kept them stable, evenly matched. She has lost her footing.

. . .

He is dirty, worn and thinner than she has ever seen him. The radio man was wrong. They were not dicey moments; they were catastrophic. It spills out of him in a rush. Engine failure, g-force, dizziness, running out of gasoline, landing unexpectedly on foreign runways with no warning, running out of oxygen, blacking out. My god. He is shaken by the risk. But, he did it.

"Proud of me?"

"Proud of you."

"That's better than a parade."

"You're already late."

HOWARD

NEW YORK CITY

Why would she want to be here? She is right to stay away. People screaming, trying to touch him. Dust, exhaust, horse manure. They call it ticker tape but really, they are throwing everything at him. Flowers, notes, coins, paper airplanes. He does not like to touch things other people have touched. Howard is sure she is listening on the radio. It is enough.

When he told her about the flights, the stories felt stale. He could not capture the fear of a stalled engine nor the exhilaration when it found an extra drop of fuel and restarted. Those terrible moments were silent and now do not fit into words. They replay in his head. He cannot make her part of it the way he wants to.

Instead, he told her that these are stories they will tell their grandchildren one day. But that didn't bring her closer either.

LAURA

NEW YORK CITY

She goes to the parade even though she knows Kate won't be there. Why would she go? More speculation if she stays away. That's their game, isn't it? Eluding the press so the press will chase harder? Kate doesn't need a parade to see him. They will celebrate tonight, alone.

Laura tries to picture herself happy. Isn't that what that doctor said to do? He's probably a quack. Anyone who charges seventy dollars an hour must be a quack. She leaves before Howard's float passes by. She does not want to see him. Only her.

LOS ANGELES

JULY 1938

Like everyone else in America, John Ford is listening to the radio. That man has done it. Stayed awake for ninety-four hours, nearly died from lack of oxygen, kept going. Goddamn. He deserves her. When John Ford sailed the *Araner* to Mexico after filming with Kate Hepburn he stayed drunk for three weeks. And then he sailed home to his wife.

KATE

NEW YORK CITY

She listens to his parade on the radio. Howard, the best airman in the world, waving, smiling, catching roses from pretty girls. Kate is sure it's awful for him. So many people. All that noise. He must not be able to hear a thing.

She switches off the radio. He's leaving Battery Park, moving up Broadway toward City Hall. It will be more of the same. He will tell her about it when he gets home. *Home.* Her home, not their home. But that is what she needs now. *Her* home. She is better here, sturdier. In her own house, in her own city. Stories to tell their grandchildren. Kate has to tell him.

But she already knows she won't.

While Howard is at the parade, Kate has her second telephone call with the playwright Philip Barry. When she first called him, she asked if he was surprised to hear from her after so long.

"Not very. I knew you would want to come back here eventually and I knew someday you would want a play."

"Not very. My eye." They crackle together. She can hear it.

He agrees. He will write something, someone for her. She just needs to tell him who she wants to be and he will write her a story to turn her into someone new. She will tell Howard when he comes back. She knows he will be happy for her.

George was right. She needed to find the right script.

HOWARD

NEW YORK CITY

AUGUST 1938

The date is arbitrary. Yes, last week he booked the airfield and the ground crew to fly back tomorrow morning but one phone call to Noah and all that is undone. Gone. Why is he leaving on this day rather than another day? Another later day after they have had more time together? He doesn't need to be back. He can work here. He can do it all on the telephone, just as he did when he followed her on tour. Then, he didn't wait for her invitation, he just told Noah to make the bookings. What's changed?

. . .

It doesn't happen the way he planned. He had wanted to fly her home to California and then give it to her when they landed. He imagined that it would be sunrise; she reminds him of morning, but the landing time would have depended on the wind speed.

Instead, he gives it to her in her bedroom in her townhouse in the city that is not his own.

"Have you had it all this time?"

"All this time."

"Those news articles?"

"Yes, someone at the jeweler's leaked it; the owner was mortified."

He should have given it to her yesterday, when they still had the night to spend together, when they could have curled together in her big white bed and made plans, talked about the places they would fly and the family they would make. But he had wanted the contrast of the gray pink dawn and the deep green emerald and it rained yesterday. Sound is compromised so light and color are important to Howard.

She said she loves it, didn't she? Loves it. Loves him. That is what matters.

Neither of them used the word "marriage." But, it is understood. Spelling it out is reductive.

. . .

She goes with him to the airfield. He drives her car. Or not really her car, Luddy's car, parked around the corner from the townhouse. That lump leaves it there in case she needs it. It irritates

Howard. Kate tells him that she will drive it back, as if he cares where Luddy's car ends up. He tries not to be bothered by driving the ex-husband's automobile. He wishes it were not such a good car.

"You will come home, when the script is done?" Home to his house, that has become their house.

"But then there will be the rehearsals?"

"You could come home for a while before the rehearsals?"

"Yes, maybe before the rehearsals."

"You don't have to do this play," he says.

"Yes, I do."

He has said it all and will not say it again. He has never said it to a woman before. Not like this, outright, flat. At the kitchen table of that tall city house, he told her he would take care of her, that she could have her own money, her own account, her own car. Whatever will make her forget it all comes from him. It is not the money, he knows that. He wishes he didn't understand so well. It is the weight and counterweight between them. And she is doing exactly what he would do. She is creating opportunity where none exists. She is making herself valuable. It is exactly why he loves her. How he loves her.

But, it is not enough to bring her back.

She stands to the side of the airstrip with her hand shading her eyes as he climbs up to the cockpit. He turns around but doesn't wave. He just wants to look at her.

. . .

As he flies, he runs through the conversation again and again until it frays and separates like ribbon. He tries to stop but can't.

She doesn't want to come back. Not yet. But, she has promised she will come back in the end. Did she promise? Or did he add that part? Yes. He is sure she promised. She will come back in the end.

CARY

SANTA MONICA

SEPTEMBER 1938

No one in this sunny city is talking about war. No one is talking about Neville Chamberlain or Czechoslovakia or Herr Hitler. They talk about the WPA and the New Deal and the Hoovervilles but not war with Germany. His mother writes that war is all anyone talks about in Bristol. Neville Chamberlain is going to Munich at the end of this month.

Cary and his mother speak on the telephone. The more often he calls, the more fluent they become. Cary calls on Sundays. His mother tells him she is glad Cary is in America, where he cannot be drafted. Cary tells her that he'll likely be overage if they announce the draft.

"Only if the war is short," his mother says. "If it goes on, like the last one, they will need every man they can get."

KATE

NEW YORK CITY

They've settled into a rhythm. They speak on the telephone at least three times a week. Kate knows his number by heart. At first she could hear his pen scratching out notes but now, she hears the keys clacking.

"Typing is faster," Philip Barry tells her.

He sends the first wad of pages. *Tracy Lord*. Her voice, the tart, abbreviated phrasing. He has it.

"But they have to like you," Philip says.

"No, first, they have to hate me and pull me down, and then come to like me. It's different. First, we have to give them room to dislike me."

. . .

The photographers are gone. No one waits outside the house. They are all in Los Angeles, looking for Howard.

HOWARD

HANCOCK PARK

"Is it almost finished?"

"Almost."

"By the end of the month?"

"This month?"

"The end of next month then?"

"Yes. By the end of next month."

Howard has kept a pillow that smells of her. He doesn't ask if she is wearing the ring.

RANDOLPH

SANTA MONICA

Cary and Randolph have always read the international news. It affects their investments. Now they listen to the BBC Empire Service as well. Last month, they moved Cary's money out of Britain and into gold. This month, they invest in companies that manufacture airplanes.

Cary switches off the radio.

"Do I bring her here?" Cary asks. He has just hung up with his business manager.

"And your brother, Eric?" Randolph asks. "And *his* mother?" Randolph is careful to refer to Mabel Alice as Eric's mother rather than Mrs. Leach or Cary's stepmother. Randolph is tactful that way.

"It's impossible to get travel visas for all of them," Cary says.

Randolph realizes that Cary has already made inquiries.

"Have you thought about going back if war does come?" If Cary goes, Randolph has already decided he would go with him. He has been trying not to ask.

Cary doesn't answer right away, which answers Randolph's question.

"Am I still British?"

"Do you feel British?"

"*Archie* is British," Cary says softly.

Would Archie enlist?

KATE

NEW YORK CITY

SEPTEMBER 1938

The whole first draft. She reads it at the kitchen table, start to finish. Yes, he's done it. Philip Barry has knocked her down and raised her up. Tracy Lord is the Kate the public believe her to be. She sends out four copies. Cary, George, Irene, and Howard. *Top Secret* is printed at the top of every page.

Yes.

Irene would love to produce it.

Cary wants to star in the film version.

George wants to direct the film version.

"Buy the film rights today," Howard says.

. . .

They do not always say good night now. Kate and Philip Barry are editing morning to night and sometimes she falls asleep before calling. She wants to speak to him, wants to tell him everything they are writing, but she can't. She is excited and happy and it feels wrong to show him that when he misses her so.

He no longer asks when she is coming back. Without her noticing, they are no longer a *we*.

. . .

They talk about the script. His suggestions are good. Howard knows how to trim a line to make it land. Kate does not tell Philip Barry which edits come from Howard.

Quietly, without any fanfare, she offers to buy the film rights to *The Philadelphia Story*. No, Philip Barry will not sell. Not for any price. He also knows this show will be a hit.

LOS ANGELES
SEPTEMBER 1938

The flood that takes the house away happens on a Wednesday. The storm is not reported here. Not before it hits anyway. It moves up the East Coast, the way that storms over there do. Kit Hepburn goes into Old Saybrook to put extra fuel in the car and buy a second bottle of milk. Bob offers to come and put boards on the windows at Fenwick but then his day at the hospital runs long and he can't make it. He telephones to apologize.

Kate is at Fenwick, reading on the porch, when the wind picks up. She switches on the radio to listen to the weather report before the electricity is knocked out. She turns the outside furniture upside down to make it heavier and takes down the sun umbrella.

By the time the storm pulls the house off its foundations and into the sound, the Hepburns are all crouching on the small inland hill. Kate is the last one out. She has to climb through a first-floor window to get back to land and her trousers are wet up to the knees. Her arms are full of photographs.

The big summerhouse sails down, hugging close to the land until it pauses, turns right, and bobs away. The Hepburns watch it go, feeling proud that their house remains upright all the way. It is more dignified. Sailing out, shoulders straight, the house is in open ocean now and never coming back. It is over. All that feeling, gone out to sea.

CARY

SANTA MONICA

He's going to do it. Neville Chamberlain will offer up Czechoslovakia to protect the "peace." What kind of peace is that, Cary asks Randolph.

Howard says the government has already contacted him about the design for warplanes and fighter jets. They want to use the H-1, his flat rivets and streamlined design. The president telephoned.

"And he doesn't want to pay for it," Howard says.

"Give it to him, Howard," Cary says. "Give him whatever he wants."

RANDOLPH

SANTA MONICA

"Will you go over if it comes to it?" Randolph asks. They are sitting on their back deck, being home, together. These days are sweeter now that they are endangered.

"I made an appointment with a lawyer last week," Cary says. "To petition the court to legally change my name."

"An American court?"

"A California court."

Randoph understands immediately. They have spoken about it before. "You want to be an American," Randolph says, surprised.

"Cary Grant *is* American."

Yes. Reinvented, built from scratch. Cary Grant has always been American.

"Your mother?"

"I will try but she will never leave England."

KATE

FENWICK, CONNECTICUT

He sends bottled water, enough for the whole town, but he doesn't come out to Connecticut. She does not ask him to. Is he waiting for her to ask? She could, but she holds back. She had thought he would want to fly in and rescue her. No. She doesn't need to be rescued. She will dig herself out. Inexplicably, the garage has remained standing. She finds a shovel and begins.

By the end of the day, she has found a bathtub and most of the family silver, sunk into the mud. But the photograph albums are gone. She wants to hear his voice but she cannot telephone him. She has no phone.

IRENE

BEVERLY HILLS

David is not worried about the war; everyone will want to go to the pictures in wartime, but he *is* worried about his new star. He must get Vivien Leigh out of Britain and MGM is not moving on the paperwork. He has registered his own company. Maybe he can push her visa application through quicker. He calls his studio Selznick International Pictures.

"Do you like the name?" David asks.

Irene has just finished getting Jeffrey off to school. She doesn't answer.

"And I have put you on the board of directors," David says. He hasn't but he meant to. He will do it today.

"No," Irene says, without looking up.

"No, you don't like the name, or no, you will not be on the board of directors?"

"No, I will not be part of you or your new company."

"But, darling, we do everything together."

"No, David, you have never joined our company, this one, the one that lives in this house."

KATE

FENWICK, CONNECTICUT

A neighbor takes them in. The Hepburns have never been popular here, have always been outsiders, but now that their house has gone, they become one of them. Kate's clothes and shoes are mud encrusted but she doesn't care. Kate, who needs three showers a day to feel clean, is happy to be filthy. She and her family work together. The press come and take photographs. Kate will not pose, but she doesn't mind either. She stands still, a kerchief on her head and shovel in her hand. The press have come to see her lose everything. That is what they want? Fine.

. . .

On the third day, they have found all they will find. It's time to go back to life and plan how to start again. Dr. Hepburn has contacted a prominent Hartford architect. Kit Hepburn has called one in Old Lyme who she likes better. Everyone agrees the foundations must be built of concrete this time.

It is time for Kate to go back to New York.

Sitting on the hillside where they eat their lunch, Kate tells her mother about the script, the play, the plan. She tells her mother about Tracy Lord, about the new Katharine Hepburn. No family, no children, a star who only ever wanted the life of a star.

Her mother understands the script and the plan. The public needs to see her apologize before they will raise her daughter up again. And then Kate will rise up to become someone unbreakable. It's a steep price to live this life but her daughter will pay it. It is what she is choosing.

"It's worth it and then I will never be in this position again. I will act, all the time." Kate throws a clod of dirt down the hill. The ground is drying. "Tracy, this new Kate, is biting and strong and not me, but she is who they think I am, who they want me to be," Kate tries to explain. To simplify. "She is who I will be from now on."

"Who you will be for them?"

"For everyone who is not us," Kate says. "I cannot be like Bob or Marion or Peg or you. There will be no happy family growing around me. I have to do this well; there is nothing else."

They are side by side, facing the water.

"I can see that you have to do this and it will be difficult. But, it won't be a small life, not a forgotten life. What does Howard say?"

"Howard. He wants the me from before." She stops. Simplifies. "He wants a whole family, a full life. It won't work."

"Has he said he wants them?" her mother asks. "Have you given him the chance to say he doesn't? Have you ever told him?"

Kate looks at her mother, the brilliant feminist campaigner who keeps herself smaller to make her husband feel bigger. Kate will never have to do that.

"No. I know he wants them. I don't need to ask him," Kate says, not looking up. "It's all over with us, and I will be alone." Sitting by the hole where the house used to be makes these things easier to say, but she still cannot look at her mother.

"Kate"—her mother's voice is gentler than she has heard since she was a child—"my darling, you are already alone. You have been alone since." She stops. "You know since when."

Even now, her mother cannot say her brother's name.

. . .

Her sister Peg is getting ready to go back to school. She likes having her big sister home, even when home is gone.

"And you'll stay in New York?"

"I'll work in Los Angeles, but yes. I will always live in New York."

She has not said it aloud until now.

PART ELEVEN

THE PHILADELPHIA STORY

LOS ANGELES

MARCH 1939

It's rare, but everyone knows right away. It's one of those shows. The kind that buzzes and crackles and is touched with that stuff that makes things go bang. It opens at the Shubert Theatre on West Forty-fourth. The audience is on their feet before the curtain starts to fall. By the time it rises again to show the actors as themselves, they are screaming. Katharine Hepburn is beloved again. She is theirs.

Her family is in the audience. They watch her, their daughter, their sister. They watch her pretend to be someone else under the hot lights. They watch her keep on pretending after the curtain falls and rises again. She is not their Kate.

Studio producers and agents have come from the other coast. They are already thinking about casting. Of course, it will be a film. Myron is there, Louis B. Mayer, George, the Selznicks, all in the first six rows. Louis B. sends a junior producer to look for Philip Barry in the intermission. He wants to get in first and is prepared to be generous. Leland Hayward is in a box just above the stage. He wants to see her up close, the line of her back, her nose, her long arms. Margaret is not with him.

Howard watches from the wings. He can hear better from there and does not want anyone to watch him watching her. He understands that she is no longer his but he wants to bring her a towel. He can see she has sweated through the back of her dress. There is whispering behind him—the lead dresser and the assistant stage manager. Standing offstage, in the shadow of the lighting rig, Howard has heard the rumors zipping through the theater. Paramount, MGM, RKO, they are all looking for Philip Barry. Howard already knows they won't find him.

The emerald ring is in his breast pocket. They are done, he understands that, and it was honorable of her to give it back to him. But he had it made for her and he will never give it to anyone else. In all the life he has yet to live, there will be no one like her. How could there be?

He will put it in her dressing room during the curtain call.

They are waiting outside the closed dressing room door. All the big players are lined up, trying to look casual, but do not be fooled, this is going to be a bidding war. Irene refuses to wait in the bar. She wants to watch her friend outsmart Hollywood.

Junior producers return. They whisper to senior producers. No one can find Philip Barry. That is because he is already at the bar, wishing he had held out and waited. But Howard Hughes is a hard man to turn down.

Kate can hear them, outside her door, all those powerful men from the town that didn't want her. And Howard, the man who swears he will want her always. She removes her makeup in long, slow strokes. The emerald ring lies in her jewelry dish. Howard must want her to have it. He designed it for her. She cannot marry him, but she will never marry anyone else. She puts on the ring.

"And you helped write it?" Louis B. says loudly, hating that this conversation is happening in a hallway.

"It is based on her," a young producer from Paramount says. "Of course, she helped write it."

"Who owns the film rights to this story?" David Selznick asks, speaking across Kate to Myron, as if Myron still represents her.

"The thing only opened tonight. The playwright, Barry, he must still own them," Louis B. says.

"No," Kate says, clearly, speaking for herself. She will not have anyone speak for her again. "Philip Barry does not own the rights to this story. *He* does."

She is looking toward Howard, who is in the corner, standing back from the crowd. She is proud that they have beat the town together.

"No," Howard says, speaking quietly, "that's not quite right."

The greedy crowd twist around to see him but he looks over their heads to Kate, standing in the center.

He speaks only to her.

"This is your story. You own it."

Love has nothing to do with what you are
expecting to get—only with what you
are expecting to give—which is everything.

—*Katharine Hepburn*

AUTHOR'S NOTE

What happened next:

IRENE SELZNICK

Irene Mayer Selznick divorced David Selznick and went on to become a legendary New York theater producer. In 1947, working closely with Tennessee Williams, she steered the original production of *A Streetcar Named Desire* to Broadway. The cast included Jessica Tandy, Karl Malden and Marlon Brando in his first breakout role. Irene Mayer Selznick died of breast cancer in 1990.

HOWARD HUGHES

During World War II, Howard Hughes became a leading defense contractor, developing and supplying aircraft for the United States military. An innovator in the field of aviation, Hughes never returned to film directing. After suffering a near fatal plane crash in 1946, Hughes also developed an entirely new model of hospital bed, an early prototype of ones used today. In order to manage the pain resulting from the crash, Hughes began taking codeine and was addicted to large doses of the drug until his death in 1976. As his obsessive-compulsive disorder worsened, his behavior grew eccentric and Hughes became increasingly isolated, moving from hotel to hotel, always staying in the top floor penthouse. Although she never resumed their romance, Katharine Hepburn always spoke warmly of Hughes. She kept their vivid love letters and the emerald engagement ring for the rest of her life.

LUDLOW OGDEN SMITH

Luddy Ogden Smith eventually married a woman named Elisabeth Albers, but he remained close to his ex-wife and her family until his death in 1979. He named his only daughter Katharine.

CARY GRANT

Cary Grant did try to join the Royal Navy at the start of World War II but was told his talents would be better used to raise funds and morale. By the time the United States entered the war, Grant was too old to be considered eligible for active service in the U.S. military. Desperately worried about his mother in Bristol, a city devastated by bombing raids, Grant repeatedly applied for permission to travel to Britain throughout the war but was denied. His mother survived and Grant returned to the city once peace was declared. Today, a statue dedicated to Grant stands in Millennium Square and Bristol holds the Cary Comes Home film festival every two years.

Grant married five times, eventually becoming a father and walking away from Hollywood in 1966, at the height of his fame. Under increasing pressure from the studios to deny any hint of homosexuality, he and Randolph Scott stopped living together sometime in the mid 1940s. Although no one can ever know the true nature of their relationship, toward the end of his life, a writer friend asked Grant about his feelings for Scott. He answered, "Have you ever heard of gravity collapse? Some people call it love at first sight." Cary Grant is remembered as one of the greatest stars of the golden age of Hollywood. Synonymous with elegance and style, he once said, "Everyone wants to be Cary Grant. Even I want to be Cary Grant."

KATHARINE HEPBURN

While Katharine Hepburn never remarried, she did enter into a long love affair with actor Spencer Tracy, who was himself already married. George Cukor did build a cottage on his property on Cordell Drive. Hepburn and Tracy were living there together when Tracy died in 1967. Hepburn took over the lease and kept it as her Los Angeles home until Cukor's death in 1983. Spencer Tracy's last movie was *Guess Who's Coming to Dinner*, filmed when he knew he was dying. Tracy's final speech of the film is said to be meant for Hepburn.

Katharine Hepburn refused to sell the film rights to *The Philadelphia Story* unless she was cast in the starring role and permitted to select both the leading men and the director. She chose Cary Grant, Jimmy Stewart and George Cukor. MGM agreed to her terms and Katharine Hepburn was relaunched as a star. She was nominated for Best Actress for her role, one of six Academy Award nominations the film received. In her career, Hepburn was nominated twelve times and won four Academy Awards, more than any other actor in history.

Katharine Hepburn absolutely refused to do television interviews, but in 1973 her friend Irene Selznick talked her into meeting with talk show host Dick Cavett. Hepburn agreed to go to Cavett's studio, just to see how it felt. They spoke and then Hepburn suggested they move forward with the interview right away with no studio audience. Hepburn did not know the initial conversation was being filmed but eventually allowed Cavett to air those four minutes of footage along with the subsequent interview. We see Hepburn reorganize the furniture, ensuring a stable surface where she can put up her foot, switch chairs so she can be filmed from her better side, ask the hair and makeup person to fix her hair so it's loose and "falling down," so she can then haphazardly pile it back up. It's part of the act. In essence, we see her stage manage and preset the interview so her manner will seem entirely impromptu and natural and she can best play the part of Katharine Hepburn. She knew what worked for her and became famous for her candid, unstudied, unrehearsed personality. Of all the primary, archival, video and biographical sources I found, these four minutes of film were among the most useful. They helped me tell a story of the woman I saw in those unguarded moments. A woman who had perfected her public-facing technique, who learned the hard way how to get to the top and stay there.

Many of the historical figures featured in this novel came to prominence just as Hollywood was becoming a more dangerous place. The Hays Code and surrounding scrutiny meant that in effect, a star could be quickly "canceled" for getting caught saying or doing something deemed transgressive. As a result, much of what we know of the sexuality and private lives of stars such as Cary Grant and Katharine Hepburn is based upon personal accounts from friends and industry insiders at the time. It is impossible to know the truth about Katharine Hepburn's intimate affairs with both men and women. Her relationship with Laura Harding remains an open question, regardless of the fact that biographers and contemporaries claim the connection was absolutely sexual. And so, while the timeline of their friendship in this novel is rooted in fact, the emotional and sexual choreography is very much a fictional creation. It is a guess at what *might* have happened.

As far as possible, I stuck to the historical chronology but there are places where dates, names and events are altered to improve pacing and storytelling. For instance, Cary Grant did not buy himself out of his contract, he simply chose not to renew it but I have adjusted the detail in service of the story. In other cases, changes were made to avoid confusion such as when two characters had the same name. With such a vast and interconnected web of characters, many professional, personal and romantic adventures I would have loved to explore did not make it into the final novel at all. Howard Hughes had several brief but high-profile romances between his liaison with Billie Dove and his relationship with Katharine Hepburn but I left them out for narrative clarity. Hepburn herself likely had a tempestuous sexual relationship with John Ford and possibly with the editor Jane Loring, among others during this time but those encounters could be entire novels in themselves.

I would have loved to write the story of Katharine Hepburn briefly fleeing to Paris in 1934 after receiving bad press. She returned on the same boat as Ernest Hemingway, who was sailing home from Europe with his wife Pauline. Allegedly, he gave Hepburn a fantastic pep talk about facing the cameras. Whatever transpired, Hepburn stepped off the boat ready to dazzle reporters. Just after Cary Grant's separation from Virginia Cherrill, Randolph Scott briefly married and then divorced but like Grant, he never moved out of their shared home. Other events such as Cary's trip to Bristol have been condensed and restructured in order to streamline the narrative. In reality, Cary Grant made multiple visits to Bristol—first to reconcile with his father and then later upon learning his mother was alive. Howard Hughes's unfortunate visit to the Hepburn home in Fenwick, Connecticut, was excluded as it has been depicted in films such as *The Aviator* and I wanted to avoid scenes that already exist in the collective imagination.

Some private moments live only in the negative spaces of missing or fragmented correspondence and I was interested in examining events that *might* have happened. We know from Luddy's letters that Hepburn was rushed to Good Samaritan Hospital in Los Angeles in January 1933. Upon her release, she quickly returned to Connecticut to be treated by her father. For narrative ease, I moved the event back to December when she was already home on the East Coast. While we don't know the exact nature of the surgery, we do know that she nearly died several times while on the operating table and that things went awry as the surgery took twice the amount of time as expected. We also know that the surgery left a scar on her "lower anatomy." It could not have been her appendix as her father had already removed it while she was at Bryn Mawr. Months later, Hepburn's friend Alice Palache mentioned in a letter that Kate was still recuperating and was extremely unwell. Hepburn biographer, William J. Mann, surmised from this information that the surgery was likely to be uterine, possibly a hysterectomy. It is interesting to note that it is only after 1933 that Hepburn is quoted as saying that she did not want children. She never publicly referenced the surgery.

Some of the unlikeliest events of the novel really happened. Howard Hughes did land on the golf course in an effort to spend time with Katharine Hepburn. Cary Grant did find out that his mother was alive and living in a mental institution decades after he left Bristol. Cary Grant and Randolph Scott also did pose for a series of domestic photographs in their shared home. The Hepburn house in Fenwick, Connecticut, floated clean off its moorings in the great storm of 1938, and Howard Hughes sent the whole town bottled water. Hughes also really did help Hepburn to outsmart Hollywood and together they bought the film rights to *The Philadelphia Story* before the smash hit play ever opened on Broadway. Hepburn went on to five decades of iconic popularity, dying at age ninety-six at her home in Fenwick.

I am hugely indebted to the vast array of biographers and film historians who have preserved so much of the cultural history of this time. For anyone wishing to read further, I would urge them to read the work of Charlotte Chandler, Anne Edwards, Scott Eyman, Barbara Leaming, William J. Mann, Patrick McGilligan, David O. Selznick, and Irene Mayer Selznick, as well as Hepburn's own memoir, *Me*.

This was a daunting and thrilling novel to write and 1930s Hollywood a glorious and storied place to mentally make camp. Katharine Hepburn is ultimately unknowable. She designed it that way. But the words I found most often used to describe Katharine Hepburn are independent, unapologetic, and original.

ACKNOWLEDGMENTS

This novel wouldn't exist without the kindness of so many people. I'm grateful to all who read, guided, and encouraged along the way. I would like to particularly thank:

Kaleem Aftab, Anita Angad, Adrienne Brodeur, Jack Brough and Jess Ronane, Louis Brough, Emma Burbank, and everyone at The Kate, Anne Burt, Lyn Liao Butler, Jamie and Linsey Deeks, Sophie and Max Deveson, Wendy Oates Devore and Chad Deal, Channon Donovan, Steph and Ed Drax, Charlotte Eggington, Amaryllis Fraser, Brian and Elias Fulton, Dr. Nancy Gade, Terri, Benjy, Amber and Chloe Garfinkle, Jennifer Garza, Jane Green, Philippa Gregory, Lauren Groff, Kristin Hannah, Patti Callahan Henry, The Margaret Herrick Library, David Katz, Martha Hall Kelly, Adriana, Simon, Felix, and Logan Kent, Alex and Katie Kerr, Cathee King, Dr. Richard King, David Kline, Megan Labrise, Ariel Lawhon, Susanna Lea, Lena Mahadeo, Marc Magsaysay, Sarah McCoy, Mike Melahn, Jocy and Brody Mello, Claire Messud, Elliotte Williams N'Dure, Celeste Ng, Naomi Nicholson, Beth Parker, Camille Perri, Digvijay and Yukiko Puar, Matt and Angela Pycha, Aron Rollin, The Billy Rose Theatre Division of the New York Public Library for the Performing Arts, John Searles and Tom Caruso, Lisa Sharkey, Alix Strauss, Adriana Trigiani, Jane Williams, Meg Wolitzer, and Jon Zeitler.

Stephanie Cabot—my spectacular agent and unwavering advocate, who flew in to help me rework the manuscript when I needed it most. Your belief in me and in this novel means everything. Thank you.

Susanna Porter, my brilliant editor—thank you for knowing

what this book needed. With wisdom, insight and so much grace, you challenged me, cheered me on, and never let me settle for anything less than the story's best self. To everyone at Ballantine—thank you for bringing this book into the world with such thoughtful and meticulous care. From navigating Adobe nightmares to chasing down the perfect pink, your kindness and generosity have been sewn into every step. In particular, thank you to Ralph Fowler, Jennifer Hershey, Kim Hovey, Anusha Khan, Melanie Muto, Taylor Noel, Sophie Normil, Jennifer Rodriguez, and Chelsea Woodward, and Briony Everroad, Andrea Gordon, and Barbara Greenberg. And to Scott Biel and Derek Walls—thank you for a beautiful cover.

Thank you to Megan Beatie, my extraordinary independent publicist, for your kindness, your clarity and your steadfast belief in this novel.

Thank you to Ash and Cliff Mello—for your bright, sharp insight and unshakable friendship. To Haley and Alana Sharp—it is a joy to watch your creativity tear through the world, and to Joan Maas—you inspire me with your kindness, presence and strength. To Kiernan Melahn—for taking such beautiful care of my family, both those with four legs and those with two. To Dr. Lindsey Westerfield, Dr. Christian Benyei, and everyone at Schulhof Animal Hospital—thank you for your extraordinary love and kindness.

To the coven—Cynthia Baker, Christina Baker Kline, and Paula McLain—for your incredible smarts, kindness, love and loyalty. Thank you for making the whole world feel possible.

And thank you to my family: to my sister Tina, brother-in-law JD, and nephews Dash and Emmett—for their unflappable kindness; my stepchildren Jesse, Martha, Edie, and Jonah—for inviting me in and making me family; my stepdaughters Maddi and Ava—for always choosing me back. To my husband Anthony—thank you for being my anchor. And to my mother—you are woven through every word I will ever write.

ABOUT THE AUTHOR

PRIYA PARMAR is the author of the novels *Exit the Actress* and *Vanessa and Her Sister*, a *New York Times* Notable Book, and is co-writer of the musical *Sylvia* (London Old Vic), nominated for the Olivier Award for Best New Musical. She divides her time between Hawaii and Connecticut with her family and four rescue dogs.

priyaparmar.net